DISOBEY

DISOBEY

by

Jacqui Rose

Magna Large Print Books
Long Preston, North Yorkshire,
BD23 4ND, England.

British Library Cataloguing in Publication Data.

Rose, Jacqui
  Disobey.

  A catalogue record of this book is
  available from the British Library

  ISBN   978-0-7505-4246-3

First published in Great Britain by Avon 2015
A division of HarperCollins*Publishers*

Copyright © Jacqui Rose 2015

Cover illustration © Simon Turner by arrangement with
Arcangel Images

Jacqui Rose asserts the moral right to be identified as the author of
this work

Published in Large Print 2016 by arrangement with
HarperCollins Publishers Ltd.

Magna Large Print is an imprint of Library Magna Books Ltd.

Printed and bound in Great Britain by
T.J. (International) Ltd., Cornwall, PL28 8RW

Acknowledgements

A huge thank-you to the wonderful team at Avon but especially to Lydia, my editor, who has been as always, so fantastically supportive. A massive loud thank-you to my family for simply just being them as well as all my friends and colleagues.

This book is to you, the readers who've come on this wonderful crazy journey with me. Thank you for your support.

'No man ever steps in the same river twice, for it's not the same river and he's not the same man.'

−Heraclitus

PROLOGUE

At four in the morning the door of the Turkish restaurant in Greek Street was kicked open. Careering into the wall, it caused the glass to smash into tiny fragments on the tiled floor. Three men waving baseball bats charged in, smashing everything in their way.

The sound of the chairs being kicked over and the tables being thrown woke the sleeping proprietor, Sarp, who'd seen and caused enough trouble throughout his own life to not hesitate to rush downstairs, cosh in hand, to face whatever danger awaited him.

Although Sarp had just had his fifty-sixth birthday, with adrenaline racing round his body he stood tall, sounding like a man much younger than his years.

'What the fucking hell?' The sight of the three Chinese men standing in the middle of his vandalised restaurant made Sarp see red and unwisely, he threw his full weight behind a punch, landing it directly in the smallest of the three men's face. The blood splattered across the room, patterning the whitewashed wall with a sea of tiny red dots.

Without a moment's hesitation, the men easily grabbed hold of the overweight Sarp, pushing him down against the sharp metal side of the bar's counter. He cried out as the steel ripped into his bulbous flesh. 'What ... what do you want?'

The cold stare of the men sent a chill of fear through him.

'We've warned you before. We told you there were no second chances. None. This time you pay up.'

'I ain't got the sort of money you're asking for. The business isn't doing that well.'

'I'm not interested in your problems. You've had long enough; I'm sure you wouldn't want anything happening to your restaurant or want your clientele to be too afraid to come here. The money's to make sure these things don't happen. To keep you safe.'

Sarp snarled at the men; his lip curling up in hatred. 'Ain't no need for protection mate; those days are long gone. We look after ourselves round here or we look after our own. Either way, we don't need the likes of you thinking yer China's answer to the Krays.'

'You're a very foolish man. Don't you understand we'll get our money one way or another; either which you'll end up paying. Don't make it difficult for yourself.'

Sarp leaned forward, wincing at the pain in his torn flesh. 'Ain't no way in the world I'm giving my hard-earned money to the likes of you. You can't just go around doing this. There are rules; laws against this kind of stuff.'

'Really? You want to talk about rules – perhaps you should be speaking to Alfie Jennings then.'

'What are you talking about? What's he got to do with it?'

'You need to ask him, but in the meantime...'

16

The Chinese man spoke with a sarcastic tone as a smirk began to pass across his face. He pulled a blade out of his pocket. With a quick movement, he slashed Sarp across the cheek, drawing a five-inch gash on his face. The largest of the men pushed past him, disappearing out of the main area and upstairs into the living quarters. A couple of minutes later he returned, dragging a screaming woman through by her hair. She cried out to the owner in Turkish, her eyes wide with terror.

Sarp shouted loudly, fear in his voice. 'Leave her alone! Leave her alone! She ain't got nothing to do with this.' He paused, seeing the look of terror in her eyes as she shook with dread. He turned to face the men directly. His voice was breathless; his words staggered.

'Okay ... okay, what do you want me to do?'

'You have forty-eight hours and then we'll be back. If you don't have our money then; kiss your wife goodbye.'

SOHO

1

They were all there. All of them. The faces of London coming together, putting their differences aside to sort out the problems hitting the streets of Soho. But as Alfie Jennings sat staring hard at Vaughn Sadler, who in turn was staring hard at Johnny and Frankie Taylor who sat belligerently in the corner with their backs turned on Tommy Donaldson who was refusing to converse with Del Williams, putting their differences aside looked like it was going to prove more difficult than any of them could have imagined.

'Bleedin' hell, anyone would think this is a flipping wake from the looks on your faces.' Lola Harding cackled out her words as she served them chipped mugs of over-milked tea in her café in Bateman Street. She smiled an almost-toothless grin but only received deep scowls in return, which only served to make her laugh harder.

'Come on gentlemen, it ain't that bad. Look at you all! Frankie, you look like a wet weekend in Margate, and Del, cop on to yourself, sitting hunched up in the corner like a crack-addicted little Jack Horner.'

She exploded into another raucous laugh, making Del scowl and mutter under his breath. 'Do me a favour.'

Lola – who was now on a roll and enjoying every moment – continued, not being put off by anyone's lack of enthusiasm towards her. She shuffled over to another of the London faces, poking him playfully in the chest. 'Then you, Vaughn; Christ darling, you look like you're about to shit out an elephant. Come on sweetheart, I expected better of you. What's there to be glum about? Okay, okay, I know there's a little bit of trouble bubbling about but nothing you can't handle. Vaughn! Come on doll. Where you've got breath you've got a smile. Vaughnie baby, give old Lola a smile.'

Vaughn glared at Lola. He could feel his face turning red as he tried to keep down his temper. Although Lola's antics hadn't brought him out in a smile, it'd certainly brought the others out in one, or rather, it'd brought them out in smirks. And it pissed him off no end – especially as the person who was grinning the most was Alfie Jennings, who was sitting opposite him in the dingy café.

Being anywhere near Alfie pissed him off. They had history. *Too* much history. Alfie's daughter, Emmie – Vaughn's goddaughter – had come to live with him and his partner, Casey awhile back, and for a short time life had been peaceful; he'd even go so far as saying it'd been idyllic, something he'd never experienced nor could have ever imagined before, but then *this* had happened. This *shit* which had hit Soho, smashing his peace like a big brass fucking band.

Vaughn sighed, rubbing his head as his hair flopped over his handsome sun-kissed face, giving him the appearance of a man twenty years his junior. Jesus, he wished he was back in his place in Surrey, tending his roses, making love to Casey or even listening to Emmie's teenage strops. Anything. *Anything*, would be better than fucking *this*.

He'd left Soho life and all it entailed a long time ago, really only coming up for social gatherings and to catch up with old acquaintances and that had suited him well. It was on his terms. Vaughn had spent too many years looking over his shoulder with his life revolving around money and violence, and finally he thought it was over. But then he'd had the call. The code of honour call from another face. The call which meant no matter how much he didn't want to be here, he really had no choice.

The call had come from Greg Bradley, an old face who still lived in Soho after seventy-eight years. Although Greg had retired a long time ago and now chose an early night and a drink of Ovaltine over any form of ructions, all his faculties were still intact and he was the ears and eyes of the place.

When Vaughn had picked up the call from Greg, he'd had no time for small talk, simply saying. *'It's Soho. We're in trouble.'*

In all his time as a face around London Vaughn had only had *the* call, once. A long time ago, when he'd temporarily settled in Spain, needing to hang low after a multi-million-pound heist, and then, like now, he'd been forced to return to Soho.

Back then it'd been the Yardies, a group of tough and ambitious Jamaicans who'd wanted to add Soho to their takeover of London. There'd been a lot of violence, a lot of claret spilt, but eventually after a few weeks, the turf war had come to an end. Soho had been reclaimed and Vaughn had gone back to Spain for a while, whilst the other faces who'd also got the call had crawled back to wherever they'd come from.

And now twenty-odd years later, the call had come through, but not because of the Yardies or any other group who thought they were tough enough to take the faces of London on. No, this time the enemy were bigger, more dangerous, more ruthless and they needed all the manpower they could get. Because, this time ... this time the triads had come.

The triads were at one time the largest criminal organisation in the world with over half a million members, based mainly in Hong Kong and China with roots dating back to centuries-old secret societies. Over the years the triads had branched out and started to operate in smaller groups, though this regrouping hadn't lessened any of their violence or criminal activities.

Groups such as the deadly Wong Shing Ho and the infamous 14k gang had exploded onto the British scene in the 1980s, bringing with them fear and intimidation, specialising in armed robbery, racketeering, smuggling, drugs trafficking and selling, as well as prostitution and gambling.

The fear that surrounded them was justified, with torture being commonplace to anyone who refused to comply or anyone foolish enough to try to stand up to them or inform the authorities. And up until now, Soho had been free from the rule of triads, with Shaftesbury Avenue serving as the invisible line dividing Chinatown from Soho. But now, everything had changed.

Vaughn tried to muster a smile for Lola but even he could feel it was crooked, a bit like the rest of the men sitting in the café. No matter how fond of her he was, the last thing he felt like doing was being drawn into any sort of conversation. All he wanted to do was decide on a plan then get the hell home.

As if reading his thoughts, Alfie Jennings piped up, a cheeky grin spreading across his face.

'Got somewhere else to go, have we mate?'

Vaughn snarled at Alfie, 'I ain't your mate, I thought I made that clear to you a long time ago.'

Alfie stared at Vaughn and although he didn't show it, what Vaughn had said cut him deeply. They once had been best friends, inseparable, and with one thing or another, no thanks to his ex-missus, he'd lost everything. His money, Emmie his daughter, and most of his friends. The money hadn't mattered; well not really, Alfie was a born wheeler and dealer, a born survivor, and he'd always known one way or another he would climb back up. The friends hadn't really mattered, most of them had been a bunch of muppets anyway. What *had* mattered was Emmie and Vaughn. His best mate and his daughter had given him the brush-off when he'd needed them the most.

He knew they'd say the reason they'd turned their backs on him was because of things he'd done in the past; mistakes he'd made with the people he'd got involved with, compromising all their beliefs, but everyone made bad judgements, hadn't they? Everyone got it wrong from time to time, but it seemed only ever to be him, Alfie

Jennings who was punished for it.

He could forgive Emmie. She was his princess and always would be, no matter what. But Vaughn. Vaughn-fucking-yesterday's-news-Sadler, well he was different. He was a piss take, one that he, Alfie Jennings would never forgive.

Alfie stood up, his six-foot-plus well-built frame looming towards Vaughn. 'Oh you made it clear. Very clear, *mate*. Leaving me with fuck all while you and that bird of yours waltzed off with me daughter like you were a contestant on fucking *Strictly*.'

Vaughn, not in the least intimidated by Alfie, stood up, so that he was nose to nose with him.

'Do yourself a service, Alf. Turn it in, and stop embarrassing yourself in front of everyone.'

'I ain't the embarrassment, but you'd like me to be wouldn't you? Oh, didn't you just love it when I was down on me friggin' hind. But that ain't the case now, sunshine. 'Cos Alfie is back. Alfie Jennings is back on top.'

'Alf, you sound like a fucking muppet. For fuck's sake do us all a turn will ya and do what Vaughn says, or at least keep it tight will ya; I don't need me ears chewing off with all this schoolgirl shit.' It was Del Williams who spoke. A big player in Soho as well as the Costa.

Alfie swivelled round, his face turning up into a sneer. 'When I want your opinion, I'll ask for it.'

Del barked back. 'No, son, I'm just going to give it to you. Wise up mate.'

Alfie's contempt was palpable. 'To quote Vaughn here, I ain't your mate.'

Del rolled up his sleeves. 'Which will make it all

26

the more easy to knock yer fucking head off.'

'Hold up! Hold up! Is that right? What's your frigging problem, Williams? If anyone is going to pull the bollocks, it's going to be me and it ain't going to be Alfie's jewels I'm holding in me hands, it'll be yours, *mate.*' Frankie Taylor bellowed his threat to Del. Besides being good mates with Alfie, he had no time for Del who, since being involved with the Russians, thought he was Al Ca-fucking-pone.

Del laughed aggressively. 'I didn't know you needed a nursemaid, Alf; I thought that was more Tommy's style.'

'Who you calling a pussy!' Tommy Donaldson scraped back his chair, entering the arena of arguing men.

'Gentlemen! Gentlemen! Please!' Lola wasn't laughing now, her voice was raised and her arms folded.

'Zip it will you, darling!' Del snapped at Lola, causing Tommy, who had always been closer to Lola than his own mum at times, to grab hold of his arm.

'Don't speak to her like that, otherwise you'll have me to deal with.'

'Oh and is that supposed to rock me fucking boat?'

Johnny Taylor, Tommy's brother-in law, began to jump to his defence.

'It ain't going to rock it, Del, it's going to...'

'Enough!' Vaughn Sadler stood up, banging his fists on the table, staring hard at all assembled. His voice was rough and edged with hardness as the room fell silent.

27

'We ain't here for a mothers' meeting, but we sure as hell sound like one. I know most of you would rather be somewhere else, but until we sort out exactly how we're going to keep Soho safe from the threat of the triads then none of us are going anywhere, unless you want to deal with me.'

Alfie's tone was sarcastic. 'Oooh! You're scaring us now, Vaughn. I don't know if I'll be able to sleep in me bed tonight.'

Vaughn, about to turn on Alfie, was stopped by Lola's soothing voice.

'Leave it, Vaughnie. You know he's being a wind up ... ain't you, Alf? Listen, can we all turn it in for now? This ain't a joke and it ain't just a threat either. There's been attacks and there don't seem to be anyone wanting to stop it. Folk are frightened, real frightened. Greg said the last time he'd seen business people so terrified was when the Krays ruled the East End. We don't want to go back to that, and besides, these triads make Ronnie and Reggie look like the Flowerpot Men. And that's why you all got the call. We need help. Soho needs help.'

Johnny nodded his head in agreement. 'Lola's right. They clearly want to come and take over and won't stop at anything until they succeed. What we have to do is stop them, and quick.'

Del interjected. 'Yeah, but why?'

Johnny looked puzzled. 'Why what?'

'Why now, why after living all these years with them in relative harmony do they want to come over to our patch? The triads have been coming and going long before I was around, but now all of a sudden they have a problem with us. It don't make sense.'

Vaughn spoke matter-of-factly. 'Maybe it does, maybe it's just a question of things changing. New people taking over.'

Del rubbed his chin, shaking his head. 'There's more to it. I'm sure.'

Alfie snapped, looking slightly uncomfortable, 'Why does there have to be more to it?'

Del looked puzzled before he frowned. 'What's your problem hey, Alf?'

'I never said I had a problem, I just think not everything's as deep and frigging complicated as you make it. Reckon you've been hanging out too much with your missus.'

A dark expression came over Del's face. 'And I reckon that...'

Before Del could get the rest of the sentence out, the door of the café was swung open by two masked men. One of them shouted, the distinct Chinese accent present in his voice, and it was clear to everyone they were the triads.

'A message for disobeying the rules.' The man threw what he was holding in his hand before rushing back out of the café. There was a loud bang, followed by a flash of light. Immediately Vaughn began to shout.

'Get down! Get down!' he bellowed as Alfie grabbed hold of Lola, pushing her to safety under one of the tables as the small petrol bomb the man had thrown exploded into the corner of the Bateman Street café.

A small fire broke out as the place began to fill with black smoke. Most of the men, save the ones trying to put out the fire with water, pulled out their guns, racing to the entrance.

Tommy Donaldson, getting outside first, watched as the two men sped off on a scooter turning right into Greek Street. The other men, seconds behind, piled out of the café, along with Lola, whose face was red with rage. She stared at everyone, her whole body shaking as tears of shock ran down her face. She spoke, her voice stripped of its usual warmth as they all stood and watched her beloved café burning.

'I don't care. I don't bleedin' care how you do it but as of right now, it stops; all of it. The squabbling, the petty jealousies, the blown-up egos, the whole bleedin' works. You lot need to start working together to sort this out. Because *no one,* no bleeding one, not even an army of Samurai-fucking-warriors will ever get away with trying to destroy me frigging café.' And with tears streaming down her face and her head held high, Lola Harding hit each of the men on their chest with her battered handbag before turning and walking away, leaving all those present feeling ashamed and less like London's feared number one gangsters, and more like reprimanded schoolboys.

2

The Turkish restaurateur, Sarp, and his wife Anna sat across the table from Alfie Jennings. They were telling him the story of what had happened the night before last – but Sarp's face told the tale more than his words did. The multi-coloured bruises covered most of his face, a large bandage covering the now-stitched gash.

'I thought they were going to rape her.'

Alf's voice was urgent. 'They didn't though?'

'No, but they could've done. They could've done anything. Worst thing is they knew it and so did I. They ain't afraid of no one. It was a game to them. They're animals, Alf. Animals.'

Fear was imprinted in their features and Alfie could see Anna was visibly shaking as she clung onto Sarp. Alfie had known them for over ten years. They were good people and they respected him as both a friend and a face.

He'd had a call from Sarp, pleading for him to go round. It wasn't the usual course of events. If there was a problem in Soho one of the smaller faces, the upcoming guys, usually dealt with it. Alfie had been around too long to have to deal with shit between neighbours or some of the Toms touting on corners to the disapproval of the business owners.

But this was different. And although he'd known straight away what it was about he was pleased

31

that Sarp had come to him; for more than one reason.

'So you see, you guys need to do something. I can't have my wife terrified. Look at her, she's in a right state. They ain't like us. They're crazy. If you don't do anything, Alf, you'll give me no option... I'll have to get the Old Bill involved.'

Alfie leaned back on his chair and shook his head. 'Come on Sarp, you know we don't get the filth involved. We look after our own. Calling the Old Bill is dead man's talk.'

Sarp stared at Alfie furiously. 'Well, tell me what I'm supposed to do then. 'Cos I don't see any of you lot giving a flying fuck what happens to Soho. It's going to rack and fucking ruin, like the rest of the country.'

Alfie raised his eyebrows. 'There's always Turkey.'

'Don't give me that, Alf. This is my country too. I've worked hard, like my parents did when they came over in the Fifties. Tell me something, is it really too much to ask to be able to sleep in my own bed at night without myself or my wife being dragged out by a bunch of hammer-wielding maniacs? You need to do something, Alfie and quick, otherwise I swear I'll go down to the cop shop, and I won't give a shit what any of you lot think.'

'Sarp, just hear me out; don't be doing anything rash. It ain't just me who won't like it. It'll be the others. Do you really want to cross swords with the likes of Del Williams and Vaughn Sadler? Give me time to sort this out.'

'And what am I supposed to do in the meantime, hey? Perhaps I should go and speak to the Taylors.'

Alfie pounced on Sarp's words. 'No!... No! Don't do that. Leave it to me and I'll sort it, but I'll sort it my way... I promise.' He stared at Sarp. There was no way he wanted him to go to the Taylors, or any other faces for that matter. Alfie needed to sort something out first or rather, he needed to go and see somebody first.

Sarp looked unsure. 'They said they'd come back. If I didn't have the money to pay them, they'd come back and really do something. They ain't messing about, Alfie.' The restaurant owner dropped his voice to a whisper. 'I'm not ashamed to tell you I'm scared; really scared. Those triads mean business.'

'Okay, you might not like this suggestion, but you need to pay them...'

'No fucking way, Alf. No way. The minute you start paying them; that's it. It's over. I'll be forever in their pocket, and they'll just keep wanting more and more until I've got fuck all left.'

'If you're six foot under you won't need to worry about money. Pay them. Keep them sweet for now.'

'No. I worked hard to get where I am, and there's no way I'm going to give tea money; protection money to people. It's crazy.'

'I know it is, but ain't nothing I can do at this moment. I'm not saying pay forever; of course I'm not, but it'll keep you and your missus safe for now.'

'I'm not sure.'

'Well, I am. You came to me for a reason. Pay

up, and I'll have it sorted for you in a week'

Sarp glanced at his wife, who looked anxious. Alfie went into his pocket and brought out a roll of fifty-pound notes. He pushed the money into Sarp's hand who nodded gratefully.

'Okay Alfie. A week, but no more.'

'Just hold on tight. I'll make sure everything is sorted.'

Sarp fell silent for a moment before saying, 'They said something. Something about me speaking to you about breaking rules. What did they mean?'

Alfie looked uncomfortable. 'I dunno. They're just talking shit. Can't listen to anything they say.'

Sarp looked suspicious. 'It's funny, they seemed so sure I should talk to you.'

Alfie said nothing, just got up to go and headed towards the door. He turned to Sarp, talking to him quietly, his voice full of reassurance. 'Listen, forget what they said. We need to concentrate on sorting you out, mate. You did the right thing by calling me. But listen, I *don't* want you mentioning we had this conversation. And I don't want you mentioning what happened to your restaurant to anybody. Do you understand?'

'I dunno, it seems odd.'

Alfie looked exasperated. 'It ain't odd. The less people know the better. I don't want word to get out we're on their case. I'll speak to the Taylors. You know Johnny and Frankie.'

'Yeah, they're good people.'

'Well I'll see what they think about it all. I'll make sure they keep an eye on things as well. Just trust me. Everything is going to be fine.' Alfie smiled at Sarp, patting him on his back as he went.

He opened the restaurant door, walking out into the bright light. He wasn't quite certain of what he was going to do but one thing Alfie Jennings *did* know was that there was no way he'd be talking to the Taylors. *This* was something he needed to sort out by himself.

3

'I'm impressed, Lin. You did well. The fire was only a warning, but one they'll take seriously. It's only a shame I couldn't have been there to see their reaction.' Mr Lee, a small unassuming-looking gentleman who'd just celebrated his sixty-fifth birthday, smiled darkly at his second-in-command. His accent, a surprise to those who met him and far removed from the obvious assumption of a heavy South-East Asian one, was Etonian in sound, and certainly not representative of his rural upbringing.

Chang Lee had been born to impoverished but hardworking parents in the poor, yet beautiful town of Zhouzhuang in the Jiangsu Province of China, which had a rich 900-year history. It was a place surrounded by water, often dubbed by the Europeans as the Oriental Venice.

Growing up in Zhouzhuang, the young Chang Lee had despised the poverty and hardship which seemed to determine and limit his family. With the harsh and controlling idealistic socialist regime of the people's republic of China, led by Mao Zedong, Chang saw the widespread famine and perishing of families due to Mao's land reforms which formed the basis of the infamous and disastrous Great Leap Forward campaign.

The Great Leap Forward had been an economic and social campaign that was supposed to change China from an agrarian economy into a leading, modern society to rival and compete with other industrialised countries in the world within a five-year time period.

From the beginning it had been a disaster, with the Maoist regime forcing millions of Chinese citizens to move and work in communes on farms or in manufacturing. Private farming was prohibited, and those who did it were assumed to be counterrevolutionaries and were either tortured or executed for it.

As a consequence of the Chinese people being forced off the land and into the factories to try to produce steel, the crops were neglected and along with the compounding effects of the floods of 1959, within the three- to four-year period during which the campaign ran, the estimated death toll was between twenty to thirty million.

When the campaign was brought to an early halt, Mao Zedong was forced to resign from his position as Head of State, but the damage had been done.

All around him Chang saw the devastating effects of abject poverty, hating, yet strangely admiring, Mao Zedong. He'd looked with disdain at his parents who had nothing and were certain to die that way, and then he'd looked at the tyranny of power and fear Mao had implemented in a once-great nation. Although Chang could see that Mao's campaign had desolated the country, it was Mao whom he admired and wanted to emulate.

The chance of following his dreams of a better life and escaping the picture-postcard town of Zhouzhuang, with its numerous arched bridges, murmuring brooks, narrow waterways and quiet simplicity, came when Chang had been just fourteen. An uncle of his had had permission from the government to travel down to Lo Wu, on the border of Hong Kong.

Travelling throughout the country in the Sixties was mostly a foreign concept to the people of China, risking death or imprisonment if caught doing so without permission, therefore Chang saw his uncle being allowed to take the refined bars of iron ore down to Lo Wu as probably his only opportunity to make the seven-hundred-and-fifty-mile journey to where China bordered British-ruled Hong Kong, the place he'd set his heart on being.

He'd sneaked into the back of his uncle's lorry, without thought or goodbye to his parents, and had lain crammed amongst the metal rungs for over a week, with barely any water and certainly no food for the whole of the journey.

When Chang had arrived in Lo Wu, he'd slept rough, hiding out in the backstreets. During the day he'd tried to glean information about how to cross the border to Hong Kong. It'd taken over a month for Chang to find out what he needed, during which time he'd stolen food from shops and broken into houses to steal money. It all came naturally to him; even though crime had previously been absent in his life it now seemed second nature, and although he was fending for himself at only fourteen, Chang was the happiest he'd ever felt.

A man Chang had met when he'd been getting something to eat had told him about the yellow waters of the Sham Chun River which flowed unceasingly under the Lo Wu bridge; the only link between China and Hong Kong.

He'd told Chang about the town of Sham Chun which stood on the river, a few miles down from Lo Wu, telling Chang about the people who'd risked their lives by swimming the river to the British side to escape communist China.

But Chang hadn't seen it as a risk as he'd listened to the tales of those that'd made it and those that'd perished by drowning or from the bullets of the soldiers who stood in the chain of sentry boxes along the shore. No, Chang had seen it as his bid to freedom.

At its widest point the river was less than a quarter of a mile across; an easy crossing to a strong swimmer like Chang. What wasn't so easy to avoid was the manned twenty-four hours a day armed guards searching the river banks for any would-be escapees hiding out until the darkness of night.

Over the next few weeks, Chang took daily trips to Sham Chun to survey the river, taking in the position of the sentry boxes and the patrolling guard's schedule, then on the 3rd July 1965 Chang hid amongst the rushes of the river, waiting for his chance to make the journey across.

Chang knew from hearing the nightly echoing

of bullets across the river that the sentries would fire at the slightest noise and the waters would be aglow and riddled with bullets, but neither this nor the stories of failed escape attempts could deter Chang from lowering himself quietly into the cold blackness of the river.

The swim across had been almost uneventful until he'd seen a family of six a few metres behind him. The youngest child had begun to cry, and had immediately brought attention to the escapees.

Without a moment's hesitation on hearing the child's noise, the guards had opened fire, killing all those present and wounding Chang in his leg. The wound had been deep and the blood had poured out into the river but Chang had continued to swim through his pain and haziness, making it across to the other side, onto the safety of British-ruled soil.

He'd blacked out on the river bank and had woken up in the back of an old van, after a kindly man had driven past and seen him lying there. The man had taken Chang to his home, a tiny, squalid apartment within Kowloon Walled City; once thought to be the most densely populated place on Earth, with 50,000 people crammed into only a few blocks.

From the Fifties the walled city had been run by the triads and this was the place Chang Lee had learnt his trade; prostitution, gambling, drug dealing, along with implementing fear and torture.

Chang had lived within the walls of the city until the government destroyed it in 1994, forcibly evicting everyone; but by this time, Chang had become one of the most feared triads – powerful and ruthless, still basing his ethos on Chairman Mao.

Chang hadn't minded leaving Kowloon Walled City, the place had become too small for him, and he too big for the place, and now he'd set his eyes on something more international; London.

In 1997, Chang found himself on a boat to England, and although the government's demolishment of Kowloon had ultimately put paid to Chang's livelihood, leaving him with no money, it hadn't mattered to him. He knew it was only a matter of time before he built himself up again, along with his reputation; but this time it would be in London.

During the next twelve years Chang had gone to elocution lessons, involved himself in the heroin business, mainly in southwest London, making money and contacts; but then the bottom had dropped out of it, and he'd turned to gambling dens amongst other things. It was then he'd decided to move to Chinatown.

Through violence and manipulation, he'd secured the monopoly in illegal gambling, and no one had dared to challenge his position – that was, until now. Until Alfie Jennings had decided to open his own casino in Soho, breaking the rules of the pact which saw the triads run all casinos and the faces of London deal with whatever it was they dealt with. And now they were going to pay. Now, the rules had changed. Now, Chang was going to take over everything, and Soho was just the beginning of their takeover of London.

Lin nodded at Chang Lee as he drew an ace in the poker game he was playing with Mr Lee's other men. 'I would've liked to have done more, show them all what fear really is.'

Mr Lee stood up from the card table. He was already ten thousand down but he liked to occasionally lose to his inferiors; winning all the time was only something a fool would want, it made you lazy. 'Slowly, Lin; slowly slowly catchy monkey. We want to do it properly. We want to force them out of Soho, like rats on a sinking boat. Soho will be ours, but patience is our path.'

Before Lin could answer, the buzzer rang. He looked on the monitors, immediately recognising the caller. It was Alfie Jennings.

Chang Lee gave a tight smile as he headed for the door. 'I think I'll leave the pleasure of a meeting with Mr Jennings to you, Lin.' He paused, adding, 'Oh and Lin, don't forget to send the flowers.' With that, Mr Lee left the room.

Alfie Jennings looked at his watch and quickly glanced around. He took a deep breath before again pressing the door buzzer of the unmarked basement office. They were taking the piss, he knew for a fact someone would be there. No doubt they'd be watching him on the CCTV cameras, thinking it was funny to make him wait. Well he'd show them. Oh yes, he was going to tell them just what he thought of their warnings and intimidation. No one, but no one was going to rip the piss out of the Jennings, especially not a bunch of noodle-eating triads.

Why should the triads have the monopoly on it

all? Alfie hadn't signed a fucking agreement saying they had the stakehold on casinos. There was enough money to go around and he not only wanted some of it, he was going to get it.

When Alfie had had the idea of opening a casino, he'd got one of his business associates to introduce him to Mr Lee, the head of the triads. He'd been polite, and asked them if he could open a casino, something he usually would never have done. He'd expected the man to say yes, but he'd just laughed in his face and given a point blank no. He'd asked three times more but he'd been warned off, something which had angered him no end, but had given him the nudge he needed; making him decide he didn't need anyone's permission to open a late-night illegal gambling den in his own club, Whispers.

It was a fucking muppet contract and of course, whoever had agreed to it had been a mug or a pussy, or both. No one would tell him what to do, and once he'd spoken to Mr Lee everything would get sorted and he, Alfie would carry on with his *get-money-fast* plan.

Of course he hadn't told anyone what he was doing, but he'd spent his life playing by the rules of Soho and now it was time for Alfie to start to think about himself. And setting up this gambling club was doing exactly that. By the time word *did* get out to the other faces that he'd opened a casino behind everyone's back, he'd be hopefully lying on the Costa del Sol with Franny, because that's what it was all about. Having enough money behind him to wave goodbye to Soho and spend the rest of his days with Franny Doyle.

'Ah, Mr Jennings, Lin is downstairs waiting for you.' One of Mr Lee's men opened the door to the basement office in Gerrard Street, Soho. He bowed courteously to Alfie, who scowled and growled at the man.

'I ain't here to see the monkey, I'm here to see the organ grinder. I want to see Mr Lee. Where is he?'

The man didn't react, simply saying, 'As I said, Lin is downstairs. He'd be delighted if you joined him for tea.'

Having no choice, Alfie followed the man along the dimly lit corridors to a white door which was opened by a smiling Lin.

'Mr Jennings, a pleasure.'

'Ain't no pleasure for me mate, where's your boss?'

'I'm afraid Mr Lee doesn't see visitors without an appointment.'

'What is he, a fucking doctor? I ain't here to get me cholesterol checked, I'm here to give him a piece of me mind, and get this sorted out.'

Lin smiled, looking amused. 'A piece of your mind; what a strange expression, Mr Jennings, a curiosity quite how that would be achieved, unless of course someone puts an axe in your head.'

Alfie's face darkened. He hated dealing with foreigners, especially smarmy ones, and the Chinese were the worst for that. To Alfie they had an air about them that made him feel they were looking down at him; that they thought themselves superior to him in some way.

'Look, keep the chat to yourself, Lin, I want to make this short. Tell Lee to back off Soho.'

Lin roared with laughter, causing Alfie to seethe with even more anger.

'And why would he do that?'

'Well if he knows what's good for him he will.'

Lin, a tall muscular man with dark eyes and poker-straight hair tied in a ponytail, was dead-pan in his response. 'Mr Jennings, aren't they the same words we gave you when you came to ask us before about opening a casino? We told you not to, *if you knew what was good for you,* yet here you are demanding that we back off. Too late, Mr Jennings; the dove no longer carries the olive branch.'

Alfie stepped forward towards Lin: 'Listen pal, I like straight talk, you can save all that spiel for the fortune cookies. I'm telling you, back off Soho.'

'You broke the rules, Mr Jennings, you should've thought about that before. All these attacks on Soho are your making. If you had let things be, left the casinos to us, then everything would have been fine.'

'That's bullshit, you would've come sooner or later. We both know that.'

Lin contemplated Alfie's words. 'Perhaps you're right, but you'll never know now the rules have been broken.'

Frustrated, Alfie shouted, 'There ain't no fucking rules, and your name's not Hasbro, you don't have the monopoly on casinos. There's enough punters to go around for us all to have a share.'

'That's where you're wrong. There *are* rules, ones which you have disobeyed, and it would be in your best interest to stop with your casino now before it's too late.'

Alfie looked curious. 'And if I did, that would make you back off Soho?'

'Oh no, like I say, Mr Jennings, it's all gone too far, but it would keep you safe. Now if you'll excuse me, I have somewhere else I need to be.'

Lin walked away but stopped, turning back round to face Alfie. 'Oh, and if it's straight talk you want, then how about this, Mr Jennings... Don't fuck with us or you're a dead man.'

'I don't get it. Why now? Why fucking make a nick after all these years?' Vaughn Sadler shook his head as he paced about in Bateman Street, speaking to Lola. He watched as his men boarded up her café; it was the least he could do. Lola didn't have the means or probably the insurance to get the place up and running again and besides it being her livelihood, Vaughn also knew how much it meant to her.

The café gave her a purpose, kept her as part of the community within the only life she'd ever known. Years ago Lola had been a Tom, working street corners and living with various pimps, and although she had been harder, tougher and not a woman to mess with, she'd still been Lola. Ferociously loyal; someone who would do anything for anybody.

'Watch what yer bleeding doing! When I want a bunch of frigging muppets fixing me caff, I'll call Disney.' Lola shouted at the men, making Vaughn smile. The fire was only superficial and it clearly was only a warning; nothing that a little work and a fresh coat of paint and a few builders couldn't

45

fix. But the one thing Vaughn knew they couldn't fix was how he felt.

Last night was a wake-up call for him. Until then, he'd seen the summons to come back to Soho as an inconvenience. But that was then and this was now, and now had just got personal.

The attacks on businesses in Soho over the last few weeks had been troubling, but nothing that had kept him awake at night. He didn't really know the owners of these places and in consequence he'd been able to keep a distance from it all, but Lola? An attack on Lola Harding, who'd been there through so many hard times with him; that was different. And if the triads wanted an all-out war, then that's exactly what they were going to get.

Lighting a cigar, something which was a relatively new habit, Vaughn continued to mull things over. He didn't get it. He just didn't get why the triads would make a move now. They'd lived in relative harmony for all these years, with Shaftesbury Avenue acting not only as a road dividing Soho and Chinatown but also acting as the separation of the two turfs.

They had an understanding, an unwritten rule about trespassing into each other's territories or challenging each other's businesses and so far it'd worked; since as far back as Vaughn could remember. So what had changed? What had gone wrong to warrant these unprovoked attacks? He honestly had no clue, but he certainly was going to find out, and when he did, whoever was behind it, he was going to stop. Once and for fucking all. And that was certainly worth coming out of retirement for.

'Excuse me, I'm looking for Lola Harding?' A man walked round the corner.

Vaughn eyed him suspiciously. 'Who's asking?'

'These are for her.' The man held a large bunch of lilies in his hand.

Hearing they were for her, Lola ran up to the man, snatching the flowers off him as her eyes twinkled in delight. 'Bleedin' hell, look at that. Ain't they beautiful Vaughnie? I wonder who they're from. I bet they're from Franny or Casey. Ain't that sweet, they knew how upset I was.' She grabbed the card inside them and began to read it but her face drained of colour.

Vaughn looked concerned. 'What is it?'

'It's from them.'

Lola shoved the card at Vaughn, who read it out loud.

'To Mrs Harding with deepest condolences. Next time you won't be so fortunate.'

Another person who was mulling things over was Alfie Jennings. He hadn't slept well. Even the presence of the beautiful Franny Doyle lying in his bed next to him hadn't given him any comfort. She was so different from any woman he'd ever been with. Fiercely independent, successful, and sharper than a fucking scalpel in surgery. And he'd done the thing he'd scorned Vaughn for and vowed he'd never do. Ever. He'd fallen in love. And what a frigging chump he felt.

Everything had turned upside down and it drove Alfie crazy. Rather than having some dolly bird or fucking some Tom, all he wanted to do was spend time with Franny, the daughter of one of his old acquaintances, Patrick Doyle. When he'd first met Franny, he'd been blown away by her beauty. Piercing blue eyes and a mane of long silky hair. But she had hated him, or so she said, though he still reckoned it was more a question of how she wanted him but just couldn't have him.

He'd thought she was a stuck-up spoilt cow, but had been cordial because of the respect he had for her father. But like everything else, things had happened, people's outlooks changed and they'd got together and been inseparable ever since, or so he liked to tell himself.

Franny did his nut in. Most birds had always wanted to chew his ear off about him not spending enough time with them. His ex-wife, Janine Jennings, had nagged him so much about having family time with her that he'd ended up buying a mansion in Essex and dumping the fat greedy bitch there whilst he played, lived and worked in Soho. But now it seemed he was having a taste of his own medicine. Because now *he* wanted to spend his time with a woman; all his time if he had his way, but now the woman he'd fallen for, Franny, who was as stubborn as a mule on smack, wanted to keep her independence both financially and personally. And he, Alfie Jennings hadn't heard such a crock of shit since 'The Chicken Song'.

Still, he had other things to worry about at this moment. The conversation with Sarp had bothered him, especially as his name was now

48

being mentioned; plus the attacks on Soho were beginning to get closer to home, and the meeting with Lin hadn't gone to plan. Though perhaps once he spoke to Mr Lee, not Lin, things might be able to get worked out, or at least Alfie hoped they would.

When the attacks had first started he'd originally thought they might be a one-off and nothing to worry about, a warning shot from the triads, but after Lola's café and Sarp's restaurant it was clear that he'd been wrong. And one thing Alfie never liked to be was wrong.

It was beginning to get out of hand, especially now Sarp was on his case and threatening to call the Old Bill and make a noise; a sure way to make matters worse. Sarp paying them off for now would give Alfie time to sort it. But like he'd said to Sarp, he was going to do it *his* way – and *his* way was certainly not going to involve Vaughn Sadler. There was no way Alfie could let him know he'd set up a casino behind his and the other faces' backs and that the attacks on Soho were a consequence of his actions.

About to pick up the phone to try to speak to Mr Lee, the doorbell of Alfie's flat rang. Looking at the monitor of the CCTV screen, he saw some woman; young, brassy, standing at the door. He sighed, that was one of the bad things about having a past like his. He'd fucked that many Toms and escorts, wives and girlfriends, it was inevitable on occasion the odd one would turn up wanting to get another taste of the Jennings.

Pulling his Ralph Lauren pink jumper over his shirt, a present from Franny, Alfie headed down the plush cream thick-carpeted stairs. The bell rang again.

'Fucking hell, hold up, this ain't Aintree you know. I'm coming!' Alfie yelled out to the unknown caller as he began to unbolt the door.

'Yes?' Alfie peered at the female caller, his good looks scrunched up in the April sunshine as he scanned his memory to recall where he knew her from.

'It's me.' The woman stood chewing gum. Alfie thought she couldn't have been older than about twenty, if she was that. She was certainly a looker though; high cheekbones, button nose, big red lips and the largest of green eyes staring out at him. She was slim yet curvaceous, and her large breasts were further emphasised in the tight red top she wore with matching miniskirt. Alfie sniffed, she was definitely a brass. A cheap one at that. Even though she was pretty he knew he must've been well cut for him to go anywhere near someone who looked that young. Jail bait certainly wasn't his thing.

'Well?' The girl pouted, then spat out her gum. Alfie shook his head. Once upon a time he remembered when women were women, whether they were an old brass or not they still didn't go round acting like geezers.

'Well what?' Alfie answered coldly.

'Ain't you going to say anything to me?'

If she wanted money, well she'd come to the wrong door and if she was looking for more of the same, well maybe once but certainly not now he was with Franny. This was the first time in his life Alfie had been monogamous, and strangely enough it felt good.

'Like what?'

'Like hello?'

'Like piss off.'

The girl rolled her eyes at Alfie. 'That's bleedin' charming ain't it? You can't remember me, can you?'

'Listen darling, do yourself a favour and go and knock on someone else's door will ya. I'm pleased to say my days of rodding are well and truly over; besides your lot are ten a penny and if I was in the market for it, I certainly wouldn't be barking up your skirt, I've never liked mouthy birds and especially not ones that look like they've still got their homework books in their bag. Now do one.'

The girl crossed her arms, scowling from under her long blonde hair, cheeks flushed with anger. 'My lot? And what is "my lot"? What's that supposed to mean?'

Alfie smirked, 'You want me to spell it out to you?'

The girl put a cigarette in her mouth and lit it before she continued to speak. She narrowed her eyes as the smoke wafted into them and began to walk away, throwing her small tattered rucksack over her shoulder. 'You know what, don't bother, me mum always said you were a wanker.'

Alfie looked stunned. Her mum? What was she talking about?

The girl turned around, sticking two fingers up at Alfie. 'See you around, Uncle Alfie, it's been a pleasure.'

Uncle Alfie? What?... Wait. Shit. It couldn't be.

Alfie shouted out to the girl as she disappeared into the crowd of milling tourists in Old Compton Street.

'Chloe?... Chloe-Jane? Wait!... Wait!' Out of breath, Alfie caught up to the girl and grabbed her arm, recognition mixed with puzzlement written over his face.

'Chloe? Fuck me girl, you've changed. The last time...'

'I know, I know, the last time you saw me I looked a flipping geek.'

Alfie's voice was warm, his eyes reflecting the same sentiment. 'I wasn't going to say that ... you've just, well, grown up, that's all.'

Chloe-Jane beamed a smile. 'Oh you mean these. I had them done last year, cost five bleeding grand.' She pointed to her large breasts, proudly sticking out her chest even further which caught the leering attention of a male passer-by, who quickly averted his eyes once he saw the steely glare of Alfie.

Alfie pulled her towards him before taking his jumper off. 'No, I didn't mean them.'

Chloe-Jane giggled as Alfie handed her his top. 'Oh Uncle Alfie, you're so old-fashioned.'

Alfie's voice was firm. 'Just put it on.'

Chloe-Jane decided it was best to do as her Uncle Alfie said. She pouted, taking the jumper begrudgingly. She liked showing off her body. Liked men looking at her. It made a change.

For so long she'd been the geeky kid in school, with second-hand clothes and second-hand care. Her mother hadn't given a shit about her. She was either boozed-up or cracked-up.

She'd lost count of the amount of times she'd gone into short-term foster homes which were a relief from the chaos of life with her mother. If it had been her choice she would've stayed with any one of the foster carers she'd been to, apart from the last ones. Chloe shuddered, remembering.

As foster carers went they'd been okay, well at first anyway. The woman, a doctor, had been harmless, though it'd been clear to Chloe that she disapproved of her. Her husband had been a lawyer and Chloe had thought he was kind. He'd taken her places, bought her things, told her she was pretty and treated her like a father would treat a daughter. Not that she knew what that was like, she never even knew who her dad was and neither did her mum. All Chloe had ever known was a procession of her mum's violent boyfriends.

The man had even bought her a puppy whom she'd named Timmy, a cute white poodle. Then on her sixteenth birthday he'd given her the best present ever. He'd offered to buy her a boob job, and of course she'd jumped at the chance.

The operation had gone well and she'd gone up to a double EE. At only sixteen, the girls at school had been riddled with jealousy as suddenly overnight Chloe was now the most popular one with the boys. It'd been the happiest time of her life – and then it'd happened. Something she should've seen coming.

She'd been asleep when her foster father had woken her up. His hands and his mouth groping at her, pulling at her body and breasts as she tried to push him off. But he'd been too strong for her and after putting up a fight, Chloe finally was overpowered and the man had forced his erect penis into her. That was the night Chloe-Jane Jennings had lost her virginity.

The next day, Chloe had packed her things and gone to sit in the offices of social services, but as she had turned sixteen, no one had wanted to listen to her – she was too old. She'd gone back to her mother's but had only lasted a further eight months before her mother's behaviour had become too much for her.

She'd slept on friends' floors for another eight months before deciding to come up to London and leave Essex behind once and for all. And it was only when she'd arrived in London she'd remembered her Uncle Alfie. Her mother's half-brother. She'd only ever seen him twice in her life. But both times she remembered vividly because of his kindness. So where better to come and stay but with him? After all, he was family.

'I hope you don't mind me turning up like this, it's just I ain't got anywhere else to go. But I reckoned you wouldn't mind me staying with you.'

Alfie stared at her. He hadn't seen this coming, and even if he had there was just no way it was happening.

'When you say stay, what exactly do you mean?'

'Like stay. Crash out at yours. It'd be only for a couple of nights.'

Alfie began to shake his head. 'I don't think that'd be a good idea.'

Chloe-Jane looked at Alfie. She had to play this delicately. She glanced at Alfie slyly. Lying came second nature to her, after all, she was her mother's daughter. Chloe chose her words very carefully.

'Well that's what my mum said, but I said you weren't like that. I said you were the sort of bloke who wouldn't mind me just turning up out of the blue.'

Alfie silently nodded. It was true. He *was* a generous, welcoming guy. He listened on as Chloe continued.

'I don't know why Emmie thinks you're 'orrible. She don't know how lucky she is. If I had a dad like you, I'd...'

Alfie smarted at hearing the name of his daughter. The idea that Emmie thought he was horrible killed him.

'When did Emmie say that?'

Chloe shrugged her shoulders, knowing it wasn't true. In fact she hadn't spoken to her cousin in years. She'd heard her mum speak to Janine – Alfie's ex and Emmie's mother – on the phone and retell all the ins and outs of what happened, but besides that she really didn't know anything about Emmie.

'Anyhow, I best be getting on, Uncle Alfie. I gotta find meself somewhere else to stay. Sorry for troubling you.'

'No! Wait! Did your mum really call me a wanker?'

Chloe shook her head and a look of relief passed over Alfie's face, though it was only short-lived. 'No, she actually called you a cunt.'

Alfie's face reddened.

'Anyway Uncle Alfie, I really got to go.'

55

'Maybe ... maybe it'd be alright for a couple of nights.'

'Really?'

It was Alfie's turn to shrug. 'I guess ... but I mean a couple.'

Chloe squealed with delight as Alfie led her back to his flat. Well what could he do? After all, she was family. And family stuck together, no what matter what. The only problem was, Chloe was trouble. Alfie could smell it a mile away.

4

The scream echoed through the building and out onto the street as if it were a gush of air, causing the late-night passers-by to stop and wonder what they'd just heard, before hurrying quickly away.

Inside one of the darkened rooms of the six-storey building Chang Lee owned in Gerrard Street, Chinatown, Mr Lee stood behind the two-way mirror. The building's ground and first floor housed a restaurant run by some of Chang Lee's men, with the higher floors used for late-night illegal gambling, and the basement where he was now, for moments like this.

Chang watched his second-in-command, Lin, screw the pliers into the cheek of Sarp.

'Open up. I said, open up!' Lin shouted loudly, his eyes dancing in excitement as he began to extract the teeth of the man whose face already poured with blood.

Mr Lee looked on calmly, not showing a hint of emotion, watching whilst a patch of urine spread further across the tormented man's bloodstained underwear. He'd seen enough.

'Stop!' The one-word well-spoken order from Lee had Lin immediately breaking off from the pain they were inflicting on the man. Lin exhaled heavily, out of breath from all the physical exertion.

Mr Lee came out from behind the mirror, walking over to the man who lay crumpled on the stone floor like a heap of old sacks.

'My men are very loyal to me. When I give an order they like to carry it out; it's a matter of honour, you see. And when they can't, it upsets them. In Hong Kong we have a code. A code in which we swear an oath to preserve the fellowship at all costs. To do all we can to uphold it. My men will go to any lengths to make sure my orders are carried through.'

Sarp growled out something inaudible as Mr Lee shook his head.

'Pride can be an honourable trait, but it can also be a foolish one and cause a very nasty fall.' Mr Lee stood up, towering over the man as he continued to talk, his tone sinister. 'What I don't understand is why. Why on earth you wouldn't just pay. We could've protected you. Looked after your business ... looked after you. But as such, you've lost everything. Everything gone. Burnt to the ground.'

Through the pain, Sarp mumbled his words of defiance.

'I ain't paying you lot nothing. Fuck all.'

Mr Lee nodded to Lin, who picked up a discarded piece of wood from the floor and played with it in his hand for a moment as Lee continued to speak.

'That's it right there. The pride coming before the fall – and as for you not paying us anything; how wrong you are. You've paid a very high price indeed.' Lee nodded once more to Lin, who effortlessly swung the wood and smashed it into the man's skull, splitting open his head. Blood and brain mass spilt out as the man started to convulse.

Mr Lee sighed, a note of resignation in his voice. 'Bag him up.'

It'd just gone three in the morning as Alfie Jennings stood outside Whispers nightclub, which he'd owned for many years. It was something he was proud of, something which was close to his heart. He'd started the club in memory of his mother who'd killed herself when he was only a kid. To this day, the image of finding her covered in blood after she'd stabbed herself in the neck with a pair of garden shears still haunted Alfie.

Although it was only a business, essentially only a building, to him it was a way of keeping his mother's memory alive and he would do anything in his power to keep it going. In fact, Alfie suspected he'd put a bullet in someone's head to keep it going.

It was one of the reasons why he had such a problem with Vaughn. Okay, Alfie had made mistakes and got involved with people he shouldn't have done when he'd got mixed up with a gang of sex traffickers a few years back. But he hadn't known the full story, hadn't known all the ins and outs of it, not really, or so he liked to tell himself. What Alfie had known was that it paid well and he had been desperate.

His decision to get involved with the gang had seen Vaughn give him an ultimatum. Pull out of the deal or cut all ties with him. But how could he have done that? Alfie had needed the money and when it looked like Whispers and everything else was about to go under, he'd begged Vaughn to help him, to lend him money – but the only thing his one-time best friend had done was turn his back on him when he'd needed him the most. For that, Alfie Jennings would never forgive him.

Alfie realised Vaughn would have a different version of events to his. There'd be accusations of how he'd mugged him over, lied to him and tried to break up the relationship he had with Casey, and maybe, just maybe Alfie *hadn't* played fair, but then he'd never said he was an angel. Besides, what Vaughn had done by pulling his hand of friendship away was in Alfie's book far worse than anything he might or might not have done.

If it wasn't for Franny he'd be still down on his luck, but she'd come through even though there was nothing really in it for her. And he was more than grateful, which was why he needed to earn big money, and fast.

Alfie was too old to get involved in heists and robberies; besides, everything had changed; there was no such thing now as a clean robbery, which was essentially a case of going in with shooters, getting the dough before laughing all the way to the Costa.

The old school way of robbing had well and truly gone; the days when people just stuck their hands up, gave you no grief or behaved like funny cunts. Yes, they were the glory days when you could take the money and run, but now everyone wanted to be a hero, everyone wanted to be in the news for stopping a robbery – so more often than not, someone got shot, and the last thing Alfie wanted to do was spend any more of his life doing bird for some have-a-go hero.

No, what he needed to do was get enough money together and go and start a new life in Marbella with Franny. He was ready to settle down, like Vaughn had with Casey. Alfie was ready for the easy life. Jesus, he never thought he'd ever say that.

He'd always thought he'd stay in Soho all his life. Around everything he ever knew. But outlooks changed, people's perspective altered and it was because of this need to settle down and start afresh with the woman he loved that Alfie had started up his get-money-fast plan.

He hadn't run any of this by Franny, he thought he'd get everything sorted first. Come to her with a solid plan and enough dough to live the life he wanted and give her everything she could ever wish for. It'd crossed his mind that she might say no, but one of the things Alfie prided himself on was knowing women, and eventually, one way or another he knew he could talk Franny round. Because no matter how independent women *thought* they were, when it actually came down to it, all they really wanted was to be looked after by a real man, and he was certainly that, a little bit of the Jennings magic went a long way. But once again everything had changed, and now Franny saying no to a luxurious life on the Costa was the least of his worries.

His plan to have a slice of the money from the gambling dens of the triads had seemed so simple. He thought it would run so easily and work so well but it had started to go wrong. Badly wrong. All he'd ever wanted to do was have a share of the riches, not take over their empire, and the amount he'd be earning, taking from them, the likes of Mr Lee wouldn't even feel it. But they hadn't seen it like that. Oh no, they hadn't seen it like that at all. And now he needed to sort it out pront-fucking-o, before anyone, especially Vaughn found out. Because if he did, Alfie knew only too well that Vaughn Sadler would make it the beginning of the end for him.

As Alfie stood in the street, continuing to mull over the scenario he'd found himself in, he watched as a blacked-out car suddenly did a U-turn in the middle of Old Compton Street. It began to speed up and head towards him. Instinct told him to get back.

Jumping into the entrance of the club, Alfie narrowly missed being hit by the car as it pulled up beside him. His heart began to race as adrenaline raced round his body. Shit. The doors of the Mercedes flew open and for a moment Alfie thought it was over. That this was it. That finally his comeuppance had caught up with him. Images flashed through his mind whilst he scrambled for his gun, knowing by the time he drew it, it would probably be too late.

With the gun in his hand and about to fire, the car, as quickly as it'd driven up to Alfie, drove away, but not before the occupants in it had thrown something out. Something wrapped up in black bin bags and bound tightly round with silver gaffer tape. It didn't take Alfie's life of crime to tell him what it was.

The relief Alfie felt at not getting a bullet in his head was tangible but short-lived as panic began to set in. He quickly put his gun away and looked round the deserted street to check if anyone had seen what had happened. Satisfied no one was about, Alfie charged over to where the home-made body bag lay.

Quickly he dragged the body into the club, using his feet to push open the doors before diligently locking them behind him. The last thing he needed was someone coming in.

His phone rang. It was Franny. She'd have to wait; Alfie didn't want her knowing anything about this and if he answered she might sense there was something wrong and as much as he didn't want to lie to her, he'd have no choice.

Turning on the lights, Alfie stood gazing down at the body-shaped parcel. There was a note taped on the bag. It was written in red. Blood. Claret. And it simply read. *This is what happen when you disobey the rules.*

Alfie crouched down and took a deep breath. He ripped open the taped bin liners, revealing a naked, tortured body. Burns and bruises marked the man's white skin. Next, Alfie began to uncover the upper part of the body. The head had been bound over and over again with thick tape, making it necessary for Alfie to use his penknife.

After a few minutes, and with the bags and tape cut away, Alfie grimaced. For all his years of violence, it still sometimes made him recoil to see someone so battered. The geezer had had it bad. Alfie could see the man's teeth had been forcibly extracted and it looked like his right eye had been gouged out with what was probably a hot poker.

Wiping away some of the man's blood with part of the torn bin bag, Alfie paused. Shit. Shit. Shit. He knew who the geezer was. It was Sarp.

The last time Alfie had seen him was about a week ago, when he'd promised to have a word with Johnny and Frankie Taylor to keep an eye out, but he'd purposely not bothered, knowing exactly who was behind the threats.

He'd warned Sarp to pay the men until it was sorted. Then it wouldn't have mattered that Alfie hadn't spoken to the Taylors – but clearly the man hadn't heeded his warning, and now he'd paid with his life. Fuck. Fuck. Fuck.

Cold sweat ran down Alfie's face. The whole situation had become out of hand, spinning out of control and it was getting nearer and nearer to his doorstep.

He'd call his men to get rid of the body; he couldn't afford to have the Old Bill sniffing about, but first before he did anything else he needed to make a call. Taking out his phone from his pocket, Alfie Jennings dialled a number.

'Mr Lee, it's Alfie. I think we need to talk.'

5

'Are you sure he said that?' Franny Doyle looked at Chloe-Jane incredulously as she laid the few clothes she did have out on the spare bed.

'Yep. He said as long as it was alright with you, I could stay for as long as I liked.'

Franny gave a small smile. 'It's not really my decision.'

Chloe chewed her gum noisily. When Alfie had brought her to the flat, no one else had been in and he'd only just managed to have time to show her to the spare room before rushing out to his club which was almost opposite the flat.

Chloe remembered he'd said something about Franny, but she hadn't really listened. She wasn't the least bit interested in any of Alfie's girlfriends. But then Franny had come in, and they'd both given each other a fright as they'd bumped into each other in the darkened hallway.

That had been two hours ago and for some reason this woman wanted to know all about her, asking her questions about her life. Chloe-Jane *wanted* not to like her but for some reason she couldn't help warming to Franny.

Chloe's eyes glinted slyly. 'But it is to do with you. Uncle Alfie said if *you* didn't mind then I could stay longer... So is it alright? Can I stay?'

Franny wasn't sure what to say. She could see Chloe was desperate. Behind the front was a vulnerable young woman who was essentially still a child. Her body was that of a woman though, albeit a glamour model. Huge breasts, almost cartoonish in look, disproportionally formed the contours of her tiny body. Huge eyes and full lips gave her sensuality older than her seventeen years which Franny was certain would attract the wrong kind of attention.

It wasn't Chloe's fault but it slightly niggled her that Alfie hadn't bothered to tell her his niece was coming to stay or even ring her for that matter. She knew she was being silly, especially as things like this never usually troubled her. Maybe it had something to do with her finally deciding she was going to tell Alfie that she'd move in with him. Perhaps it was selfish, but the idea of having someone else in the flat whilst she adjusted to giving up her independence hadn't been what Franny had imagined.

But then what was she supposed to do? Chloe was Alfie's family and he didn't have much of that, and if she was going to be with Alfie long term, well that made Chloe her family too. And reading between the lines, it was clear Chloe had had a difficult time of it.

Franny could tell Chloe was proud, just like Alfie, but she hoped the girl would eventually open up to her. She knew through experience what could happen if problems and secrets went unresolved. She also knew what it felt like to be lost.

Franny smiled at Chloe, suppressing a sense of foreboding. 'Yes Chloe, of course you can stay as long as you want.'

Chloe couldn't contain the sound of excitement in her voice. Franny was clearly an easy touch. Before she knew it she'd have her eating out of her hand. Things were beginning to look up. 'I'll pay my way.'

Franny looked sceptical. 'Don't be silly, you haven't got any money. Besides, Alfie wouldn't expect that. You're family.'

'I will though, then there'll be no problem.'

'There'll be no problem anyway.'

'Are you sure?'

'Of course I'm sure, it'll be lovely and I'm sure Alfie will feel the same.'

'No way. No fucking way. Do I look like I've got baby-fucking-sitter written all over me boat?' Alfie Jennings did not need this at all.

'But I've told her now, Alf.'

'Well un-fucking tell her, Fran. I ain't got time for this shit now. And who's going to fork out for her? Muggins here. I don't even know her and I'm supposed to cop the bill for her? It's bad enough having to fork out for me ex and me daughter who I never see but who still wants to spend me money, let alone some waif from me half-sister.'

'You can be really horrible sometimes, Alfie.'

'So you like to keep on telling me, but I like to see it as being real. I ain't having someone leeching off me, family or not. So you can tell her she ain't staying here.' Christ, this was the last thing Alfie needed. What happened to Sarp had really shaken him up, and he didn't want to have to worry about anything else. He had to think about what to do, and having Chloe here wasn't going to help one little bit.

'Alfie, come on!'

'Franny, listen, I've got a lot going on right now, babe, so when I say no, I mean no. I can't deal with it at the moment. So just get rid, will ya.'

Chloe-Jane listened at the door as Franny and Alfie argued. Her heart was sinking. She'd hoped against hope that unlike the majority of people in her life, her uncle might actually want her around. But clearly she was wrong.

'I'm not going to do that. If you want to, you tell her. I'm not going to do your dirty work for you, Alf.'

'Fine then, I will.' Alfie headed for the door but Franny grabbed his arm, holding him back.

'Alfie, no! Wait!... You can't.'

'Firstly, I can and I'm going to, but secondly, how come you're bothered; what's it to you?'

Franny frowned, annoyed. This was the part of Alfie which irritated her and sometimes made her doubt the relationship. He could be so compassionate at times, but then there were times when he was like this. Ignorant. 'What do you mean, what's it to me? She's your niece and she's just a kid, plus it's obvious she's got nowhere to go.'

Alfie snorted.

'I hate it when you do that, Alf.'

Alfie looked surprised. 'Do what?'

'Snort when you know I'm right.'

Alfie's roar of laughter made Chloe jump but she continued to listen, her resentment towards her uncle growing greater. 'You ain't right, babe. She's a player.'

'She's a seventeen-year-old kid, Alf.'

'Yeah, a seventeen-year-old kid who wouldn't look out of place on the cover of *Playboy*.'

Everything about this moment made Franny want to walk out and go back to her own flat. She hadn't yet told Alfie about her plans to move in with him and the way the conversation was going she didn't know if she ever would.

'Why do you have to be like this, Alfie?'

'Like what?'

'Don't play the innocent!'

Alfie shrugged, he hated it when Franny became difficult. He was used to birds giving him grief; usually when they did he'd just leave them to it and go and find some Tom to fuck or play a few games of poker to get his mind off it. But with Franny he couldn't do either. Knowing that *he*, Alfie Jennings, was locked down by a woman pissed him off and fascinated him all at the same time, which in turn made Franny even more attractive to him.

'Play the innocent! I'd say if anyone had then it's Chloe. Don't you see Fran, she's properly played you. I said to her she could stay for two nights only.'

Franny shook her head, picking up her coat and bag. Even though it was the early hours of the morning, she wanted to go home to her own bed. She didn't feel like being around Alfie tonight. 'I'm not stupid, Alf. Of course I know she's playing me. But don't you see she's got nowhere else?'

'Well she ain't staying here.'

Franny stood opposite Alfie. She studied his

handsome face and gave him a sad smile.

'Then that makes two of us then.'

Alfie raised his voice in annoyance. 'You what?'

'You heard me, there's no way I'm going to stay here if you throw her out.'

Alfie's old school instinct kicked in and he growled at Franny, a sneer coming over his face. Love was one thing, but this was another. He was basically being blackmailed by Franny and he didn't like it. Not one fucking little iota.

'Sorry darlin', you may be the woman who's grabbed me heart but I ain't letting you grab me balls. No one but fucking no one tells Alfie Jennings what to do.'

Franny stepped in towards Alfie. Her voice was calm but cool. 'Alfie, I'm not telling you what to do, quite the opposite in fact. I'm telling you what *I'm* doing. Give me a ring when you've stopped being such a prick.'

Franny swung open the living room door, coming face to face with Chloe who had heard every word of the conversation.

'Get your stuff, Chloe, you can come and stay with me.'

The surprise on Chloe-Jane's face mirrored that of Alfie's. Chloe looked first to her uncle, then to Franny and back again. 'You mean it?'

'Of course.'

'No she don't. This is about me.' Alfie's voice was loud and although she ignored it, Franny could sense some hurt in his voice. She swivelled round to look at Alfie.

'I don't know if anyone's ever told you this, Alfie, but the world does not revolve around you.

Contrary to what you think, this *isn't* about you. This is about Chloe, your niece. Remember?'

Alfie began to panic, this was the last thing he'd expected. 'You walk out of here and you won't be walking back in. You hear me?' The moment the words came tumbling out, Alfie immediately regretted them, especially saying them to someone as fiery and stubborn as Franny Doyle.

Although Franny knew that Alfie didn't really mean what he'd just said, her eyes flashed with anger. He was behaving like a spoilt child. 'Is that what you really want, Alfie?'

It was the question Alfie Jennings hoped that Franny wouldn't ask. Either way, the answer would make him look like a cunt. If he answered it with the truth – which was, of course he didn't want her not to come back, in fact he didn't want her to go – he'd look a soft cunt and he'd be open to any sort of female manipulation in the future. The other way he could answer it was with a lie, which would be to tell Fran that, yes he meant it and she could piss off out of his face. If he told her that he'd not only look a cunt, for the first time in his life he knew his heart would break, so instead, Alfie Jennings did what he'd done whenever he got nicked. He stayed silent. After all, it was his right.

Franny glared at him. 'Fine, well if you haven't got anything to say, Alf, Chloe and I will get off. You know where we are when and *if* you decide to wind your neck in.' And with that Franny marched out of the room, with an excited-looking Chloe next to her.

The front door banged and Alfie rushed across

to the window, watching as they walked down the street. He wondered if Franny could feel him watching. There was a huge part of him that wanted to call her back, but his stubbornness and male pride wouldn't allow it.

He'd been right about Chloe, she was trouble, and now the thought began to creep in that Franny was too. But then show him a woman that *wasn't* trouble, and he'd show them a man. Alfie sighed. Maybe it was better like this. Yes, he'd make Franny sweat for a couple of days, bring her back to her senses and have her scratching down the door to come back. It'd also give him time to concentrate and sort out all this mess with the triads.

As Alfie continued to gaze out of the window, he caught a glimpse of someone looking up. He couldn't make out who it was but he was certain of one thing. Like everything else in his life at the moment, it probably meant only one thing. Trouble.

6

'Uncle Alfie! Uncle Alfie! Open the bleedin' door will ya!' Chloe-Jane banged hard on the side entrance of Whispers nightclub. Two days had passed since the last time she'd seen her uncle. And although no doubt he'd been in a huff, getting his bollocks in a twist, as arguments went, it was nothing. She was used to having stand-up rows, followed by fisticuffs. Broken bottles and drunken slurs thrown about by her mother and her boyfriends; that had been Chloe-Jane's life, so a few choice words were no reason to harbour a grudge. As well as this, she wanted something from Alfie.

About to bang on the door again, it was swung open by a startled-looking Alfie, something which didn't go unnoticed by Chloe-Jane.

'Alright mate!' She grinned, trying to peer over Alfie's shoulder. 'Up to no good, are ya?'

Alfie scowled. 'Has anyone ever told you you've got too much chat? Anyway what are you doing here? I thought you'd be somewhere else causing trouble.'

'Ain't me causing trouble. What's going on in there, 'cos whatever it is I bet Franny don't know nothing about it?'

Alfie stepped out into the alleyway, making sure the side door of the club was closed behind him. He shoved her gently on her shoulder. 'Piss off, will you. I don't need you buzzing around here like a fly on a pig's arse. So do one.'

Chloe-Jane looked nonplussed. 'Can't understand what Franny sees in you.'

'Well it's a good job it ain't nothing to do with you, ain't it? What is it you want anyway? Oh don't tell me, money...' Alfie went in his pocket and took out a roll of twenty-pound notes. 'Go on then, how much do you want? How much will it cost me for you to go on your merry way?'

Chloe-Jane looked affronted. 'I don't want yer money!'

'No?'

'No.'

'Then what?'

Chloe-Jane folded her arms, reminding Alfie of his ex. 'I want a job.'

Alfie roared with laughter. 'A job, in my club?'

'Yeah, what's wrong with that?'

'Now I know you're taking the piss. For a start, my club is a classy joint and the way you dress it'd make it look like it was a knocking shop for misfits and secondly, giving you a job would mean I'd have to trust you and I don't, not one tiny bit.'.

Having developed a thick skin over the years to survive, Chloe-Jane was not put off. 'Oh please Uncle Alfie, I won't let you down, I promise. I'll work *really* hard, just give me a chance.'

'I gave you a chance and what have I got to show for it? I'll tell you. Me missus up and left, and now I'm in the dog house and you're like the cat that's got the cream.'

'Look, all I want to do is pay my way.'

'And there's me thinking you're a freeloader.'

'I ain't, and I know Franny said I didn't have to pay, but people get fed up don't they?'

'That's the first sensible thing that's come out of your mouth. Ain't nothing for nothing in this world, you need to learn that, Chloe-Jane.'

Chloe's tone was laced with a bitterness far surpassing her age. 'You think I don't know that? From the time I was thirteen I was having to pay my way at home, and if I didn't, me mum would chuck me out or call social services to come and get me.'

A flash of shame briefly crossed Alfie's face,

thinking about Chloe-Jane's life. He'd half suspected his sister had neglected her but he'd done nothing about it. But then, it wasn't his fault was it? He'd had his own problems and there was no point in beating himself up about it now.

'So that's why I want a job, 'cos I reckon if I pay Franny, she can't say anything and won't get rid of me.'

Alfie leant forward. 'And that's why I ain't giving you a job. Because the sooner Franny comes to her senses the better, and we can all get back to normal. So like I said, do one, 'cos you're not going to make me feel bad about it because it ain't my fault you've got nowhere to go.'

Never one to be able to keep her mouth shut, no matter how hard she tried, Chloe-Jane retaliated, sticking her two fingers up as she turned away. 'And it ain't my fault you're a prick.'

Alfie watched the ball on the roulette table go round and round. The place was packed and all thoughts of Franny and the annoying Chloe-Jane began to fade. He had been supposed to meet Mr Lee, to sort things out, but he'd cancelled so until Alfie heard from him, why not keep pushing ahead with his venture? The damage had been done anyway, so what harm would a few more quid in his pocket make?

The room was packed with illegal gamblers and there was an air of excitement about the place as wealthy businessmen from all over laid thousands of pounds on the table, losing it in a turn of a card or a spin of the wheel.

'Hey! Alfie!' The voice sounded from behind

him and before Alfie had a chance to turn round properly, he felt a punch land at the back of his neck, complete with knuckledusters. He leapt back as his men ran forward, swinging with his fists at the suited men. The other punters in the club ran over to the exit but it was blocked by a large group of Chinese men who'd somehow got in through the double-locked doors.

Immediately the men started attacking the terrified punters. Nunchucks and coshes, chains and knives were bandied round. Alfie caught sight of a rich American banker being stamped on by three of the perpetrators. Blood poured from the man's face as he screamed at them to stop.

Alfie ran over to the far side, but was grabbed by a Chinese man with an ability to fight far superior to Alfie's. The man roundhouse-kicked Alfie's face, splitting open his lip and loosening one of his back teeth in the mix.

The next blow to Alfie, apart from to his pride was to his nose. A grinding of cartilage sounded as Alfie saw all around him his men being overwhelmed by the triads.

The side lunge to Alfie's knees brought him down to the ground and he yelled out in pain as his head hit the sharp side of the corner of the bar. He felt the warmth of his blood trickling down his neck. It was all beginning to get blurred now and the room began to spin around. The people's outlines began to fade in and out. Double vision halted any attempt for Alfie Jennings to fight back. Another pain hit him, this time in the stomach. The blow winded him and he struggled to breathe as he reached out to the wall to try and drag himself up. The boot to the back of his head saw Alfie sprawling on the floor. The next moment, he blacked out.

7

'Will you just sit down, Vaughn!' Casey Edwards sat at the kitchen table in Lola's flat watching her soon-to-be husband pacing up and down. He'd been pacing for the last hour and a half, ever since he'd got the phone call from one of his men, and it was now playing on her nerves. 'Vaughn, please! Can't you go and pace somewhere else?'

'I'm thinking.'

'Well can't you think in the car, I thought you wanted to get back home?'

Vaughn swung round to look at Casey. She was so beautiful and he was a lucky man, but she needed to understand things had changed. Everything had changed. And he wasn't going anywhere, not until this was all over.

He'd just got a call from one of his men, letting him know there'd been some trouble at Alfie's club, and also that Sarp, the Turkish restaurant owner from Greek Street, had gone missing. As for Alfie's club, he didn't know what was going on there but apparently something about a casino had been mentioned.

Vaughn shook his head as he thought about it. There was no way Alfie could really be so stupid, so fucking muppet-like as to open a casino right under the noses of the triads. No, he might be a lot of things and do a lot of things, but that? To bring the devil to the door, knowing it wouldn't be just him who would be in the firing line. No, surely not.

Alfie had sat there and seen the state Lola was in when the triads had thrown a warning fire bomb in the café. He'd been as angry as the others to think the triads were coming on their territory. There was no way it was an act. Vaughn's men must have got it wrong about the casino. Or they better have got it wrong. Because if they hadn't, this stunt of Alfie's would certainly be his last.

'You go, Cass. I'm going to stay in Soho.'

Casey looked amazed. One of the things she loved about Vaughn was that he'd put all his old life behind him. He hadn't seemed to miss his old life like so many of the other retired gangsters; he'd been satisfied to take it easy.

Casey had played hostess many times at the lavish dinner parties she and Vaughn had at his sprawling Kent mansion, listening to the retired faces who could no longer cut it or who no longer had the edge to stay; all dissatisfied and unable to take to civilian life. But Vaughn had been different; he'd found peace outside the world of violence and multi-million-pound deals. But since the attack on Lola's café last week he'd become obsessed with catching up with the people who'd done it. Almost overnight, the Vaughn Casey she had known changed into a hard ruthless man, set on revenge.

'Vaughn, this isn't a one-man crusade. What

about the others, they can help sort it out as well. There's Del, Johnny, Alf...' The moment Casey began to say Alfie's name she immediately regretted it, as she saw the look in Vaughn's eye. His voice was cold and agitated.

'Alfie? Are you fucking serious? That man's caused enough grief, wouldn't you say, Cass?'

Casey decided to remain silent. Vaughn and Alfie's history went way back. At one time, at the height of Vaughn and Alfie's friendship breakdown, Alfie had told Vaughn he'd slept with her. And although Alfie Jennings had eventually admitted nothing had happened between him and Casey, it was still a sore spot for Vaughn when she talked about Alfie with any form of affection or positivity.

'Well, Cass?' Vaughn stood in front of Casey. She could see he was pushing for a fight, which would be his excuse to stay in London without having to discuss it with her. Well she wasn't going to be goaded. If he wanted to stay in Soho then she wasn't going to let him put it on her. She remained silent, staring at Vaughn.

Eventually Lola, having finished consuming a runny egg sandwich, broke the silence.

'Listen Casey, Vaughnie is just doing what he knows best. He's old school. Them triads need to be stopped and put in their place. This is Soho. *Our* Soho. Me and Vaughn's. All of us have been round here as long as me memory will take me back. It's where we belong. It's all some of us know; all some of us want. You're not from round here, love, so it's different for you, harder for you to understand. But this is our home and we'll do anything to protect it. So let Vaughnie do what needs to be done.'

Casey shook her head. 'Lola, you know I love you like my own mum, and you're right I'm not from round here, but neither is Vaughn, not anymore. He's moved on. I'm not asking him to turn his back on you or Soho, I'd never do that, but he needs to leave it to the others, take a step back.'

Lola shook her head, her warm smile cutting through her craggy wrinkled skin. 'Cass, it's in him. Soho is in his blood. No matter what, that will always be the case and no matter how much he loves you, Soho will always come first.'

Casey was about to object but as she watched Vaughn walk out of the room without saying a word, something told her Lola might just be right.

The AA meeting in Greek Street was empty, save for an old man and a twenty-something skinny woman whose eyes gave away her hard life. But it wasn't the people Casey had come to see, it was the sense of support she felt when she walked into the hidden meetings which could be found in every town. These sobriety meetings had saved her life. Stopped her from destroying herself when nothing else could reach her.

But as she'd got better, she'd relaxed, hadn't bothered attending so many meetings, and that had been fine, but one morning last month she'd woken up and from nowhere the cravings had returned. That overwhelming sense of needing a drink. No matter what. No matter how much it hurt her or anyone else, the need to feel the burn of the alcohol hit the back of her throat had become overwhelming.

The cravings which in the past would've led to her putting herself in compromising situations with men and drugs were the demons which had brought her to Soho in the first place. Casey had come searching to put the past right, and whilst doing so had put herself right. Her life had gone from unmanageable to downright good. Life had come together. Her life finally had a purpose, and of course then there was Vaughn. She loved him and that love wouldn't have been possible if she was still a drunk. A lush. He was again part of the reason she needed to stay sober because if she didn't, it wouldn't be a question of *if she might* lose Vaughn, it would just be a question of *when*.

But how could Casey tell him that their life and her sobriety were in danger of collapsing because of a craving? An urge so strong that in the past, when she'd been married to her first husband, she'd found herself sleeping with strangers just to get a drink.

Even at the time Vaughn had never really understood, although he'd tried. Although he'd seen Casey battle to stay sober, he couldn't really get his head round the fact that booze came before most things, including him at times.

So here she was, sitting in a darkened basement, desperate to keep clean. But it was hard, so hard; if it wasn't for the relationship with Vaughn she wasn't sure if she'd have the strength to go another day without having a drink.

8

Casey and Franny sat in Lola's newly refurbished café in Bateman Street.

'Well, what do you think, ladies?' Lola sat down by the two women, admiring her new set up. She'd been proud of it before, but this, she thought, *this* was the dog's bollocks.

Casey, who'd worked in Lola's café before she'd met Vaughn, smiled at the flamboyance of the tiny workman's café. Gold and black chandeliers hung from the ceiling. Bright red tables and chairs had replaced the old wooden ones, the work counters were now a loud zebra print and the walls were painted lime green, with large silver-framed photos of Soho in the Sixties.

'Well, it's different.'

Lola grinned proudly. 'It ain't quite finished yet, but then I blame Vaughn. Can't get hold of him. He promised he'd get one of those moose heads for me. I think it'd look lovely over there near the door. What do you think?'

Casey raised her eyebrows, her full red lips twitching with a smile. 'Tell me you're kidding.'

Lola looked shocked. 'Kidding? Why would I do that?'

'It's just that ... well, don't you think it might be a bit OTT?'

Lola stood up, clearing the empty tea cups. She shook her head in dismay. 'You've never had any taste, Casey. It's all the rage; latest thing.'

'A moose head?'

'Oh yeah, I saw it in a magazine; they had photos of Hampton Court.'

Casey's eyes widened. 'They had a moose head in Hampton Court?'

'Well it weren't a moose head exactly; it was a deer's head. But I've never liked them things; their eyes are too close together. Gives me the heebie-jeebies. Anyway, moose, deer; they're all a bit classy ain't they? And if Henry the eighth can have one on his palace wall then so can Lola's café.' And with that, Lola shuffled off, delighted at the admiration on Franny's and Casey's face.

Casey watched Lola for a moment before turning to Franny, her smile not reaching her eyes. 'How's your new lodger?'

'Chloe-Jane?'

'Yeah.'

'Messy! I'm sure I was never that bad when I was her age, but then I'm not really surprised; by all accounts she's hardly had an easy life, she's had to fend for herself most of it. But she's sweet. I like her.'

'How long's she staying?'

Franny grinned. 'I dunno, she's talking about giving me money for her upkeep, I think she's worried I'm going to kick her out any day soon, poor kid.'

The women fell silent, then, making sure Lola was out of earshot, Franny whispered, 'What's going on, Cass?'

Casey looked down at the table. 'Oh, nothing

much. Usual stuff. Vaughn's got a bee in his bonnet.'

'About Alfie?'

'About him and other stuff. Things aren't so good.'

'With Vaughn?'

Casey hesitated.

'Cass, you can trust me. We're friends. Whatever it is, I won't say anything. I promise. I know what it's like when you've got no one to talk to.'

'Thanks Fran, it's just... I know I can trust you, but it's difficult. Apart from you I haven't got anyone else. I can't talk to Lola because it wouldn't be fair, you know with her being close to both of us, and I obviously can't talk to Vaughn...' Casey trailed off.

'Then tell me.'

Casey's eyes filled with tears as Franny reached across the table. 'Cass, *please*. I'm worried about you. You haven't been yourself lately. Tell me what's going on.'

Everything in Casey wanted to tell Franny about how the urge to drink was making her feel. But her shame stopped her. Franny wasn't like her. She seemed so sorted; she'd gone through so much, yet she'd done it all without a crutch and had only needed the support of her friends. Yet here Casey was, still fighting the booze and her demons. Still waking up with the overwhelming urge to go out and get drunk.

'Is it Vaughn; Cass, and all this stuff in Soho? I know you want to be loyal to him, but what are friends for if you can't lean on them? I won't say anything.'

Casey looked up at Franny. It was easier to agree with her friend than tell her the truth, though it wasn't a complete lie. Things *were* strained with Vaughn, but it was difficult to know how much was actually him, and how much was Casey. Vaughn had been pushing her away, but then she'd been doing the same with him. He couldn't find out what was going on. He just couldn't.

Feigning a smile, Casey spoke to her friend. 'Yeah, that's right. It's Vaughn. All this stuff with Soho has got right under his skin. He's like a different man.'

'Try not to worry, Cass, Alfie's no better. He's roaming around like he's got a rod stuck up his arse... It'll be okay; if it's any comfort, I know Vaughn loves you. But if I can give you any advice, Cass, it'd be this; talk to him. That's what gets me and Alfie through the tough times. We talk to each other, and above all we don't have any secrets.'

9

Mr Lee stood by the window, wondering quite why the English were so foolish. There seemed to be a common thread which ran through them, a thread of misplaced pride – or as he liked to call it, stupidity.

He'd warned them. Warned them that the trouble wasn't necessary, and could have so easily been avoided. All they'd had to do was abide by the rules. How easy. How simple; yet as Mr Lee stared in contempt at the bloodied and battered Alfie Jennings lying on the floor, it was clear to him, *simple* was something the English didn't like.

Sitting down on the large purple velvet chair, Mr Lee crossed his legs, making him look smaller and more diminutive than he usually did.

'It's a shame we couldn't meet under better circumstances. I was very much looking forward to our discussion later on in the week, but as Robert Burns said, *the best laid schemes of mice and men.*' Mr Lee paused, flicking off a stray piece of ash from the large cigar he was smoking. 'When my men told me you'd decided to continue with your little venture, I thought it best to cut my trip short and have that chat sooner rather than later. I'm sure you understand. And I can only imagine you've got a good reason for disobeying my rules.'

Through his swollen, bruised eyes, Alfie glared at Mr Lee. 'Ain't no one going to tell me what I can and can't do, especially from a fucking *kitchen sink.*'

Mr Lee looked puzzled. 'Kitchen sink?'

Alfie sneered defiantly. 'Chink.'

Chang Lee's face expression hardened. He leaned forward and addressed Alfie, speaking quietly. 'You see, Mr Jennings, it's comments like those that I can't ignore. It never ceases to amaze me how foolish people are.' Mr Lee nodded his head to Lin and another of his men who walked across to Alfie. They yanked hold of his arms, pulling at his hands as Mr Lee stood up. 'You

85

leave me no choice, Alfie, and to think all of this could have been avoided.'

Mr Lee nodded again, watching as Lin brought down the machete on Alfie's forcibly spread fingers. Blood splattered out everywhere along with Alfie's scream as his little finger was cleanly cut off. His body jerked in shock as what looked like a river of blood streamed out from the mutilated hand.

Mr Lee bent over and picking up the severed finger, walked over to Alfie.

'Hopefully now you'll get the message, Mr Jennings and if you haven't, there's always the other nine.' He went to walk away but stopped short of the door. Turning round, he threw the finger at Alfie with a grin. 'I think you might have more need of that than me.'

10

'Here you are. I got this for you.' Chloe-Jane handed Franny eighty pounds.

Franny looked curious. 'What's this for?'

'It's for you. For me board and lodgings.'

'I told you, there's no need. Really Chloe, I'm happy for you to stay.'

Chloe-Jane shrugged her shoulders. 'I just want you to take it.' She pushed the money into Franny's hand. *'Please.'*

'Where did you get it from?'

'I ain't robbed it, if that's what you think.'

'I don't think that.'

'It's me money I saved to come here. I told you I was going to give you some.'

Franny shook her head, going across to the other side of the kitchen to make a cup of tea. She opened a packet of dark chocolate biscuits, offering one to Chloe-Jane who proceeded to take several, much to Franny's amusement.

'Listen, Chloe, why don't you keep the money? You'll need it when you move on.'

Chloe-Jane bristled. She wanted to yell at Franny that that was the point. She didn't *want* to move on. She wanted to stay, because aside from the fact she liked it with Franny, she had nowhere else to go. With a sad smile, Chloe replied, 'Well until then; take it, it'll make me feel better.'

Franny looked doubtful. 'If you're sure.'

'I am!'

'Okay, what I'll do is, I'll put it up here in this tin, and for any reason you want it back just take it. No questions asked. Deal?'

'Deal, and I'll give you eighty pound a week from now on. I don't want to leech off anyone.'

'Well I appreciate that, Chloe. Thank you.'

'It's no problem. No problem at all.'

It was getting dark as Chloe-Jane walked along Brewer Street, watching as the passing men ogled at her and the women gave her a look of scorn. She wore a low-cut pink top with nothing underneath, erect nipples obvious under the clinging material. Her tiny white miniskirt skimmed the bottom of her buttocks, and her high patent yellow shoes gave a swagger to her walk.

'Fancy a drink, darlin'?' A large, sweaty passing workman hollered out to her from his van.

'Not with you, mate, I'd rather stick me head down the khazi and drink from there!'

The van sped off beeping its horn, leaving Chloe to cross the road at the junction of Brewer and Glasshouse Street.

Hanging out on the corner, a car pulled up. A man in his late fifties rolled down the window. His voice was low and Chloe could hear a Northern accent.

'You doing business, love?'

Chloe nodded, quickly looking around before getting in.

11

'Just fucking sew it back on. I don't care how you fucking do it, but there ain't no way I'm ending up like frigging Anne Boleyn.' Alfie grimaced at the hospital doctor as he clutched his wrapped bloody hand to his body.

'She had eleven fingers, not nine, and it was her head that was cut off, not her hand.' Chloe-Jane smirked at her uncle as she chewed on the constantly present piece of gum.

'I'll chop your bleedin' head off if you don't shut it,' Alfie growled at his niece. Why the hell Franny had brought her along, fuck only knew and it pissed him off no end.

'Alfie, there's no need for that.' Franny spoke,

not unkindly.

'Me hand's fucking been chopped off and she wants to give me a fucking history lesson, do me a favour!'

'One finger isn't exactly your whole hand, Alf.'

'No? Well it fucking feels like it, you should try it someday. And look at the state of me boat, do I look like a person who's just sat watching telly all day?'

Franny stared at Alfie, taking in his cut and bruised face. When she'd got his phone call asking her to come and see him, she'd been surprised and secretly pleased, thinking his male pride would have made it difficult for him to phone so soon. She'd been about to tease him about it but there'd been something in his voice which had stopped her. So instead she'd just listened, hearing the edge of urgency and panic in his voice. When he'd told her he was in the hospital, her stomach had tightened and she'd rushed to see him, bringing a complaining Chloe-Jane, who'd been very mysterious as to where she'd been, with her.

When Franny had opened the blue faded hospital curtain, she'd been shocked at the sight of his battered appearance.

She'd arrived in casualty full of sympathy but when she'd asked him questions about what had happened, Alfie had been rude and evasive, and Franny's warmth had turned to what Alfie always called her *bitch stance*.

'Perhaps a bit of sympathy would be nice. Ain't too much to ask for.'

'Well when you start behaving decently and

answer my questions, maybe I'll give you some.'

'Has anybody told you you've missed your vocation? You should've been the Old Bill, do you go around giving everyone the third degree?'

'No, only you when you're being childish.'

Even through the pain, Alfie managed to stare at Franny incredulously, not quite believing what he was hearing. He'd called her assuming she'd be distraught with worry and concern, he'd even half suspected that she'd come to her senses, apologise and stop the stupid point she was trying to prove with Chloe-Jane. Sympathy. A little bit of TLC. Surely that wasn't too much to ask for? A man wanting a bit of care from his woman. It should be a given; man provides for woman. In return, woman cares for the man and tends to his every need. That's the way it was. Should be. And that'd been the case since the beginning of time and it would always be – unless the woman on your arm went by the name of Franny flipping Doyle. It was just his luck. Just Alfie's fucking luck to fall in love with an independent, man-hating, beautiful, fiery woman. On top of which, he now had only fucking nine fingers to his name.

'Do you think you'll be able to sew it back on?' It was Franny who spoke to the doctor, voice full of concern, which only added to Alfie's annoyance. She was able to air her concern and flicker her eyelashes at the handsome casualty doctor, but not for him.

'I'm not sure, it really depends on the replantation team.'

'Fucking hell, what am I? A frigging hydrangea? This ain't *Gardener's World* you know, mate.'

'Ignore him, he often gets like this when he doesn't get his own way.' Franny smiled as she talked to the doctor who gave Franny a sympathetic look in return, making Alfie seethe even more.

Alfie decided he wouldn't stand for this anymore and sprang up from the hospital trolley, ignoring the pain which was only slightly helped by the injection of painkillers he'd been given earlier. He grabbed the man by his good hand, pushing past Chloe-Jane who stood back trying to make eyes at the doctor, who was by now too busy trying to stop Alfie attacking him to notice.

'Alfie! Alfie, get off him!' Franny's voice was pitched high as she shouted at Alf, pulling on the back of his bloodstained sweater.

'Maybe I can help.' A deep voice sounded from behind. Franny turned round, expecting to see a hospital security guard, but instead she came face to face with Vaughn Sadler followed by Del Williams.

Vaughn pushed past Franny, grabbing hold of Alfie by the scruff of his neck. 'You've got some fucking explaining to do.'

It took Alfie only a second for his brain to realise what was happening and another second for his face to blanch momentarily, before he leapt into action.

He twisted his body, ignoring the pain of his injuries from the triad attack. Using his shoulder, he slammed into Vaughn who staggered backwards, surprised at the strength of the injured Alfie Jennings. As Vaughn fell into the hospital sluice trolley, propelling the steel surgical instruments to the floor, Del Williams stepped forward to help, lunging angrily towards Alfie, but a sudden pain stopped him, sending shockwaves through Del's body. He held onto his head.

'Fucking hell!' Del shouted out in pain as Chloe-Jane stood with a metal tray in her hand.

Del turned to stare at Chloe, seeing the security guards rushing over to see what the commotion was. He snarled at her. 'What the fuck did you do that for?'

Chloe-Jane shrugged, looking first at Alfie, then at Del who'd she'd struck hard across the head. 'He's family. And family stick together.'

An hour later, Franny sat in the waiting room drinking what she suspected was the worst cup of coffee she'd ever had. Either that, or it was the bitter taste in her mouth she'd suddenly developed as she listened to Vaughn and Del tell her their suspicions about Alfie, who lay oblivious under anaesthetic in theatre.

'It ain't even bang out of order, Fran, what he's done is worse. Much worse. He's got involved with them triads, or at least he's been part of the reason they've launched their attacks on Soho. He went against the rules, Fran, opening up a casino behind our backs. Everyone knows that's off limits.'

Franny bristled. 'If it's true.'

Vaughn and Del glanced at each other.

'Don't look like that, guys, we don't know it's true.'

Frustrated, Vaughn stood up, gesturing widely with his hands. 'Oh come off it, Fran, you know what a fucking muppet he is, this has got Alfie Jennings written all over it. Anything that goes wrong and there's even a sniff of Alfie's name, you know he'll be right in the centre of things. Ain't no smoke without fire, or in this case, ain't no smoke without Alfie. It's always been the same. You know that.'

Franny's face flushed with anger. She spat out her words, surprising herself at how protective of Alfie she felt. 'This isn't about what's happening in Soho, Vaughn, this is about you. Everyone knows you've got a problem with Alfie, and this is your way of getting back at him.'

'Don't be such a stupid cow, Fran, didn't you see what shit he got your father into? I don't know how you can bear to let him near you.'

Franny's slap to Vaughn's face shocked everyone, apart from Chloe-Jane who had seen it coming. The only other person Chloe had known do that had been her mother, just before she'd drunkenly laid into her, often leaving her too bruised to go to school the next day.

Chloe-Jane stepped behind Franny, showing her solidarity to her newfound friend as well as her uncle. He wasn't her favourite person by any length but it was one thing for Chloe-Jane to think Alfie was a god almighty prick, but it was an entirely other thing for someone else to.

Vaughn's fury showed in his eyes. Who the hell did Franny think she was? This was men's business, not women's. He'd had a lot of respect for her at one point, the way she'd handled herself when the shit had hit the fan with her father, Patrick. She'd also been a good friend to Casey which of course he'd appreciated, but now? Now he was losing respect for her and if she wasn't careful, Franny would lose the respect of the other London and Soho faces she'd known since she was a child.

Franny's voice was steely.

'Don't you dare speak about Patrick.'

'Why not, truth hurts.'

Franny stepped forward, closing the space between them. Franny stared at Vaughn, wondering how he'd changed from the sweet perfect gentleman to a hardened embittered man. When Casey had called her in tears, worried about the way Vaughn was acting, she'd reassured her friend it was probably nothing and had convinced Casey just to put it down to Vaughn having a bad day. But as Franny stood in front of him, it was clear this was far from a bad day.

'The only truth here, Vaughn, is whatever vendetta you're riding on, you better get off it and real quick. You don't run Soho – those days are well and truly over, whether you like it or not. Go up against Alfie and you'll go up against me.'

Vaughn laughed scornfully. 'Oh and that's supposed to frighten me how?'

'I don't expect it to frighten you, Vaughn, you're too stupid for that. What I do expect is for you to back off from Alfie until you know the truth, because if you don't you'll regret it.'

'You two deserve to be together. At first I couldn't quite see how you and him could work, but now I see it, Christ do I just.'

'Maybe instead of worrying about Alfie and me, perhaps you should be worrying about your own relationship.'

It was the first time Franny saw Vaughn bristle. His eyes darkened. 'What's that supposed to mean?'

Franny began to walk away. 'You tell me.'

'I said, what's that supposed to mean?'

Ignoring Vaughn, Franny opened the waiting room door but felt her arm being held. She stared down at Vaughn's grip before staring up into his face. 'Get your hands off me.'

'Not till you tell me what you meant.'

'You heard her, get the fuck off her.' Chloe-Jane stood with a chair in her hand a few feet away from Vaughn.

'Get your dog to back off, Fran.'

Franny, who'd just been about to tell Chloe-Jane to put the chair down, angrily reacted to Vaughn's comment. 'Who the hell do you think you are, Vaughn, speaking to her like that, she's just a kid? What's happened to you?'

Chloe-Jane continued to hold the chair in a threatening manner, trying to decide whether or not to feel affronted by Franny calling her *just a kid,* or to be touched by Franny sticking up for her, a rare occurrence in her life. Deciding on the latter, and without a moment's more hesitation, Chloe-Jane swung the chair at Vaughn, screaming at him hysterically.

'She said get off her! Fucking bastard! Get off!'

Seeing Vaughn's head begin to bleed and sensing Chloe-Jane was about to hit Vaughn again, Del intervened, grappling the chair off her. He pulled it from her hands with a strong tug, managing to release it from her grip in one go. But like a wild feral cat about to lose its prey, Chloe-Jane pounced on both Del and Vaughn. Fingernails scratched at skin, teeth bit into flesh as she yelled a stream of profanities.

Franny moved forward, dragging Chloe-Jane off the men. She wrapped her arms round her as she pulled her away, battling as Chloe tried to break out of her hold and back to the men.

Franny shouted loudly. 'Chloe! Chloe-Jane! Stop! Stop! Just calm down.'

Chloe-Jane turned to Franny, her face expressing hurt and frustration. 'Did you hear him though? Did you hear what he said?'

Franny nodded. 'I did and he was wrong, but you've got to calm down. You can't go round hitting people as and when you feel like it.'

'But he grabbed hold of you. He wouldn't let go. He can't do that, can he?'

'No. No, he can't.'

Del spoke up. 'He can if you're taking the piss. What do you want him to do, Fran? Let you talk shit about him and Casey?'

Franny's eyes flashed with anger at Del.

'Has it come to you having to fight Vaughn's battles for him now, Del?'

Del scowled. He didn't need this shit, he'd rather be back home in the Costa with his family, but he, like everyone else, had received the call to come and help. So now he was here, Del wanted to resolve it all as soon as possible, which didn't mean having to argue the toss or get clouted across the head by some bird. He'd had enough of that being married to his ex-wife, Edith.

'Turn it in Fran, Vaughn's right, you're acting

like a silly cow. What you need is a reality check and what missy here needs is a hard spank on the arse.'

It was like a flame to a petrol can and Chloe-Jane exploded. 'Is that fucking right, mate? And what? You think you're the one to do it do you? Fucking perv, get off on the thought of young girls having their behinds tanned do you? Go on, frigging try it and see what you get.'

Del sighed. Even though he was furious with Alfie for what he'd brought onto Soho, a part of him couldn't help but feel sorry for him. This girl was trouble. Trouble and loud-mouthed, and if Franny wasn't careful, it wouldn't be just Alfie who'd bring down her world, it'd be Chloe-Jane.

'Listen sweetheart, think whatever you like, it ain't going to make an iota of difference to me, but I'm telling you if you carry on like this, you'll make lots of enemies. And the kind of enemies you'll make around here, I wouldn't wish on even you.'

Franny turned her attention from Vaughn to Del, speaking in a low hushed tone. 'Is that a threat, Del? Because if it is, you better take that back right now.'

Del shook his head. 'You know how it is, Fran. What you playing at? She ain't even your family, but you're happy for her to destroy the relation-ships around you with the likes of me and Vaughn.'

It was Franny's turn to shake her head. 'If my relationship with you is so easily broken, maybe I'm better off without it. And as for her not being family; you're wrong. She's Alfie's family, which makes her mine. So if you've got a problem with her, you've got a problem with me.'

Chloe-Jane once again couldn't help feeling delighted with what Franny had just said, but this time she didn't try to hide it. Standing in the tiny hospital waiting room, she grinned as Del and Vaughn looked on. For the first time in her life she felt wanted, and no one but no one was going to take that away from her. If anyone tried, Chloe-Jane was going to make them wish they hadn't. Oh yes, she would make certain of that.

12

Franny sat in Lola's kitchen. She looked around at the tired orange paisley wallpaper and brown tiles and although it certainly was in need of re-decoration, there was something comforting about the familiarity of the place. Days gone past of happy times with her father, memories of late-night chats with friends, and crying through difficult times over cups of tea. It was all here, here in this room.

'Do you think it's true, Lola? Do you think Alfie is the reason why the triads attacked Soho?'

Lola Harding, dressed in a cheap designer knock-off dress, plonked a cup of steaming hot tea in front of Franny. Her expression was sympathetic.

'Listen Fran, I love Alf, we all do, even Vaughnie does in his own way, but both you and I know he's

98

a chancer. Old school he is, always ducking and diving like the rest of us, but unlike the rest of it, he takes it too far. He gets greedy. No, don't look like that Fran, you know I'm telling the truth. Ain't got no reason to lie to you. You and I go as far back as when you were a baby, and I've never told you an untruth and I ain't going to start now. See sense darlin'. Alfie needs to stop what he's started; he's making enemies everywhere, those triads will kill him if he's not careful, and I don't want to see something happen to him.'

Franny bit her lip. She didn't want to argue with Lola, especially as she was still upset from the attack on her café, even if it now looked a hundred times better than it ever did. Casey had told her that Lola had called Vaughn up several times demanding high-spec fittings and fixtures for the café which certainly wasn't reminiscent of the cheap and grimy decor it'd had previous to the attack.

'What is it all of a sudden about everyone wanting to be enemies? We've all been friends for years and now all that's changing. The Soho I used to know is disappearing, Lola. All the good times we had aren't there anymore. Do you remember how we always got together on Sundays? Me and my dad and my Uncle Cab, Del, Vaughn, Alfie and the Taylors. And then there was you and...'

'Any bastard I'd fallen for that week.' Lola cackled, reaching out to take Franny's hands into hers over the kitchen table.

'The picture's changing, Lola and I can't help feeling sad; it's like we're all being written out of a story and it's time to go our separate ways.'

'Fucking hell girl, remind me to invite you round again won't you when I need cheering up? Christ, you make a funeral march sound cheery.'

Franny laughed, tears of mixed emotions brimming up in her eyes. 'Thank you, Lola.'

Lola looked surprised. 'For what?'

'For making me laugh, for being here ... for being you.'

Lola blushed, then winked at Franny. 'You soft cow, you certainly take after your father. The gift of the gab he had, or as I like to call it; bullshit.'

The two women burst into laughter. The evening light faded as they both hung onto the memories of the past, both uncertain of the future.

13

'Well wake up then. Talk about fucking milking it. I'm surprised you ain't got bleedin' udders.'

Alfie Jennings slowly opened his eyes to see Chloe-Jane leaning over him. He croaked, his mouth dry from the anaesthetic.

'What the hell are you doing here? Where's Franny?'

Chloe-Jane looked slighted. 'Well that's flipping nice ain't it, next time I won't bother nicking these grapes for you.' She threw the bunch of red grapes at Alfie and began to walk away.

'Oi! Chloe. Wait up girl.' Alfie called her back, noting how quickly and eagerly she turned round.

A tiny shot of guilt hit him. Maybe he'd been too hard on the girl. 'Listen, I wanted to say I saw what you did back in casualty, whacking Vaughn like that. Some of the hardest men wouldn't have even done that.'

'I ain't scared of no one.'

'Well, maybe you should be.'

Chloe-Jane looked puzzled and genuinely interested. 'Why? You ain't.'

Alfie nodded his head in agreement. It was true what his niece was saying. The only person he'd ever been afraid of was his dad when he'd been a kid, as he'd savagely beaten him on an almost-daily basis. But Alfie's fear had turned to fearless hatred on the day his mum had killed herself and soon it was his dad who'd been afraid of him.

'You're a girl, it's different.'

Chloe-Jane scoffed. 'This ain't Victorian times you know.'

'Listen, if you're going to give me another history lesson, save your bleedin' breath. I never learnt fuck all in school and I don't want to start learning now.'

'Has anyone ever told you you're an ignorant pig?'

Alfie grinned. 'Yup, plenty, including Franny. Did you come with her?'

Chloe-Jane took the piece of gum she'd been chewing and stuck it on her leg enabling her to tuck in to the bunch of ripened grapes.

'Nope, and you should be grateful she ain't here, Uncle Alfie.'

'Why?'

'Because if you think it's painful having your

101

finger chopped off, imagine how it's going to feel when you have your balls sliced off.'

Alfie closed his eyes again, he was tired and the last thing he needed was the chattering of a teen-ager but it didn't stop him being curious as to what Chloe was talking about. He turned his head and opened one eye. 'And why would I want to imagine that, hey?'

Chloe-Jane grinned. ''Cos Franny is going to whip them off when she sees you.'

Alfie snapped. 'What the fuck are you talking about?'

'She knows.'

Alfie paled slightly. 'Knows what?'

'Ain't no good lying, Uncle Alfie, I know, just like everyone else does.'

Alfie pushed himself up, pain rushing through his hand. Panic began to rise inside him and a defensive tone was evident in his voice. 'Like I said, I ain't got a clue to what you're talking about.'

Chloe-Jane shrugged, stood up to go. 'Okay, well suit yourself. Don't try to tell me I didn't warn you.'

'Wait! Okay, okay, you've had your fun and now you can stop playing your games.'

Chloe-Jane looked the picture of innocence. 'Oh, I'm not playing games, Uncle Alfie.'

Alfie Jennings spoke through gritted teeth. His voice was hushed. 'What do you want from me, Chloe?'

Chloe-Jane looked genuinely surprised. 'From you? Nothing. I'm here to help you.'

Alfie looked stunned, before bursting into

laughter. 'Fuck me, I ain't that desperate.'

The pain in Chloe's eyes pulled Alfie up. He hadn't meant to upset her, but it was absurd that he, Alfie Jennings would need the assistance of his wayward niece. 'I'm sorry, Chloe. But I've never heard anything so ridiculous.'

Chloe-Jane wiped away the tear she felt running down her cheek. 'Well you won't be saying that when they catch up with you. You should've heard them talking.'

'Heard who?'

'Del and Vaughn was telling Franny all about the casinos you've been running behind everyone's back. They're blaming you for the attacks on the businesses in Soho and on that old bird's café.'

'Lola?'

'Yeah, that's her. Apparently because it's Lola, one of your own the triads turned over they're wanting revenge, and when they found out you were involved in it...' Chloe-Jane stopped to pull a face, drawing her finger across her throat, gesturing it being cut. Alfie gulped.

'Well thank you for that, Chloe, it's made me feel a lot better.'

'No problem.'

'I was being sarcastic ... and do you have to frigging munch those grapes like a bleeding combine harvester? It's getting on me nerves and I need to think.'

Ignoring Alfie, Chloe-Jane continued popping the grapes into her mouth, chewing loudly in between her continuing conversation.

'So what are you going to do then? 'Cos how I

see it, them two muppets are going to be putting you in the ground.'

Alfie looked amazed. He gestured his arms widely. 'Have you come to wind me up?'

'No, as I said, I've come to help you.'

'And why would you do that?'

''Cos I like it here. I like Franny ... and I guess you're alright, but it's as near to feeling like family as I've ever had. And I don't want to lose it.'

Alfie stayed silent. Chloe-Jane had been down in London for less than a couple of weeks but she'd latched onto Franny like a baby on a tit. He supposed he could understand. Understand how it was when you had nothing and no one around you to care whether you lived or died. He'd been lucky he supposed, at least he'd had his brother, Connor, when he'd been growing up. Chloe-Jane had no one. No one apart from him and Franny.

'Listen, I appreciate you offering help and everything but...'

'You better start talking! And quickly. I want to know everything, and don't try to lie, Alfie. Don't even think about it, because you'll wish it was only Vaughn and the others you had to run from.'

As Alfie Jennings looked at Franny Doyle standing furiously at the end of his hospital bed, waiting for him to tell her what was going on, he thought about Chloe-Jane and what she had said. Perhaps having her help wasn't so stupid after all. But now all they needed to do was come up with a plan...

14

The girl lay quivering naked on the rusting old bed. Track marks in her arms. The heat of the room made the three onlookers undo the top buttons on their overly starched shirts. In the darkened corner, Mr Lee sat silently, watching with simmering anger, as one of his new investments looked like they were going to pass out.

Over the years his involvement in the sex trade had grown, as the internet had; becoming more lucrative than extortion money, and certainly safer than drug money. He'd started off years ago in the heroin trade, and at one time in the Nineties the business had been booming. But over time, the government clampdowns and not having the financial ability to pay off the border patrols had crushed the trade, so Lee had begun to invest more and more in prostitution.

With the explosion of the internet and the massive demand in web pornography he'd been able to make more money than he ever did with drugs. At first, most of the images were still, but now everything was live streaming. He'd dealt with all ages, then realised underage pornography was where the real trade and money was. For a while, it had been easy to cover their tracks without ever worrying being caught, but as police technology had grown, so had the likelihood of being traced, especially if dealing in very young girls.

In a way, the police were onto a losing battle. The war against the world's online pornography was something the governments would never win, but it didn't stop them trying, especially when it came to cracking the gangs who dealt in kiddie porn. Not wanting to be traced or caught but still wanting to earn the sort of money the online porn industry brought in, Mr Lee decided to up the age of the girls.

And although most of the girls were runaways, handpicked from the streets, or groomed from care homes, he'd recruited girls who looked like they were over the age of consent; this way the online police generally left him alone. In the unlikely event they did ever bother trying to track him down, the constant re-routing of the proxy server and complex encrypted data stream enabled him to hide his identity and tracks, bypassing the surfing restrictions. By the time they did catch up, he had already moved his streaming to another server, only for the cat and mouse chase to start all over again.

What Mr Lee enjoyed so much about the live web porn was the ability to have the girls situated in any part of the world, in any part of a street, in any part of a home, which again gave him the sense of being untouchable. If there was a raid, Lee would be nowhere to be seen and it'd be the pimps, the fathers, the friends of the girls who'd be taken into custody, leaving him free to make his main source of income from web pornography instead of extortion.

The reason why Lee was present on this live

stream shoot was to do with the way they were going to film the girls. Sex and sex alone had started to become too mainstream; every other person was filming their wives or girlfriends in their back bedrooms and as a consequence, he'd begun to lose money. And one thing Mr Lee hated was to lose money.

People had become desensitised to seeing straight sex, girls on girls or even anal sex. It'd become routine. An everyday occurrence to switch on the computer and see pop-ups of websites advertising sex. What wasn't an everyday occurrence was the corner of the market he'd newly stepped into. The reason why Lee was sitting here now.

He'd been in the business long enough to know what the clients wanted and he was going to give it to them. They wanted to see pain, hurt and ultimately fear in the girl's eyes. They wanted violence, living vicariously through the masked men who'd inflict the pain on the girls. Wishing they were the ones, doing it, but knowing they couldn't, they were willing to pay however much it cost to watch it and in their own way be a part of it. Having a girl with some glazed expression, disconnected to the pain and the torture inflicted on them, wasn't what they wanted, which meant they'd take their tastes elsewhere. And there was no way *he* was going to sit by and let that happen.

'I thought I told you to only give her a small amount of diazepam, not fill her up so she looks like some crack head. It's bad enough we have to cover up her arms from all that shit she bangs up. When you do a close-up the on-liners need to see she's feeling it, not anesthetised.'

Lin, who'd worked for Mr Lee for the past ten years, working his way up the ranks, spoke. 'We only gave her two tablets, but it seems to have knocked her out. It's probably the mix of drugs.'

Chang Lee narrowed his eyes

'I don't care what or why it happened, just do something about it. We're going to start the live streaming in the next half an hour, and punters won't want to pay for a girl who can't join in on the action. I wanted you to take the edge off so it could last longer, not mess up the whole of the streaming.'

Mr Lee watched Lin shake the naked girl, whose head lolled back as he tried to wake her up. The pimp he'd purchased her from had re-assured him she was clean and worked hard. So far there seemed to be no evidence of any of that.

Chang called out, 'Put her feet in freezing ice water, which should do it. If not you'll have to use one of the Romanian girls. Next time, I won't be so understanding.'

Half an hour later, the girl had been changed and Mr Lee sat back as the first of the masked men walked into the makeshift bedroom. It was a simple scene. Girl sleeps on bed as masked intruders come in. No script required. No words needed. The action and the screams would do. The directive of the men was to hurt, not kill. Cut, not disfigure. Rape, not mutilate but apart from that – apart from that there were no rules. No limitations when the word sounded.

'Action!'

15

'What did you say to her? Come on, what did you say?' For the second time that week, Vaughn Sadler paced about Lola's kitchen. 'Well?' Vaughn slammed his fist on the table, shaking the pots off it.

'Bleedin' hell, Vaughnie. Calm down, sweetheart.'

Vaughn snapped at Lola. 'How the hell can I calm down, Lol, when Casey here is mouthing off to the whole of Soho about our relationship?'

'Oh turn it in, Vaughn, Casey hasn't done that.'

'Hasn't she? Then you tell me why Franny-flipping-Doyle was telling me I was having problems in my relationship?' He stared at Casey, who wouldn't look at him. Vaughn didn't need this. Anger and hurt filled his veins, but if he were to be honest with himself, his overriding emotion was humiliation.

The idea that Franny would be insinuating there was something wrong with his relationship with Casey drove him incandescent with rage. Vaughn was a proud man. A private man when it came to relationships; but more to the point he didn't want Alfie Jennings to think there were problems between him and Casey. And knowing women like he did, there was no way Franny would have this gem of gossip without telling Alfie.

'Well?' Vaughn's handsome face shone with

annoyance as he stood over Casey.

Casey sighed, her long auburn hair falling over her face. She knew there was no point in arguing. Vaughn seemed determined to push her away, he didn't want to see reason and the attacks on Soho almost seemed insignificant compared to his determination to bring Alfie down.

'I'm talking to you, Casey!'

'Yeah and she's listening. Bleedin' hell, Vaughnie, I wouldn't be answering you either if you were breathing down me neck like a snorting bull. Leave her alone.' Lola poked Vaughn in his back, causing him to have to take a deep breath to prevent him from turning round and giving Lola what for. He was sick of women. Sick of them. He'd done better when he'd not bothered with them. He yearned for the days when he'd take a bird or two home, fuck them and everyone had a good time and the only thing they'd leave behind would be their Alan Whickers.

'It's okay Lola.' Casey glanced toward her shoulders and shuffled off to switch the kettle back on.

'I didn't tell her anything, Vaughn.'

'Well she had a lot to say for a person who knows nothing. I don't think you can realise how it felt. I looked a right fucking chump in front of Del...'

It was all too much for Casey. 'Is that all you care about, Vaughn? What you looked like? What Del Williams thought about you? I thought you were better than that. Clearly I was wrong.'

'That makes two of us then. I was wrong. Very wrong to think I could do this. Do us. I think the best thing we can do is call it a day. Before it gets nasty. I wouldn't want that. I wouldn't want to lose you as a friend.'

'Is that what you really want?'

Vaughn's face twitched. He knew he was being stupid, he knew that their relationship was slightly strained and had been for a few weeks due to Casey's refusal to talk to him about what was going on with her. But that was all it was, a little strained. There was certainly no need for this course of action he was now about to take, but he couldn't help himself, he couldn't stop his mouth moving and saying something he didn't really mean. That was his problem, he was stubborn and hot headed. 'Yeah, that's exactly what I want. It's finished, Cass. It's over.'

Casey held Vaughn's stare before she found herself standing up, almost robotically. She didn't hear Lola's voice call her back. Didn't see Vaughn's expression of regret at what he'd petulantly said. All she could think about was having a drink, and she knew just where she was going to go and have it.

Franny stood at Chloe-Jane's bedside. She needed answers and she needed them fast.

'Chloe-Jane, just tell me what Alfie said.'

'I don't know what you're talking about, Uncle Alfie said nothing; only thing he gassed about was his finger.'

'You're lying to me. Alfie gets that same glint in his eye when he's not telling the truth.'

'I ain't lying.'

'Well if you aren't lying, why are you all of a

111

sudden saying that you were with Alfie the night he had his finger cut off? You and I know very well you were asleep in the guest room. Don't let Alfie get you to do things you don't want to. Come on Chloe, tell me what's really going on.'

Chloe-Jane pulled a face. She was used to lying. It was easy. It was something she'd been brought up to do. Something she'd been *told* to do. All through her life there was someone who wanted her to lie for them. So lying wasn't the problem. The problem was lying to someone she liked. Chloe-Jane had never done that in her life.

She turned her head away from Franny, looking at the prettily decorated walls which had silver and pink metallic swirls delicately painted on them. The whole of the room was lovely, filled with expensive Venetian mirrored furniture, large swathes of dusky pink silk dressing the windows and vases of lilies dotted around.

Chloe-Jane didn't think she'd ever seen a room so beautiful in all her life, but not only was she seeing it, she was lucky enough to be in it. And if she had it her way, she'd stay in it forever. To be able to stay though she had to be able to please both Franny and Alfie. And that wasn't going to be easy. On the surface it might seem like they had the same views and ideas, but they were poles apart. Alfie was like her, a chancer, a ducker and diver. Somebody who put himself first. Chloe-Jane understood him, and men like him, but Franny was different.

Although Franny had been brought up by her father, Patrick Doyle, who according to Alfie had been both a gentleman and a successful face, who'd taught Franny all the ins and outs of the business, including how to pick a pocket, break a lock, and crack a safe, Franny was a life force of her own. And Chloe-Jane liked her. To Chloe, Franny was a lady, a real proper lady, something she hoped to be one day.

'Well? I'm waiting.' Franny's voice cut through Chloe-Jane's thoughts.

Chloe got up and walked into the en-suite bathroom which only last week had been a tidy luxurious marbled room and now was a chaotic mess of teenage make-up, hairspray and false tan. Franny sighed at the large orange stains of St. Tropez on her white Ralph Lauren bath towels. She tried again. Her tone was firm but as always when she spoke to Chloe, the warmth and the care spilled out.

'It's no use ignoring me, Chloe, and pretending I'm not here. Until you tell me what the truth is, I'm not going anywhere. You heard what Del and Vaughn said Alfie was up to, if it's true... Well...'

Franny broke off.

Chloe-Jane looked at Franny. 'Would you be mad with him, if he *had* been involved with that Chinese geezer?'

'Mad with him, Chloe? I'd be more than that.'

Chloe-Jane suddenly looked very vulnerable. 'Would ... would you finish with him?'

Franny smiled at Chloe's terminology; it sounded like they were at school again. Sounded like it but certainly didn't feel like it. This was serious. If Alfie *had* played a part in all the trouble and had told her, she'd have serious doubts how they could go forward in their relationship. However, if Franny found out he'd played a part in it and was willing to lie about it, then it would be well and truly over. Or as Chloe-Jane liked to put it, she'd *finish with him.*

'Well, would you?'

'Would I what, Chloe?'

'Be with Uncle Alfie if he set up the casino behind everyone's back.'

'No I wouldn't, Chloe. I couldn't be anywhere near him. I spent all my life being lied to by people I loved, and when I did eventually find out, it nearly destroyed me, and Alfie knows it. He knows what happened. He saw what lies did to me. How the bottom dropped out of my world. So, no. No, Chloe. There's no way on this earth I could be with someone who would be willing to lie to me, in fact, I'd probably up and go. It's really only because of Alfie I'm still here in Soho. I've got an uncle, well he's not my real uncle but I love him like one. His name's Cabhan Morton, he was best friends with my father, they did everything together. Well he lives in America now; North Carolina. It's beautiful out there; I love it, it's just by the coast. You'd like it, his house goes onto the beach. Well he's always asking me to go out and live with him, and I've always said no, the time wasn't right. But it appeals to me more and more, and if Alfie and I didn't work out, there'd be nothing to keep me here.'

Franny didn't see the flicker of hurt cross Chloe-Jane's face. Although she'd only been around a couple of weeks it stung to think Franny didn't feel the same way about her. It was silly she knew.

Stupid. If she was Franny, she wouldn't care about her either. To Franny she was just a kid; Alfie's problematic niece coming to cause trouble.

Worse still, if Franny found out that Alfie was involved, or more to the point shit deep in it, she would pack up and go to America. And if her Uncle Alfie hadn't wanted Chloe-Jane around before, he certainly wouldn't want her around if Franny wasn't here anymore.

There was nothing else for it. Chloe-Jane had to do something. She had to lie, to make sure that Franny was none the wiser. No matter how much she didn't like it or however much Franny had just told her lying had almost destroyed her life, to keep her in Soho was worth the lie.

With a smile on her face, Chloe-Jane popped a gum into her mouth. 'I swear Franny, I'm not lying. The only reason why I didn't tell you before I was with Alfie was because I thought you'd be mad at me. I thought you'd think badly of me and throw me out.'

Franny shook her head. 'I don't know what impression I've made, Chloe, but I wouldn't do that. We've all been young once. I used to sneak out all the time when I was your age, and I always thought I'd got away with it when I came back in. I'd sneak back into bed and just as I was, bang, the light would go on, and there would be my father sitting in the corner, ready to give me what for. So you see, it's something we've all done and besides, you're not a child, you can come and go as you please. As long as you're safe, that's the main thing.' Franny paused, looking at Chloe-Jane, sincerity in her eyes. 'You would tell me if

Alfie's put you up to this wouldn't you? I know what he's like. I mean, he...'

Chloe interrupted. 'He didn't. I was with him. Honest. I wouldn't lie to you. I know I didn't tell you, and I won't do that again and I'm sorry. What Del and Vaughn are saying, it ain't true. I was with him in the club and there wasn't any casino. Nothing like that. Just a lot of old fogies sitting around being boring. Then all hell broke loose and some Chinese fellas came running in, shouting the odds. Saying stuff like they wanted money. Alfie told me to run, so I did. But it weren't his fault. He didn't want you to know 'cos he didn't want you to worry, I guess. So all that shit them two muppets are saying, it's just gossip. They're trying to make trouble. Reckon they're jealous of Uncle Alfie and that Vaughn fella, he's just mad 'cos his bird wanted to bang Alfie a while back.'

Franny raised her eyebrows. 'Is that what Alfie told you?'

'Sort of. He said that Vaughn had never got over the fact Casey liked him first, and even if nothing happened, he could tell she wanted it.'

Bemused, Franny smiled. 'Your uncle is un-believable.'

'So you see, all this stuff they're saying ain't worth even listening to.'

Franny got up from the bed and walked over to the window, watching the throngs of people going about their business. The past few days had been a nightmare, not knowing the truth about Alfie's involvement. She was hoping, praying it wasn't true, but she couldn't quite believe how

116

relieved she felt now she knew the truth.

Maybe it was just the climate of things and the paranoia everyone was feeling as to why Vaughn had into his head Alfie was involved in this whole mess; unless of course he really was just wanting to turn everyone against Alfie, but she'd worry about that later. For now she was just happy. 'Thank you, Chloe for telling me the truth. It means a lot ... actually it means everything to me. I know I couldn't have dealt with it if Alfie had lied to me. It took me a long time to trust him after everything that's happened in my life, so it takes me a long time to trust anyone, but somehow I think you're going to be the exception to the rule. In fact, you already are. It's odd Chloe-Jane, because I don't know you at all, yet for some reason I already trust you.'

16

Del and Vaughn sat drowning their sorrows in the tiny Spanish restaurant off Brewer Street. Neither of them had spoken for the past hour, and neither of them were planning to either. They sat lost in their thoughts, not seeing the police cars or the tourists rushing by, not hearing the loud flamenco music on the sound system.

Although neither had said, both of them in their own ways felt like it was an end of an era. Soho would always be in their blood, but things had changed. People had moved on. Friends had died and their kind of crime had got lost in a culture of technology and guns.

Once this was all over, they'd have to re-evaluate what direction their lives were going in but for the time being, they needed to work out the here and now.

For Vaughn the here and now was Alfie and Casey. And for Del, it was the phone call he'd just received. Even though he lived in the Costa he still had businesses here and last week one of the regular girls had gone missing. He'd presumed she'd taken off on her own accord, sneaking off in the night to avoid paying back the money she owed him, and had marked it down as win some, lose some and not put any more thought into it, apart from knowing she couldn't ever show her face round Soho again. She'd been out of his mind until now.

According to his men, she'd just been dumped from out of a car; naked, hands bound, and with the word 'Disobey' scratched into her back. His men had tried to question the girl, but apparently she couldn't remember anything; either that, or she was too scared to talk.

It was clear the triads were behind it, and they'd stepped up their game which was not only worrying, but also something that needed to be stopped. But the only way of stopping it was to get to the man at the top, and whoever he was, he was keeping a low profile. Perhaps what they needed to do was buy some more time. One of the ways to do that was to start paying the tea money, the extortion money the triads were asking for. If they did that the attacks would stop, and although they'd be temporarily out of pocket it would give them the much-needed time they were after.

Del could get his men, along with the others, to find whoever it was, whilst keeping Soho safe. And once they'd found the people behind all this chaos, then he'd have his. Oh yes, he'd make them wish they'd never uttered the word, Chinatown.

Satisfied with his plan, Del's thoughts began to move to Alfie. He hadn't been told for sure it was true but there was no doubt in his mind that the rumour mill of Soho was right this time. Alfie had caused a lot of problems over the years for all of them, but this one; this one took the fucking biscuit. This one was Thames river stuff. Floating with the fishes.

About to break his silence and discuss his ideas with Vaughn, Del's phone rang. At first he ignored it, but the caller continued to ring back, the persistent ring of *Mission Impossible* echoing round the restaurant.

'For fuck's sake Del, do me a favour.' Vaughn growled out his words, nodding his head towards the phone.

Begrudgingly, Del reached for it. 'Yeah?' It was Lola. Her voice sounded hysterical. 'It's happened again, Del, it's happened again!'

'What has, Lo?'

'It just went off with a bang!'

Del scowled. 'Lola, slow down; you're not making sense.'

'Them lot; them triads. They've burnt down one of the Taylors' clubs; the one in Dean Street.

Smoke everywhere. The fire engines are here now, they don't know if anyone's inside but Johnny and Frankie Taylor, they're going ballistic. Where are you? You've got to come down.'

Del's voice was urgent. 'How do you know it was the triads, Lola?'

'Oh come off it, Del; where have you been, who else is going to start blowing up the place, especially as it's the Taylors?'

Del nodded his head without saying anything. It was true. Only a fool or someone very brave would take on the Taylors. Returning to the call, Del spoke. 'Okay, Lola. I'll be down there in five minutes. I'll bring Vaughn with me.'

The two men ran along the streets of Soho, pushing the crowds of people out of their way. They could see the thick grey smoke billowing up in front of them, mixing into the blue skies of Soho. Dean Street was on fire.

Ahead, they could see the police and fire engines along with the yellow tape cornering off the whole area. There was a large crowd, curious to know what had happened, and at the very front of it, Del could see the irate figures of Frankie and Johnny Taylor. Not only that, he could also hear the loud booming voice of Frankie as he spoke to the emergency service workers gathered.

'I don't give a flying fuck what your health and safety rules are, mate. This is my club and I want you to let me the hell in... *Now!*'

The fireman glanced around nervously, hoping the nearby police officer would come to his assistance. 'Sir, I'm sorry but you'll have to stand back. No one can go down there. It's dangerous, and for all we know there could be another explosion.'

Frankie Taylor gave the man a flinty stare. 'You're too damn right there'll be another explosion; and it's standing right in front of you. Let me through, otherwise...'

'Leave it Frankie, it's not the geezer's fault. He's just doing his job.' Vaughn's voice cut through the chaos of the group. Frankie swivelled round.

'When I need a nanny I'll ask for one, until then, leave me and mine alone.'

Vaughn didn't say anything. They hadn't spoken since the night in Lola's café when they'd swapped angry words, and the last thing he really wanted to do was have a stand-up row. He didn't have the energy to start something with the Taylors.

Backing down, Vaughn conceded. 'You're right. Take no notice of me. The last thing you need is me chatting shit in your ear at a time like this. I wasn't thinking. For what it's worth I'm really sorry about the club. We'll sort this.'

'Too fucking right we will. Someone is going to pay; big time.'

The men fell silent, watching the emergency services fighting against the flames. Vaughn rubbed his face, contemplating the past few days. It was all a mess and if he was truthful he wasn't handling any of it very well.

'Have you heard the rumours?' Frankie spoke to Vaughn.

'I take it you're talking about Alfie.'

Frankie nodded. 'Is it true?'

'I reckon so Frank; I know you and him are close. But my contacts tell me he's running a late-night casino. Which means...'

'Which means he's the cause of all of this.'

Vaughn shrugged his shoulders. 'I'm afraid so.'

'I love Alfie; ain't never really done nothing to me. We've always got on, had a laugh and he's been good to my boy when he was going through all that shit with his missus, Maggie. But Alfie of all people should know you don't disobey the rules.'

'So what are we going to do?'

'Well there's nothing else for it. We pay him a visit. The old school way.'

17

Alfie Jennings' finger was hurting. Or the lack of it. The surgeons had told him they'd tried their best to save it; done all they could, but for one botched-up reason or another, they hadn't managed to save fuck all. And in Alfie's opinion they were taking the piss. So – here he was, discharged from hospital, standing behind the bar of Whispers with nine fucking fingers, and didn't he just feel a cunt.

He began to think about Chloe-Jane. She was a bit of a mystery, and he wasn't sure if that was a good thing or a bad thing. He'd treated her badly, for which he wasn't proud, yet she'd bounced back and had come to his aid when he'd needed it; standing up to not only Vaughn and Del but also sticking by him and giving him an alibi whilst Franny sniffed about.

Alfie wasn't sure if he would've been as loyal at her age, especially if someone hadn't given him the time of day. But he guessed Chloe-Jane was a chip off the old block. She was, after all, a Jennings.

She'd properly pulled through for him when she'd told Franny he'd had nothing to do with the casino and nothing had been going on. The only worry now was the possibility that she thought he owed her a favour. Alfie had thought about giving her a job in the club like she'd asked, but knowing women like he did, there was a strong possibility she'd end up reporting all the comings and goings to Franny. And that was the last thing he wanted.

Franny had been cool, verging on the cold, with him, which Alfie didn't mind admitting pissed him off. There really wasn't much sympathy from her, even now he'd exonerated himself. He wasn't going to forget this in a hurry. How she'd been suspicious, non-trusting and downright cold. Yes, he was certainly seeing Franny through fresh eyes, and perhaps she wasn't wife material after all.

He was about to begin to feel sorry for himself again when a voice cut through his self-pity.

'Hello, Alfie.'

Alfie looked up, surprised.

'What are you doing here?'

'Well that's a nice welcome. I hope you don't

123

greet all your clients like that? What did you do to your finger?'

'It's a long story. Let's just say, the NHS ain't what it used to be.'

Casey Edwards stared at Alfie. She couldn't remember the last time she'd been with Alfie on her own. Everything that had happened with him in the past had always made her keep her distance, especially as the animosity between Vaughn and Alfie had been progressively getting worse over the years. So the only time she'd been in the same room as Alfie was when there'd been a large social gathering. As if reading her thoughts, Alfie spoke.

'How long's it been, Cass? You and me like this.'

Casey cut her eye at Alfie. 'We've never been a *you and me*.'

'Oh come on, stop being an uptight ass. Anyone would think you had a thing for me.'

Casey stared at Alfie incredulously. 'Tell me you're kidding.'

Alfie's handsome face lit up. He burst into laughter. 'Do me a favour. What's happened to your sense of humour? I'm with Franny now you know that. You missed the boat, babe.'

Once again Casey looked horrified and once again Alfie burst into raucous laughter. 'Got you again!'

'Has anyone told you that you're a prick?'

Alfie smirked but warmth shone from him. He'd liked Casey at one point; she was a bit of a sort, and in truth he'd been riddled with jealousy and disbelief when she'd picked Vaughn instead of him. But that was then. That was before he was with Franny, and no one could shine a light anywhere near her. 'Yeah they have, in fact, Franny asked me the same old question the other day. I suppose that's why you're here? Because of Franny? I know she's pissed with me but just tell her I really didn't have anything to do with it.'

'I'm not here because of Franny.'

Alfie frowned. 'So why you here then ... oh don't tell me. Vaughn. Vaughn sent you to do his dirty work. Well you can tell him from...'

'He didn't send me... Vaughn didn't send me.'

Alfie was puzzled. 'If Franny didn't send you and you ain't doing your old man's dirty work, why are you here?'

'Do I have to have a reason?'

'Come on Cass, it's not like we ain't got a lot of water under the bridge. What's going on? I'm surprised Vaughn let you come here ... he does know you're here doesn't he?'

Casey said nothing.

'He doesn't know does he?'

Casey went to leave turning quickly away. 'I better go.'

'No!... No, Cass, stay. Listen, it's none of my business what you do. Let me get you a drink. What's your poison?'

'Whiskey.'

Alfie grinned. 'No come on, what do you want?'

'I told you; whiskey.'

'Seriously Cass, what do you want?'

Casey stared at Alfie. She noticed her hand was shaking slightly. 'I'm being serious, Alf. Pour me a whiskey.'

Alfie spread his arms wide, a sympathetic look on his face. 'Come on Casey, you know I can't do that.'

Casey pushed her humiliation to the side. 'This is a bar isn't it?'

'You know it is.'

'So pour me a drink, Alfie. If you don't, I can always go elsewhere.'

Alfie was in a quandary. Once upon a time he'd be like the cat who got the cream to see Casey diving head first off the rocks. But he'd changed. Or maybe it was a question of Franny had changed him. Either way he wasn't going to be a part of it.

For all his gripes with Casey and Vaughn they'd been good to his daughter, Emmie. Letting her stay and be part of their family. As much as it hurt that Emmie didn't want anything to do with him, it was good there were people looking out for her, so Alfie certainly couldn't risk blowing her stability apart by being complicit in Casey going back on the booze.

'No, Casey; I'm sorry.'

Casey glared at Alfie. She didn't appreciate what he was saying but she continued to listen as a slight suspicion came into his voice. 'What's going on, Cass, why did you come here? Of all the places you could've gone for a drink? Why choose here?'

'Why not?'

Alfie scratched his head. He wasn't sure what he was supposed to do. Back in the day when he and Vaughn were on friendly terms he would've called him to let him know what was happening, but obviously now that was impossible.

'Listen Casey, why don't you get off home and try to get some shut-eye?'

'Don't treat me like a child, Alf. I don't need a nursemaid.'

'Then if you don't need a nursemaid, grow up and see what you're doing. You've got a life now, things are going well for you. Why bleedin' sabotage it hey? You were a right mess when I first met you; a lush. But that's well and truly behind you now. So do us all a favour and don't go back there.'

'Have you finished lecturing me yet? When I want the guide to life according to Alfie Jennings, I'll look in the nearest charity shop... And seeing as you won't serve me, I'll serve myself.' Casey pushed past Alfie and went to the end of the bar where she knew the whiskey was stored. Apart from Lola's café, Whispers bar and club was one of the first places she'd worked when she'd come down to London, so she knew the place well.

Alfie glowered. 'You're really looking to press that self-destruct button aren't you? Well fine. Fucking fine. Have it your way. Do your worst, darlin'.' He stood back, staring as Casey screwed open the bottle of Jack Daniels and poured it into one of the glasses sitting on the side.

As she put the glass to her lips, Alfie shouted, 'Cass! Are you sure girl? Do you really want to go down that road?'

Casey held the glass to her lips. She didn't say anything, and for a moment held eyes with Alfie, before knocking back the whiskey.

An hour and a half later, Alfie had decided not to open the club. Instead he sat at the bar silently watching as Casey became loud and brash. Her beautiful eyes were glazed and her speech was slurred as she recounted a hotchpotch account of her life for the second time.

Never a particularly patient man and having never really approved of a woman being drunk, Alfie was beginning to lose patience.

'So that's when I met Vaughn ... do you remember, it was in here, or I think it was. Or was it in Lola's café? Can you remember, Alf? Oh no, it was...'

Alfie interrupted abruptly. 'Enough Cass! Fuck me, you've been chewing me ears off for a couple of hours, and to tell you the truth, darlin', I've never liked women's chatter. I certainly don't like it when they've got a drink inside them. So do us a favour and keep it shut. Better still, go and clean yourself up.'

Casey's eyes filled with tears, giving cause for Alfie to roll his. A drunk emotional bird was not what he needed.

'Alfie... Please, you don't understand, me and Vaughn, well I ... I ... oh Christ, I think I'm going to be sick.'

Alfie ran round to Casey, dragging her up from the chair. 'Not in here you're not. Swallow it down until I get you into the ladies for fuck's sake.'

Casey draped her arms around Alfie's neck. He turned his head, pulling a face as she spoke, the stench of alcohol overpowering. 'I love you,

Alfred Jennings.'

'You don't and it's Alfie not Alfred and you stink.'

The drunken howl from Casey blasted into Alfie's ear. 'I don't stink! I don't.'

'Alright darlin', keep it down. Let's get you into the bathroom.'

Alfie had only managed to get halfway across the dance floor when he heard a voice behind him. One that he knew, and one that he could certainly do without hearing.

'What the fuck is going on here?'

Slowly, with Casey still draped around him, Alfie turned round. Standing by the bar was Vaughn.

Always one to try to play things down, Alfie chirpily greeted Vaughn. 'Alright, mate.' He paused as Del Williams and Frankie Taylor walked into the club. Shit.

'Well, what have I done to deserve this pleasure?'

Del piped up. 'Oh, plenty.'

Panic began to rise in Alfie but he was long experienced not to show it. 'Listen guys, why don't we all sit down and have a drink.' He held his smile but it didn't go unnoticed that Vaughn hadn't said anything, instead continuing to stare on in horror.

Alfie decided that ignoring the fact he had Casey clinging onto his neck in a semi-conscious stupor was maybe the best ploy. 'So gentlemen, like I say, just help yourself. It's all on me. I haven't bothered to open up tonight, what with everything going on. I thought it was best because of the way things were.'

'Have you heard about Frankie's club?' Del spoke, also feeling uncomfortable at the sight of Casey in front of him. It was embarrassing, but seeing as everyone else was choosing to ignore the fact that Vaughn's missus was sprawled across Alfie, he didn't think it was his place to say anything either.

Alfie looked puzzled. 'No. What happened? I've been here most of the time.'

Del narrowed his eyes. 'What? You didn't see or hear anything?'

'Nope.'

'Well it's been scorched. Blew up like a fucking petrol can.'

Alfie paled, feeling the weight of Casey on his neck. Before he managed to say anything, Vaughn broke from his trance, yelling loudly.

'Are you all taking the fucking piss? Ain't your eyes working?'

The men put their heads down and said nothing as Vaughn continued to rant, walking forward to confront Alf. 'What's your game, Alfie? What have you done to her? What is it, hey? You can't have her in the normal way so you have to drug her up?'

'Hey Vaughnie, you've got it all wrong.'

'Don't fucking Vaughnie me. What have you given her? Come on...'

Alfie encouraged Casey to sit down on the nearest chair which she did unsteadily, enabling him to square up to Vaughn.

'I'd stop right there if I were you, mate. I've done fuck all to Cass.'

Vaughn's face reddened with anger. 'No? Then

130

tell me why she looks like a crack head on a bad day?'

'Maybe it's because she came looking for a drink like she was a camel in a desert. Begging me, fucking begging me she was, to give her some booze. What didn't she tell you? Seems strange that she couldn't come to you; says something when your missus has to come to me.'

'Shut up Alf, what yer doing, mate? You looking for an early grave, son? 'Cos spiking me missus with fuck knows what is sure going to get you there.'

Alfie's face was scornful. 'Look at yer, Vaughn; you're embarrassing yourself in front of everyone. You look a right mug. Think about it. Why would Casey be here if she didn't come on her own accord? Are you saying I kidnapped her and brought her here? Do me a favour. Face it, your missus would rather come and booze with me than be with you.'

The words were like a shockwave going through Vaughn's body. He leapt forward, grabbing hold of Alfie's collar. With a swift flick of his head, he headbutted Alfie, splitting open his skin just above his eyes. Blood spurted out, covering Vaughn with a splash of red before he began to grapple Alfie.

Adrenaline rushed round Alfie's veins; he pushed Vaughn hard, giving him no chance to attack back. Expertly he brought down his elbow; grinding it down. Ignoring the blood dripping down his forehead which blurred his vision, Alfie smashed the glass sitting on the table.

With the jagged edge of the glass, Alfie prepared to slam it into Vaughn's mouth but he felt his arm being pulled back.

'Give it up Alf!' Del bellowed as he yanked Alfie off Vaughn.

'Get the fuck off me!... Get off me!'

Del snarled as Vaughn stood back up, wiping his face. 'This is going to be the last of your worries when we've finished with you.'

Alfie spat his words at Del. 'Ain't that nice, Vaughn's got his Flower Pot Men to fight his battles.'

The blow to Alfie's stomach winded him, and for a minute he couldn't get his breath as the sharp splintering pain gripped hold of his body. Eventually he managed to stand up and faced the three men.

'What is this, guys?'

'It would be easier all round if you stopped the games, Alf. We know what you've been up to.'

Alfie feigned innocence. 'I don't know what you're talking about. It might be okay in your book for you lot to come round here talking shit, but it ain't okay in my book.'

Vaughn stood nose to nose with Alfie. 'Give it up. I've known you for too long not to know when you're spewing bullshit. Ain't worth lying to us.'

'Fuck me, it ain't the Flower Pot Men, it's the Three Stooges. Whatever you guys have got blown up your ass, you're barking up the wrong tree.'

Del spoke again. 'Alf! Alf! Give it up. We know, pal. We know what you've been up to with the casino and breaking the rules between the triads and us.'

'Well then you know more than me.'

The backhand from Del drew hard across Alfie's face, busting both top and bottom lip. His expression was hard and steely as he glared at Alfie, his tone low. 'This isn't a joke, Alf. You've fucked up here; big time. You've brought more shit to Soho than an elephant in a circus.'

'Fuck you!' Alfie, defiant as ever, stood firm as Del continued.

'You must know why we're here. Alf, you know you can't disobey the rules and get away with it. You've brought carnage into Soho, and for what? A few shillings. You also know what happens when you betray those close to you.'

For the first time, Alfie genuinely felt uneasy. His voice gave away his anxiety as it wavered. 'What ... what are you going to do?'

Del pulled out a gun from his jacket pocket. He pulled back the trigger. 'It'll be over in a minute.'

Forgotten for a moment by the others, Casey, who was sobering up and aware of what was happening stood up, albeit slightly shakily. 'Have you lost your mind, Del? You can't go round just shooting people because you feel like it.'

Vaughn cut Casey a stare. His voice was solidified with anger. 'Stay out of it Casey! I'll deal with you later.'

'Excuse me?'

'You heard. Don't embarrass yourself or me. There's a conversation to be had about what the fuck you were doing here, but for now, get out of here.'

Casey Edwards, like a lot of the women in Soho, was strong and fiery and objected to being ordered about, especially when it was from Vaughn.

'Who do you think you're talking to? I'm not one of your men.'

'No, because they wouldn't act like a slut.'

Casey slapped Vaughn across his face, hard.

'Whatever your problem is, that is the last time you speak to me like that.'

Del spoke to Vaughn sympathetically. 'I'll give you a minute.' He moved away, but spoke to Alfie as he did so. 'But you. You stay where you are.'

Vaughn grabbed hold of Casey's arm, shaking her with enough strength for her head to jerk forward. His voice was a whisper. 'You never change, do you? Couldn't keep it up, could you; the good girl image too hard for you, Cass? Look at the state of you.'

Casey pulled her arm away. 'Whatever you do or don't think about me, Vaughn, it's no longer any of your concern. Remember? *You* were the one who finished it. Oh and whilst you're here, why don't you take this.' With a large tug, Casey pulled off her yellow diamond ring and threw it at Vaughn, who stood feeling as if a large freight train was about to hit him. He refused to let his emotions get the better of him, and decided to concentrate on what was about to happen to Alfie.

His tone was hard and icy.

'Get out, Cass.'

'Don't you dare lay a hand on him, you hear me?'

'I said ... get out!'

Slowly, Casey began to back away. She looked at Vaughn, then Del and lastly at Frankie before she began to run.

18

Chloe-Jane sat on Franny's bed, going through photographs. 'Who's that then?'

'That's Patrick; my father when he was little.'

'He's a bit of alright ain't he?'

Franny smiled. 'Oh yeah, I think the ladies loved him, but he wasn't really interested. As much as it's a cliché, he really only loved my mum.'

'You don't get fellas like that anymore; once they get your knickers off, you don't see them again.'

Kindly, Franny asked, 'Have you ever thought of not getting your knickers off, Chloe?'

Chloe-Jane looked amazed at Franny's suggestion. 'No! What good would that be? They ain't going to like you if you don't put out, are they?'

'But they don't really like you if they just sleep with you and then don't want to have anything to do with you afterwards.'

Chloe-Jane burst into laughter. 'You're so funny Fran, you sound dead old-fashioned.'

Franny knew when she was on a losing battle and carried on looking at the photos of her life, taking herself on a trip down memory lane. As she continued to look, Chloe-Jane's phone rang.

'Hello? Chloe listened to the caller on the other

end of the line. After only a minute, she put down the phone.

Neutrally Franny spoke. 'Who was that?'

'Who was what?'

Franny, who hadn't been really interested in who was calling Chloe, suddenly began to get curious. She stared in bemusement. 'Chloe. The phone call, who was it?'

'No one... Unless you call my mum someone. She wanted money. That's the only reason she calls me.'

Franny's face was full of sympathy. 'I'm sorry, Chloe.'

Chloe-Jane smiled at Franny. It was strange having someone to care for her, and it was hard to get her head round it. 'Oh, don't worry about it. You get used to it.'

'You shouldn't have to ... you're not going to give her any, are you?'

Chloe-Jane smiled as she pulled on her pink denim jacket. 'No. Probably why she put the phone down on me... Oh well. Listen, I'm off out now. I'll see you later.'

Franny saw the sadness in Chloe's eyes as she walked out of the room. A moment later she heard the front door open and close leaving her in the silence of her flat.

It was only recently Franny had learnt to be able to be at peace on her own and not have to keep busy until she fell exhausted into bed. The memories of her life had haunted her but now they comforted her, and lately she'd relished the solitude instead of run from it. Not that she minded Chloe-Jane staying; the idea of a kid of

136

seventeen having nowhere to go apart from her uncle's girlfriend made her feel sad.

Franny had been lucky with her upbringing. Full of love. Full of laughter. Having her father Patrick and her Uncle Cabhan dote on her. Lavishing her with gifts and supporting her in everything she did, as well as teaching her how to look after herself.

About to look through more photographs, the doorbell rang. Then it rang again.

'Okay I'm coming... Hold on,' Franny shouted out as the person began to bang on the door.

Assuming it was Chloe-Jane, Franny opened the door with a smile which froze when she saw, Casey looking hysterical. Hysterical and drunk.

'You've got to come!' Casey's voice was urgent.

'Where? Why, what's happened? Are you alright, Cass? What the hell's happened?'

'It's Alf.'

Franny's face drained of colour. Her mouth began to dry up as fear rushed through her. 'Is he alright? For fuck's sake, Casey, tell me what's going on.'

'Vaughn, and the others; they're in the club with him. They're saying it was because of him the triads have started all the attacks. And Del...' Casey began to trail off but Franny grabbed hold of her, frantic to find out the details.

'And Del what? Come on Cass!' Franny's voice was loud as she gleaned the information from her friend.

'Del – he's got a gun.'

Thoughts and memories rushed through Franny's head. Images of what had happened to her father were triggered as she stood staring at Casey in silence.

'Franny! Come on, we have to do something.'

Snapping out of it, Franny nodded her head, but to Casey's surprise she didn't immediately run to the club. 'Wait there, Cass.'

'But...'

Franny didn't bother waiting to hear what Casey had to say. She ran back up the stairs, two at a time. Charging into her father's old bedroom.

Quickly moving the large leather cream chair to where the wardrobe was, Franny climbed up on it, giving her leave to reach the top of the doors. She reached up, feeling about on the top of the maple wardrobe. Right at the back, she found what she was looking for.

Pulling the small bag down, she jumped back off the chair, unzipping the small holdall. And there it was. Inside, right at the bottom was her father's Colt .380 Mustang.

Finding most of the streets were still blocked off, Franny and Casey ran along the outside of Soho. They were both out of breath as their hearts beat fast. Ignoring the crowds, Franny pushed through, knowing time wasn't on her side – or more to the point wasn't on Alfie's.

Cutting through the small alleyway into Wardour Street, the women finally found themselves at the top of Old Compton Street, where Whispers nightclub was.

'Do you think we're too late?' Casey panted to Franny.

'I dunno... I hope not... Christ, I don't want to

think like that. I can't bear it. Come on, let's go in the back way.'

'What are you going to do?'

Franny looked at Casey square on then proceeded to pull out the gun from her jacket pocket. She cocked the striker on the gun, ready for action. 'I'll worry about that when I get there. But whatever happens, do as I say and make sure you stay behind me.'

19

Chloe-Jane sat in the front seat of the old brown Ford Fiesta. The punter she'd picked up wanted a blow job. So she'd got in the car, agreed on a price; a fiver, and then sat in silence as they sped along Theobalds Road, turning left at Grays Inn Road before hitting the gridlock of King's Cross.

She chewed on her piece of gum and thought about how many blow jobs it'd take her to get the eighty pound to give Franny. Chloe-Jane had never been great at maths, and by the time the punter pulled up at the car park behind Goods Way in King's Cross, she'd convinced and depressed herself thinking five into eighty was thirty-three which meant excluding this one, she'd have to give another thirty-two blow jobs to get the money.

Chloe-Jane sighed as she gave the man a sideways look. She shivered. He had thinning brown greasy hair with a ridiculous sweep-over and his thick rimmed glasses were ugly and harsh in their appearance, making his already small eyes look even smaller. His fingers were short and pudgy, as was he, and Chloe-Jane knew she'd have to brace herself to get through the next ten minutes.

They parked up and immediately the man locked the door, causing Chloe to get nervous. She hadn't brought anything such as a penknife or razor to be able to fight him off, so she could only hope he wasn't a complete nutter.

The man leered at her, licking his lips as he gawked at her large breasts. With hurried movements, he unzipped his trousers, going into his pants to pull out his erect penis as if he was dipping his hand into a tombola at a summer fete.

'Go on then.' He nodded encouragingly to Chloe-Jane who shook her head fervently.

'I ain't sucking it without a condom.'

The man's eyes darkened. 'Don't mess me about. I don't take kindly to piss takers.'

Chloe-Jane held her ground. 'That's not what we agreed; I don't do bareback, not with me pussy or with me mouth.'

'I said, do it, you fucking bitch!' The man was red-faced as he shouted at Chloe, holding onto his penis with one hand whilst he prodded her with the other.

Chloe-Jane's eyes filled with tears. 'I said, *I don't do it without a condom.*'

Chloe didn't see the slap across her face coming; she only felt it. A quick hard sting, burning up her right cheek. She yelped and held her bitten-nailed hand on her face.

'Let me out!... Let me out, *please!*'

'Not until you do what we came here to do.' The man grabbed hold of Chloe's hair, pulling it hard and trying to force her head down to his swollen penis. She fought hard – she was good at that, she'd been fighting all her life – but the harder she did, the harder the man's punches were.

She could feel the man's hands around her neck now as her breath became shorter and raspier, and she sensed she might pass out any moment.

With one big final effort, Chloe-Jane twisted her body around, managing to bring her teeth down into the man's arm.

'You fucking bitch!' The man let go and immediately Chloe pulled away. Turning her whole body round, Chloe brought up her knees and kicked at the car door with all her might. The door of the Fiesta crashed open and Chloe-Jane jumped out of the car without looking back, running towards the main road.

That had been an hour ago. Chloe-Jane sat, shaken, in a rundown pub just off Tottenham Court Road. In front of her was a neat glass of vodka. Things definitely hadn't gone as planned and to make matters worse she now had a black eye to show for it.

She'd been frightened. Really frightened. She had truly thought the man was going to hurt her, but as awful as it was, the alternative was almost worse. The alternative was not being able to pay Franny her eighty pounds. And that wasn't even an option.

Knocking back the vodka, Chloe, about to get up and order another one just so she could calm

141

her nerves, was abruptly joined by a young girl at her table who was probably no older than herself.

'Mind if I sit here? I don't want that dirty bastard over there to think I'm touting, I've had enough for today. Makes the skin crawl. He won't leave me alone. Hands bleedin' everywhere. Last week I gave him a blow job so now he's acting like me and him are an item. Bleedin' nut, he's a punter not frigging Prince Charming... Oh my name's Jodie by the way.' The girl smiled at Chloe who smiled back warmly, then plonked herself down on the worn-out pub sofa.

'I'm Chloe-Jane.'

The girl paused. She was short and fat, dressed in a tight blue jumpsuit which was clearly too small for her giving her a very obvious camel toe. Her short bobbed hair was dyed peroxide blonde with an added pink streak down the side. Her face, although plain, held the warmest of blue eyes.

'Good to meet you, Chloe-Jane. Where are you from? I haven't seen you about. Are you new? Have you come from care? Where you stopping?' Jodie's questions were non-stop as she went from one to another without so much as a pause.

'I'm stopping with my uncle's girlfriend.'

Jodie pulled a face. 'Oh God, how's that? Is it a shitty nightmare? I once stayed with my dad's girlfriend, we ended up fighting at four in the morning. Police had to come in the end. Haven't seen either of them since.'

'No, she's nice. I'm lucky; it's more my uncle who's a bit of a wanker, but he's alright. He's family, innit.'

'Well that's good. So how come you're here? When did you come to Soho? Do you have any brothers or sisters? Do you fancy another drink? What did you do to your eye?'

'Some fella did it, but I've had worse.'

Jodie leaned in closer to Chloe, her curiosity lighting up her eyes. 'Was it your pimp?'

'My pimp?'

'Yeah... I'm guessing you're on the game.'

Chloe-Jane sat up, feeling insulted by Jodie's assumption, no matter how true it was or was not.

'What makes you think I'm touting?'

Jodie looked genuinely amused. 'Oh come off it, you couldn't advertise it any more if you had a neon sign on your head. I spotted it the minute I saw you.' The girl paused, thinking for a moment before adding, 'You ashamed of it or something? Don't your boyfriend know you're down here doing it?'

Chloe snapped, 'It ain't nothing to do with fellas. And I certainly ain't got a boyfriend or a bleedin' pimp.'

Jodie looked at Chloe, clarification etched all over. 'Oh, you're gay.'

'No I ain't gay, I'm just saying that you can't go around saying people are on the game when they ain't.'

'So you saying you ain't?'

'I'm saying I might not be.'

'Well either you are or you ain't.'

Chloe-Jane sighed, annoyed but somehow feeling like she needed to answer Jodie's question.

'Well ... er ... I...'

Jodie began to rummage in her bag for her asthma pump. 'Well you're either a whore or you ain't, which one is it? You should know.'

Chloe-Jane was about to object again but instead she burst into laughter. There was a refreshing quality about Jodie. It'd been a long time since Chloe had had a friend. Jodie looked like she was someone who enjoyed having fun, and fun was something that'd been missing in her life recently.

Chloe gestured to Jodie's empty glass. 'You want me to get you another one?'

Jodie looked around the dark grim pub, seeing the punters, the old man in the corner sleeping with his brown hat pulled over his eyes. She shook her head. 'Nah, how about we go somewhere else? This place is like being in a bleedin' graveyard ... come on!'

Chloe-Jane and Jodie hurried out of the pub, giggling as if they'd known each other for a long time.

As they walked down the street, Chloe-Jane was busy talking and didn't notice Jodie give a thumbs-up to a man sitting in a darkened car on the other side of the street.

'So tell me the truth, are you on the game?' Jodie shouted above the sound system to Chloe.

The alcohol Chloe had been drinking had her talking more than she usually would, especially to someone she hadn't known for more than a couple of hours. 'It ain't full time, I'm really only doing it because I can't get a job and I have to

144

find a way to pay for me keep, otherwise I'll be out on the street.'

Jodie nodded her head, understanding what it was to have nowhere to go and no one to care for you. 'And this bird you're living with, would she throw you out if you didn't have the money?'

'Well she said she wouldn't, but what's to say she won't change her mind? It's easy to say that, ain't it – and if me own mum can throw me out, a complete stranger certainly can.'

'So how long you been doing it then?'

Chloe shrugged. 'On and off since I was thirteen, but not full sex, not then. It was just hand jobs and maybe the odd blow job here and there, but then last year I started going all the way 'cos I needed more money to give to me mum. When I came back from temporary foster care, she was shacked up with this new boyfriend who was a boozer like her, and 'cos they were doing fuck all, they didn't have the money to keep up with their drinking habits. So they relied on muggins here. But then I got fed up of it, and I came down to stay in Soho with me uncle. What about you?'

'I've been on the game since I was eleven. It was really from the time I went into care. My mum OD'd on heroin. Anyway, I got into it through some mates, and as me dad had used me as his sex doll before I went into care, moving on to clients seemed easy really. Especially as I was being paid for it. Only thing is the money was shit and the risks were too big... Can't tell you how many times I got beat up. Then I met this person and they introduced me to this geezer, the money's brilliant and I don't have to worry about some bastard

145

trying to rob or rape me.'

Chloe sat forward, interested in what Jodie was saying. 'What kind of good money?'

'Really good money ... look.' Jodie opened her bag, showing Chloe a bulging envelope.

'Bleedin' hell! There must be...'

'A grand there.'

Chloe looked impressed but also curious. 'So how come you were in that grotty pub then if you're earning money like that?'

Jodie shrugged. 'Sometimes it's nice to get away. Do me own thing for a while; you know what I mean?'

Chloe-Jane didn't say anything, but she knew exactly what Jodie meant. She wished she could get away from everything. Soho was supposed to have given her a fresh start but instead she'd found herself going back to her old ways. And she hated herself for it.

A wave of sadness came across Chloe-Jane and suddenly she felt very lonely and very lost. The nearest thing she had to calling somewhere home was Franny's. And to continue living there she needed money – but without a pimp to keep her safe, Chloe-Jane knew how difficult it'd be to sustain a life on the game. But perhaps Jodie was the key.

Slightly hesitantly, Chloe spoke. 'Do you ... do you think you could introduce me to this person?'

'What person?'

'Whoever you're working for. Do you think they'd have something for me?'

'Maybe. I guess I could ask. Why don't you meet me tomorrow, then I'll have had a chance to talk

146

to them.'

Chloe's face lit up. 'Really?'

'Yeah, really. Take my number and I'll meet you here at two.'

Jodie Wright walked out into the street ten minutes after Chloe-Jane had gone. She waited for a few minutes before a car drew up beside her. The blacked-out window slowly lowered.

'Well?' The man spoke to Jodie.

'She's perfect. I think you'll like her.'

'Do you think she'll be up for it, or rather, up to it?'

Jodie nodded. 'Yeah, she's desperate. She needs the money.'

'You've done well, Jodie; you know how to spot them.' The man passed Jodie an envelope. 'If it works out with her, you'll get the rest of it.'

Jodie grinned. 'Thank you ... thank you, Lin.'

20

'Shhh! Be quiet!' Franny warned Casey as they snuck along the back corridor of Whispers.

'Are you sure about this, Fran?'

'No, but I'll be less sure if you keep going on about it.'

They edged forward, feeling their way in the darkness. As Franny went to open the door at the far end, she froze, hearing raised voices. Del. Vaughn. And yes, she could hear Alfie's voice as well. Franny, anxious to get to Alfie as soon as she could, whispered to Casey.

'Come on, let's go.' She was about to go through the door but felt herself being held back by her friend.

'No, not through that way, Fran... We need to go up and through the back stairs, then we'll come out near the stage.'

'Okay, show me but let's hurry.'

Franny followed Casey as they raced up the stairs and along yet another dark corridor full of Alfie's stolen goods.

'Are you sure this is the right way, Cass?'

'Totally. Don't forget I worked at the club for a while.'

Franny didn't reply. She had forgotten that, but it gave her a renewed sense of purpose and security as she chased down the corridor.

A couple of metres in front of her, Casey stopped. 'It's through here, but we have to be really quiet because the stage is on the other side of the door.'

Franny held her gun in her hand. She took a deep breath, looking at Casey. 'Stay here.'

'No way! I'm coming with you. Vaughn wouldn't do anything if I'm here.'

'Wouldn't he?'

Casey looked horrified. 'No, he wouldn't.'

'Let's see then, shall we? Come on. And remember what I said. Stay behind me.'

Casey nodded as Franny went towards the door. She took a deep breath, then opened it slowly, listening to the men talk.

'So how do you want it, Alfie? 'Cos you ain't

walking out of here, mate.'

'If you're going to do it just fucking well do it, but I ain't admitting to anything. I ain't done fuck all wrong.'

'Oh turn it in will ya? Talk about tell a Jackanory. We know, Alf. Ain't you got no pride? Do you want the last words that come out of your mouth to be a lie? Well, do you?'

'How many times do I have to tell you, Vaughn, I ain't lying... Del, you got to believe me; this is all conjured up by him. Can't stand to see me doing well. Think about it. I'm the perfect fall guy. Who was it that told you, hey? It was Vaughn. Who did he say told him?... It was his men. So you can't trust it. He just wants to get rid.'

'Bullshit, your time's up, Alf, it's time to kiss goodnight.

'I don't think so.' Franny walked onto the dimly lit stage in the nightclub from behind the red velvet curtains.

'What the fuck?' Vaughn spoke as Del, Frankie and Alfie looked on, amazed.

'Hello gentlemen.'

Del turned to Vaughn, his face turned up into a snarl. 'Your fucking missus must have gone and opened her mouth.'

'What the fuck did you want me to do? Stop Casey leaving the club?'

'Yeah, well that would be better than this.'

Vaughn turned away from Del. 'Oh do me a favour.'

'You should have more control of your bird.'

'Oh, you mean like you and your missus? Last time I heard she was selling her ass, and you were crying to anyone who'd listen.'

Del yelled, jumping at Vaughn. He grappled him in a head lock, eyes flashing with anger.

'You're a prick, you know that! A fucking prick!'

Vaughn managed to push Del off. Both men stood opposite each other in a stand-off, panting.

'What's this gentlemen, fighting within the ranks? Don't you know that's the number one mistake?' Franny's voice was cool and calm.

'What the hell do you want, Franny? This is man's business.'

Franny burst out into mocking laughter as she glared at Frankie Taylor. 'Man's business, Frank? You sound more like a bunch of fishwives squabbling between yourselves. It's pathetic. How you lot ever became faces, I don't know.'

'If you know what's good for you, Fran, you'll get out of here.'

Franny smiled, her tone unwavering in its defiance. 'You of all people should know I've never known what was good for me, Vaughn. My father always said the same thing.'

Vaughn walked closer to the stage where Franny stood. 'Get out Fran, don't make me do something I'll regret.'

'What's that then, hey? What are you going to do? Come on Vaughn, follow through with that threat of yours.'

'Do as he says, Fran.' Alfie's voice cut through the air.

'Listen to your old man, Fran.' Del encouraged Franny to go, with a gesture of his head to match his words.

'Oh, I'm not going anywhere, not without Alfie anyway.'

Del shook his head. 'No can do, babe. You know the score. Don't make it harder for everyone.'

Franny raised her eyebrows. 'Me, Del? *I'm* making it harder? I don't think so.'

Vaughn interrupted. 'Enough Fran! You know what he's done. Lola's, the Turks in Greek Street, Frankie's club to name but a few. He's fucked too many people over, too many times. And now we know the truth about the casino, it's over.'

Franny's voice was stony. 'You don't know the truth, Vaughn. You wouldn't know the truth if it hit you between the eyes.'

'Stop being naïve, Fran.'

'I trust Alfie. He wouldn't lie to me.'

It was Vaughn's turn to burst out into bitter laughter. 'For an intelligent woman you're very stupid.'

'Oi! That's my missus you're speaking to,' Alfie growled at Vaughn.

'Then tell her the truth, Alf. Tell her what you've been doing. If you love her the way you say you do, show her some respect so she don't look a fool and lose our respect as well.'

Alfie gritted his teeth as he listened to Vaughn. As much as he hated the geezer, he had to concede to what he was saying. If he could put it right not for himself but for Franny, he would want to be able to tell her the truth but for now, all he could do was continue telling her a lie. And yes, he was Alfie Jennings and somehow, some-way he'd sort it out, but he wished things could be different.

151

So Alfie being Alfie, like he had done all his life, put on his best front, looking Vaughn directly in his eyes as he did so.

'Piss off, Vaughn. You know I was with Chloe-Jane when this so-called casino night happened. Problem is even though I've got a fucking sound alibi, you won't have it, but I ain't dancing to your tune, mate. No fucking way, sunshine. Me niece has told her the truth. *I* told her the truth. I told you *all* the truth and if you want to shoot an innocent man; go on. Go ahead and do your worst.'

Del, highly irritated at this point, shouted, 'Well I don't believe a frigging word of it. And I ain't got all day. Do you want to or shall I?' He looked over at Frankie and Vaughn but as he was doing so, they heard the unmistakable sound of a safety latch being pulled back.

'I don't think so. Now move away from Alfie. Put your hands in front of you ... right out... Del, drop the gun... Now!... Vaughn, don't move. I said, *don't move!* Hands in front. In front.' Franny pointed the gun at the men, experience and survival instinct in her whole being.

'Don't be stupid, darlin'.' Vaughn spoke up.

For a moment, Franny ignored Vaughn, turning her attention to Alfie, who was stunned to see Franny pointing a Colt 380 at three of the biggest faces in London. She was truly a bird in a million. And then some.

Franny interrupted Alfie's thoughts as she talked to the men. 'Now as you said, I'm going to make this easy. Alfie is going to pick up the gun, and then he's going to leave with me. I'm going to lock the doors so you can't follow us, and sadly for you, gentlemen, you won't be going anywhere till I send one of Vaughn's men to let you out tomorrow morning. And as I can't trust any of you to just let this lie; it'll be the last you see of us, and don't bother trying to come after us, because you'll just be wasting your time. So it's goodbye from me, and it's goodbye from him ... Alfie.'

Franny nodded to Alfie to go and retrieve the gun lying on the floor. As he went towards it, Vaughn pushed forward, barging Alfie out of the way. Franny fired a warning shot in the air, but the two men fought on, Alfie scrabbled along the floor, reaching out for the gun which spun like a roulette wheel. Just as he touched it, he felt a kick to the side of his face as Vaughn's boot smashed into him.

The kick stunned him, giving Vaughn the opportunity to grab the gun himself.

'Alfie, run! Alfie!' Franny screamed out his name. She couldn't shoot, not now there was a possibility she might hit Alfie; he needed to separate himself from Vaughn.

'Stay back Del, and you Frankie.'

Amidst the chaos Alfie heard Franny shouting, giving him the renewed energy to haul himself back up from the floor, rushing towards Franny on the stage.

Vaughn fired at him. It missed, allowing him to dive behind the table before charging towards the stage and towards Franny. He bolted to her and as he did so, he saw Vaughn aim towards him ... and Franny.

'No, Vaughn!... Don't!' The cry was drowned out by the loud shot, but as the person rushed forward, it was too late for Vaughn Sadler to realise what was happening. Too late to stop the bullet as she dropped to the floor, a pool of blood around her.

'Casey!... Casey! Oh my God, Casey!'

Vaughn cried out as the others charged forward, circling around Casey. With his eyes wide open in terror, Vaughn fell to his knees and cradled Casey's head in his lap. He looked at the others' equally horrified faces.

'What have I done?... What have I done?'

21

Mr Lee watched the monitor. He was pleased. The girl had terror carved into her face, both metaphorically and literally. Things had been going well, and the streaming of online sadism was racking up the dollars in the bank.

The only problem was getting the girls to appear in it. He'd tried the druggies who'd do anything for a bit of crack cocaine, but they'd been so drugged up they couldn't even feel the pain, which was of course no good. As for the trafficked girls, he'd thought about it but like the dealing of underage girls, it was too risky. He couldn't be sure if the police or families were looking for them, and if they were spotted, there was no doubt they'd try to track them down and be on his trail.

No, Lee wanted girls who were willing but without anyone caring whether they were hurt or scarred or lived or died, and from what Jodie had told him of this girl she'd met at the pub, she certainly fitted the bill.

Mr Lee sipped his tea; black not green, he'd never been partial to green, too much like the taste of fish for his liking. He was a PG tips man; he'd never had a complicated palate.

Sighing, he turned his attention back to Jodie. He'd met her in much the same way as he was about to meet this new girl. He'd paid girls who'd worked for him in the past to go out and find some *fresh meat*. Jodie had been perfect.

The girl was a runaway from care, abused by her father, vulnerable and desperate for that eternal quest of feeling like she belonged. And because she'd been touting herself since she was a kid, she had been up for anything and everything. But things had got out of hand one night with one of the punters who got their kicks from fucking the girls with hard, sharp objects. He'd got carried away and left Jodie with multiple anal and vaginal injuries.

To his surprise though, Jodie had kept her mouth shut and refused to even converse with the police. She had been loyal to Lee. Loyal because she'd had no one else. He was her everything.

Jodie didn't have Stockholm Syndrome, where the hostage expresses empathy and sympathy as well as positive feelings towards their captor, sometimes even to the point of protecting and identifying with them. No, it was clear to Lee that

155

Jodie had traumatic bonding; strong emotional ties that develop between two people where one of them has all the power and intermittently harasses, beats, threatens, abuses, or intimidates.

As a result, she would do anything for him and for her reward he had recruited her to be *the* recruiter, and she had shown herself to be astute and intuitive to be able to spot the right girls. But then, they did say like attracts like, vulnerable attracts the vulnerable – or in other words, whores attract whores. Jodie was just another throwaway commodity to him, something that could be used, but Lee knew to Jodie he meant far more.

'Mr Lee?' Lin stood by the door.

'Yes, what is it? Make it quick.'

'I've just had word from one of our sources that the flies are going to eat the spider. Alfie Jennings' days are numbered, in fact they're over today. Apparently his own colleagues, the other faces, are making him pay. Do you want me to do anything about it?'

Mr Lee stood up, leaving his half-drunk cup of tea. He thought for a moment he should leave them to it, let them fight amongst themselves, but then, he could never resist putting the cat amongst the pigeons.

22

'Chloe-Jane?'

'Hey you! I didn't think you'd call me.'

'I said I would didn't I? What do you take me for?' Jodie laughed down the phone.

'I dunno. You know how people say they'll call but never do, I thought that's what you'd do.'

'But why wouldn't I call if we're going to be meeting at two o'clock tomorrow?'

Chloe-Jane didn't say anything for a second. She was so used to people letting her down that she imagined she was going to show up at two and Jodie would be nowhere to be seen.

A big smile spread across Chloe-Jane's face. 'I'm glad you called, Jodie.'

'Good, 'cos I've got some good news for you. I talked to that fella and he probably will have some work for you. I told him all about you and he wants to meet you.'

Chloe-Jane squealed with delight. 'You ain't fucking me about?'

'No I ain't.'

'Promise. This ain't a wind-up?'

'No Chloe, it ain't.'

Chloe-Jane's eyes filled with tears. She felt stupid but she didn't care, this was the best news she'd heard in like forever. She'd be able to pay her way without worry. Finally she'd be able to call a place home. 'You really spoke to him. You really did that for me?'

Jodie answered, but her voice seemed more distant and reflective than it had been before.

'Yeah Chloe-Jane, I did that for you... Listen, I better go.'

'Hey Jodie? Are you okay?'

'Yeah I'm fine... I'll see you tomorrow.'

'Okay, I–' The phone went down and for a moment Chloe sat motionless before she jumped up and down on the bed, feeling like the happiest girl in the world.

Fifteen phone calls later, Chloe's mood had turned from joyous to being well and truly fed up. She'd been trying to get hold of Franny but her calls kept going through to voicemail; she'd wanted to tell her about her good fortune, albeit sparing the details of what she was going to do; not that Chloe entirely knew herself, but whatever it was she was certain it wasn't going to be something she'd want to tell Franny.

Having tried Franny, Chloe had then attempted to contact Alfie. And again it was to no avail. Deciding that she really did want to share her news, Chloe picked up her jacket and headed off to Whispers club.

Walking up to the main entrance of Whispers, Chloe found the door was shut, which was odd as she knew the place was supposed to be open on Tuesdays.

Going to the side entrance of the club, down the small side alleyway, Chloe banged on the door. No answer. She banged on it again. 'Oi! Uncle Alfie, are you in there? Uncle Alfie.' Chloe continued to hammer on the door. Sighing, she was about to walk away but she heard the clatter of footsteps coming from inside.

'Uncle Alfie! It's me, Chloe-Jane.'

The steel metal door swung open and Chloe gave a grin. It was Franny.

'Hiya, Fran, I didn't think...'Chloe-Jane stopped as she looked at Franny's drawn face. She saw the fear in her eyes, and then she saw the blood.

'What's happened?... Are you hurt?... Franny, you're covered in blood. Franny! Is it Alfie? Did he do something to you; did he?'

Franny gazed at Chloe-Jane, she whispered her words in a trance-like state. 'No, it's not Alfie... He's alright, it's my friend ... my friend, Casey.'

Chloe still didn't understand. 'What's happened, Franny?'

'You better come in. I don't walk to talk out here.'

Chloe-Jane didn't hesitate to follow Franny through the steel door but she jumped as it slammed behind her, which drew a curtain of darkness in the corridor. Never having been a fan of the dark, Chloe stretched out in front of her. 'Franny, I can't see, where are you?'

Chloe didn't receive an answer, and knowing something was very wrong, she didn't pursue it, only tried to stumble forwards as her eyes adjusted to the dark.

She followed Franny to the end of the hall, where there was a door, a crack of light shining from underneath.

'Don't say a word, Chloe.' It was all Franny said to her as she opened the door to reveal the grouped circle of men standing across the other side of the room.

There was Del Williams, Frankie Taylor, Alfie and Vaughn Sadler but there was something strange; different about them. As Chloe approached she saw what it was. Like Franny, they were all covered in blood.

Chloe-Jane froze, and if it wasn't for the fact Franny was now holding her hand she would've run, terrified at the scene in front of her. Before she had the chance to say anything, Alfie spoke up, though his voice wasn't harsh.

'Chloe-Jane, what are you doing here?'

'I was looking for you; well, Franny. Neither of you answered your phone. What's going on?... Uncle Alfie, what's happened?'

Alfie turned to Franny, exhaustion in his voice. 'Why did you let her in?'

'She was hammering on the door. I couldn't leave her outside, could I? I actually thought it was Doc.' The doctor who Franny referred to had seen all there was to see in Soho; he'd healed the wounds of most of the men who stood in Whispers club, he'd tended to the wounds of Franny's father, Patrick, to Frankie's son, Johnny, to Lola's ex and long-deceased husband, Oscar Harding. He was the first port of call, someone everyone trusted, someone who'd keep his mouth shut.

'Shut up!... Shut up!' Vaughn's voice boomed out, tears streaming down his cheeks. He looked around at the assembled company, and shook his head. 'What are you talking about... It ain't the doc we need, it's a mortician.'

The circle of men opened up and Chloe saw for the first time what everyone was talking about. There, lying on the floor in a pool of her own blood, was Casey.

Chloe put her hands over her mouth to stop the scream coming out. 'Is... Is she dead?... Is Casey dead?'

No one uttered a word. About to ask again, more hammering was heard on the door. Chloe-Jane looked around; frozen in horror.

'Shall I?... Shall I...' Without bothering to finish her sentence, Chloe ran. Back along the corridor, back through the darkness, to the side entrance where she'd first walked in. She threw open the door, seeing a small man standing there. Guessing it was the doctor, she gestured him in. 'Come in... Come in, they're waiting for you. Please hurry!'

Chloe turned and ran back to the others. 'He's here!... The doctor's here!'

She turned, wanting to scream at the pace of the man and having to fight against the urge to drag him along faster. Her words spilled out. 'She's here!... She's over here!' Chloe pointed at Casey.

'I think it's too late. Even from here, I can see your friend is dead... I'm sorry.'

Frankie Taylor stared. 'What...'

The man smiled. 'Sorry, I should have said; I'm Lin. I understand you were looking for Mr Lee.'

With the grace of a man who was honouring the dead, Vaughn Sadler scooped up Casey's body. So light. So beautiful. So still.

161

'Vaughn...' Del reached out to him, but stopped, unsure, unable to find the words.

'Vaughn...' Franny tried, but her stomach knotted, gripped in a vice-like hold. She couldn't bear to look.

'Vaughn...' Alfie attempted, but his words faded into unspoken pain.

'Vaughn...' Frankie ran up to his friend as he got to the far end of the room, but dropped back as Vaughn shook his head.

'Leave him Frank, let him take her up to the flat to say his goodbyes,' Del called out to Frank, who understood perfectly what was going to happen, and why Vaughn needed to have some time alone with Casey, because in less than an hour it'd be like she never existed. The cleaners – Vaughn's clear-up guys – would come in, get rid of any evidence. Get rid of any trace, and then they would take the body. Casey's body would go somewhere no one would ever find her. Where no one would ever know. There'd be no flowers. No gravestone. Nothing. And as hard as it was, however cruel it seemed, that's how it had to be. They all knew it, Vaughn knew it, and even Casey had known that. Because that was the life. That was the life they had all chosen to lead.

23

'You?... How do you have the fucking front to come in here? Get out, or I won't even think about putting a bullet in your head.'

Lin, who was now surrounded by eight of Mr Lee's men, who were all armed and had come in directly after him, smirked. 'Or you'll what? You know how it works. Do you really want to start a full-scale war? By all means, if that's what you want. I know Mr Lee wouldn't be averse to it. You see gentlemen, the troubles you have at the moment you've clearly brought on yourself. It's very much of your own making; you do understand that, don't you? This could have all been avoided.' Lin paused, looking around, he stared at Alfie then slyly added, 'Mr Jennings, isn't it? Help me out here, I have a very bad memory for faces. Where is it we've met before? Perhaps you can put your *finger* on it?' He grinned, making Alfie very uncomfortable. 'No?... Not to worry, I'm sure it'll come to me in due course.'

Alfie stared in horror. What was happening was worse than any nightmare. Casey laid dead... Dead! Fuck, only an hour or so ago she was trying to grab a drink off him.

Since he was young Alfie had surrounded himself with criminals who dealt in killings; gangland and otherwise, but ironically it still didn't prepare you for it when it was close to home. And fuck only knew, Casey Edwards lying only a few feet away from him was certainly close to home. Too close.

And if that wasn't nightmarish enough, Lin, the man who'd come storming in to his casino night, the man who'd chopped off his finger without a blink of the eye was standing there, goading him.

If his game was to cause trouble, then by the way Frankie and Del were glaring at Alfie, Lin was certainly doing a very good job.

'I can't believe she's dead. Franny?' Chloe's voice wailed through the tense atmosphere of the room. 'I thought... I thought he was the doctor. I thought he'd come to save her. Franny...' Chloe's eyes brimmed with tears as Lin stood quietly watching and listening.

'I know... I know sweetheart, don't worry. I can't believe it myself. But I think you should get out of here. Go on, Chloe, go home. This is no place for you.'

'But...'

Del, overhearing the conversation, interjected angrily. 'What fucking difference does it make now hey, Fran? You let the kid in when you should've been sending her home in the first place. You're a fucking joke.'

Fran's eyes flashed, but it was Chloe-Jane who got there first. 'Just leave her alone won't you. Can't you see she's upset?'

Del, having had enough of Chloe-Jane at the hospital, grabbed hold of her arm, pulling her towards the entrance. 'Out! Out! Don't try and give it. We're all upset. We're all...' It was Del now who trailed off. He couldn't believe it had happened either.

'Get your hands off her! Now!'

'Do one Fran, just do one.'

There it was again, the trigger of the gun being pulled back and Franny's tone turning threatening. 'I said; get your hands off her now, Del.'

Del Williams turned to Franny and shook his head as he let go of Chloe-Jane and pushed her forward. 'You'll regret this, Franny. Oh and congratulations, you've succeeded in making me your number one enemy. Make sure you sleep well tonight; it's probably the last time you will.'

'Like I said, we're out of here. Me and Alfie. You can have Soho. Have it all.'

Mr Lin butted in. 'Very wise... I think that's the most sensible thing you could do, Mr Jennings, I'm sure Mr Lee will be delighted to hear it.'

Alfie hissed at Lin, 'Get out of here!'

Lin looked amused. 'And just as it was getting interesting.'

'I said, get out!'

Franny shot Alfie a strange stare. What was going on? But before she could start figuring that out, another wail came from Chloe-Jane, but this time it wasn't about Casey. Her eyes showed a startled frightened child. 'You're leaving?... You can't. You can't leave.'

Franny held onto Chloe-Jane's hand, bringing her in close so Del or Frankie couldn't hear.

'Don't worry; you can stay in the flat. I won't be doing anything with it for a while. But I'm sure you'll have moved on by then anyway.'

Chloe shook her head. 'No!... You can't.'

'Chloe, calm down.'

But Chloe was beside herself. 'You can't go... You can't go and leave me. I'll have a job. I can pay me way... Please. I can...'

Franny shook her head. 'Chloe, this isn't about you. Look around at what's happened, even if we wanted to; we couldn't stay.'

'Uncle Alfie! Please!'

Alfie Jennings looked astonished. What the hell was the matter with the girl? Oh fuck, of course. It was probably the first time she'd seen a dead body and definitely the first time in these circumstances. What the fuck was Franny doing letting her in like that? The poor kid. His niece might be a pain but she certainly didn't deserve to see the stuff tonight.

Alfie winked at Chloe-Jane. 'Listen babe, I know it's been a shock, but you'll be alright girl. I would've given the world at your age to be on me own in a cushy flat. No one to tell you what to do, no one to give you grief. I long for that meself at times.' He grinned, then whispered in her ear, 'I appreciate everything you've done.'

Chloe didn't listen. 'Take me with you... I can come with you. I'll do whatever you want me to do. I'll cook, clean... Please.' She looked over at Franny.

'Franny, just say yes, just let me.'

'Chloe, you're just in shock. Everything will be fine. It's like Alfie says you'll be fine, and I'm betting you'll even have fun.'

'Don't leave me... I ain't got anyone else.'

Grabbing hold of Chloe, Franny pulled her completely away from the others, closely followed by Alfie.

166

'Chloe, I'm sorry but I have to go away. *We* have to go away. Me and Alfie. It won't be safe for us to stay here. I love Alfie, and Alfie loves me so we both have to go. He's my family.'

'He ain't your family. He's my family. Mine!'

Franny looked shocked. 'Chloe!... Please, you don't have to be like that.'

'Then stay... Stay.'

Franny glanced at Alfie who was taking the easy option of saying nothing.

'I can't stay. Alfie needs me, all the other faces have turned against him. For some reason Vaughn has started this vendetta, and it's only going to get worse. They don't want to hear the truth. We've told them Alfie's had nothing to do with breaking the rules. *You've* told them. And it's because of that I have to go.'

'You're leaving because they won't believe Alfie?'

'Yes, Chloe. That's exactly right.'

'Well then you need to stay, because Uncle Alfie lied to you.'

24

'Where is she?' Lola ran into the corridor of Whispers, letting herself in by the spare set of keys she held for Alfie. Doc had been in her café, admiring her new décor as she told him about her varicose veins and wondered if he could do anything about her bunions when the phone call had come in about Casey.

Both she and Doc had set off at a pace, but like everyone that day, they'd been diverted and had ended up going the long way via Shaftesbury Avenue to get to the club.

A moment behind her came Doc. Grey-haired and red-faced. 'Where is she?' Doc spoke to Del, repeating Lola's concern.

'It's too late, Doc... She's dead.'

'No... No, she can't be. This is Casey we're talking about. Casey. She's a fighter.' Lola spun round to look at everyone; refusing to accept what Del had just said.

'I'm sorry, Lola... I really am.'

'Well, where is she? I want to see for meself, Frank. Tell me where she is?' No one was forthcoming, but Lola saw the flicker of an unconscious glance towards the internal door which led upstairs.

'She's upstairs ain't she?... She's up in the flat.'

'Lola, leave it ...Vaughn's up there...' Del spoke but Lola had no intention of leaving anything. She sped forward, looking like a woman half her age.

Hurtling up the stairs, Lola barged into the flat without knocking. 'Casey!... Casey, love. It's me, Lola. Casey!...'

Not seeing anyone, Lola made her way through to the next room. 'Casey!... Ca–' Lola's words froze like icicles in the air. There in front of her was Vaughn, sitting on the bed, soaked in blood, with Casey lying motionless next to him.

Vaughn looked up, his eyes red from the painful tears he had cried. 'Lo... Lo...' He couldn't say

168

any more; instead he stared ahead in tortuous grief.

Lola spoke to Doc who was already by the bed. 'He's in shock; give him something... Oh my God, Vaughn.'

Doc had been highly trained as well as highly skilful in his profession before he'd turned to the more lucrative business of gangland doctor – which included everything from taking bullets out of people, handing out false death certificates to delivering babies born to mistresses of the married faces of Soho who needed to keep a low profile. Now, he shook his head, as he leaned over and examined Casey.

Doc looked up at Vaughn with a start. 'Vaughn... She's alive... Casey's alive!'

The scream from Lola had the others running up the stairs and falling over themselves to see what the noise was all about.

Franny urged Lola to tell her. 'What's happened? Lola, are you alright?'

'She's alive. Doc says she's alive.'

Del frowned. 'That's impossible, how can she be?'

Doc put his stethoscope away and stood up, getting out his phone. 'She is... Barely, but you'll have to get her to hospital. Now.'

Del noticed Doc begin to dial a number. 'What are you doing?'

'I'm calling an ambulance.'

Del walked across to Doc, pulling the phone out of his hand. 'I don't think so.'

Lola couldn't believe what she was hearing. She snatched the mobile phone away from Del, giving it back to Doc. 'What the hell's got into you? Casey's alive... Don't you understand?'

'I understand, but if you think for a moment we can afford to phone the flashing lights, you've got another think coming. The police will turn this place upside down, they'll come knocking and we'll all get nicked. And I'm sorry but I ain't risking it, I've got my own family. I'm not serving a stretch for anyone.'

'So we're just going to stand here and let Casey die?'

'Of course not, I'll take her to hospital; drop her off, no problem.'

Doc piped up. 'You can't take her, didn't you notice all the roads and streets are blocked off because of what happened at Frankie's club? There's no way you'll get through. Only an ambulance will. It's the only chance she has. And it's touch and go anyway; she's lost so much blood already. It's your call, Vaughn.'

Franny shook her head, horrified. 'Just do what's right, Doc, we're wasting time.'

Del snarled at Franny. 'What's right? If you were looking to do what's right, why are you even here? Ain't nothing right about the world we live in, you know that, and it's never bothered you before, but now all of a sudden you want to do the *right* thing because it suits you. Well sorry darlin', things don't work that way. Rules are rules, disobey them and everything gets fucked up.'

With no one else having their mobile phones on them, having run straight to Whispers, Lola gave an order. 'Doc, phone the ambulance... Now!'

170

He nodded, and began to dial.

'I said, I don't think so.' Del urged caution.

'Phone them, Doc. It's fine.' Vaughn who hadn't said anything till now, stood up, his legs threatening to give way. He looked around and even though he spoke to everyone who was assembled, he stared at Del, not letting him break his gaze. 'Tell them what happened. Tell them everything they need to know. Whatever it takes.'

'You're making a huge mistake, Vaughn.'

Vaughn glared at him. 'I don't care how much it costs me, I'll do time. I'll do anything to keep Casey alive. Doc, go and make that call.'

Doc nodded and took the phone into the next room, closing the door behind him.

'What are you playing at, Vaughn? Do you really think I'm going to let you bring me down with you?'

Vaughn stepped closer to Del. 'You've known me long enough to know that I'll keep your name out of it.'

'And you've also been in this game long enough to know that ain't how it works. The Old Bill won't stop at just that, they'll be sniffing around and they won't stop unless they have us all bang to rights.'

Vaughn's expression was one of sadness. 'They always say you find out who your friends are when the shit hits the fan, and it's well and truly hit. Fuck knows it couldn't hit any harder. And I can see clearly who my friends are.'

'Whatever Vaughn, but I swear to God, you bring me down and you'll not live to see next week; be certain of that.'

Vaughn's jaw clenched. 'It's a shame you feel like that, Del. I'll tell them it's a domestic. Then they won't be looking for anyone else.'

'Tell them what you like, but you know as well as I do that now Doc's told them Casey's been shot, any minute now, the armed response unit will be here and I'm not hanging around. I'm going back to Spain, my life's there with me missus and the kids; whatever happens to Soho now isn't my concern...' Del quickly headed for the door, but he paused as he got to Franny. 'Tell Alfie, I won't forget what he did ... and that goes for you as well, Fran.'

There was silence for a moment before Frankie spoke, slightly embarrassed, slightly in a hurry.

'I'm sorry Vaughn; I'm the same, I'm out of here too. I can't afford to be found here, especially as one of my clubs has been torched. They're going to start sniffing; it looks well suss... I'm going to lie low meself, I'll probably head off to Spain as well, but good luck, and I wish Casey all the best.' Frankie Taylor stared at Vaughn, feeling emotional. It felt like an end of something really special, but he wasn't going to hang around. There was no way he was going to do some bird. He wanted to end his days lying next to his wife, not next to some hairy prison cell mate.

He smiled, patting Vaughn on the back, knowing he had to hurry if he wanted to be clear out of it by the time the Old Bill came. 'If it's any consolation, Vaughnie, I would've done the same for me missus, and so would Del, no matter what he says; we all would.'

Five minutes after all the others had left, Vaughn Sadler stood in the flat above Whispers nightclub. He bent down to kiss Casey on her lips. 'Come on Casey. Come on baby, I know you can do it. I know you can pull through. Do it for me... For us... I'm sorry.'

He stood up with his hands in the air as he listened to the thunder of feet charge up the stairs. *'Hands up... Get down! Get down!... On the floor, I said on the floor... Spread your legs...'* The armed response team bellowed out their orders to Vaughn as he saw Casey being stretchered away out of the corner of his eye. The rest didn't matter. All that did was Casey was going to get a chance; some kind of chance of getting help.

So now when the police officer shouted out, 'What happened?' and kicked him in his side, Vaughn was willing to say, 'It was me, officer... I shot her. I shot Casey Edwards.'

25

'Get out! Get out!' Franny Doyle shouted as she threw clothes into a bag.

'What you doing?'

'What do you think I'm doing, Chloe-Jane?... I'm packing your stuff.'

Chloe-Jane burst into tears for the second time in five minutes.

'I'm sorry Fran... You've got to believe me, I'm

so sorry. I never meant to hurt you. Never.'

Franny pushed the last of Chloe's clothes into her small bag. 'Believe you? Isn't that what I did before? And look what happened. I warned you. I warned you not to lie to me.'

'I only did it because I thought it'd help Uncle Alfie... I thought if you knew what he did you'd leave him...You said that you'd go to America if he was involved in the casino night... So I thought...'

'You thought what, Chloe? You thought you'd get involved in somebody else's relationship. Two people you don't even know.'

Chloe retorted, 'I do know him! He's my uncle! He's my family.'

'Oh come off it, Chloe-Jane, when was the last time you saw him before you came here? Go on, *tell* me.'

Chloe-Jane shook her head, putting her head down as her tears dropped onto the floor.

'I can't.'

Franny knew she was being harsh, but she was also too angry and too hurt by Chloe and Alfie to care. Not that she knew where Alfie was; he'd done a disappearing act in the club along with Lin when everything was going down.

'Why not, Chloe-Jane? What can't you do?'

'Tell you. I can't tell you the last time I saw him... He never bothered to come and see me, but that don't mean he ain't my family. He is and he always will be.'

Franny protested, 'I doubt he'll want to know now. You've messed things up from both ends. You lied to me and the way Alfie will see it, you grassed him up. It's over, Chloe. He said you were trouble and he wasn't wrong.'

'Why are you saying these things? Why?'

Franny's face was red with anger. 'Because your lies nearly cost my friend's life; and that's still in the balance. She could still die. Don't you see, Chloe, your lies have caused a lot of people to get hurt? Think about it, Chloe-Jane, if you hadn't lied to me, telling me that Alfie wasn't involved in the casino night then I wouldn't have gone round to Whispers. Do you understand what I'm saying? I wouldn't have bothered, and then nothing would've happened to Casey.'

Chloe was distraught. 'Franny... Please.'

Franny's voice hardened as the images of Casey lying on the floor in Whispers flashed into her mind. 'No, it's not *please Franny*. Like I keep telling you, it's over. I want you gone and I don't want to see you again.'

Chloe-Jane held onto Franny; tugging at her sleeve like a young child. 'I'm sorry!... I'm so sorry, Franny, please. Please don't throw me out, I ain't nowhere else to go... I got nowhere else to go.'

It hurt Franny to see such a vulnerable girl in such turmoil. But her weakness towards the situation only lasted for a moment; she knew she couldn't live her life in the heart of such lies. She didn't want to be around people who could hurt her. And Chloe-Jane had.

'I'm sorry Chloe, I've said all there is to say. You need to leave now.' Franny put her hand out to Chloe-Jane. 'Can I have my keys back?'

'Fran...' But the look in Franny's eyes made Chloe stop. She'd seen that kind of look before.

175

The look that said it was pointless. The look that told her it wasn't worth putting up a fight any-more.

Going into her pocket, Chloe pulled out the key, placed it gently into Franny's hand then turned and walked out of the flat, into the darkness of Soho. Alone once again.

'Well?' Mr Lee waited for Lin to close the door behind him. They were streaming live and the sound of the girl screaming wasn't conducive to discussions.

Lin, feeling a bit of food in his back teeth, rolled his tongue in his mouth. 'More interesting than either of us thought.'

'I'm intrigued.'

'You were right. Certainly the cat was amongst the pigeons. Vaughn Sadler's girlfriend was shot.'

Mr Lee stood up as if he'd just received an electric shock. 'I didn't give you orders to do any-thing. Just go and see what was happening I said but now...'

Lin grinned, interrupting. 'Not me. They had done it to themselves...'

Self-satisfied, Mr Lee nodded. 'And so they fall.'

'I got word from one of our sources that the only one left in Soho is Alfie Jennings.'

'Ah, yes, the irrepressible Mr Jennings.'

'What would you like me to do?'

Mr Lee walked across to the window. Watched the leaves fall from the tree. How apt. How like the leaves the faces of London were. So quickly they'd dropped and divided. He hadn't expected it to be this easy.

And as they had run and dropped Soho, Mr Lee would run and pick it up. Pick it up and do with it as he saw fit. And there was nobody to get in his way, nobody except...

'Get rid of him. Get rid of Alfie Jennings, permanently.'

Lin raised his eyebrows. 'In any particular way?'

Mr Lee smiled. 'As painful and drawn-out as possible.'

26

Alfie Jennings sat in the waiting room in the hospital, his head in his hands. He didn't even want to contemplate the past few hours' events. He couldn't. He had lost everything. Yes, he still had his money from the diamonds he'd sold from a robbery, given to him by Franny some time back, well for the time being anyway; but what good was money when everything you held dear had vanished or collapsed?

'Oi, is there any word yet?' Alfie called to the passing nurse.

'I'm sorry, there's no news yet, Mr...'

'Jennings.'

Alfie went into his pocket and brought out some money. Taking a quick look round to make sure no one was watching, he pushed the money into the woman's hand. 'Find out, will ya?'

The nurse, tired from her long shift, sighed

irritably. She stood back, distancing herself from the money. 'I'm sorry, but that won't make a difference.'

Alfie's anger was palpable. 'Won't it?... Well how about this... And this.' He threw more money at her, pulling fifty-pound notes out of his pocket and showering the nurse with them as if it were confetti. 'Here you are, love. Not enough hey? Why don't you take it all? Go on ... take it. If it means you'll tell me what's happening with Casey; take the frigging lot.'

The nurse raised her voice to be heard over Alfie. 'Mr Jennings!... Mr Jennings! It's not about money.'

'No?'

'No... If you can just calm down, then I can explain.'

Alfie was now almost beside himself. 'And you couldn't have done that before hey? You couldn't have fucking explained before?' He kicked out at the blue plastic chair, not really thinking anything of it until a split second later when an extraordinarily sharp pain shot through his toe and into his foot, sending shockwaves of excruciating agony up his leg.

He held onto his leg crying out, 'Fuck ... fuck ... me fucking toe.'

The nurse, unmoved by the display in front of her, gazed in contempt at Alfie. 'You should get that looked at; you could've broken it, but then that's what you get for kicking chairs that are fixed to the floor. It's also one of the reasons why we did it, because of people like you.'

Alfie gazed up at the woman with fury in his

178

eyes. 'This is funny to you?'

'No, not at all. In fact, far from it. Now if you'll excuse me, I have patients who I need to see to, and as I said before you broke your own toe, there's no news. Casey is still in surgery, as she has been for the past two hours.'

Alfie was about to pursue his gripe with the nurse but he heard a familiar voice behind him. One he could do without hearing.

'What the fucking hell are you doing here? You're not wanted. Go on; go.'

Alfie turned around, unable to completely ignore the throbbing in his toe. 'When you run the hospital, or even have a say about my life, Lola, you can tell me what to do. Until then, and I'm going to try and put this as politely as I can... Do one. Fucking do one, so help me God I'll...'

'You'll what, Alfie?'

'Yes, I'd be interested in hearing what you'll do too, Mr Jennings.'

Two voices were heard behind him. Alfie swivelled round to see Franny, who was in the process of turning round herself to see who'd spoken.

'Hello Mr Jennings, good to make your acquaintance, I've heard a lot about you. The name's Detective Spencer, I'm Detective Teddy Davies's replacement. You remember him don't you?'

Alfie didn't say anything but oh yes, he remembered Detective Davies alright. Who couldn't? The man had been as bent as a U-bend and as full of shit as one. Davies had been in Del Williams' pocket for quite some time before things had turned nasty between the two of them.

Detective Spencer turned his supercilious attention to Franny. He smiled unconvincingly, though it was hidden under his greying moustache.

'Ms Doyle, isn't it? I think we've met before.'

Franny snapped at Spencer, giving him a cold stare. 'Yes I know, when you arrested my father on a false allegation, wasn't it?'

The detective sneered. 'I like to call it unproved; *false* is rather a strong word, don't you think?'

'I don't think anything about you, Detective Spencer, now if you'll excuse me, I've come to see my friend.'

'Not so fast, Ms Doyle, I need a word, but before I do the faces just keep popping up from the past. Lola? Lola Harding.' The detective paused to roar with feigned laughter. 'Who'd have thought hey? Who'd have thought you'd still be alive and kicking?'

Lola shook her head. 'You're scum, Spencer, always have been, always will. You make Davies look like Snow White.'

Spencer turned back to Franny. 'Perhaps we can go somewhere quieter?'

'I've got nothing to say to you.'

'That's where we differ in opinion. Shall we?' Spencer gestured to the visitors' room.

'Is this official, detective?'

'No, just routine enquiries.'

'Well in that case, I'll tell you again, I've got nothing to say and anything *you've* got to say, you can say it here, in front of everyone.'

Infuriated and determined to push on with his questioning, Spencer glared at Franny, hissing his words. 'Ms Doyle, where were you when Casey

180

Edwards was shot?'

Franny turned away, refusing to look in Alfie's direction. 'Detective, I've already…'

'We've charged Vaughn Sadler with attempted murder. And depending on if Ms Edwards gets through the night, it well may be murder.'

Franny, Alfie and Lola all baulked but it was Alfie who spoke. 'You're taking the piss. You lot are taking the fucking piss. He would never hurt Casey; he loved her.'

Spencer's voice was sarcastic. 'Well I'd hate to see what he did when he didn't want to hurt her.'

Franny interrupted. 'Where are you keeping him? Who's representing him?'

Detective Spencer looked at his watch. 'All in good time, Ms Doyle, I've got an appointment with a Big Mac. I'll be back on duty in an hour, we can talk then.'

Ten minutes after Detective Spencer had gone in search of his midnight McDonald's, Franny, Lola and Alfie sat outside the ICU department, having been informed that Casey had come out of surgery.

'Happy now? Are you happy now?' Lola's voice was loud and full of passion and for a minute, Franny thought she'd have to tell her to keep it down, but it soon dropped to a hoarse whisper. 'Look what you lot have done.'

Alfie, not in the mood for anyone, and needing time to think, growled at Lola. 'What the hell are you talking about?'

'I'm talking about you. You, Frankie, Del and even Vaughn. All the lot of you. You were supposed to come and help Soho, not bring chaos on it. I loved you Alfie, Franny loved you; we all did but you screwed us all over by getting involved with the casinos when you knew better. We've given you chance after chance and we did it because we cared. We hoped that one day, you'd sort yourself out and show us it was worth sticking by you, but instead you went on your own selfish path, and now look. Casey's life is hanging in the balance, the others have upped sticks and gone, and the triads are breathing on our necks like a teenager in the back row of the movies... Even your niece, Chloe-Jo...'

'Jane. Chloe-Jane.'

'Jane, Jo, you know what I mean, Alfie, don't be smart. Even Chloe-Jane got caught up in all of this.'

At the mention of Chloe-Jane's name, Alfie rolled his eyes. Franny tried to push the guilt she'd been feeling for the past couple of hours away.

'They've all gone. All of them, and now it's only us. How the hell are we supposed to keep the triads at bay?'

Alfie said nothing, he felt ashamed. Not that shame would help anyone, all it did was allow him to feel sorry for himself.

'Alfie, I'm talking to you.' Lola angrily pushed on.

'I know and I'm listening but what the fuck do you want me to do?'

Franny whipped round. 'Perhaps do something that you haven't done before; be a man. A real man.'

Alfie looked bemused; of all the things she could accuse him of, not being a man wasn't one of them.

Reading his thoughts, Franny continued. 'Oh please, don't look like that, Alfie. Anyone can walk around banging their chest and threatening people with a gun, but the mark of a real man isn't what they do when all is well, it's what they do when things get tough. It's then you see the true colours of a person.'

'Fran, listen; I feel me balls are being squeezed and I don't know which way to turn for trailing crap with me. I'm sorry, okay. I know that's not what you want to hear but I am, let me explain why I did it.'

Franny shook her head, sadness filling up her eyes. 'There you go again, Alf, making this about you and singularly you. Don't you see, I don't care *why* you did it, or why you felt the need to lie to me when you knew perfectly well lying would break us. You and I are over. Get that into your head, because all that energy you're wasting on trying to figure out how you can come up with an excuse about why you did this or that could be better used to figure out what we're going to do.'

'Fran, look, you and me, well we...'

'Stop! Alfie, stop! There you go again; you're trying to talk about us. Us is no longer. If you want to do something for me, do this; pull your self-pitying, self-indulgent head out of your bullshitting ass and help us find a solution for Soho, Casey and Vaughn.'

Like a man on a self-destruct mission, Alfie

183

opened his mouth and let his hurt show in his words. 'Vaughn... Oh I see, that's how it is. You and Vaughn. When did it start, Franny?'

'Excuse me?'

Franny couldn't believe what she was hearing and even though Lola didn't want anything to do with Alfie at the moment, she couldn't help but stand behind Franny, signalling him to keep his mouth shut. But to no avail.

'Don't give me the wide-eyed innocence, Fran, it all makes sense now. You and Vaughn. That's why Casey had gone back on the treacle ain't it?... What's the matter, Fran, hit on the truth have I? And there's you talking about telling the truth.'

Franny stood with her mouth open, and although Alfie suddenly felt what he was saying was something he shouldn't, he carried on regardless. 'You see, sadly for you, Franny, I spoke to Casey and she couldn't look me in the eye when I asked her what was going on. I can see now the girl was covering you; poor cow, for what? So she can be laying in intensive care tubed-up to the nines.'

The fury and volume of Franny's voice surprised everyone in the waiting room. 'How dare you! How dare you insinuate I'd do something only a lowdown dog such as yourself would do? I don't know why Casey didn't come and tell me she was struggling, but whatever the reason, it isn't because I was boning Vaughn. You don't get it, do you? It was you, Alfie, you I loved. I was happy with you, all I wanted was to be with you and all I asked for was the truth. Is that so hard,

184

is it? No, don't answer that because whatever comes out will be a lie, and I don't want to hear any more lies. Now get out, go. 'Cos I never want to see you again. *Never*. Go to the Costa like the others, go to Essex, go to the moon and back for all I care, but don't come near me again.'

And like his niece, Chloe-Jane had seen just hours before, Alfie saw the look in Franny's eyes that told him she was serious. It was over. It was pointless saying another word.

Turning round without a goodbye, Alfie Jennings walked out of the ICU, determined never to talk to Franny again.

Lola put her hand on Franny's arm, she smiled. 'So that leaves you and me then.'

Franny nodded. 'Then you and me is what it'll take.'

27

Chloe-Jane hugged her knees tightly as she hid behind two stinking bins in the alley behind Oxford Street. She sat shivering on the hard concrete surrounded by the overflow of the rubbish as the rain drenched through her clothes, dripping down her back and soaking into the top of her pants.

She raised her head up to the night sky, feeling the drops of rain sting against her face. The smell of the bins was making her feel sick but she was too frightened to come out of her hiding place, at least until morning.

The streets at night were unsafe; they were dangerous. She had learnt that the hard way. The last time she'd slept rough, she'd been jumped on, and if it hadn't been for the passer-by she would've been raped, or worse. She'd been lucky that night; she'd come away with only a loose back tooth caused by the man's fist smashing into her face.

The stranger who'd helped her had taken Chloe-Jane back to his bedsit, but instead of giving her a safe, warm haven for the night, he'd locked her in, calling her names and insisting on her giving him oral sex.

She hadn't thought she'd be back on the streets, or rather she'd *hoped* she wouldn't. She'd really believed that *somehow*, somewhere there'd be a life she could carve out for herself. And if there was a place where she'd thought that was possible, it had been Soho, with her Uncle Alfie. But it'd all gone so wrong. So horribly wrong. Chloe-Jane put her head in her hands and began to sob again.

It was so cold. Her hands were part-way between numb and freezing. She didn't think she could make it through the night feeling this way. She had to do something. The idea of waiting there for God knows what to happen to her in the shadow of the night had her pulling out her phone.

Her hands shook; freezing fingers dialling the number. As soon as it was answered, Chloe-Jane started talking.

'Uncle Alfie... No please, don't put down the

phone. Please, listen to me... I'm sorry.'

'What the fuck do you want?'

'Can... Can I come and stay with you?'

'Tell me... Tell me you ain't being serious, Chloe?'

'I ain't got anywhere else to go.'

'And you thought you'd call me because...'

'...Because I need you.'

Alfie had had enough of women. Every bird he'd ever come across; every encounter with them, it'd always led to this. Ear ache. Grief, and ultimately a fucking great big guilt trip. But he wasn't going to accept it, no way was he was going to accept responsibility for this.

To Alfie, this was all Chloe-Jane's fault. If it hadn't been for her turning up and stirring things, then opening up her mouth, he and Franny would still be together.

'Do me a favour Chloe, you really are taking the piss. How you have the gall to call me or are you coming back for second bites? What is it that you're going to destroy this time, hey babe? My house, my money, my daughter, me? Oh no, you already did that. Come on Chloe, do your worst. Come on, put the bullet in... What?... Got nothing to say?'

Chloe-Jane *didn't* have anything to say, because she couldn't. She just couldn't. The loathing she heard in Alfie's voice cut her deeply. Broke her heart. He had been her last chance. Quietly and without any fuss, Chloe-Jane locked off the phone, putting her head back in her hands once more.

'What have we here then?' The cold water being sprayed onto Chloe-Jane had her scrambling up from her concrete bed. She spluttered, gasped and coughed and for a moment she didn't know where she was.

'Get up you lazy tramp!... Come on, move it.' The road cleaner shouted angrily at Chloe.

'Sorry... Sorry, I'm going.' Chloe tried to gather her things; her bag and the jacket and jeans she'd used as a pillow stuffed into her arms.

'Too late darlin'.' Nastily the man cackled as he held the cold water spray, dousing her down in cruel pleasure.

'Please stop it... Please stop it.'

The sweeper, now joined by his colleagues, continued to taunt Chloe.

'I've always loved a wet t-shirt competition! Take some of that dirt off her! Tramp! Tramp!... Come on love give us a smile... What's the matter you fleabitten bitch, I thought you'd be pleased to get a shower!'

'You bastards! Leave her alone!' A loud voice was heard and the men turned around to see a woman swinging a broomstick.

'What the fuck...' The men shouted and ducked all in the same moment as the first blow to the head with the broom handle landed clean on the tallest of the road sweepers' head.

'You crazy bitch!'

'Oh you haven't seen anything yet! Now get out of here, before I really lose it.'

With the men gone, Chloe-Jane looked up at the woman who had helped her. 'Thank you... Thank you.'

'Listen, why don't I rustle up a nice bit of

188

bacon and eggs for you, and perhaps if you're lucky a piece of my special fried bread; can't beat a bit of fat to block up the arteries in the morning... Come on Chloe-Jo, you'll be alright.'

Chloe-Jane looked at Lola, seeing not the old woman she'd seen before, but a woman whose eyes said she'd seen many things but had come out the other side carrying warmth and love with her.

'Jane. It's Chloe-Jane.'

Lola frowned looking puzzled. 'Alfie said it was Jo; Chloe-Jo, I'm sure he did, yes I can hear it now, Chloe-Jo.'

With a big effort, Lola helped Chloe off the ground, pulling her up. 'Bleedin' roll on, I ain't what I used to be. Me back's knackered, still it could be worse, I could've lost me looks.' Lola cackled, showing off her almost-toothless grin. She smiled at Chloe, but it was tinged with sadness. 'Chloe-Jo, I'm sorry what happened with Alfie and Fran.'

Chloe shrugged. 'Don't worry about it. I brought it on myself.'

Lola grabbed Chloe by the shoulders. She shook her. 'Don't you say that! Don't you ever say that! I never want to hear that out of your mouth again. It *wasn't* your fault. None of this is your fault. You got caught up in the middle of something you didn't understand. I love them both but they had no place letting you get involved. You're just a kid, and I know what it's like to be out on your own on the streets. I know what it's like to have no one.'

Chloe-Jane sobbed her heart out and as she

189

did, Lola pulled her into her. 'Now come on, dry them tears. Like I said, I'm going to take you to mine and get you something to eat. You can get yourself washed, dried and cleaned up. We'll get you back to looking like a princess again. And it won't be a problem for you to stay the night. Just one, like.'

Chloe-Jane almost knocked Lola over in her excitement. 'You mean it? I can really stay?'

Lola laughed. 'Of course I mean it. But listen, I can't tell Franny. I don't think it'll go down well with her at the moment.'

Chloe's face dropped. 'You mean you're going to lie to her.'

Lola looked hurt. 'Ain't nobody said anything about lying. No... No, I'm not going to lie to her, I'm just not going to tell her the truth, which isn't quite the same, is it?'

As Chloe-Jane walked down the street, wondering quite why Lola was armed with a broomstick at all, she knew Franny wouldn't see it like that. No, she wouldn't see it like that at all.

28

'Another piece?' Lola held a burnt piece of fried bread over Chloe-Jane's plate. She was happy to see the girl eating. She could never understand the girls of today who thought there was something sexy about making themselves look under-nourished and hollow-eyed. When she had been

Chloe's age, it'd been all about the curves, now it was all about the scrag and bones.

'Thanks, Lola but I've got to go and meet someone; chance of a job.'

Lola sat down next to Chloe, picking at the rind of her bacon. 'Yeah, what's this all about; you kept this quiet.'

Chloe-Jane smiled; she'd had a long bubble bath, complete with candles. She'd washed and dried her hair and Lola had let her wear a pair of True Religion jeans and a black fitted Gucci shirt she'd found amongst the pile of stolen clothes Lola had apparently got from some of the girls who worked in the sauna in Brewer Street.

'It's nothing really, I met a girl in a pub and she said she might be able to get me some work.'

Lola frowned, not really liking the sound of it. 'And what exactly will you be doing? You know you can't trust people.'

Chloe-Jane smiled. 'It's all above board.'

'So what is it, 'cos as far as I can see jobs don't grow on trees? Maybe I can find you a few shifts at the café, once Fran has calmed down of course. It ain't a bad gig, Casey worked for me and she had no complaints.'

At any other stage in her life, Chloe-Jane would've leapt at the chance of working at Lola's caff, a few shifts here and there, but after what had happened with Franny, the idea of getting close to someone again frightened her. She'd get a job on her own, that way no one could take it away from her.

'Thanks for the offer, but I think this is a sure thing. And don't worry, it's just a marketing job, you know, promoting clubs and bars.'

Lola nodded cautiously. 'Are you sure, 'cos it's not good trying to pull the wool over my eyes because I am the bleedin' wool. I see everything love, and I've been everywhere.'

'I know Lola, but it's fine. Really ... but thank you, thank you for everything.'

Lola wafted Chloe away. 'You soft cow. Christ knows what you'd be like if I'd made you some of me scotch eggs.'

'I better go, I'm meeting my friend at two.'

'Well like I say, there's no problem with you staying here tonight; I always like a bit of company, but as I said...'

Chloe-Jane smiled at Lola. 'I know, Franny can't find out.'

'That's my girl. I think you and me will get on just fine, Chloe-Jo.'

Half past two came and went and there was still no sign of Jodie. Chloe-Jane was about to start to despair when an unmistakable voice was heard coming from the other side of the bar.

'Chloe-Jane, Chloe-Jane, Christ almighty you'd never believe the trouble I had getting here. You look tired, are you alright? How's that uncle of yours? Did you see the news yesterday? They showed Soho; I thought of you. Oh that's a nice shirt, me friend had one like that, not as nice as yours though, think she got hers from Primark. Have you had anything to eat, I'm starving. Do you know anywhere round here to eat?'

Chloe-Jane burst into laughter so hard she had to hold her sides. Since the last time she'd seen

Jodie so much had happened and she'd been sucked into things she certainly didn't want to be a part of. So it was good to see Jodie; really good.

Instead of answering any of the questions, Chloe-Jane just hugged her friend. 'It's great to see you. For a moment there, I thought...'

'What? You thought I wasn't coming? I'm as good as me word I am, unless of course me word is bullshit.'

'So when are we meeting him?'

Jodie winked. 'You're eager, he'll like that. He always likes girls that are.'

A slight cold worry ran through Chloe-Jane, but she pushed it away, trying to ignore it.

'What do you mean?'

Jodie grabbed Chloe-Jane by the arm, pulling her towards the exit. 'Oh don't worry. I'm just being silly. Come on then if you're coming. He don't like to be kept waiting.'

Although it was only four o'clock, the dark basement of the tall six-storey building in Gerrard Street they were in made it seem much later. Chloe-Jane could smell something that made her want to be sick. She wondered if it was coming from the restaurant she'd seen on the ground floor of the building, with its array of powerful smells. Crispy belly pork, duck and what looked like a squashed deep-fried goose had hung from hooks in the window and Chloe had decided nothing could've looked less appetising.

'Are you sure it's down here?'

Jodie answered from the darkness, and Chloe

could imagine her smiling. 'Of course I'm sure, I'm not taking you on a tour of the London dungeons you know.'

Chloe didn't say anything, mainly because it was exactly how it felt. Damp, cold walls and eerie sounds reminding her of the day one of her foster parents had taken her for a day out at the popular tourist attraction. If she didn't know better, she would've certainly said that they were there, rather than underneath one of the buildings in Chinatown.

'Are we there yet Jodie, I've never been keen on the dark.'

'Baby!'

Chloe was about to protest but Jodie opened a door into a large room, which was also dark, but certainly nothing like the labyrinth of corridors they'd just come along.

'Jodie, it's good to see you, and who have we here?' A man's voice came out of the darkness making Chloe-Jane grab hold of Jodie in fright.

'It's the girl I told you about, Chloe-Jane.'

'Bring her nearer.' Mr Lee spoke out from behind the two-way mirror. It was important for him at this stage not to be seen.

Chloe was pushed forward by Jodie into the middle of the room where she stood feeling more exposed and self-conscious than she had done in a very long time. The eeriness of talking to someone she couldn't see made her feel nervous.

'Jodie tells me you're interested in working for me.'

'Yes, I need to get meself a job.'

'Then why haven't you?'

194

'I've tried, but things haven't been so easy...'

'And how do I know you're a good worker?'

'I am, I'll work really hard. I don't care what I do. I'll do anything.'

'Really? That's a huge statement to make.'

For some reason, Chloe found herself blushing. She shrugged, not quite sure what she was supposed to say. 'I dunno.'

'Take your clothes off, Chloe.'

Chloe's head whipped round to stare at Jodie, who looked away. 'I ... I...'

'Right, well I can see you're wasting my time, Chloe. I don't think there's anything more to say. Jodie will show you out; thanks for coming.'

'No, wait! Wait! I need this job.'

'I don't think so.'

'Please, I'm a good worker.'

Mr Lee's tone was full of scorn. 'So you say, Chloe, but as we've all just witnessed, what you say and what you actually do are two different things.'

'What do you mean?'

'What I mean is you've just told us that you're willing to do anything, yet when I tell you to do the simple task of taking off your clothes, you can't manage to do that. How am I supposed to employ you now?'

There was a desperation in Chloe's voice. 'It was just a shock, that's all. I wasn't expecting it.'

Mr Lee laughed. 'What were you expecting, Chloe? A job in a hotel?'

'No... No.'

'Do you really think you can earn the sort of money that Jodie's earning by waiting tables?'

'No, of course not, it's just...'

'Just what, Chloe? Wouldn't you like to earn enough money to be able to rent your own flat, even buy one?'

Chloe-Jane listened, both intrigued and apprehensive. Having her own place was something she dreamed of, something that she'd thought of since she was a kid. A place of her own; somewhere where no one could throw her out, somewhere where no one could sneak into her bedroom at night and hurt her, somewhere where no one could take away the keys.

So as Chloe-Jane stood in the darkness, unable to see more than three feet in front of her, she decided whatever it took, whatever this man told her to do, it was worth it. Worth it to be safe. Worth it to have a place called home.

Slowly, but determinedly, Chloe spoke.

'Let me start again... Give me another chance. I won't let you down...' And without another word, she began to undress.

29

Alfie Jennings looked across the park, watching the royal keeper's car being driven carefully across the bumpy ground towards him. With his head banging from the scotch and the dry hot air which had pumped out all night from his car heater, the last thing he wanted or needed was to have an encounter with some official telling him he needed to move on. He just wanted to be left alone and continue feeling sorry for himself.

He'd slept in his car and had turned off his phone, not that anyone was going to contact him. Not now anyway. How things had got this far, he didn't know.

Alfie rubbed his chin, feeling the stubble. It was probably best if he went to the store to pick up a razor and have a shave in the gents before he faced the world; it was one thing feeling rough but looking rough was an entirely different matter; he still had an image to keep up.

Standing outside his Range Rover for a moment to stretch his legs, he looked out across Richmond Park, thinking about Franny and how not so long ago he'd have been waking up next to her; and making love to her, instead of waking up in his car miles from home.

Shit. He wanted to talk to her. He really did, but he couldn't quite take the rejection if she didn't want to know him anymore. His thumb for a moment hovered over the speed dial button, but the idea of listening to her hostile voice was too much, especially with a painful hangover. Perhaps he'd call her later.

Getting back in his car, Alfie felt the heat hit him, making him feel weary again. He looked in the driver's mirror and saw his bloodshot eyes staring back at him. His skin looked pallid and dehydrated.

Lately he'd noticed how his face had started to show lines and the surprised comments had stopped when he told people his age, but no one could mistake his age today; looking at himself now, he looked like he was ready for his bus pass.

Women; they'd a lot to answer for. That was the cause of his problems, or any man's for that matter. Scientists blamed men's early heart attacks, strokes, premature ageing and even death on poor diet, smoking and excess drinking, when the root of the problem, Alfie was convinced, always went back to a woman.

He'd had a lot of friends and lost a lot of friends over the years, all from different backgrounds and different cultures, but the one thing in common, the one thing that pissed them all off, the one thing that had them tearing their hair out and ailed them, was women. Somewhere at the heart of every transgression was a woman; whether it was to do with money, sex or someone's downfall, it always seemed to be the female of the species who was at the root of the cause.

Still deep in thought, Alfie Jennings put his Range Rover into gear and sped off out of the park, not noticing the small blue car begin to follow him.

30

'Would you listen to this crap?' Franny sat on the edge of the table in Lola's café, looking at the newspaper, addressing no one in particular. 'Gemini; today a mysterious stranger brings you good news and with the moon in Jupiter your worries will be eased... Could you spout any more rubbish to me?'

'I take it you don't believe in star signs.' Lola raised an eyebrow.

'Well let's put it this way, if it read, Gemini; today you'll wake up to the familiar sound of the road works, get stuck on the Euston Road behind an HGV lorry, followed by a row with a traffic warden for wanting to park near my own house, then Lola, I might say there's something in it.'

Lola laughed, gathering up the plates on the table as Franny continued to look at the paper.

'Okay, how about a crossword, Lola? You any good at them?'

'Try me.'

'Okay, here you go; one down. An error of judgement; eight letters.'

Lola fell silent as she became a picture of concentration, before a wide smile crept on her face. 'An error of judgement... That's easy... Marriage!'

Franny laughed. Lola was the perfect tonic. 'What is it about us, hey Lola? Why do we make men our downfall? You'd think we'd learn, but we never do. We're strong, independent, intelligent women, yet each and every time, we let men ruin our lives. Behind every problem there's a man.'

Lola looked at Franny. 'Oh I wouldn't say that, Fran ... I'd say in front of it, to the side of it and bleedin' on top of it.' She grinned at her friend before sitting back down next to her.

'Look love, it'll be fine, you and...'

'Don't say it. Don't say, *me and Alfie will work it out* because we won't. We just won't. He lied to me and I don't do lies. He knows that.'

'But…'

'No, no I don't want to talk about him… I don't suppose you've see any sign of Chloe-Jane, have you?'

Lola shifted in her seat. 'No, why would I?'

Franny shrugged. 'I dunno… I was just hoping. Put my mind at ease I suppose. I feel bad about what happened. If I knew she was okay, then…'

'She's fine.'

Franny sat up straight, narrowing her eyes as she looked at Lola. 'What do you mean?'

'I … I just mean she's a survivor, ain't she.'

'Do you know something?'

'No … no; I'm just saying, girls like Chloe-Jo will find a way to get through.'

'It's Jane.'

Lola turned round, looking annoyed. 'Where? Because I want a word with that cheeky cow. She's been going round saying me and Doc have something going on, plus she still owes me a score.'

'No, not Jane from the sauna, I mean, it's Chloe-Jane.'

'Where?'

'No, I mean. You said… Actually, forget it.'

Lola shook her head. 'You need to get some rest, love, you ain't making sense.'

Franny smiled, getting up to go. 'You would tell me if you heard anything? She caused a lot of bother but I'd hate it if anything happened to her.'

'Nothing will. She'll be fine. I'm sure of it.'

Franny Doyle stood watching the machine breathe

for Casey. There'd been no change, which she couldn't tell if it was a bad thing or a good thing. The doctors and the ICU nurses hadn't been forthcoming with any information either.

'No change?' A voice came from behind Franny. She turned round to see Detective Spencer's smug expression.

'You tell me, detective, after all that's your job. Why are you here anyway?'

'The same reason as you.'

'We both know that's not true.'

Spencer shrugged. 'You're right.'

Franny walked away, she didn't have anything to say to this man. He was a vulture. Yes, he had his job to do but the enjoyment the man got from seeing others' misery was hard to stomach.

'We're going to throw the book at him you know.' Spencer talked in a monotone manner as Franny stared through the glass of the intensive care ward.

'It was an accident.'

'Really? I thought you weren't there. Because according to Mr Sadler, he and Casey were the only ones there. Which does seem strange, especially as the club is owned by Mr Jennings, but then you'd know that, wouldn't you?'

'Everyone knows that.'

Spencer joined Franny at the window. 'The thing I don't understand, Ms Doyle, is why Mr Sadler was there in the first place.'

'Why wouldn't he be? It's a bar after all.'

'But why that bar, Ms Doyle? Especially as Mr Sadler and Mr Jennings didn't get on, yet he finds himself in that bar with Ms Edwards.'

'I don't know. You'd better ask him.'

'I have, and now I'm asking you. Why would a man go to a bar which is owned by a man he detested? An empty bar. No clients. No owner. Yet there's Mr Sadler upstairs in the flat of Whispers. Who let him in? And why was the place like the *Marie Celeste?* None of it makes sense, Ms Doyle, none of it.'

'You're the detective.'

'You know what I think? I think there were other people there. I think it wasn't as simple as Mr Sadler's saying it was. I think he's covering for someone, Ms Doyle; after all where did the gun go to? That's the thing about guns, they don't have legs.'

Franny shrugged. 'Who knows, stranger things have happened.'

'I'm going to find out who and what really happened, Ms Doyle, and when I do...'

Franny interrupted. 'Don't tell me, when you do, you're going to throw the book at them as well.'

Spencer sneered. 'Jennings, Williams, Taylor, all lying low, all at the same time? All out of British jurisdiction or un-contactable. Don't you think that odd?'

'Haven't you ever heard of coincidence, detective?'

'When you've been in the game as long as I have, you get to realise there isn't such a thing as coincidence. So if you do speak to them, tell them I'll be catching up with them for a little chat, and when I do, if they've got anything to hide, then...'

Franny turned to walk towards the exit. '...That book's going to come flying. That's an awful lot of books you'll be throwing, detective, but if I were you, I'd hold off with the Waterstone's vouchers... Oh, and I'd be careful who you go round accusing, otherwise you might wake up one day to find that gun has walked right into your room.'

31

The gates of Belmarsh prison opened and slammed behind Franny, making her shudder. Of all the prisons in and around London, she found Belmarsh to be the worst. Not because of the actual building but rather it was the sense of overwhelming hopelessness coupled with the almost visible tension amongst the prisoners. And it was here Franny found herself waiting to see Vaughn.

She wasn't sure if he'd see her; after all she was certain he'd blame her for everything that had happened, as well as being part of the reason why he was sitting in a cell.

Franny watched the other prisoners' wives. A group of women who made the journey come what may to sit for two hours opposite the man they'd chosen to be with, for better or for worse.

Franny always divided them into categories. There were the ones who were done up to the nines; head to toe in designer gear, and there were the frazzled ones, elbow-high in kids and debt as they took on all the worries of the outside world on their own. Those who took it in their stride; this was their life and it'd never change; visiting their banged-up partners was as familiar as going to the supermarket. And then finally, there were the ones – if you looked carefully enough – who had the look of relief on their faces; finally their old man was behind bars, unable to cause any more grief, pain or hurt, and whether it was for one month or ten years, the day their partner had been imprisoned and started their sentence was the day theirs had finished.

'Franny.'

Franny looked up to see Vaughn standing in front of her.

'Hi, it's good to see you.'

Vaughn didn't say anything. He sat down, slumping in his chair looking like a broken man.

'How is Casey?'

'She's stable. I've been trying to get some information out of the doctors but they don't seem too keen to divulge anything.'

'Has she woken up yet?'

Franny shook her head, taking in the tiredness around Vaughn's eyes. 'But she will. I'm sure of it.'

Vaughn's tone was scathing. 'Really? And how can you be so sure, Fran? Last time I heard you weren't a doctor.'

Franny didn't say anything. It was true. What did she know? And it was stupid to try to comfort Vaughn with empty words. 'I'm sorry... I'm sorry for everything.'

Vaughn stared at Franny, but there wasn't the hatred there that had been present only a week or so ago, just sadness for what had once been. 'You should've trusted me, Fran.'

'I thought Alfie was telling me the truth. I know it sounds stupid, but I thought he and I had something special, and you were so angry with him. So hostile, I thought...'

'...I had a vendetta against him.'

'Yes, but you can see why. There was all that history between you and him and you seemed so different. Everybody did, but you, Vaughn. You seemed to be driven by hatred. I didn't recognise you ... and neither did Casey.'

For a moment Vaughn's jaw clenched, annoyed at what Franny was saying; but maybe there was some truth in it. Perhaps if he'd listened more to what Casey had been trying to tell him about his behaviour, maybe he wouldn't be in this predicament now.

'Did she say that?'

Franny was silent for a minute. She certainly hadn't come here to rub salt into any wound and the last thing she wanted to do was hurt Vaughn any more than he already was. But she wouldn't lie to him, because that's what had got them all there in the first place. Secrets and lies.

'Yes, but she loved you, Vaughn. That was a given.'

'And her drinking. Did she tell you about that?'

'No... No she didn't. I wish she'd been able to share it with me. Let me know she was struggling.'

'You and me both, Fran. You and me both.'

'It's such a mess. I don't even know where to begin. Oh before I forget, Lola sends her love and she wants you to know that being banged up is a pretty poor excuse for not getting the moose head for the café that you promised her.'

They both laughed; warm, gentle laughter driven by the memories of the days gone past and the time they'd all spent together. The struggles they'd had and the heartbreak they'd shared over the years.

Franny sighed. 'I didn't know it would get to this. What can I do? What do you want me to do? How can I make this better for you, Vaughn?'

'There's nothing to do, Fran. I've got to take the bird; ain't nothing else for it. And anyway, it ain't like I didn't do it.'

'It was an accident.'

'Yeah, one that's seen Casey end up in a coma and Soho open to anyone who wants it. Don't you see, Fran, the game's up, sweetheart. It's over. As long as Casey comes through, that's all that matters to me; I'll take whatever comes after that. Ain't no wriggling out of this. Del was right, if I'd started saying it wasn't me, all I would've done was bring everyone else down with me. It would've given them an excuse to go fishing, and you know as well as I do, there's plenty to catch.'

'It might have been okay.'

'Don't Fran, you know how it is. If I'd run when Doc called the ambulance, not only would I have left Cass on her own but they would've torn Soho apart, arresting everyone from Toms to pimps to dealers to the faces. And if I'd said the others were

206

there, they would've had them down as accomplices. You know that. And if you'd stayed, well, who knows.'

Fran leaned in to Vaughn, whispering as well as covering her mouth with her hand in case any of the prison staff could read lips, as occasionally she'd heard of them being able to.

'I picked up the gun. It's in a safe place.'

Vaughn smiled wryly. 'Thanks, but I don't think them not having the gun will make much difference, seeing as I've admitted doing it and seeing as Casey has a bullet in her chest.'

'Then tell me what to do.'

'Go home. Go home, Fran and put your life together. Start afresh, forget about me and trying to make things right. And if I were you, I'd get as far away from Soho as I could.'

32

'*Harder. Harder. Use your fists. That's better. Use the strap. Harder. Jesus, this isn't Nickelodeon.*' Mr Lee fed the instructions through to the live streaming as he sat in the next room.

'Don't you think that's enough?' Jodie bit her fingernails as she watched Chloe-Jane on the monitor.

Mr Lee turned round, hostility dancing in his eyes. 'Excuse me?'

Jodie stammered, her eyes wide with worry. 'It's just... It's just, she's new at it. Can't you go easy on her? It's her first time and he's hurting her.'

Mr Lee laughed nastily. 'And how is this anything to do with you? Correct me if I'm wrong but wasn't it you who brought her here?'

'Yeah, but I like her.'

Mr Lee mocked her. *'I like her. I like her...* The next thing you'll be telling me is she's your friend.'

'She is.'

'If she was your friend, why would you bring her here?'

Jodie looked confused. 'Because you asked me to find someone.'

Mr Lee stood up, taking and squeezing Jodie's face in his hands. 'Exactly. And I've told you before, Jodie, you don't need friends. You've got me. Do you understand?'

Tears rose in Jodie's eyes. She nodded, her voice tiny. 'Yes.'

'Yes what Jodie, yes what?'

'Yes, Mr Lee.'

Mr Lee threw her back, sending her flying. Jodie crashed down onto the floor. Sprawled amongst the chairs, Mr Lee kicked her hard in her side. 'And don't you forget it, Jodie. I was the one who cared for you. I was the one who took you in when no one else wanted you. That's true, isn't it?'

Jodie hugged her knees, rocking through the pain in her side. 'Yes ... yes.'

'And if it wasn't for me, you'd be back on those streets, doing God knows what and with God knows who. Is that what you want? Because if it is, you're free to go. Go on; the door's open. I don't want to keep you against your will. In fact,

I'll pack your stuff now.'

Mr Lee walked towards the door. A moment later Jodie jumped up, clung to the back of Mr Lee's jacket. 'No, please! Please, I'm sorry. I know you've been good to me.'

'Do you, Jodie? I don't think you do.'

There was desperation in Jodie's voice. 'I do! I do! Just let me stay. You're the only one who cares. I ain't got no one else.'

'I think you're ungrateful, Jodie. I'm not surprised nobody else wants you. If I had a child like you I'd get rid of you too. Why should I let you stay?'

Jodie started to shake. 'Because I love you.'

Mr Lee smirked, stroking Jodie's face. 'And this is the way you show it, by telling me you've got friends. I thought I'd be enough for you, Jodie; but clearly I'm not.'

Jodie was fully hysterical now. 'You are! You are! Please give me another chance.'

'Chances, Jodie, you're always looking for chances.' Mr Lee paused, watching the monitor for a time. He turned and smiled. 'Okay Jodie, I can't be like everybody else. I can't be cruel and turn my back on you, so you can have your last chance, but I don't want to hear any more about you having friends. We've got each other. Remember that, Jodie. The only person who cares is me. Without me, you've got nothing and I'm all you need.'

'It hurts.' Chloe-Jane looked at Jodie as she sat in the bath above the live streaming room.

'It will.'

209

Chloe looked at Jodie. 'What's the matter, Jodie? Are you mad at me?'

Jodie stared, watching as the water turned red with blood. Watching as Chloe-Jane's back welted up. 'No, I'm just saying it will hurt. What do you expect?'

'Jodie, what's going on?'

'Nothing, okay? Nothing. You're here to work and so am I.'

The cuts on Chloe's back seemed to hurt more with Jodie's coldness and she wasn't entirely sure if the reason she was crying was all down to the burning pain in her back or down to the fact Jodie was being strange with her.

'Please, Jodie. What have I done? I thought we were friends.'

Jodie swivelled round, turning her back on Chloe-Jane, not letting her see the tears in her own eyes. She scoffed. 'Friends? Why would we be friends? I've got enough friends without having someone like you hanging about... Now hurry up, I'll be downstairs. Mr Lee has left your money.'

'Jodie!...' The door slammed shut, leaving Chloe-Jane alone in the bath, wondering why the idea of the money waiting for her downstairs didn't make her happy.

'And where have you been, young lady? I've been worried out of me mind.' Lola stood, hands on hips, dressed in a nightgown which looked like something she'd stolen out of a Victorian museum.

'Sorry.'

210

'Is that all you have to say? Me mind was racing; there's a lot of bad things out there. Not that I have to tell you that.'

'I know Lola, and I really am sorry.'

Lola backed down, switching on the kettle. 'Well you're here safe now, that's the main thing. How did you get on with the job?'

Chloe-Jane forced a smile, still feeling the burn in her back.

'Fine. I got on fine, it was really good. And I got paid.'

Lola raised her eyebrows. 'Already?'

'Yeah, cash in hand. Look...' Chloe-Jane opened her bag and proceeded to get thirty ten-pound notes out.

Lola whistled but her face turned quickly to a frown. 'Listen love, I wasn't born yesterday. Money like that isn't earned by promoting a few clubs and pubs.'

'You're right, it wasn't just that. I just didn't know if you'd approve or not. This fella, he deals in designer bags; nicked ones. And I got lucky, I managed to sell three of them for him. So that's my cut. Sorry, I should've told you.'

Lola studied Chloe's face. The girl looked tired but she didn't look like she was lying. And she supposed there was no reason why it wouldn't be true. She knew a lot of girls who sold knocked-off stuff and they got a good cut, so why not Chloe?

Lola's face broke into a smile. 'That's wicked, Chloe. What a touch. I'm pleased for you. I knew you'd be okay, I told Franny just as much.'

Chloe's face lit up. 'You saw Franny?... How is

she? Did she mention me at all?'

'She did actually. Obviously I didn't tell her I'd seen you, but she was worrying whether you'd be alright. I assured her you would, and look, I was right, wasn't I?'

There was such hope in Chloe's voice as she spoke. 'Do you think I should call her?'

'No baby. Just leave her alone. She's hurting and I know it sounds harsh but I don't think she'll want to hear from you. Maybe in time, but not now.'

Chloe-Jane put her head down. 'Lola.'

'Yes, love?'

'Do you think I could stay here till I can get meself a place of me own? I can pay you. I can give you a hundred a week'

'I don't know, love, it's awkward. What with Franny.'

'Please, Lola.'

Lola sighed. She didn't want to have to lie to Franny but the girl had nowhere to go, and she seemed a good kid. A good kid with rotten parents. And it wasn't fair. The girl needed a break, a chance to get herself on her feet whilst she saved up for a place of her own. Well why not? And what harm was it doing anyone? And if truth be told, Lola could do with the money.

Business had been down for a while. Too long in fact. She had to compete with the big chains of coffee shops popping up all over the place, so a hundred quid a week would be a touch.

'Why not? It'll do no harm, but I'll have to keep it quiet. Just until it all calms down.'

'Thank you, so much. I owe you.'

Lola grinned. 'Don't owe me love, just pay me.' And with that, Lola gave Chloe-Jane a huge hug, not noticing the pained expression on her face or the blood seeping onto the back of her top.

33

Alfie sat contemplating what he was going to do next, as he had been for the past hour. And the answer he came up with was just the same as it had been last night and first thing that morning. He didn't know, and the more he didn't know the more it frustrated him, and the more he felt like wringing someone's neck, preferably Chloe-Jane's.

Part of him deep down knew he was being ridiculous blaming her for everything. But then, what did it matter if he was being ridiculous? Everything had gone pear-shaped anyway so blaming a seventeen-year-old kid seemed appropriate, given everything he'd been going through. He also knew he was feeling sorry for himself, but who else would if he didn't?

Here he was sitting in his semi-furnished, semi-finished house on the wrong side of Basildon with no one giving a flying fuck about him. His daughter, Emmie didn't give a crap about him, in fact he'd heard she'd gone to Sydney to visit some of his ex-wife's relatives. Fuck knows he didn't even know she had relatives in Australia, but then nobody told him anything. He didn't know what the others were going to do. He didn't know if Franny would ever speak to him again, and he didn't know if Casey was going to make it. And that was all before he started on the *ifs* and *buts* of him and Vaughn.

Alfie gave a start. He was sure he'd heard something. Slowly he got up, trying to avoid the worst of the old wooden floorboards which creaked and groaned underfoot. Shit, there it was again. The sound of breaking glass.

Looking around, Alfie grabbed the nearest thing he could find to a weapon, which wasn't very much, unless an umbrella and a hot water bottle counted.

The sound of more glass being broken had Alfie running across the landing towards his bedroom which led to his en-suite bathroom. From there he could access the fire escape and make his way to the outhouse which held his shotguns. Fuck. Why hadn't he brought them into the house? He'd been naïve to think that Del Williams and Frankie Taylor wouldn't have come after him.

Getting to the bedroom, Alfie Jennings pushed it open, and froze. There was somebody in there. He turned, charging back across the landing, hoping to get to the stairs before whoever it was caught up with him.

Alfie ran down the stairs two at a time and scrabbled round the corner towards the back door; along the corridor, past both sitting rooms and through the kitchen.

Shit. Pulling at the handle, Alfie found the door was locked. With no other choice, he smashed his

214

fist through the glass pane, not spending any time acknowledging his torn flesh and the blood which oozed out.

With the delicate pane shattered all over the tiled floor, Alfie dragged one of the kitchen chairs to climb on, hoping it would make the scramble through the door frame less precarious.

'Mr Jennings. We meet again.'

The words immobilised Alfie and it took him a few seconds before he dared to turn his head towards the voice. There, standing with three other men was Lin, Mr Lee's henchman and the man who'd taken delighted pleasure in hacking off his finger.

Alfie's blood ran cold and instinctively, he began to scramble through the window.

'Pointless, Mr Jennings. Completely pointless. If you wouldn't mind me making a suggestion; perhaps it'd be advisable to come down from there. You could do yourself a mischief. Isn't that the expression?' Lin smiled as he watched Alfie standing with one foot on the chair whilst his other leg stretched over the jagged glass on the mid-section of the door, only just able to stand on the ground outside on his tiptoes.

He walked over to Alfie. 'You don't look very comfortable there, Mr Jennings. Here, take my hand.'

Alfie snarled. 'I'd rather cut it off.'

Lin grinned. 'Really? Well that can be arranged.' He clicked his fingers to one of the men standing behind him. The man produced a large machete out of the inside of his jacket and passed it to Lin.

Alfie's face blanched. He felt genuine fear and

215

beads of sweat begin to drip down his back.

'Worried, Mr Jennings? I wish I could say you needn't be, but then I'd be lying.' Lin raised the machete, bringing it down towards Alfie's skull.

Alfie screamed out in terror covering his head and bobbing down away from the blade, but the blow to the head didn't come. What did was the sound of Lin's laughter, along with a scorching, searing pain between his legs. In his terror, and his instinct to duck away from the attack, Alfie Jennings had forgotten the broken glass door pane he stood astride, which now cut with torturous agony into his penis.

Through his pain, Alfie could hear Lin talking. 'What did you go and do that for, Mr Jennings? I wouldn't have brought the machete down on your head. That would be too quick, too easy. What we've got in store for you is going to last for so much longer.'

34

Chloe-Jane picked up her bag and started to creep out of Lola's flat. She didn't want to wake Lola and even though it was still quite early, she needed to get out of the flat to clear her head.

She hadn't slept well and had been awake most of the night. No matter how hard she'd tried, she hadn't been able to get what had happened to her at Mr Lee's out of her head. It had all been such a blur, and not just because of the wine they'd given her to calm her down before they'd started. Far from it, they'd only allowed her to have one glass, telling her if she had more it might ruin her performance.

She hadn't known what they'd meant, but afterwards, when she'd thought about it, it was obvious they'd wanted her to be as alert as possible for the paying viewers.

She was still in shock. Not because she didn't know these things went on, but she'd had no idea she was going to be part of it. She'd assumed she'd be having sex with one or two men, perhaps even another girl thrown into the mix. But it hadn't been that, far from it. In fact, no one had had sex with her at all. It had all been based around pain. The kind of pain she didn't know had existed till last night. The pain in her back was still excruciating and when she'd laid in bed, every time she turned over it had jolted her into being wide awake.

When Chloe had managed to fall asleep for a little bit, she'd woken up to find her open sores stuck to the sheet and she'd had to peel herself off the bedding as if she'd had a giant plaster stuck to her back.

To make herself feel better she'd looked at the money, but the same thing had happened as yesterday. Instead of delighting her and exciting her like she'd thought it would've done, all it did was depress her more, which didn't make sense. It was what she'd wanted; an opportunity to be able to save up and get a place of her own. Buy clothes. Buy food, even travel. It was what she had wished for most of her teenage life, but now it might actually happen she didn't feel anything. Anything apart from the empty hole inside her, which had been there as long as she could remember.

Quietly opening the front door, Chloe-Jane breathed a sigh of relief. The last thing she wanted to do this morning was to have to converse with Lola, and answer questions about her job which would inevitably mean having to lie. And she was sick of it. Sick of lying to people who believed in her and cared. Her lies had already ruined her relationship with Franny and the last thing Chloe-Jane wanted to do was have the same thing happen with Lola.

Halfway down the low-rise block of flats' communal corridor, Chloe heard a familiar voice behind her. 'Hey, what's all this missy? Were you trying to get off without saying goodbye?'

Chloe turned to see a bleary-eyed Lola standing at her front door.

'Sorry, I didn't want to wake you. I had to pick up a few bits and then I've got to go to work. Oh, I left your money on the kitchen table in an envelope.'

'What about a cup of tea and a cigarette? Can't beat that for starting the day. I don't know what I'd do without me B&H.'

Chloe smiled, wishing she could do exactly that. But she couldn't. She didn't want to hear any more lies coming out of her own mouth. 'I'd love to but I've got to go. I'll see you later, Lola.'

Chloe headed down the three flights of stairs to the entrance. At the bottom, she heard Lola calling.

'Have a good day and be careful, Chloe-Jo.'
Chloe smiled, calling back up to Lola. 'It's Jane.'
'Well send her up, I want a word.'

Half an hour later, Chloe-Jane walked down the road, still chuckling at Lola. It was funny when she'd first met her, she'd got the impression she was a minging old cow, but she'd been so wrong. Lola was quite the opposite. She was warm, funny and caring. Just like Franny. Thinking about Franny made Chloe have to take a sharp intake of breath.

It still hurt and she was still ashamed that she had lied to someone who had been so kind to her. Her Uncle Alfie on the other hand had been a bit of an idiot to say the least – but then there must be something about him other than what she'd seen for Franny to be in love with him.

As much as Chloe-Jane missed Franny, she was pleased not to be in the middle any more though. She'd hated being in-between her and Uncle Alfie. And what had happened to Casey, she didn't like to think about. The memory of Casey lying in the pool of blood flashed through her mind constantly and she was too afraid to ask Lola if she was going to pull through.

Sighing, Chloe stopped to pull out her phone. She'd been told to call Jodie and wait by the pharmacy in Glasshouse Street, and from there she'd be collected by her friend to take her to see Mr Lee.

Not that she felt Jodie was her friend anymore. She'd behaved so weirdly. And although she'd only known Jodie for such a small time, Chloe had really thought they could've been the best of friends.

'Hello?' Jodie's voice sounded muffled.

'Jodie, it's Chloe-Jane.'

'I know who you are, you come up on my caller ID.' There was silence.

'Jodie?'

'Yeah?'

'I thought you'd gone.'

There was a moment's silence before Jodie spoke. 'I didn't think you'd be coming back.'

Chloe didn't say anything. The thought of not going back had crossed her mind as well. But then what? She'd be in the same predicament as she was before, and perhaps, just perhaps she'd get used to it, like she had with any of the bad things that had happened to her in her life. And after all, it wouldn't be forever. The most it might be would be a few months, and by that time she would've saved up enough to pay a few months upfront for a flat.

'Why not?'

Jodie's voice was flat. 'Because of what they did to you.'

Chloe-Jane's reply was equally as flat and devoid of emotion. 'It's work, ain't it.'

'Yeah, I guess... Where are you?'

'Glasshouse Street.'

'Okay, I'll be there in about fifteen minutes... Chloe-Jane?'

'Yeah?'

'You don't have to.'

Chloe was puzzled. 'Don't have to what?'

'Come back. You don't have to come back... I

can tell them you decided to go back home. It's not too late, Chloe. You can still change your mind.'

'What do you mean?'

'Nothing, it doesn't matter. Listen, I'll see you in fifteen minutes.' The call was cut off without a goodbye, leaving Chloe-Jane to stand in the middle of the busy street, wondering quite what her friend had meant.

'Is it sore?' Jodie touched Chloe's back.

'Yeah, but I think it looks worse than it is.'

Jodie burst into laughter. A warm childish giggle. 'How do you know what it looks like if it's on your back?'

Chloe, delighted her friend was talking to her properly for the first time, giggled too. 'I used a mirror, silly.'

'Was it a big one?'

'The mirror?'

Jodie's face became serious. 'No, the strap, was it a big leather strap he used?'

Chloe Jane shivered. 'Not really, but it had a small razor on it. That's what made the cuts.'

Jodie closely inspected Chloe-Jane's back. Her fingers traced the welts and bruises, the tiny cuts and lumps. 'I'm sorry, Chloe.'

Chloe turned to her friend, seeing the kindness in her eyes. 'What for? You've got nothing to be sorry for.'

'I have. I shouldn't have picked you. In the pub that night, I picked you for a reason. It was written all over your face.'

'What was?'

Jodie looked ashamed and her eyes filled with fresh tears. 'That you had no one. I should've left you alone, Chloe. You shouldn't be doing this.'

'No Jodie, I'm pleased you did. I'm pleased you picked me. You've given me a chance. There's no way I'd earn the kind of money I'm going to earn here. I can get me own flat... Hey, maybe we could share a flat.'

Jodie's face was full of fear. 'Listen Chloe, I have to tell you something, they...'

'What's all this then?' One of Mr Lee's men walked into the room, followed by Mr Lee himself. He let his acolyte do the talking. 'What were you talking about?' His tone was sharp and he stared at Jodie, who blushed profusely and stumbled to find the words.

Chloe-Jane spoke quickly. 'She was telling me that I was lucky to be here, that there were a lot of other girls who'd love to earn the kind of money I am.'

The man looked towards Jodie, watched by Mr Lee. 'Is that right?... Jodie, is that right? You know how I hate it when you don't answer.'

Jodie glanced at Chloe, then back to Mr Lee's man. 'Yeah that's right. I just wanted to make sure she kept her word about doing a good job for you.'

'I'm glad to hear it, now hurry up, we're streaming live in five minutes.'

The two men walked out of the room and as Chloe went to follow, Jodie grabbed her arm.

She spoke in a whisper. 'Here, take this.'

'What is it?'

'A tablet; it'll help numb the pain. It works quite quickly.'

Chloe smiled weakly. 'Thank you.'

'But don't tell them I gave you anything.'

Chloe took the tablet out of Jodie's hand, swallowing it down. She met Jodie's eyes. 'Of course not, I promise. Friends don't rat on friends.'

Jodie sat in the darkened room, next door to where the live streaming was taking place. She couldn't watch the monitor. She knew what was happening, but she didn't want to see it. She didn't want to see the terror and pain in her friend's eyes, so instead she sat with her eyes shut tightly, hands over her ears, trying to block out Chloe-Jane's screams.

35

Lola sat in the front room of her flat, feeling slightly uncomfortable, jumping at every single sound. When the door buzzer had gone only a few moments after Chloe had left, she'd thought it was Jane from the sauna with her twenty quid, so she'd buzzed her in, waiting to give her a piece of her mind. So it came as a huge shock when she opened the front door to see Franny, armed with a couple of chocolate croissants.

'You don't mind if I come in do you? I could do with a chat.'

Normally she wouldn't have minded at all, in

223

fact she would've enjoyed the company but as things stood, having Franny anywhere near the flat made Lola feel very uneasy, and as the morning had progressed, her unease hadn't waned.

'Lola, are you okay? You seem distracted.'

'Oh, don't worry about me. The usual stuff...'

'Want to share it?'

Lola wafted Franny away with her tea towel. 'No, ignore me. Tell me about you. How you doing?'

'I went to see Vaughn.'

'And?'

'The moose head might be a bit tricky.'

Lola laughed. 'Is he keeping his spirits up?'

'As well as can be expected. He's worried about Casey. I think once he knows Casey will be alright, it'll be easier.'

'That goes for all of us.'

Absentmindedly, Franny looked around the room. There was always a calmness about Lola's place. 'What's that?' She frowned, pointing in the far corner of the room.

'What's what?'

'The bag. That's Chloe's bag.'

Lola's face paled. 'Chloe's bag! You want to get your eyes tested. That's mine. I've had it for ages. Shows how much notice you take.'

But to Lola's horror, Franny stood up and walked towards the bag. 'It *is* hers. Look, that's the badge she insisted on getting the day I took her to the zoo. She was like a little kid.' Franny picked up the bag and had a quick look inside. She turned to Lola, a puzzled expression on her face. 'This is her stuff... What's going on, Lola?'

There weren't many times Lola couldn't find anything to say, but over the past couple of weeks she'd found herself stuck for words on more than one occasion, and this moment was no exception. She smiled, shrugging her shoulders, feigning ignorance.

'You've got me there. I must've picked up Chloe's by mistake.'

Franny stared at Lola incredulously. 'From where, Lola? Where did you *happen* to pick up Chloe's bag by mistake instead of yours?'

Lola's shoulders drooped. 'Okay, listen, don't get mad at me. It's just...'

Before Lola had a chance to say anything else, the front door opened and Chloe-Jane walked in, looking tired and unwell. All three women looked at each other, but it was Franny who spoke first.

'Has she been staying here?'

Lola answered, trying to soothe the inevitable betrayal Franny was about to feel. 'It's not how it looks.'

Franny shot Lola a hard stare. 'How does it look, Lola? Because how it looks to me is yet another one of the people I cared for and who I thought cared for me has gone behind my back.'

'She had nowhere to go. Come on Franny, what was I supposed to do?'

The hurt was palpable in Franny's eyes. 'Talk to me. That's what you were supposed to do.'

'I'm sorry Fran, I felt caught in the middle.' Lola went to hug Franny but she pulled away.

'You weren't caught anywhere. I asked you if you had seen Chloe.'

'I know you did but I didn't know how you

were going to react.'

'Yes you did, Lola; you knew exactly how I was going to react; otherwise you would've told me. Didn't you think about how I would feel?'

'Of course I did, but be fair darlin', she had nowhere else. You're hurting, I know that but this ain't like you; normally you'd be the first one to help.'

Franny laughed bitterly. 'And just look where it got me.'

'Maybe I should go.' Chloe spoke nervously.

'Maybe you should.' Franny stared at Chloe-Jane.

'Fran, you're wrong. Give the girl a break.'

'Like she did me? Like she did Casey?'

Lola's voice became firm. 'That's out of order, Fran; she was only doing what she thought was best. She had no malice. Come on, you must be able to see that.'

Franny hated herself for the way she was being. She should be encouraging Lola to help Chloe; after all, Chloe staying with Lola didn't affect her in the slightest, and in fact it would put her mind at rest knowing the girl was safe. And yet knowing all this didn't seem to make the slightest difference. 'No, I can't see that. All I can see is one of my closest friends going behind my back.'

'Listen, I don't want to cause any more problems. I'm sorry, I never meant to hurt no one, and I don't want to put you in an awkward position.' Chloe-Jane took her bag gently out of Franny's hand. She then turned to Lola; kissing her on her cheek. 'Thank you Lola, thanks for having me.'

'Chloe, wait!' Lola ran after Chloe as she headed for the door. 'Please wait, Chloe.'

'Really, it'll be fine. I'll be fine. I don't want you falling out with Franny, not over me.'

'But...'

'Lola...' Chloe smiled, stopping herself from crying.

'Maybe I can talk her round.'

Chloe shook her head. 'It won't work.'

'Where will you go though?'

'My friend Jodie; the one who helped me get the job. I can go and stay with her.'

Lola looked relieved. 'And will she be alright about you staying?'

'Yeah, she'll be fine.'

'Well at least you've got that job to go to, ain't you? You'll be able to get a flat of your own before you can say Foxtons.' Lola fell silent then warmly added, 'I wish it could be different. I just...'

'I know... Listen, I better go. I'll see you around.'

'Hey, don't be a stranger.'

Chloe didn't answer or turn round. She walked away, not allowing herself to consider that she might never see Lola or Franny again.

'I told you. I told you that you can't trust anyone. What did she say to you? Cheeky cow must have thought it was funny. Did you tell her where to get off? Did she cry? Did *you* cry? I hope you never; I hate it when they think they've got the better of you. Are you gutted? Have you had anything to eat?' Jodie's questions fired down the phone as Chloe-Jane sat on a bench in Green Park.

'Jodie, can I stay with you?'

'With me?'

'Yeah, I wouldn't ask you if I wasn't desperate.'

'I dunno, it's difficult.'

'It wouldn't be for long, I can crash on the floor.'

Jodie's voice was apologetic. 'It ain't you, Chloe, it's Mr Lee. He sometimes checks on me at night.'

'That's odd ain't it, why does he do that?'

'Dunno, just the way it is.'

'What time does he come round?'

'About ten.'

'Then how about I come about eleven?' Chloe could feel her heart racing. She was desperate. There was a long pause before Jodie finally answered.

'Okay.'

Chloe-Jane screamed, making the nearest passer-by turn round in fright. 'Really?'

Jodie's laughter carved into her words. 'Yeah, really! You're so funny Chloe, but listen, we've got to be so careful.'

'I will. I won't utter a word.'

Jodie suddenly dropped her voice. She spoke in a whisper. 'Someone's coming, I have to go, but meet me at the corner of Weymouth and Beaumont Street at eleven-thirty.'

The line went dead and Chloe-Jane knew she had a few hours to kill. She was pleased she didn't have to go to work for the next couple of days; it would give her wounds time to heal. The tablet Jodie had given her had worked. Although it hadn't taken all the pain away, it'd taken the edge off it without making her look out of it, and Mr Lee had seemed pleased. If she could get through the next couple of months, then she'd be able to not only find a flat but also find another job.

For the first time in a long while, when she thought about the future it didn't fill her with dread. With a renewed sense of hope, Chloe-Jane pulled out her phone to do something she'd been putting off; to make peace with Uncle Alfie.

36

Alfie Jennings couldn't see anything, but he could feel it. But this time he could sense something else apart from the pain. He could feel his phone vibrating. Through the lost hours and his agony, Alfie had forgotten he had his phone tucked away in his sock and it was the first time it'd rung since he'd been wherever he was. He was surprised the battery wasn't flat but he guessed with no calls and him unable to use it, it would have lasted longer than usual. The thought that only one person had noticed or bothered he'd gone was something he didn't want to dwell on. Though in a way it didn't matter how many people had called him because he couldn't answer it anyway.

His hands were bound to the cold damp wall and his feet were unable to move from the position he was in.

They'd tied him up and left him, and the torture of not knowing what was going to happen made him feel like he might go mad. But he supposed this was all part of their game. The mental torment sometimes was worse than the actual physical pain inflicted.

After all Alfie should know – it was something over the years he had used to extract and intimidate enemies and associates alike. But now the terror of the unknown was pointing his way. The idea if Lin did come back, he'd know it was for one purpose only. And if he didn't come back, Alfie would slowly starve to death.

The last thought struck a nerve, terrifying and charging him into action. 'Help!... Help! Help me!' His words floated up but the sound was trapped within the thick walls. He pulled at the chains which cut deep into his flesh. The pain in his back shot through him, tearing at his muscles as the pressure of his body being immobilised on the cold concrete floor began to weaken his skin, splitting it open to make raw fresh wounds.

'Uncle Alfie, it's Chloe-Jane. Call me back, I want to talk to you... Oh, and I'm not looking for anywhere to stay, if that's what you think. I just want to say I'm sorry.' Chloe locked off the phone. She'd kind of guessed her uncle wouldn't answer, but she'd keep trying until he did. There was no way he was getting out of this one. He was going to talk to her, whether he liked it or not.

37

'Chloe! Chloe!' Jodie waved to Chloe who was standing on the corner of Beaumont Street near Paddington. Chloe's face lit up as she saw her friend.

'Hi! Thank you so much for this. I wouldn't have asked if I wasn't desperate.'

'Well that's nice innit, you only asked me because you're desperate!' The girls both giggled, holding hands as they walked down the street, looking much younger than they really were.

'I thought you lived in Chinatown?'

Jodie pulled a face. 'No, why did you think that?'

Chloe shrugged her shoulders, not quite knowing the reason why she'd assumed that. The times she'd gone to do the live streaming, Jodie had met her then taken her to a car which had been waiting for them, and from there she'd been blindfolded, having no idea where they'd taken her, but she'd always assumed it was in or around the Chinatown area, where her first meeting with Mr Lee had been. But that had been all a guess, because she hadn't ever seen anything – when they'd arrived at the destination, they'd taken Chloe along dark corridors and then eventually to the room where she'd get ready to do the live streaming.

'Dunno, just thought you did, that's all.' Again

231

the girls fell about laughing, happy in their own world.

Five minutes later, and with Chloe having taken no notice of the route Jodie had taken, they came to a large building on the rundown borders of Paddington and Edgware Road, which was less of a block of flats and more of an office building. The bottom windows had been boarded up, with security posters warning intruders not to enter. A large metal fence ran round the side.

'This is it.'

Chloe looked surprised. 'Here?'

'Yeah.'

Chloe-Jane smiled. 'Cool.'

'But you have to be really quiet. There are other girls who live here – if they see you, one of them's bound to tell Mr Lee.'

Chloe looked curious. 'Who are the other girls?'

'Oh, they're mostly from Hong Kong. I don't really have much to do with them because they don't do the live streaming, they're mostly mules. Smuggle drugs in exchange for a place to stay in London. Most of them are heroin addicts, they're forever shooting up on the stairs. Gets on me tits.'

'Do they get paid a lot?'

'I doubt it, they'd probably do it for nothing as long as they were going to get a bit of smack at the end of it all. Guess it's not a bad gig coming over to another country, but I wouldn't do it. Too dangerous, if you get caught, you're looking at time!' Jodie exaggerated the last word so much it sent Chloe off into fits of laughter again.

It felt good to laugh and being with Jodie made

life worth living. And maybe, just maybe what Chloe was having to do was worth it. Not because of the money, but because she'd met Jodie. And she couldn't put a price on friendship; as she was slowly discovering, friends were sometimes better than family.

'Come on, but watch your step – it's really dark, but I can't risk putting the lights on.'

Chloe didn't say anything. She took hold of Jodie's outstretched arm, using it to guide her in the darkness.

Not being able to see, Chloe made sure she kept hold of Jodie's hand tightly. The dark frightened her for many reasons. As a kid, the moment the lights went out she knew bad things were going to happen and the fear of it had stayed with her ever since.

She could hear drops of water and the muffled sounds of people talking, though she wasn't sure if it was coming from outside the building or from directly above her.

'Jodie!' She called out her friend's name for reassurance.

'Shhh! We're almost there.'

Chloe did as she was told and fell into silence, following behind for another couple of minutes until they got to a large door. Jodie spoke in a whisper.

'Wait here, I'll go and make sure that the coast is clear. If I don't come back in a minute, it's only because some of the other girls are about and it's not safe.'

'Don't leave me here! Can't I come with you, say I'm a friend visiting or something?'

Jodie was firm. 'No, I've already told you. We're not allowed to have anyone here, and if Mr Lee finds out...' Jodie trailed off.

Chloe-Jane decided not to push it anymore. There was no way she wanted to get Jodie into trouble. 'Okay, but don't be long ... promise.'

'Promise.'

'Pinkie promise?'

Jodie giggled quietly. 'Yes, pinkie promise.'

The metal door creaked open and then slammed shut, leaving Chloe-Jane alone in the darkness. For a moment she felt frozen to the spot, as she listened to the sounds which seemed louder and eerier now Jodie had gone.

She tried to distract herself by thinking about nice things, but she couldn't really think of one. Her legs began to shake and standing up wasn't helping. So, just as she was deciding it was better to sit down than stand up, Chloe-Jane heard something which made her freeze. There it was. She wasn't certain at first, but she could swear it sounded like someone shouting. She listened again, straining her ears to hear whatever it was properly.

Perhaps it was Mr Lee, shouting at one of the girls, or even Jodie. Perhaps Mr Lee had caught her sneaking about and had demanded to know what was going on. Maybe Jodie needed her help.

Slowly, Chloe-Jane shuffled back towards the metal door where Jodie had gone through, but the shouting seemed further away when she stood there. She moved back to her original spot. And yes, yes there it was, louder and clearer. And it was coming from down one of the corridors.

Bravely, Chloe tried to quell her fears and took a deep breath before slowly, cautiously, moving forward along the corridor, hoping her eyes would eventually get used to the dark.

The idea had crossed her mind to use her phone light but she was frightened somehow it'd be seen. Using the wall to guide her, Chloe paused, listening again for the cry. There it was, but this time not only could she make out that it was someone shouting, she could make out the words. *Help me! Help me!*

Chloe-Jane shivered, fear creeping over her entire being. The largest part of her wanted to run, to get out of there and pretend she hadn't heard anything, yet the part of her that had helped her survive over the years and kept her going when all around was falling apart made her push on further into the darkness.

A minute later, Chloe could feel she was in a larger space; the air felt different and the corridor branched off into others. She listened, wanting to know which way to go, but the cry had stopped. And as the time ticked by, Chloe began to question herself. Had she been imagining it? Had it just been her fear of the dark which had taken over? Hearing things and feeling things, just an elaborate reaction to her fear of the dark? But then, there was only one way of finding out.

With her heart racing, Chloe-Jane whispered her curiosity. 'Hello? Is there anyone there?' No reply. She waited a moment before speaking again, but this time she voiced her question slightly louder.

'Hello?' And then there it was. Coming from deep within the labyrinth of hallways, a faint voice, replying. *'Help! Help me!'*

The second the reply came, Chloe-Jane began to panic. It could be anybody, doing anything. Fear raced round her mind and Chloe turned to run, but her terror made her forget which way she'd come; disorientating her in her alarm. Right, it was right. No, left – maybe it was left. She staggered along, tripping and grappling her way along the passageways.

Chloe swivelled round, lost and alone, listening to the cries for help. She covered her ears, trembling and frantic, not wanting to hear the voice.

'Chloe! Chloe-Jane!' Jodie appeared out of nowhere and grabbed her, her tone furious as she shook her. 'What the hell are you doing here? I told you to stay where you were. Why did you move? I've been looking for you for ages. Do you want to get me in trouble?'

The relief Chloe felt made it nearly impossible for her to speak. 'No... No... I'm sorry.'

Jodie held up her phone to Chloe's tearstained face. 'What were you doing here?'

'I ... I heard something.'

Jodie snapped at Chloe. 'What do you mean, you heard something?'

'I heard someone shouting for help.'

A look of worry flashed in Jodie's eyes. 'Don't be silly. You're just imagining it. I told you you were a baby.'

'I'm not, I really did hear...' Chloe-Jane stopped. 'There! Did you hear that! It's coming from down there. Someone's in trouble.'

Jodie's voice was flat and cold. 'I didn't hear anything.'

'You must have! Listen, you must be able to hear it!'

Jodie's eyes narrowed, her tone low, almost threatening. 'I said, there's nothing to hear.'

'But...'

'But nothing, Chloe. There's nothing to hear. Now come on, before I change my mind about you staying with me.'

As Chloe-Jane walked behind Jodie, she began to wonder quite how much she should trust her new friend.

38

Two days had passed and Chloe-Jane had been holed up in Jodie's room. They'd had a near-miss when Mr Lee had decided to make an unexpected visit and she'd had to hide under the bed whilst he reprimanded Jodie, shouting and telling her off as well as trying to humiliate her by making her stand naked whilst he told her off about how messy her room was. He'd stayed in the room for over half an hour and by the time he'd left, Jodie had been in tears, and Chloe had a terrible case of pins and needles from being under the bed too long.

Today she was back at work, and although the trepidation of what was to come sat at the bottom of her stomach like a sickness, the more imminent, impending fear was what or rather *who* was in the darkened corridor below Jodie's room.

Chloe had tried desperately to push it out of her mind, trying to tell herself it was no concern of hers, but the more she tried, the more prevalent the thought became.

'So, if you wait at the corner, near Paddington Station, we'll pick you up there. But make sure you keep your mouth shut about staying here. The driver may look like he can't speak a word of English but he has better vocab than me.' Jodie smiled warmly.

Chloe returned the smile; weaker and cooler. Ever since Jodie had denied hearing the cries for help, Chloe had been cautious. Cautious about everything and anything she said to her. She'd tried to speak to her about it yesterday, but one of the other girls living across the corridor had knocked on the door.

As Chloe-Jane put on her jacket, she tried again, needing answers. 'Jodie, you know the other night, I didn't mistake what I heard. There *was* someone there.'

Jodie turned round, her face contorted in anger. 'What did I tell you? Didn't I say there was no one there?'

'Yes, but...'

Jodie raised her voice. 'Just leave it! Leave it, Chloe, you don't know what you're messing with.'

'So there *is* someone there. I knew it. You know it too What's going on, Jodie?'

'I didn't say that. Why are you trying to twist my words, Chloe? All I've done is be a friend to you and you come here wanting to start trouble. Now leave it ... leave it, before it's too late.'

But Chloe-Jane couldn't. She couldn't dismiss the mix of anger and fear on her friend's face.

'Jodie. What is it? Who is it?'

Jodie grabbed her bag, pulling her arm away from Chloe who was trying to hold onto her. 'No. No, I won't be tricked into talking about this. Just stop it; *please.*'

'Tell me what's going on; if you're in trouble we can get out of here. We can go now.'

Jodie began to cry but the anger was still in her voice. 'Stop! If you're my friend as you say you are, then stop. For me. I'm begging you, no more questions.'

Chloe was shocked at Jodie's tears. She nodded her head. 'Okay... Okay, I'll leave it.'

Jodie wiped away her tears. 'Good... Good, now come on, we'll be late.' She walked out of the room, closely followed by Chloe, who was deep in thought. She wasn't going to leave it. In fact she was going to do quite the opposite.

She was going to find out exactly what Jodie was hiding.

Chloe-Jane lay on the bed, watching the red flashing light on the camera letting her know that it was being streamed live. She watched as the hooded man walked in, leather and metal stud strap in hand, and as the first strike cut into her skin, she closed her eyes, feeling the pain but disconnecting from her body, pretending she was in some faraway place, somewhere safe, just as she had done as a child when the ones she had trusted had hurt her the most.

In the next room, Mr Lee watched the monitor. Standing next to him with a frown on his face was Lin, wondering quite where he'd seen the girl on the bed before.

39

She had made up her mind. She was going to find out once and for all. And as Jodie slept in the bed and she lay on the floor, Chloe-Jane was going to take this opportunity to find out who and what was in the darkness below.

She knew Jodie was sound asleep; she'd taken a couple of the pink tablets she kept on her at all times, and within ten minutes she'd fallen into a deep oblivious sleep.

Slowly, Chloe-Jane got up, creeping to the door. She put her ear on it, listening to make sure none of the other girls were about. Satisfied there was no one there, Chloe opened the door; making her way down the dimly lit stairwell to the ground floor.

Once at the bottom, Chloe looked around. The place was asleep, and with the metal door in front of her, she knew it was now or never. Putting her fears to one side, Chloe opened the door, stepping into the darkness.

The moment the door slammed behind her, Chloe-Jane began to regret her decision. What the hell was she thinking? Jodie had been right, she should leave well alone. It was one thing thinking about it, but an entirely different matter actually being here. With fear getting the better of her, Chloe-Jane went to open the door, but she paused as she heard the distinctive voice of Mr Lee. She couldn't quite make out who he was talking to or what he was saying, but there was no way it'd be safe for her to try to go back to Jodie's room now.

She waited for Mr Lee to go but he seemed to be standing directly on the other side of the door. And then an awful thought struck her. What if he decided to come through this corridor instead of the front way? It was a possibility, because although this was the way the girls and Jodie used to come in and out of the building, Jodie had mentioned how on occasion Mr Lee would come the back way, thinking he might catch the girls out doing something they shouldn't.

There was no other thing for it; she had to keep moving. But quietly. So, so quietly. He was only on the other side of the door and if he heard her move, about he was sure to look and find her...

Chloe decided not to switch on the torch light on her phone yet, it was too risky and knowing the floor was clear of anything to fall over, she made her way, tiny step after tiny step, making sure each movement was controlled and silent.

It took almost fifteen minutes of cautious steps as opposed to the minute or so it had taken to walk to the end of the corridor a couple of days ago. But it was worth it to keep silent. When Chloe felt confident she'd put enough distance between her and the metal door she switched her phone light on.

Taking a deep breath, Chloe called out quietly. 'Hello!... Hello! Is anybody there?' At first she heard nothing and then, there... There it was. The calling. The cry in the darkness. Weaker this time. Quieter, but still distinct. She stood listening, hearing the direction of the sounds of despair.

That way. It was definitely coming from there. Walking forward, Chloe-Jane, determined now and assisted by the light, walked closer to the calling. *Help!... Help me!*

'Hello?' Chloe-Jane called out.

The feeble, broken-sounding voice abruptly became louder, stronger; and Chloe could hear the injection of hope in the words. *'Hello! I'm here!... Help!'*

'Hold on, I'm coming. I can't see much. Keep talking, so I know I'm going the right way.'

'Here... I'm here. Over here... Help ... please, help.'

Chloe followed the voice, the sound of it guiding her along a partly flooded corridor. The water came up to almost the top of her shoe as it seeped into her pink and yellow dolly pumps and it was all Chloe-Jane could do to stop herself from screaming at the large rat scuttling past.

Suddenly Chloe-Jane could see exactly where the voice was coming from. Standing in front of a large black rusting door, she spoke in hushed tones.

'Hello? Can you hear me?'

'Yeah... Yeah. You need to get me out.'

Chloe leaned on the door, not wanting to shout but allowing whoever it was to hear exactly what she was saying. 'How... How, the door's locked.'

'Look, you need to go and get help. If they come back, they'll kill me.'

Chloe-Jane froze, before bursting into tears. Her whole body shook. 'Uncle Alfie... Uncle Alfie, is that you?... It's Chloe-Jane.'

40

Chloe-Jane ran along the corridor, back along the passageways, thinking about how she was going to get her Uncle Alfie out.

It was no good going to ask Jodie. She was part of it, Chloe-Jane was sure of it. The way she'd been angry with her when she'd asked if she'd heard her Uncle Alfie's cries. The way she'd pretended to hear nothing when they'd walked along the passageways, the fact that Jodie had tried to stonewall her into thinking all was well, when all the time Uncle Alfie was locked up and held as prisoner.

But why? What had happened? What had he done? And why did Jodie cry? Was she afraid? Did she know what Mr Lee had in store for Alfie? Perhaps she was afraid the same thing would happen to her? There were so many questions but Chloe-Jane didn't have anyone she could ask.

So now the problem was, what was the best thing to do? Calling the police was out of the question; she knew well enough that even if the police did believe her, which was of course doubtful, they would come and knock on the door asking questions before they even began to think of a search warrant. By the time they did decide to make a move, Mr Lee would've definitely got rid of all traces of her uncle.

No, what she needed to do was to get help but to make sure Jodie didn't suspect anything – if she did she was bound to inform Mr Lee, and there was no way she could contemplate the consequences of that. The other thing Chloe-Jane was aware of was she didn't know how much time she had, and that was the worst thought of all.

Getting to the metal door, Chloe-Jane checked Mr Lee wasn't still about. Giving it a couple of moments before she opened the door, Chloe sneaked back up the stairs. There was no way she was going back to sleep but she had to be there when Jodie woke up, so as not to bring any suspicion.

Chloe-Jane wasn't due in to work, so she could spend the day sorting out help – quite what that would be, she didn't know, but whatever it took she would do it.

41

'Lola!... Lola!' – Chloe-Jane banged on the door frantically. She'd tried Lola's mobile and the café but it had been shut so, assuming she'd be at her flat she'd run the whole way, only to find there was no answer.

'She ain't in love, gone to the hospital for her veins.' Lola's next-door neighbour came out into the corridor, dressed in a thick pink towelling dressing gown.

'Do you know when she'll be back?'

The woman shrugged. 'Beats me love, all I know is she went out at about eight this morning... Who shall I tell her called?'

Chloe-Jane began to run back down the communal hallway towards the staircase, shouting as she went. 'Tell her Chloe, and say ... say I need to talk to her; urgently.'

At the bottom of the stairwell, Chloe got out her phone. If Lola wasn't about, she needed to speak to Franny. Before she dialled, Chloe decided to withhold her number, that way there was more chance of Franny answering.

'Hello?'

'Franny, it's Chloe, listen–' The phone went dead. In despair, Chloe phoned again, and once more it was answered cordially. 'Hello?'

'It's about Uncle Alfie, he's...' The call was cut off. Locked off by Franny.

Chloe-Jane began to run but as she did so she dialled the number again. This time it went to voicemail. Deciding it was better and safer not to say what had happened, Chloe-Jane left just a brief message. 'Franny, please it's urgent. You have to call me.'

With her phone now in her pocket, Chloe picked up her speed, running towards Soho. If Franny wouldn't answer, then she would go and find her.

Arriving in Dean Street, Chloe felt her phone buzz. Quickly pulling it out, she answered.

'Franny?... Listen, it's about Uncle Alfie... Franny?' The line was silent for a moment and then Chloe heard the chirpy voice of Jodie.

'Who's Franny? Is that the woman you were talking about? Is that your uncle's girlfriend? What's up with him?'

Chloe-Jane pulled the phone away from her ear in horror. She looked at her screen; she hadn't known it was Jodie – her screen had been broken last week when she'd dropped it on the stairs of Lola's flats. Shit.

Chloe-Jane's heart began to race. Had she given the game away? Did Jodie suspect? She didn't sound like she did but then, she would never have expected that Jodie was involved in something like this. She had to be careful; Jodie was sharp.

Taking a deep breath, Chloe began to talk, trying to keep her voice steady and nonchalant. 'Oh hey Jodie, I didn't know it was you. My screen's not working properly. What's up?'

'Nothing, just wanted to see where you were.'

'I... I'm... I'm just...' She looked around. There

was no way she was telling Jodie she was in Soho. 'I'm in Kilburn High Street; just doing a bit of shopping. I thought it was about time.'

There was another pause, before Jodie spoke. 'So what's going on with your uncle?'

'Oh nothing. It's my cousin's birthday and I was trying to get in touch with him so he can pull his finger out to get her a decent present, but no such luck. That's typical, so I thought maybe Franny might be able to help. Oh well, it looks like it'll be down to me to sort it...' Chloe bit her lip, hoping she'd done enough not to raise any suspicion.

'Cool, listen what time are you going to be about later, maybe we can grab something to eat?'

Chloe frowned. Jodie knew they weren't supposed to be meeting till tonight but maybe she'd forgotten. 'I'm not sure, how about I call you when I'm through shopping and stuff?'

'Okay, well I'll see you later.'

The phone clicked off and Chloe breathed a sigh of relief, hurrying off towards Franny's flat, not noticing she was being watched by two people in a car. Jodie and Mr Lee.

'Well?' Mr Lee stared at Jodie.

'I don't think she knows anything.'

'How can you be sure?'

Jodie continued to watch Chloe-Jane as she walked away into the distance. Her voice was quiet as she talked. 'Because she would've told me. She thinks I'm her friend.'

The door of Franny's flat was flung open, but

standing in the doorway wasn't the person Chloe-Jane was expecting or wanting to see. 'Is Franny in? I need to speak to her.'

Franny's housekeeper, Janet, stared with as much hostility as she could muster. 'No.'

Never having got on with her during the short time she'd stayed at Franny's, Chloe stuck a gum in her mouth along with her hands on her hips and a bold look on her face. 'I ain't got time for games. So is that a, *No, she ain't in* or, *No, I can't speak to her?*'

The housekeeper took her time to answer, but eventually she did, replying curtly. 'Both.' And with that, the door was shut with a loud bang.

Chloe knocked again on the door, and almost immediately it was flung open. 'Look, can you tell me when she's going to get back? I really need to talk to her. Do you think she'll be back this evening?'

The housekeeper, having no desire to continue opening and shutting the door, gave Chloe the information she was looking for. 'She's gone away. She'll be back next week.'

Chloe turned and walked away. Next week. That would be too late. Tomorrow might even be, she didn't know; but what was very clear to her was she'd never felt so alone in her life.

Standing in the middle of the street, Chloe-Jane began to panic. She had no idea what to do, where to go for help and all she could hear were her uncle's cries for help in her head. She began to shake. It was hopeless.

Sitting down on the wall outside Starbucks in Wardour Street, Chloe started to cry. She held her head in her hands and through her fingers she saw her teardrops falling onto the pavement.

But after a moment an idea began to form in her head. It was crazy. Stupid. But what other choice did she have? And why not?... Why not? She had nothing to lose and everything to gain. So with a renewed hope, Chloe-Jane jumped up, hailing the nearest cab.

42

'You're not being serious? Is this some sort of a fucking wind-up?' Vaughn Sadler stared at Chloe-Jane, who was sitting opposite him in the visiting room at Belmarsh.

'I need your help.'

'How did you even know I was here?'

'Lola mentioned it, and because you're on remand I didn't need a pass.'

Vaughn shook his head. When the screws had told him he had a visitor he'd thought it was Franny again or perhaps even Lola, but Chloe-Jane? Not in a million years. The truth was when they'd told him her name he'd not had a clue who she was, but curiosity had gotten the better of him, so he'd agreed to the visit. It was only when he'd walked into the visitors' room he'd recognised her and it was only the fact the wing was on lock down that he hadn't turned right around and walked out.

Vaughn leaned in to Chloe. 'What the hell do you want.'

'It's Uncle Alfie, he's in trouble.'

That was it. They were all the words he'd needed to hear for him to get up and ask to go back to his cell; lock down or no lock down.

He glared at Chloe with contempt. 'You really are taking the piss.'

'No!... Please, please don't go. Just listen ... listen to me.' Hysteria lifted Chloe's voice into a loud cry, making the prison officers begin to walk over. Vaughn signalled, letting them know everything was alright which had the desired effect.

He sat down, whispering angrily. 'Look around you, Chloe. What do you see, darlin'? I'm in a prison; a fucking prison! And you know why? You know why I'm in a prison looking at a stretch? Because of Alfie. I'm here because of him, and you...' Vaughn had to stop to take a deep breath to calm himself down. '...You have the audacity to come and tell me he's in trouble. Well so am I, Chloe. So am fucking I.'

Chloe wiped away tears with her sleeve. 'I know, and I'm sorry; but I need your help. I ain't got anyone else to ask.'

'Have you ever wondered why that might be, Chloe?'

Chloe-Jane looked puzzled. 'I dunno.'

Vaughn's face was flushed red. 'Well, let me tell you. Alfie Jennings is a fucking piss take. He's lived his life always looking out for number one. Always willing to sell everyone else out, but you know you can only do that so long, until it all comes home to roost. And boy has it just. So if

Alfie is in trouble, it's a long time coming.'

Chloe was beside herself. 'What can I do? What can I do to get you to help?'

'Even if I did want to help, which I don't, I'm in here. Ain't nothing I can do from here.'

'But you know people. You know people who can help. Maybe you can call them ... or maybe I can.'

Vaughn laughed bitterly. 'It ain't a game what I do. It ain't a game what the people I know do, so do you really think that you can come in here and start asking for telephone numbers like you're phoning round about a Christmas party?'

Chloe put her hands over her face, and it was a minute before she was able to look at Vaughn. 'He's being held in this place near Paddington, some guy called Mr Lee, he...'

Vaughn sat up in his chair, interrupting Chloe. 'Mr Lee? Are you sure?'

'Yeah, why? Do you know who he is?'

'I know who he is, but I ain't ever met him.'

'He's a slimy bastard. He makes me skin crawl.'

Vaughn looked surprised. 'How come you know him?'

Chloe couldn't meet Vaughn's eyes. She shrugged, looking around the visitors' room.

'Chloe?... *How* do you know him?... You do know he's a dangerous man?'

Tears filled up in Chloe's eyes. This isn't what she'd wanted to do. Not at all. She hadn't wanted to cry, she'd wanted to convince Vaughn to help her but here she was, blubbing away and behaving like a baby. She could hear her mum's voice in her head, telling her as she always did –

251

especially when it'd been to do with one of her mum's boyfriends trying it on – not to cry. '*What have you got to fucking cry about, Chloe-Jane? You've got a roof over yer head ain't you? It's me who should be crying; me old man would rather sleep with you than me? How do you think that makes me feel, Chloe, when I know you tart yourself up and encourage them? So don't you dare start with them tears like a baby. Don't you dare cry.*'

'Chloe ... I'm talking to you.' Vaughn broke into her thoughts.

'I ... I did some work for him.'

Vaughn looked around, then leaned in, fascinated by this revelation. 'What do you mean you worked for him? You do know he's part of the reason why Soho is being taken over?'

Chloe didn't know any of this. All she knew was Jodie had introduced her to him, and all she cared about was sorting out Uncle Alfie. So Chloe-Jane answered as she always did when she wasn't sure what she should say.

'I dunno.'

'Well I do, Chloe, and I'm telling you right now, that guy is dangerous.'

'So will you help me then? Will you call some of your people?'

Vaughn thought about it for a moment. But only for a moment. What did it matter if Soho was taken over, he'd probably never see it again anyway. And as for Alfie, he could rot in hell.

Standing up, Vaughn looked at Chloe. 'No, no, I'm sorry I can't help you.'

Chloe flushed with anger. 'You mean you won't.'

'Yes, that's exactly what I mean.' Vaughn turned to walk away, but stopped, and turned back; real concern showing in his eyes. 'But Chloe, you need to stay away from that man. You hear me? Stay away from Mr Lee.'

Half an hour later, Vaughn sat in his cell, musing everything over. He refused to acknowledge the look of terror in Chloe's eyes. The girl was trouble. He refused to acknowledge her trembling body language. She'd brought it on herself. He refused to acknowledge her heartfelt pleas. She was a game player. Fuck. Fuck. Fuck. It was no good. She was still just a kid.

Going into the secret compartment in his mattress, Vaughn Sadler pulled out his prohibited phone. He needed to make a call.

43

Chloe-Jane stood outside Franny's flat. The lights were all off, and if she knew one thing about Franny's housekeeper, she knew she would've clocked off early. Going to the bottom of her bag, Chloe pulled out a key. Although she'd given Franny the key back, she'd had a copy made. Old habits die hard.

When her mum had thrown her out and demanded her keys back, which she did often, Chloe had always made sure she had a spare set, allowing her to sneak back in to get dry clothes or even food. So when Franny had first given her the door key, without really giving it much thought, she'd had a set cut for herself.

Turning the lock, Chloe let herself in. Even though the housekeeper had told her that Franny was away, her heart was still racing as she entered the dark hallway. Hearing no sounds, Chloe made her way up the stairs. At the top, she turned right, going down the corridor to the last white door at the end.

Taking a deep breath, Chloe pushed the door open and stepped into Franny's room. Looking around, her eyes darting everywhere, Chloe-Jane ran over to the tall wardrobe, dragging the bedside chair closer to it. Standing on it, Chloe felt on top of the wardrobe, pulling down the holdall right at the back.

She opened it, rummaging in the bag, but to her utter despair what she was looking for wasn't inside. She wasn't going to cry. She wasn't going to cry. But where was it? She knew it had been there a couple of weeks ago. She had seen the gun with her own eyes. And now it was gone.

Another old habit. Each time Chloe-Jane had gone to a new foster carer, she'd checked out her environment, knowing and in a way needing to find out all there was to know about the new place and the new people she was staying with. It had made her feel safe; well safer at least.

Knowing whether there was a hidden stash of porn, a bag of drugs or just seeing photos of the family on their holidays helped Chloe understand more about her new home. It allowed her to judge whether she needed to be on high alert, whether she needed to put a chair in front of her door at night when she went to bed or whether she could simply relax and know everything was going to be alright. And however much she'd liked Franny, that was what Chloe-Jane had needed to do when she'd stayed with her, and that was how she'd seen the gun, tucked away on the top of the wardrobe. But now it was gone.

Jumping off the chair, Chloe began to search around. She looked under the bed, on the dresser and eventually started to pull open drawers, carefully at first, but as her desperation built, so did her recklessness. She searched through clothes and scarves, letters and keepsakes, throwing them out and onto the floor.

Having no luck in the bedroom, Chloe made her way through to the walk-in-closet. Again she pulled at clothes, suitcases and shoeboxes; determined and frantic to find the gun. It was her only hope.

Running through to the lounge, Chloe went through the desk. There were photos, jewellery, and a bundle of fifty-pound notes. There were an array of keys, a diamond bracelet and other precious items, but none of it was of interest to Chloe.

Nothing. There was nothing which could help her. She had to think. The kitchen; maybe Franny had put the gun in there.

Diving into the handmade cupboards, Chloe pulled everything out. Pasta, rice, biscuits and multi-vitamins; all thrown and spilling onto the marble floor. The cupboard with all the crockery in it was the last place to look through.

Seeing nothing besides the expensive cut glass and tea sets, Chloe, about to go through to the bathroom to search, froze. Right there, tucked behind the decanter at the back was a small flap at the back of the cupboard.

With a lurch, Chloe stretched her arm further in, trying to get to the flap. In her haste she knocked the glasses over, sending them flying to shatter on the kitchen floor.

Chloe, focused only on what was behind the flap, pulled it open. And there was what she'd been looking for. Franny's gun.

'What the hell do you think you're doing?' The voice behind Chloe-Jane startled and terrified her all at the same time. It was Franny.

Chloe whipped round, relief on her face. 'Fran, Fran, I'm so pleased you're here... It's Alfie. It's Uncle Alfie.'

Franny stared at Chloe, unable to say anything as she looked around. Her entire kitchen had been ransacked. Food, letters, bills and broken crockery strewn everywhere. Forcing her eyes away from the floor, Franny spoke angrily.

'It's not enough for you to mess about with people's lives, you have to rob them as well.'

Chloe's face drained. 'No... No... Oh my God, no, it ain't like that.' She paused to look around. 'I know it seems like that, but I was looking for something.'

Franny's eyes flashed. 'In *my* house! You were looking for something in *my* house!'

'You weren't in.'

Franny shook her head in amazement. 'So

what? You thought you'd break in? Have you heard yourself, Chloe?'

'I'm sorry.'

'Sorry! I got a call from Vaughn, saying you might be in trouble, but clearly he's got it wrong. He obviously don't know you've taken up burglary.'

'I didn't break in. I used keys.'

'What?... Oh, this gets better.'

Chloe shifted on the spot. 'I... I...'

Franny's voice was loud and furious. 'Actually, I don't care! I don't want to hear it, Chloe, only for the fact I don't see eye to eye with the Old Bill I'm not calling them... Now get out, before... Oh, just get out, Chloe!' The hurt showed in Franny's face as she grabbed Chloe by her arm.

Chloe pulled away, staggering backwards. 'I ain't trying to upset you, Alfie's in danger. Mr Lee has got him. He's got him locked up.'

'So that makes it fine to burgle my house?'

Chloe shook her head. 'No, I wasn't, I swear. I was looking for this.' Chloe pulled out the gun from the cupboard. Franny froze, her voice dropped to a whisper.

'Put it down, Chloe... Put down the gun.'

Chloe cocked her head to the side, pain in her voice. 'I'm not going to hurt you.'

Franny stepped towards her. 'Chloe, give me the gun, sweetheart.'

In a tiny voice, Chloe replied. 'No.'

'Chloe! Please!'

Tears fell from Chloe's eyes. 'I need it.'

Franny reached out again to her, slowly; making

257

sure she didn't make any sudden movements. 'No... No you don't. It's dangerous, Chloe. It's loaded and it can hurt you. Look what happened to Casey.'

'I ain't stupid.'

'I know you're not. Nobody's saying you are. All I'm saying is, give me the gun.' Franny took another step towards Chloe.

'I can't. Uncle Alfie needs me.'

'What are you talking about?'

'He needs me, he's in trouble, he...'

Franny interrupted. 'Chloe, look...'

Inconsolable, Chloe raised the gun, not wanting to hear anything more. She pointed it at Franny. 'No, I'm sorry, I never wanted it to be like this. But you ain't going to help me, are you?'

'Chloe, listen to me. You don't know what you're doing, sweetheart. These are dangerous men you're dealing with. Alfie may be your uncle, but he's a face, Chloe. Money, drugs, turf war, people getting killed. That's his world; he's a part of it all. It's what he does.'

'I don't care, he still needs me, whoever and whatever he does. So will you help?'

'Chloe, we can't. *You* can't, you'll end up getting hurt.'

'I don't care.'

Not taking her eyes off the gun, Franny pressed on, desperate for Chloe-Jane to see what she was asking and wanting to get involved with. 'Chloe, please. Perhaps I've been too tough on you, maybe I didn't see how you felt through all of this, but Alfie doesn't need anyone apart from himself.'

Chloe shouted hysterically, her whole body shaking. 'You're wrong! You're wrong! What do you know? You never heard him. You never heard him crying for help. You don't know what it's like to need help and there's no one to come and help you. You don't know how it feels...' Chloe trailed off, unable to speak through her sobs.

'This isn't about you, Chloe. I know you didn't have anyone, and I'm so sorry. You didn't deserve that, but you can't confuse the two, babe. This is Alfie, you can't...'

Franny's words were like a slap to Chloe. She lifted her head up, staring angrily. The gun still pointing at Franny.

'I know this ain't about me, Franny, but unlike you, I ain't holding a grudge against me Uncle Alfie. So I want you to put your hands up and turn around. Do not move, and let me go. Like I say, I'm sorry Franny, but Uncle Alfie needs me and ... and ... and I need him. He's all I've got. Don't you understand that? He's all I've got left.'

44

Chloe-Jane sat in the back of the cab, willing the driver to go faster but ending up having to resort to the direct approach. 'Oi mate, can't you rev this up a notch? I'm in a rush.'

The cabbie, having perfected over the years the, *I don't give a fuck how much in a hurry you are,* look, glared at Chloe-Jane in the driver's mirror.

'If you'd rather walk, be my guest, love. I can't go any faster.'

Before Chloe had time to argue back, her phone rang. 'Hello?'

'Hey Chloe, it's Jodie, where are you?'

'I should be there in a few minutes.'

'Okay, good. Mr Lee's been on the war path, so we've got to be careful.'

'Has he gone now?'

'Yeah, he left about an hour ago... You okay? You sound stressed out.'

For a moment, hearing Jodie's voice on the other end of the phone was such a relief, but then Chloe remembered. Remembered she couldn't trust anyone, especially Jodie. 'I'm fine. Just tired from shopping.'

'Did you get anything?'

'No... Listen, I've got another call coming through, I'll see you in a minute. Shall I meet you at the corner of Beaumont Street as usual?'

'Yeah, okay.'

Jodie put down the phone. Her face was throbbing from where Lin had punched her.

'Well?' Mr Lee sat next to Lin in Jodie's room.

'She's on her way.'

Chloe-Jane switched over to the in-coming call. 'Chloe?... Chloe?' Franny's frantic voice sounded in Chloe's ear.

'Chloe, listen to me. Tell me where you are. I'll come and get you. It doesn't matter what happened, we can sort it out. Just tell me where you are, or get in a cab and come back to my flat.'

'I'm sorry Franny, I can't do that... Goodbye.'
Chloe put the phone down, watching the traffic
go by as she felt the gun in her pocket.

Jodie stood on the corner of Chilworth Street as
she had for the past thirty minutes. She looked
over to the waiting car, seeing the figures of Mr
Lee and Lin. The passenger window slowly was
lowered, and Lin spoke, angrily. 'I thought you
said she was coming.'

Jodie shrugged, trying to look nonchalant.
'Maybe she's changed her mind.'

'Then if she has, it'll be down to you.'

'Look, she didn't say anything. Maybe she's just
decided not to bother anymore and gone back to
her mum's.'

Lin shook his head. 'And you don't think that's
strange?'

Jodie pulled a face. 'No, she was always talking
about going back.'

'If I find out you're hiding anything...'

'I ain't. I told you everything didn't I?'

Lin stared at Jodie. It had taken him a while to
figure out quite where he'd seen the girl, Chloe,
before. But then it'd come to him. Whispers
nightclub, the day the woman had been shot.
She'd been there with Alfie and now what he
wanted to know was, why.

He'd thought about making Alfie talk, but he
was enjoying the fact he was languishing, no
doubt terrified in the basement of the building.

He hadn't mentioned to Jodie about the girl
being in the nightclub; he hadn't told her anything. He didn't entirely trust the girl. All he'd

said was he wanted to talk to her, see what she knew. Jodie had been evasive but after he'd reminded her who was in charge, she'd let it out of the bag that she'd been letting Chloe stay.

Harmless perhaps, although Jodie had disobeyed the rules in having her to stay and she'd been lashed on her back because of it, but maybe that was all there was to it. One friend helping another out, and it was just an innocent coincidence. On the other hand, maybe there was more to it – but there was only one way to find out.

'Try calling her; see where she is. I want to talk to her.'

Jodie nodded, watching Lin put the window back up. She pulled out her phone, but instead of pressing the dial button, she simply lifted the phone to her ear, pretending to talk to Chloe.

Perhaps by now, Chloe-Jane would've gone back to wherever she came from. Safe and unharmed. Perhaps when she hadn't turned up on the corner of Beaumont Street as arranged, Chloe would've hung around for ten minutes or so and realising that she wasn't coming, gone home, or gone anywhere, as long as it wasn't here.

So as Jodie stood on the corner of Chilworth Street instead of Beaumont Street, pretending to talk on her mobile, she crossed her fingers, hoping that Chloe-Jane was long gone.

On the other side of Paddington, Chloe-Jane was far from long gone. She'd waited on the corner of Beaumont Street for over an hour, surprised and agitated Jodie hadn't arrived. After trying Jodie

262

on the phone several times and only getting her voicemail, Chloe-Jane had made her way to the building where Jodie lived. And here she was, standing outside.

Chloe-Jane was terrified, as well as confused. She didn't understand why Jodie hadn't shown, but then, it was probably as she'd suspected. Jodie wasn't to be trusted.

Making her way down to the back door where the entrance for the girls was, Chloe looked around. There was nobody about which was something, but it still left the problem of how she was going to get inside.

Walking around the outside of the building, Chloe saw it was impossible to climb through any windows; most of them on the ground and first floor were boarded up, and the others which weren't had steel bars protecting them.

As Chloe went round towards the back of the building, she noticed an aluminium grille on the side of the wall. A ventilation outlet. It was small, probably no bigger than two foot by two foot but if she could get the cover off it, it would allow her to enter the building.

Quickly going over to it, Chloe investigated further. Through the grille she could see the basement was now dimly lit, helping her see where she needed to be.

The top two corner screws of the grille were bolted tight into the concrete but the bottom ones had almost eroded; brown rusting screws barely able to hold the steel in place.

Looking round, Chloe saw a bit of wood. She hurriedly picked it up and began to use it to lever the grille away from the wall, lifting it open; giving her access to the dark basement.

Checking around again to make sure the coast was clear, Chloe lay on the ground, wriggling to squeeze herself through the tiny hole. The fit was tight. Too tight, and at first Chloe didn't think she'd manage to get through. She scrabbled back up and turned herself round, entering this time head first, instead of feet first.

Managing to push herself in enough to grab hold of the inner walls, Chloe heaved herself in; closing her eyes as she dropped hard onto the floor below. She landed on her wrist awkwardly and a shooting pain drove through her arm.

Giving a moment for the pain to pass, Chloe pulled out the gun in her pocket and tried to get her bearings. If she was at the back of the building, that would mean the entrance the girls used should be over to the right. From there, hopefully she'd be able to find her way to where Alfie was.

There was a temptation to call out to her uncle, but she had to be certain there was no one around. With her heart racing, Chloe-Jane shrank into the walls, afraid someone would come round the corner and see her.

Getting to the end of one of the corridors, she paused for a moment, suddenly seeing the steel door in front of her which led through to near where the girls slept. She'd gone too far and missed the turning but at least now she could find her way back.

Turning round, Chloe heard a noise behind her. She froze as the steel door began to open; with trembling hands she raised the gun as she squinted through half-closed eyes, too afraid to look, too afraid to see who it was.

Piercing screams were heard as two Chinese girls stared at Chloe holding the gun.

'No!... No!... Please, I'm not going to hurt you.' The girls continued to scream as Chloe begged them to be quiet. If they carried on, somebody was bound to come.

'Please!... Please!... You've got to keep quiet. Look, Shhh! Quiet!' The girls clung onto each other in terror, not understanding what Chloe was trying to say. They began to back away and suddenly the thought came to Chloe that if she let them go, they'd go running to get help. But what was she supposed to do? How was she going to stop them? She couldn't risk them raising the alarm.

'Stop!... Don't move!' Chloe pointed the gun, and although there was a language barrier between them, there was certainly no mistaking what having a gun pointed in their direction meant.

'Hands up ... hands up...' Chloe signalled her meaning to the girls who immediately nodded, moving forward into the darkness of the corridor.

The girls, having fallen silent now walked in front of Chloe. She pushed them deeper into the corridors, hearing their whimpers which hid her own. She had to keep her mind on Alfie, and nothing else. Once she found him, she'd feel better; safer. He would know what to do and where to go.

Venturing on, Chloe-Jane continued along in the depths of the basement. This was it, she was sure of it. Feeling slightly more confident that no one was around, she held the gun in one hand and her phone in the other to guide her, calling out in a whisper. 'Uncle Alfie?... Uncle Alfie?' The Chinese girls turned round looking puzzled, as if Chloe was giving the instructions. She shook her head, smiling warmly at them as adrenaline continued to charge round her body.

'Not you ... not you, my Uncle Alfie. I'm trying to find my Uncle Alfie.' The girls said nothing, but from out of the darkness, Chloe heard a voice call back.

'Uncle Alfie? It's Chloe.' She listened carefully under the watchful eyes of the two girls.

'Chloe!... Here!... I'm here!'

Pushing the girls in the back with her hands to make them hurry forward, Chloe turned right. Seeing the door, she ran forward, speaking through it with urgency.

'It's me, I'm here... Tell me what to do.'

Alfie's voice was weak but still hopeful. 'Chloe, listen to me, tell whoever you've got there to help you crank the door, it's thick but from what I can see it's old and a crowbar should do it.'

Chloe didn't say anything as her uncle's words sank in.

'Chloe?... Clo? You still there?'

'Yeah, yeah I'm still here but ... but it's only me. I'm the only one here.'

Alfie sounded frustrated. 'Well, go call them back. Hurry Chloe, the sooner we get the fuck out of here the better. It ain't safe, sweetheart.'

'No, you don't understand. It's only me. I'm on me own.'

The long protracted silence burnt into Chloe and the two Chinese girls looked confused as Chloe leant her head on the door and burst into tears. 'I'm sorry. I tried ... I really did. I went to see Lola, I went to see Vaughn and...'

'Did you go to see Franny? She'll help. You should've gone to see her.'

'I did! I did! But she wouldn't help.'

Alfie was desperate. 'You should've tried harder. Why didn't you try, Chloe?'

'I did, I swear but–' Chloe stopped, she didn't want to say any more. 'Listen Uncle Alfie, I don't know how long we've got, Mr Lee is bound to be about.'

'Well we're fucked, ain't we?'

'No, no, I've got a gun. I got it from Franny's house.'

'Okay, what I need you to do is shoot the lock out. It'll probably take a couple of shots but the door's old and it'll no doubt give. But you need to stand back, Chloe, there'll be a ricochet from the bullet as it hits the door.'

'What do you mean?'

'If you ain't careful, the bullet will bounce back on you; in other words you'll shoot yourself... Now hurry up, Chloe.'

Chloe-Jane looked at the gun, then at the door; she had no idea how to use it, and what her uncle had just said scared her.

'You ready, Chloe? And listen, shoot down, don't forget I'm on the other side of this door.'

'Uncle Alfie, I don't know how...'

Alfie interrupted. 'Take off the trigger lock; it's a button on the side, just slide it along.'

Chloe fumbled at the gun, her hands shaking. Unable to see what her uncle was talking about, she began to panic. 'I can't... I...'

'Look on the side, Chloe. It's on the side!'

'Okay, I see it... I see it now.'

'Right, now your strongest hand should hold the gun high on the back of the grip. Put your other hand firmly – real firmly babe – against the exposed part of the grip which ain't covered by the gun hand... All four fingers of your support hand should be under the trigger guard, okay? Then stand with your feet and hips shoulder width apart, and bend your knees slightly, Chloe. Make sure you're standing at an angle to the door, then press, don't pull the tri–'

Chloe fired before Alfie had finished his sentence. One. Twice. Three times. Sending out sparks and flashes of light to illuminate the corridor. The sound of the gun mixed with the bullets hitting the door reverberated in the chamber of the passageways, loud and almost deafening, causing all three girls to scream and cover their ears.

But it'd done the job. The door swung open and Chloe-Jane ran into the tiny cell-like room. The stench of urine and faeces hit her, but she didn't react, she didn't want her uncle to see her recoiling.

As Chloe went towards Alfie, she suddenly remembered the two other girls. She swivelled round to see them running down the corridor. She shouted, desperate for them to stay, knowing they'd go and call for Mr Lee. 'Stop!... Stop! You've got to stop!'

Chloe's face was the picture of panic. She wasn't sure whether to go after them. Looking to her uncle for help, she spoke. 'What shall I do?'

'Quick, just get me out of here. Someone's bound to have heard the shots.' Alfie gestured his head, confused as to who the girls were. But there wasn't time to worry about that. They needed to get out of there, pronto.

'How?'

'What?'

'How Uncle Alfie, how am I going to get you out of them chains?'

With the aid of the phone light, Alfie stared at his hands and feet; he could see now they'd been shackled to the wall with metal chains. 'You have to do what you did with the door. Shoot the chains so they'll separate from the walls, but this time be careful. That's an eight-shot magnum revolver, so you can't waste bullets. You've already used three. Then you'll need four for here, and that leaves one. We need to keep one; just in case. You understand what I'm saying, Chloe?'

Chloe-Jane nodded her head. Visions of Mr Lee approaching flashed through her mind and for a minute fear began to take hold of her, stopping her from moving.

'Chloe!... Chloe! We haven't got much time, you're doing well girl. You're doing well.'

Chloe looked at her uncle, tears glistening in her eyes. Her voice was childlike and quiet. 'Am I?'

'Yeah girl, and when I get out of here, you and me are going to take a trip away somewhere nice and hot.'

'Really?'

'Yeah, but we have to go ... now Chloe. Come on girl...'

Wiping her face, Chloe pointed the gun at the first chain, she squeezed the trigger at the same time as squeezing her eyes shut. Alfie shouted as the chain fell to the floor.

'That's it girl!... Now the next one!' Chloe did the same to the next chain, freeing Alfie's other hand.

Although the chains were still on his wrists, and the chains still attached to them were still connected, it didn't hinder him in taking control of the situation. 'Give me the gun, Chloe, I'll do the rest.' He winked at Chloe as she gave him the gun, and expertly shot both chains out, freeing himself from his restraints which were connected to the wall.

'Help me up, Chloe, I don't think I can stand on me own.'

Chloe charged over to her uncle, supporting him as he staggered up to his feet. The smell was overpowering and she had to swallow hard so as not to be sick.

Even though the pain ran through Alfie and he had to clench his jaw tight, fighting the desire to cry out, he was still aware of his condition. 'I know I don't smell too clever...' He was about to say more, but a loud sound came from outside. They both looked at each other.

'Quick Chloe, do you know the way out of here?'

'Yeah, but it's probably the way they're coming.'

'There's got to be another way round... Think

Chloe, think.'

The sounds down the corridor sounded as if they were becoming louder; nearer. There were voices added to the mix now. They had to go.

'It's dark and there ain't that many ways round but when I was looking for you, I got lost in another tunnel which leads round rather than straight on. I'm not sure where it goes but it's dark and it'll make it easier to hide.'

'Then let's go.' Alfie started to move but alarmingly he couldn't go anywhere near the speed he needed to go at. The heavy chains dragged along behind him, making it impossible for him to go fast or silently.

Chloe looked at Alfie. 'What are we going to do?'

'Just keep moving, Chloe, you go ahead. Here, take the gun; you know how to use it now, if anybody tries to stop you getting out; use it.'

'No!... No! I ain't leaving you. And you ain't going to make me.'

The voices were almost here now. 'I'm not giving you any choice. I want you to go; go and don't look back.'

'No, I won't leave you. Don't ask me to leave you. Come on...' Chloe helped Alfie who hobbled along, surprised and unused to anyone sacrificing themselves for others.

They made their way down the passageway as fast as they could. Chloe tried to pick up Alfie's chains to stop them from trailing. 'Go left Uncle Alfie! Left!'

They continued, rushing, down the corridors. They heard the voices behind them.

'Mr Jennings, it's pointless running... There's nowhere to go. Hand yourself back now, it'll only get worse... And Chloe, Chloe-Jane, I thought better of you; I gave you a job and this is how you repay me.'

Alfie looked shocked. He whispered to Chloe. 'What's he talking about?'

Chloe didn't say anything. She pushed on, terrified and hoping any moment they'd see the vent opening. She was sure it was near. It had to be... It just had to be.

Turning the corner, a crack of light broke through into the dark. Relieved, Chloe yelled out.

'There!... Uncle Alfie, there it is.'

Alfie and Chloe-Jane picked up their speed. The vent gap in the wall was only a few feet ahead. 'Quick, Uncle Alfie.'

Alfie stopped in his tracks, his hope beginning to fade. 'There's no way I'll be able to get through there, Chloe!'

Chloe didn't know what to say. She hadn't thought of that. All she'd thought of was that was their way out. Petrified, she clung onto Alfie. 'Uncle Alfie, what are we going to do?'

Alfie started to speak, but as he did, Chloe-Jane stumbled backward and began to scream. Right behind them was Mr Lee.

45

'What did she say?' Franny paced up and down in Lola's flat.

'She didn't. She... She just said she was working for some geezer who promoted clubs.'

Franny angrily turned on Lola. 'And you believed her? Why the hell did you do that?'

Lola didn't say anything. She'd never seen Franny so irate. 'Well?'

'What do you want me to say, Fran? I believed her, why wouldn't I?'

''Cos... 'Cos she's Chloe. And we know she tells us what we want to hear. Didn't you think to quiz her more, Lola? Didn't you care?'

It was Lola's turn to be angry. In all the time she'd known Franny, she'd never had an argument with her, but there was no way she was going to sit here and let Franny make out she didn't give a damn about the kid. 'Of course I cared, so don't bleedin' give me that, Fran. This ain't about me caring and you know it. You know you feel shit about the way *you* treated her.'

'Me! Me treated her? I gave her a place to stay when no one else did.'

'Yeah, until you got hurt, then you didn't want to know.'

'That ain't fair, Lola; what was I supposed to do?'

Lola stood up, and walked over to where Franny

was standing. 'You were supposed to see her for what she was. A kid. Caught in the middle of you and Alfie. Desperate to be loved. Desperate for someone to care whether she lived or friggin' died. Desperate to be part of a family. You know where I found her the day she came and stayed with me? Do you?'

Franny shook her head.

'In an alleyway off Oxford Street, sleeping rough and being hosed down by some bastards who got their kicks that way.'

'I ... I didn't know.'

Lola shook a finger at Franny. 'No, *you* didn't ask. *You* were caught up with how it made you feel. Well it was Alfie you should've been digging out, not Chloe; but she was an easy target weren't she?'

'No... No, she...'

Lola was on a roll and refused to listen to anything that sounded anything remotely like an excuse. 'Don't give me, *no*. Don't think about what *she* did. Think about what *you* did. Start with you, Franny. And once you've done that, then start with me, 'cos I'm no better. Look at me and what I did. I offered her a place to stay and because I didn't want to upset you I let the poor cow walk out. What I should've done is said, *Fuck you Franny, she's staying whether you like it or not,* but like you, I took the friggin' easy road. And I swear... I swear if anything happens to her, I'll...' Lola began to cry; something she could count on her fingers she'd done over the years. The life she'd led didn't have a place or space for tears. But this. This was different. She wasn't crying for herself, she was crying for Chloe.

'Lola, I'm sorry, I...' Franny went to comfort Lola but she shrunk away, holding her head high; a determined expression on her face.

'No... No, I don't want comfort. I'm fine, it ain't me who's in trouble is it? I think we've both indulged ourselves too much don't you? And that goes for all of us. You, me, Alfie, Vaughn, Del, Frankie; we've all lost who we were. Somehow, somewhere along the line we forgot what's important. We forgot we stick together, no matter how hard, how tough it gets. We stick together. After all, we're family.'

Franny's phone rang, breaking the moment.

'Answer it Fran, it may be her.'

'Hello?... Hello, Chloe?' Franny fell silent, listening intently to the call, with Lola almost hopping from one foot to another, anxious to hear the news. Eventually Franny hung up.

'Well? Who was it? Fran ... who was it?'

Franny blinked a couple of times, emotion threatening to overwhelm her.

'It was the hospital... It's Casey. She's woken up.'

46

'Hello girl. You gave us a fright there. Did you ever think to duck?' Lola grinned at Casey, delighted to see her friend awake and having been assured by the doctors she'd be alright.

275

Still weak, Casey smiled back. 'I thought about it but decided what the hell, what's a bullet between friends.'

'Vaughn will be pleased.'

Casey turned her head, looking out of the window. 'How is he?'

'Banged up.'

Casey turned quickly to look at Lola; too quickly, as her wound knotted angrily under the stitches, sending out a sharp pain. 'What are you talking about?'

'He admitted it was him. Told them it was a domestic.'

'But...'

'Look honey, you know the score. He was trying to do damage limitation, he couldn't bring the others into it. Basil the Detective has been sniffing round.'

'Who?'

'Spencer, you know the one. Thinks he's bleedin' Poirot, got the friggin' tash and everything, though in truth it looks more like he's got some bird's muff stuck on his face.'

Casey giggled. 'What's he after?'

'To send Vaughnie away; he's been after the lot of them for ages – got something to prove.'

'What can I do?'

Lola sighed. 'It's difficult. He's obviously after a statement from you. Thing is, if you say you can't remember anything it won't help, 'cos Vaughnie's admitted he did it.'

'But it was an accident.'

'Don't make no difference. Silly bastard said it was a domestic, which means it was deliberate.

276

He's been racked with guilt, Cass, it's like he needs to punish himself. If he had it his way he'd be swinging from the gallows in Soho Square whilst I did me knitting by his feet.'

'What about if I said he didn't do it?'

'The thing is babe; he did. And if you start saying he didn't, they're going to want the person who did. They'll rip Soho apart and bring as many people down as they can. They'll stop at nothing. So you see, to Vaughnie this is the only way.'

'What about the others?'

'Like I say, no one wants to do time for something they didn't do, especially as we're all getting older. Del and Frankie, even Alfie, they all want out, like Vaughnie did before all this started. There's only so much living on the edge you can do before you have to decide whether to walk away or come crashing down.'

Casey was distraught. 'But they're always going on about sticking together.'

'Cass, listen, don't upset yourself. It'll work out ... somehow. Just don't talk to anyone for now.'

'Okay. So, what else has been happening?'

'How long have you got love, because by the time I've finished telling you, you'll wish you were back in that coma.'

The door opened, interrupting the two women. Lola looked up. 'Oh hello! It's the great mouse detective. It didn't take you long to hear she'd woken up. What did you do, fly here? Like a bleedin' vampire, feeding off people. By God, Edward Cullen had nothing on you.'

'Who?'

'*Twilight,* you should watch, perhaps you can

pick up tips.'

Detective Spencer sneered at Lola. 'I'm here to see Ms Edwards, I'd appreciate if I could have a word with her on my own.'

Lola stood up, giving Casey a kiss. She winked. 'Right beautiful, I'm out of here. I'll see you tomorrow ... and stay away from that tash, you don't know where it's been.'

47

'Just stay back, 'cos make no mistake, pal, I'll fire right in your fucking head.' Alfie Jennings stood facing Mr Lee. Face to face. Gun to gun.

'Likewise, Mr Jennings, but the question is who'll go down first. I've always liked a gamble; my odds are on you ... or Chloe here.'

Alfie began to back away, his gun aimed firmly on Mr Lee and another one of his men. Out of the corner of his eye he could see a turn in the passageway. If Chloe could make it, then she might have a chance.

Mr Lee laughed. 'Where you going?... I told you there's nowhere to go.'

Alfie didn't say anything as he continued to back away. As they approached the corner, he shouted to Chloe. 'Run Chloe, run!'

Chloe hesitated.

'Run... I said run!'

Still Chloe didn't move. Alfie boomed out his instructions again but this time he did something he thought he'd never do. He turned the gun on her.

With the magnum pointed at her he screamed at her. 'Get out of here!... NOW!'

Chloe ran. Ran harder than she'd ever run in her life. Her chest began to hurt as her fear clutched her, and shortness of breath attacked her senses. She was running blind, unsure of where to go and then she heard it ... the gunshot. 'Uncle Alfie!... Uncle Alfie!'

Chloe whipped around towards the sound of the shot but as she did so she immediately banged into something solid. *Someone* solid.

'Hello Chloe-Jane, we haven't been introduced properly, but I'm Lin. Good to finally catch up with you.' And with a swift expert blow, Lin knocked Chloe-Jane out cold.

Chloe-Jane lay in a room so dark she didn't think it was possible. She couldn't see anything, all she could feel was a throbbing pain in her face and terror in her heart.

She had no idea where she was. Or what had happened to Alfie. All she knew was she was tied up. Tied up, cold and terrified, and there was no one to help her and no one to hear her scream.

Although he didn't know it, Alfie Jennings was in the room next to his niece. He was bound and gagged, unable to move or see. When he'd been in the passageway he hadn't heard Lin sneak up behind him, he'd been too focused on Mr Lee. A big mistake and something he'd never normally have done if he'd been on the mark. He'd missed his chance, Chloe's chance, though he hoped she'd been able to get away. He had to believe she had. Anything else would've been too unbearable to contemplate.

Lin had brought down a piece of wood or something equally solid on his back, knocking him off balance and sending him crashing into the wall. Alfie had dropped the gun, and it'd gone off as it'd hit the floor; using up his last bullet and using up his last chance. And now all there was left for him to do was wait. Wait for his fate.

48

Mr Lee stared at Lin, who held Franny's gun in his hand. He threw it down to the side before picking up a can of Coke. 'What are we going to do with them?'

Mr Lee shrugged. 'We need to get rid of them as soon as possible. Without a trace.'

'Of course.'

'Don't of course me. I thought that's what you were going to do in the first place.'

'It was, *it is*. I just wanted to take my time.'

Mr Lee slammed down his hand. 'Last time, you taking your time nearly cost us, Lin.'

'This time I'll do it as it should be.'

Mr Lee nodded his head in approval. 'It's gone on too long, I don't want you playing games. Like I told you before, I want you to get rid of Mr Jennings; permanently.'

'And the girl?'

'Especially the girl.'

Mr Lee turned and stared at Jodie who was crouched in the corner, shivering. Her face was swollen and bruised; her lip bloody. He crouched down to her. 'Next time you bring trouble in here, I'll finish you off in the same way your friend's going to end up. Do you understand me?'

Jodie nodded, causing Mr Lee to squeeze her face harder. 'I said, do you understand?'

'Yes...Yes Mr Lee. I didn't know. I swear I didn't know anything about it.'

Mr Lee let go of Jodie's head, slamming it on the wall behind her. She yelped, though she didn't cry. He sneered at her, sighing at the trouble caused. Although Jodie was stupid, he believed her. There was no way she could have kept up the lie. The lashes to her back would've sorted out the truth from the tale. And after thirty-odd painful strikes to her back, Jodie still insisted she hadn't known there'd been a connection between Alfie and Chloe.

'Lucky for you, Jodie that I'm willing to take your word for it, otherwise Lin here would've taught you one of *his* lessons.'

Jodie flashed a glance at Lin, who stared at her with hatred. 'What's... What's going to happen to her?'

Mr Lee answered in a nasty voice. 'To your friend, Jodie?'

'Yes. What's going to happen to Chloe?'

He grinned, slamming his foot into her. 'Wait and see, Jodie, wait and see.'

49

The moment the doors opened, Franny ran in, barging past Lola who was being lined up and security checked. There wasn't a moment to waste. Every second felt like an eternity and until she found Chloe, Franny was sure it would feel like that forever.

Sitting there, Franny held Lola's hand, who thought it wise not to say anything. Franny was in a state. Neither one of them had slept, and had stayed up wondering and worrying about Chloe.

'Lola, do you think he'll know anything more?'

Lola bit her lip. She didn't want to give any false hope, and Franny was clearly looking for anything to hang her hat on. 'I dunno love, let's see what he says and take it from there.'

Hysteria rocketed into Franny's voice. 'Take it from there? What's that supposed to mean, Lo? How can we take it from there if he doesn't know anything?'

Lola could see how much Franny was hurting and she could also see how powerless she felt. 'Come on, love. If anyone knows what to do it's Vaughnie. That's why we're here, isn't it?'

Franny breathed deeply. 'Yeah, you're right.'

Lola spoke carefully as she asked Franny the next question. 'And what about Alfie? You ain't mentioned Alfie at all. You must care what's happened to him.'

Franny fell silent, she didn't know what to think. She'd been pushing the thought of Alfie away. Pushing the idea that he was hurt and needing her help to the back of her mind, and when she did think of it, she'd boxed it under the heading of, *it's the world he lives in,* but as she sat there now, in the light of everything that had happened she realised she did care.

Franny put her hands over her face. 'Oh God, Lola. It's a mess. Everything's such a mess. What was I thinking?'

Lola pulled Franny towards her, she whispered in her ear. 'I know pet, but we'll sort it. Christ knows how, but we've managed to ride out hard times before ain't we?'

'And maybe our luck's run out.'

'And maybe it hasn't. We'll do all we can to find them and bring them back safely.'

Franny sat up. She stared at Lola, her heart heavy. 'And how am I supposed to forgive Alfie? All this chaos is down to him and I feel partly responsible for it.'

'I know love, but forgiving Alfie doesn't mean you condone what he's done, it doesn't mean you have to fall back into his arms. It means you can free yourself. To forgive someone is the biggest gift you can give to yourself. Believe me, I know. Do you remember me ex-husband, Oscar Harding?'

'Yeah.'

'Well then you'll remember what a mean bastard he was, and that's only the start of it. I hated him for so long but eventually I realised I was hurting meself. It was eating away at me but the moment I decided to forgive him, it freed me. Let me get

283

on with my life.'

'But I feel like I'd be giving in.'

Lola smiled. 'No, love. Forgiveness is a strength, not a weakness.'

'But don't you think he deserves everything that's happening to him?'

'Oh come on love, neither of us think that; not really. You don't really want anything bad to happen to him. Plus, it ain't your place to decide what punishment is fitting.'

Franny looked puzzled. 'What do you mean?'

'I mean, you've turned your back on Alfie and said you want nothing more to do with him. Okay, we get that, we understand that, but to leave him to the lions? To leave him for them triad lot to do what they like with him? No, no, Fran that's wrong, and you know it is.'

Franny continued to cry. 'I know it is, Lola. Oh Christ, what have I done?'

'You've been human, like the rest of us.'

'And now what?'

'And now... And now, we're going to ask Vaughnie here to help us... Hello love, how's tricks?' Lola stood up and gave Vaughn a huge hug. He nodded his head to Franny.

'Hello ladies, good to see you. I seem to be more popular inside than out.'

Lola's eyes lit up, delighted she could bring Vaughn some good news before they got down to business. 'She's awake. Casey's woken up.'

Vaughn slumped in his chair from the sheer relief and, like Franny had done earlier, put his head in his hands. He could only just get out his words. 'And ... and is she going to be alright, Lo?'

'Yes Vaughnie, she is. How about I shed a tear for both of us, 'cos I know this certainly ain't the place to be welling up like a Milly Molly Mandy.'

Vaughn roared with laughter. That was exactly right. And exactly what he'd been thinking. The desire to cry at the news of Casey was overwhelming, but he'd had to fight against the urge to do it. Belmarsh prison was no place to be shedding tears, not unless you were looking for trouble, and that was certainly something he wasn't seeking to do.

'She's good, she asked about you. Oh and that copper Spencer's been asking questions. I told Casey to keep it shut for now, which she will.'

'I don't blame her if she won't, I can't see her forgiving me.'

Lola shook her head, taking a sip of the prison tea she'd purchased earlier and which had now gone cold. 'What is it with you lot and forgiveness? One person thinks they can't, another thinks they shouldn't, another thinks they won't. Bleedin' roll on. Everyone needs their heads banging together. We forgive each other because we love each other, we care for each other and above all, because we're family.' Lola stopped and looked from Vaughn then to Franny, and grinned, adding, 'Here endeth the lesson... Go on, carry on, I've said me piece.'

Franny turned to Vaughn. 'Did Chloe say anything more?'

'I already told you everything she said. You trying to find Alfie?'

'No... Well, yeah, both of them.'

Vaughn looked surprised; concern in his voice

285

as he said, 'What do you mean, both of them?'

'Chloe took it on herself to go and get Alfie.'

'Fuck, why did she go and do that?'

'Why do you think, Vaughn? She came to all of us and no one would help her; she loves Alfie.'

Vaughn's puzzlement showed. 'She don't know him.'

'Look, Alfie's her family. He's her uncle and that means something to her.'

'Even after the way he treated her?'

Lola interjected. 'Yes Vaughn, even after everything, and that's the tragedy of it all. There's all of us who are older, should be wiser and certainly should know better than to hold grudges against our own, and there's Chloe-Jo, who's had the roughest of starts and no one to give jack shit about her, still caring for others. Puts us to shame.'

The three of them sat silently for a moment, reflecting on their own behaviour and the enormity of the task ahead to find both Chloe and Alfie.

Vaughn looked at Lola; his words firm and resolute. 'What can I do to help?'

50

'You've got to be joking?' Del Williams sat on the well-kept lawn of his villa, sipping sangria whilst listening to the person on the other end of the phone. The Marbella sun beat down on him but he felt a cold shiver run over him.

'There's no way I'm coming back... I already said I...' The phone cut off and Del stared at the mobile; bemused, annoyed and torn. And being torn pissed him off no end.

'What's up, Dad?' His daughter, Star, stared at him, finishing off her collage of shells.

'Nothing.'

She looked at him, cocking her head to one side. 'Well that ain't true, is it? You always get that frown in the middle of your forehead when something's up.'

He laughed. Star had always been straight. It was something he loved about her. She and his partner, Bunny, were his life. He was lucky, and he wanted it to stay that way, but the call ... the call had made him think. He spoke affectionately.

'Well that was Lola, remember her?'

'The one who made them rotten scotch eggs?'

'Yeah that's the one. Well she wants me to go back to Soho and help her find someone who's missing.'

Star's eyes widened. 'Who?'

'A kid; well she's seventeen, eighteen.'

'And why has she asked you?'

Del shrugged. 'I guess 'cos there's nobody else.'

Star looked back down at her shelled master-piece, distracted once more by her artwork but speaking with a tone of inevitability. 'Well there ain't nothing else for it then, is there?'

Del didn't say anything as he watched Star. He smiled to himself. What was the saying? *Out of the mouths of bairns.* Star was right. There ain't nothing else for it.

Frankie Taylor stared at his wife, Gypsy, who was meticulously folding his clothes in his Louis Vuitton suitcases. 'Oh come on Gypsy, let me stay, how can you want me to run off back to Soho?'

Gypsy Taylor put her well-manicured hands on her hips. She sighed at her husband, loving and being exasperated by him all at the same time. 'It ain't a question of wanting you to go back, of course I'm going to miss me teddy bear. Who's going to keep me warm in bed, hey?'

'No one I bleedin' hope, not unless he wants a bit of gangland punishment.' They both laughed, before Frankie became serious once more. 'Look Gypsy, it's a big ask to want me to go over there and risk everything. I've got us to think about.'

Gypsy shook her head. 'I spoke to Lola.'

Frankie's voice was full of sarcasm. 'Oh great.'

'This Chloe-Jane, she ain't got anybody else.'

'Well that ain't my problem.'

'But it is you see. 'Cos whether you like it or not, she's family.'

Frankie looked amazed. 'Are you having a bubble? Family? Since when? You've been watching too many re-runs of *Oprah.*'

'Drop me out, Frank. You ain't half hard work at times. You, me; well all of us have been through rough times, and we've been lucky enough to have our friends to rely on.'

'And when our friends turn us over?'

'Then we forgive them and move on. If I hadn't moved on from all the things you've done...'

Frankie put his hand up and winced. The last thing he needed was to give his wife an excuse to list all his indiscretions and mistakes. 'Alright, I get it, but don't see how that makes Chloe family. She's got a right vicious tongue on her.'

'Babe, what's got us through is by sticking to-gether. We all go so far back; we've shared every-thing, lost a lot, hurt a lot, but by Christ haven't we all loved and laughed a lot? We are what we are today because of each other, and we can't separate our lives from one another. Where one starts, another one begins. That's what family is; and that's what makes us who we are, and Chloe-Jane is a part of that now.'

Frankie grinned, accustomed to his wife sound-ing like a self-help book. 'Fuck me Gyps, that's a bit heavy, ain't it?'

Gypsy rolled her eyes. 'Failing that sinking into your block head, Frank, I'll put it to you straight. She's a kid, she needs your help and there's no way you ain't going back. There ain't nothing else for it.'

Frankie winked. 'Well why didn't you say that in the first place, woman?'

51

It was gone midnight and Jodie sat wide awake in the corner of the room. Although she was tired, there wasn't any question of her going to sleep. The whole place was in darkness and everything was quiet. But she wanted to wait. Wait for a little while longer before she made her move.

Standing up, she went to the window, looking out onto the street below. It was deserted save a car driving past and a couple of late-night revellers. She looked up at the clock. Time had never felt so slow, yet the speed of her heart racing gave her the sense that something was about to happen; hurtling her along, unable to stop it.

She touched her face. It was sore, as was her back, as was every part of her, yet it didn't seem to matter. Not now, not any longer. Things were about to change, and although Jodie was scared, she was ready. It had been a long time coming.

Looking at the clock once more, Jodie looked around. She arranged her things, neatly and as required by Mr Lee. Her cuddly dog, a present she'd got from Mr Lee when she'd recruited Chloe-Jane, sat on her pillow.

Her feelings for Mr Lee sometimes confused her; at times she hated him, at times she thought she was madly in love, but one thing she was never confused about was the fact that she needed him. And any time she thought about or had tried to get away from him, she had always come back, but this time... This time it was going to be different. This time she was finally going to break free. Picking up the toy, Jodie looked at it, held it to her, closing her eyes for a moment, letting thoughts and feelings sweep over her. Then she took a deep breath and threw it in the bin before turning away, opening the door, without looking back.

The hallway was quiet and Jodie crept up the stairs. One flight. Two flights, avoiding the creaky old floorboards. She paused a couple of times as she ascended the stairs, making sure no one was coming; making sure she didn't draw any attention to herself.

Getting to the top, the highest part of the building which was the fifth floor, Jodie covered her mouth and nose. The dust was thick and it caught in the back of her throat. The last thing she wanted was to have a coughing fit.

The hallway was lit up by the moonlight, a world away from the dark basement below. Jodie could see well, and she walked down the hall avoiding standing on any of the piles of rubbish strewn about or on any of the needles left by the Chinese girls after they'd had their fix.

At the end of the corridor was a door, and carefully Jodie opened it, pausing before she entered. The room was empty but it led to another door. The anxiety in Jodie began to rise as she tried to calm herself from what she knew was behind the door.

Slowly, Jodie pushed down on the silver handle, wincing at the tiny sound it made. Once the handle was fully pushed down, Jodie creaked open the door. It was dark; the curtains were drawn and in the far corner, Jodie saw the sleeping figure of Mr Lee. Jodie knew he had a house somewhere in Chelsea but often he slept here, once telling her that he'd spent his early years in a crowded, noisy tenement back in Hong Kong and so found it difficult to live in the quiet and splendour of his Chelsea home. It was the only time he had ever spoken to her about his life.

Jodie tiptoed across the room, holding her breath, terrified the sound of her breathing would wake him up. Her legs felt heavy as the burden of fear weighed her down. Her eyes darted around the room, then fell on what she had come in for. There on the desk by the side of Mr Lee's bed were the keys which would open the door to freedom.

She crept forward again, stopping and starting at every snore and grunt. A dangerous game of Mr Wolf, a game where the stakes would mean something unthinkable.

She'd known Mr Lee was a heavy sleeper; often he'd ordered her to bring him food or a drink and when she'd brought it up to him he'd been heavy in slumber which had made it nearly impossible to wake him up. But now as she skulked across the bare-floored room, the idea Mr Lee was a heavy sleeper didn't comfort her at all.

Jodie glanced at Mr Lee, checking for certain he wasn't stirring. She reached across, leaning; stretching, not wanting to get closer than necessary. Her hand touched the cold metal, her fingers wrapping round the keys. She had to be certain she gripped them properly. She had to make sure when she picked them up they lifted smoothly, silently. One chance.

Her hand shook, trembling round the keys. She could feel it sweating, and each time she made up her mind to lift the keys away, a sea of panic rose inside her, hindering her from being able to go through with it.

She had to stop thinking. Just do it... Just do it. So with one determined effort, Jodie scooped up the keys, gripping them so tightly they dug into the palm of her hand. And now she'd got them, she needed to go. As quickly and as quietly as she came. The overwhelming desire to run drove through her, but she shouldn't; couldn't.

If Mr Lee saw her now with the keys in her hand, then there was no getting out of it. No excuse which could justify her actions.

Slowly, slowly, slowly, Jodie edged away. Backing off, backing away, with her eyes never moving away from Mr Lee. Feeling for the door behind her Jodie's heel banged into the chair; the clatter, although not loud, was loud enough for Mr Lee to utter a moan. Jodie stiffened and she could feel her knees trembling. She didn't know what to do; whether to take the chance and move or to stay rooted to the spot; waiting, hoping he'd settle down again.

Jodie looked at the large white-faced clock on the wall, watching the second hand go round, and as she watched it she knew she *had* to; wanted to, finish what she'd started.

With a quick close of the eyes before she made her move, Jodie took a large step backwards, determined to get out of the room as quickly as possible. One more step took her to the large empty room, and even though she was still as quiet as she could be, she picked up her pace.

Once outside and in the corridor, Jodie began to run. Back along the hallway, past the rubbish and needles, taking the stairs three at a time. She skidded round the corridor to the second-floor landing, did a quick check behind her and made her way along to the far end to a black door.

She began to look through the bunch of keys in her hand. Her fingers fumbled as she hurried to find the right one; many a time she'd had to use them when Mr Lee had asked her to store things in the room, but now under pressure all the keys looked the same to Jodie. She tried the large silver one but it didn't fit. Then the next one, a smaller version of the first. She was sure it was this one, but again the key didn't fit. She refused to panic as she continued listening out for evidence of anyone stirring.

Her fingers continued to jumble through the keys and Jodie was aware of the rattle which sounded and echoed around the hall. Her hand was shaking so much she could hardly manage to fit the key in the lock. She turned it and immediately she heard a click. The door was unlocked.

Exhaling to steady herself, Jodie pushed open the door.

52

Chloe-Jane turned, startled by the light and by whoever it was entering the room. Terror and panic took hold of her, her eyes wide with fear. She screamed, but the gag cutting into her stopped the noise from sounding out. She pulled on her restraints, feeling them dig into her wrists. Instinctively, she wriggled her body in a frantic, hopeless attempt to get away from her tormentor. And then she heard it.

'Chloe!... Chloe-Jane, it's Jodie.'

Chloe stopped moving, and stared as more light broke into the room. What did she want? Why was she here? The questions shot through Chloe's mind as she felt her hands being untied.

'Chloe, I'm going to get you out of here, but you can't make a sound.'

Jodie pulled the gag off Chloe, but she didn't say anything. She only stared at her. How could she trust Jodie now? Was this some kind of game? Would Mr Lee be waiting outside the door?

Jodie untied Chloe's last restraint on her foot. 'Chloe, come on. We've got to go.' But Chloe didn't move; there was no way she was going with Jodie, no way. Wherever she wanted to take her, she suspected it would be somewhere worse, if that was even possible.

'Please, Chloe... What you doing? You've got to go... Now!' Jodie crouched down and pleaded with Chloe-Jane but she sat huddled up in the corner, not moving; barely blinking. Jodie tried again, desperate to persuade her friend to move.

'If you stay here, you'll get caught, Chloe... They'll come, and then there's nothing I can do. Do you understand what I'm saying, Chloe?'

Again, Chloe chose to stay silent but this time, Jodie jumped up. 'Stay there, Chloe... Just stay there.'

Jodie ran out of the room, turning left to where the other door was. She hurriedly went through the keys, occasionally checking behind her. It took four attempts until she found the right one to open the large grey door.

Flinging it open, Jodie stepped inside, then ran across the room and crouched down.

'I'm Jodie, Mr Jennings, I'm here to get you out. Chloe-Jane's in the next room, but she's in shock, and she's refusing to leave. We have to hurry...'

Jodie used the penknife in her pocket to untie Alfie's ropes. He, like Chloe-Jane, was almost in too much of a state of shock to move and needed help from Jodie to scramble up.

'Where is she? Where's Chloe-Jane?'

Without answering, Jodie led Alfie out into the corridor and into the room where Chloe-Jane was. She hung back by the door, watching to make sure no one was coming.

Alfie crouched down to Chloe, taking her face in his hands.

'Hello darlin'.'

Chloe-Jane could only manage a weak smile, but her face lit up as she looked at her Uncle Alfie.

'Now, you need to listen to what I'm saying... Jodie here is going to help us to get out.'

Chloe's voice was small. 'We can't trust her.'

Alfie stroked Chloe's hair. 'We can, darlin'. And if we can't what have we got to lose? And anyway, I'm here. Ain't no one going to hurt you when I'm around.'

'I ... I ... I don't know.'

'Well, I do. And what about that holiday I'm going to take you on, hey? If we don't move our backsides, ain't no one going anywhere. And perhaps, your friend here can come with us ... can't you babe?' Alfie turned to Jodie who smiled, but there was sadness in her eyes. He turned back to Chloe, continuing to soothe her.

'So come on sweetheart, let's go whilst we still have the chance.'

'Please, you've got to hurry.' Jodie spoke to both Alfie and Chloe.

'Okay, babe we're coming; ain't we Chloe-Jane?'

Chloe-Jane nodded, getting up slowly. She walked to the door, stopping by the side of Jodie. For a moment she didn't say anything, then she took her hand and smiled, holding her friend's gaze. 'Thank you, Jodie.'

Jodie didn't reply, unable to trust herself to hold back the tears, instead she looked at Alfie.

'Follow me, but you have to be real quiet. We'll go to the main entrance to get out, it's the quickest way but it's also past some of the girls' rooms.'

Alfie nodded, leading Chloe out of the room with him as Jodie went on ahead. At the end of the corridor, Jodie signalled for them to stop.

'Wait, let me check there's no one there.' She crept out to the main stairwell, looking up and down the stairs, making sure there was no sight of Mr Lee or any of the girls.

'It's fine. Let's go.' Jodie waved her hand, leading them down the stairs, quietly, quickly, on alert to any possible danger. She waited for Alfie and Chloe – who were slightly behind – to catch up, and taking Chloe-Jane's hand, she guided her down the last flight of stairs.

'We're nearly there, Chloe, we're nearly there.' Chloe squeezed Jodie's hand, seeing the main entrance door in front of her now.

Jodie didn't need to fumble through the keys,

she knew which one it was. She'd watched Mr Lee on many occasions. Taking the largest silver key, Jodie could feel her heart begin to beat faster as she turned the lock. It clicked. Open. Open to freedom.

'Go!... Go on!' Jodie pulled the door wide, and as Alfie and Chloe began to run through the door, she pulled something out of her pocket and shoved it into Chloe's hand.

Chloe stared at Jodie, alarm embodying her whole being. 'Aren't you coming?'

'Yes... Yes, but give me a minute. I'll follow you... Go on! Go on!'

Chloe-Jane looked bewildered. 'Jodie!... You've got to come.'

'I am... I am, but you need to go, I'll wait to make sure no one's coming. I know what I'm doing.'

'But...'

Alfie grabbed Chloe-Jane, and began to pull her. 'Come on.'

'Go Chloe, I'll be right behind you.' She turned to Alfie. 'The best way is to go back round the building, down the alleyway and keep following it until you get to the main road.'

Alfie nodded pulling Chloe-Jane with him. The next moment, the two of them began to run.

Jodie watched them disappear. She whispered the words to herself and smiled. 'Goodbye Chloe-Jane... Goodbye.'

Closing the door, Jodie slowly walked up the stairs. Not worrying now whether anyone saw her, or anyone heard her. She had done what was needed to do, she had made sure her friend was safe, and now there was only one more thing left to do. And she was ready.

53

'Where is she?... Where's Jodie?' Chloe-Jane cried hysterically as the cab driver drove them back to Soho.

Alfie looked out of the window. 'I don't think she's coming, babe.'

'What do you mean?... She said she would... She said she was coming. We've got to go back. We've got to go back!'

'Chloe, are you crazy? We can't go back, we only just got away with our lives. If we waited for her any longer ... well...' Alfie trailed off, unable to say anything reassuring.

Chloe shook her head, and then she remembered Jodie had shoved something in her hand. It was ridiculous but in the chaos, she'd just pushed it in her pocket and hadn't thought about it. She pulled it out. It was a letter. Pink, with her name written neatly on the envelope.

Quickly she ripped it open.

Dear Chloe-Jane,
By the time you read this, I imagine you'll be back at home. Home ... wow! That's a nice thought Chloe, to think of you back where you belong, with your family. I know how important they are to you but I

also know how lucky they are to have you, like I was lucky to have you as my friend. Don't forget that Chloe. Don't let nobody tell you that you ain't special. You're the best friend I ever had and being with you made me happy. And I ain't been happy for a long time, until you came along of course. Chloe, please forgive me for letting you down. I should never have picked you but I knew I would like you straight away. And although the reasons for picking you were for the wrong reasons I'm glad I did, otherwise I would never have got to know you. I'm sorry for everything Chloe, but most of all I'm sorry that I won't be able to see you again. I know you'll be alright and I know you would have wanted me to come with you, but it ain't where I belong. But I'm okay, you made it okay for me. Promise me you won't forget me and please don't be sad Chloe-Jane 'cos you and me have been sad too long. I love you.

Jodie xxxxxxxxxxxxxxxxx

Ps. Don't let that Uncle of yours be a knob.

54

Knowing that Chloe-Jane was going to be okay made Jodie feel much better. And now here she was, sitting at the window of her favourite room at the top of Mr Lee's building after she'd managed to open the door with the set of keys she'd got hold of.

From there she could see all of the rooftops,

all of the cars and people below, unaware she was there watching them as they went about their business. Many a night she'd slunk up to this spot, doing nothing but sitting and thinking, then Mr Lee had discovered her there sometime last year and he'd kept it locked from that time on. This was the first time she'd been there since.

Jodie sighed, a calm peace resting on her young shoulders.

She locked the door, then pulled a chair to the middle of the room and climbed onto it. She lifted her jumper up, making it easier for her to pull the belt from the loops of her jeans. With the belt in her hand, Jodie calmly threw it over the exposed metal beam before making a noose with it.

She placed her head in the noose then adjusted the belt to sit under her jaw, resting just on her neck. She closed her eyes for a moment, at peace for the first time in her life. Opening them again, Jodie took one last glance around the room and without another thought, she stepped off the chair. It was finally over.

55

'Please, Franny; *please*,' Chloe-Jane begged both Franny and Lola as she sat up in bed.

'No, love. It ain't sensible.' Lola looked at Alfie, who'd washed and changed but still looked in a

301

bad way. He hadn't said much when he'd rung the bell and stumbled in with Chloe. He'd asked to see Franny who'd she'd called straight away and who'd come without hesitation.

As for Chloe, she hadn't said anything either. She and Franny had run the girl a bath and helped her to get washed, and that's when they'd seen the cuts and bruises on her back.

'What's that love? What happened?' Lola had stared, open-mouthed in horror as she saw Chloe's back.

'Nothing; it ain't anything.'

Franny had then taken Chloe's hand and urged her to talk, insisting that she tell them what had happened. It'd taken over half an hour to persuade her to say anything, and then she had simply said:

'They did it... They did.'

'Who honey, who are they?' Franny had pushed some more, but Chloe had said nothing else – until now that was, but none of them were any the wiser of how and what had happened to her.

Alfie interrupted, realising that Chloe was desperately worried about Jodie. 'Sweetheart, it ain't a question of just being able to go and get her. She had her chance to come and for whatever reason she decided not to. It was her choice.'

Chloe-Jane shook her head. 'No, Uncle Alfie, you don't understand, she wasn't happy there. The only reason she was with Mr Lee was because she had nowhere else to go. The stuff we had to do...'

Chloe stopped and looked round the room, all eyes on her. Franny walked over to the bed, sitting down on it gently.

'What stuff, Chloe?'

'I dunno.'

Franny took her hand and urged her on. 'You do know, Chloe. Whatever it is, you can tell us. You won't be in trouble.'

Chloe chewed on her lip. She wanted to tell them what had happened to her, she really did. But what if she told them and they didn't want her around them anymore?

'I don't know... I...'

Alfie decided to take control. He marched over to the bed and sat down, staring in Chloe-Jane's eyes. 'I haven't said thank you yet, darlin'... Truth is, I'm not quite sure how. Me words ain't good enough and they ain't big enough but if you put your hand on me heart you might be able to feel it bursting. Look, feel... Can you feel it, Chloe?' Alfie took her hand and placed it on his chest. 'You risked your life for me. You did that, Chloe. You found me in that basement and you promised to come back for me with help, and when you couldn't find any, then you still came back regardless. Do you realise how brave you were, babe? You took on them bastards like you was bleedin' Wolverine, and there's no way I can really pay you back for what you did.'

'No, but make sure you make him try, he can start by getting that tidy little pink Chanel handbag up in the window of Selfridges.' Lola cackled, smiling at them both.

Alfie continued, winking at Lola, and trying not

303

to catch Franny's eye. He was too ashamed of himself. 'She's right, Chloe, I will try, and I haven't forgotten about that holiday I said I'd take you on. I'm a man of me word... Okay, sometimes that hasn't always been the case, but I'm going to look after you and that don't just include designer gear, it includes making sure you're alright. And that means not letting you keep secrets. Fuck knows, Chloe, they'll come back and bite you in the end; just look at what's happened to me. So go on, darlin', tell us, whatever it is.'

Chloe looked round at them all, then took a deep breath before saying, 'It was sex stuff. Bad stuff. Like for the internet.'

Alfie clenched his fists. 'Go on, Chloe, carry on.'

'I thought it would be the usual, you know, the stuff you get with normal punters.'

'What do you mean?'

Chloe glanced at Alfie. She put her head down. 'You know – when I was working the street, it was just the normal stuff like blow jobs, full sex and anal sex.'

Franny gasped, but she quickly put her hand over her mouth not to make Chloe think she was judging her. How could she have missed it? It was so obvious now that Chloe was saying it. She should've spotted it a mile away, and Franny was ashamed to think it, but maybe the reason she didn't see it was she'd wanted to bury her head in the sand and not have to deal with anyone else's problems.

'So when Jodie asked me to...'

Alfie interrupted, his voice loud. 'Jodie asked you. I knew that little tramp would've had something to do with it.'

'*Please* Uncle Alfie, it wasn't like that. Jodie was my friend. She was as caught up in it as me.'

'But if she hadn't got you involved in the first place, Clo.'

Chloe looked at her uncle, desperate for him to see what she was trying to say to him. 'It wasn't as simple as that. And don't forget, she was the one who got us out of there. Without her, we'd be dead.'

Alfie didn't say anything else as the words resonated. 'Anyway, Mr Lee didn't want the guys to have sex with me, he wanted them to hurt me.'

Lola shook her head, she'd seen a lot in her time; after all she'd been on the game herself but it had never been any of that kinky stuff and when anyone had come along wanting to do all that sado shit, she'd run a mile. 'The sick fuck, you want to string him up, Alfie.'

Franny spoke, trying not to let her voice quiver. 'And is that what made all the marks on your back, Chloe?'

Chloe nodded. 'Yeah, the geezer did it when we streamed live on the internet.'

Lola chipped in again. 'And people pay for this stuff? They want to be locked up. I've said it once and I'm sure I'll say it again but that bleedin' internet has brought them crawling out of the woodwork in their droves. And as for that Mr Lee...'

Chloe's voiced raised. 'Exactly Lola, and that's why we have to go back and get Jodie. It ain't safe for her, especially as he'll know that it was her who let us out.'

Franny looked at Alfie, it was the first time she'd spoken to him. 'She's right, Alfie. We can't leave a young girl there. It ain't right.'

Alfie thought for a minute or two. It was all a mess and he knew now he was the cause, and he also knew he wasn't going to make any more excuses when it came to taking responsibility for it all. As much as this Jodie sounded like she'd been the one to encourage Chloe-Jane to get involved with Mr Lee, he wasn't going to turn his back on her. As Chloe had said, not everything was as simple as it seemed.

'Okay, but we can't just go storming in, we have to do this right.'

Franny agreed. 'The best thing we can do is wait for the others; Del and Frankie, to come; They should be here tomorrow by the latest. That way we can put our heads together.'

Chloe looked startled. 'Tomorrow?... We can't wait till then. We've got to go back now!'

'Calm down, Chloe, I know it's hard but it's for the best. Alfie knows what he's doing and with the help of Frankie and Del, I'm sure we'll bring her back.'

Chloe burst into tears again, but this time Franny held her in her arms as she cried through her words. 'I'm begging you, please let's go tonight.'

'Honey, we can't. It's not safe. Trust me, it'll be alright, won't it Lola?'

Lola looked dubious but didn't say anything; she certainly didn't want to add to Chloe's anxiety. She wasn't sure it would be – people like Mr Lee didn't take kindly to people getting one over on them and if she knew anything, Lola knew he'd want somebody to pay.

56

Alfie sat on Lola's couch in the dark, deep in thought, and slightly anxious about the imminent arrival of Del and Frankie. He wasn't particularly looking forward to seeing them; he was ashamed and sorry. Sorry for all the fucking crap he'd caused... But how was he supposed to tell them that? How would he, a face, a man who'd traded on his reputation of invincibility and being a hard-edged bastard, apologise and allow himself to show the kind of remorse appropriate?

Alfie sighed to himself. If he were honest, he was surprised they were coming over, but then a lot of things had surprised him lately, no more so than Chloe-Jane.

What he'd said to her earlier hadn't even come close to how he felt. He'd treated her badly, treated her like a second-class citizen and a person who just spelt trouble. Alfie shook his head, continuing to gaze out of the window. How ironic, how fucking ironic to think of Chloe-Jane as someone who caused trouble when he himself often seemed to be at the heart of any trouble.

He wished he could find the words to show Chloe just how incredible she was, but that was one thing he'd never been great at. Yes, he'd been good with his fists; breaking bones and stamping fear wherever he went. He was good at wheeling and dealing; making and losing millions only to make them all over again, and of course he'd been good, no, he'd been awesome with the ladies – but that was a given, he was after all Alfie Jennings – but words. Shit, words were the one thing which had always eluded him.

'Hey, mind if I join you?'

Alfie jumped slightly, he hadn't heard anyone come in the room. He smiled, awkwardly.

'Yeah, of course.' He shuffled up to the end of the couch, pushing off Lola's piles of magazines onto the floor.

'Silly question, but you okay?' Franny sat down looking directly at Alfie who stared back; stuck for what to say.

'Listen Fran, I... I...'He stopped, feeling a prickle of sweat break out on his forehead. He tried again. 'Look, what I mean to say is... I... I...' He paused again, despairing at himself. Ah fuck it, what was there to lose? What if he did look stupid? After everything that had happened, was it really worth worrying about?

Taking a deep breath, Alfie blurted out his words.

'I love you. And I'm sorry, and I know that won't make no difference to you after I lied and well, everything else. I'm an idiot, but you know that already. You're the best thing that's happened to me. You *and* Chloe-Jane. I don't deserve either of you and it's shit that it's taken all this stuff with Mr Lee to make me realise what a wanker I am. I had me reasons for doing the casinos; I thought if I got enough money, you and me could leave Soho and start a new life somewhere. I've never wanted to settle down with anyone, until you. And it was stupid because I wasn't thinking about anyone except meself. I didn't care what happened to Soho, to the others, or if I was disobeying the rules, even though I knew what would happen. All that mattered was I got what I wanted. So there it is... Shit Fran, I love you and I need you to forgive me, 'cos I don't want to live me life without you.'

He stopped, feeling embarrassed. He waited for Franny to reply but she said nothing and it nearly killed him to sit patiently. Eventually, she spoke.

'Alf, I love you too, but I need time. I can't just pretend it all didn't happen. I didn't come and help you, did I? What does that say?'

'It says you were pissed off and rightly so, babe. You'd had enough of me, of all of it. I don't blame you, Christ knows you're only human. You put your neck out for me with Vaughn and the others, and I chopped it off. Ain't nothing for you to feel bad about. Will you think about it? About us?'

Franny put her head down. 'I don't know, so much has happened.'

'All I'm asking is for you to think about it, doll. Will you do that?'

'Okay, I'll think about it. But don't push me on it, and I'm not making any promises.'

Alfie smiled. 'That's good enough for me, girl... And Fran?... Thank you.'

57

Alfie woke after a terrible night's sleep on Lola's couch. He looked at the clock; it was almost eight and everyone was still asleep. It was tempting to make himself a cup of tea but he had somewhere to go, and as much as he wanted to put it off, he couldn't.

Going to the bathroom to throw some water on his face, Alfie thought of Franny. Although he hadn't heard exactly what he wanted to hear from her, it was a start. It could have been far worse; he knew that, and Alfie was grateful she'd listened. But as for giving her time without pushing her on it, he wasn't sure if he could restrain himself. All Alfie wanted to do was get back to how things were, and one way or another he was going to achieve that.

The traffic had been frantic, as Alfie had been when he'd screamed at the lorry driver who'd cut him up, but he was here now – even if a very large part of Alfie Jennings wished he wasn't.

'Thanks for seeing me.' Alfie spoke sheepishly.

'Make this quick.' Vaughn pulled up the chair and sat down opposite.

Alfie gazed round the prison visitors' room. 'Good to see you, Vaughn, you're looking well.'

Vaughn sneered. 'Is that supposed to be funny?'

'No... No, I just thought you were.'

'What? Is the break doing me good?'

Alfie shifted on his seat. 'I didn't mean it like that, you know I didn't.'

'I don't know what you meant, but I do know you're looking like shit.'

A few weeks ago, Vaughn's comments would've wound Alfie up to the point where he wanted to put his hands round his neck and squeeze tightly, but now, what the hell, it didn't matter; none of it did and besides, it was true. He did look like shit. Alfie also felt like it but at least for the most part, it was over.

'I'll give you that one, Vaughn, you won't believe the last few days.'

'If you're telling the story; you're right, I won't.'

The men fell silent, with Alfie having to battle not to begrudge how much like hard work Vaughn was making it for him. Okay, he didn't expect him to make it easy; but Christ, he was blackballing everything he said.

Aware he needed to get back to Lola's before the others arrived, Alfie pushed through with what he'd come to talk about.

'I'm sorry, Vaughn... Okay, I'm really sorry.'

Vaughn gazed at him. 'For what?'

Rubbing his head with exasperation, Alfie spoke, still with patience in his voice. 'You ain't making this easy on me.'

'You don't really expect that?'

'No, it's not my place to expect anything, but I would like you to listen.'

'That's all I seem to have been doing over the past week. So go on then, how's the kid? I spoke to Franny last night, she said she was safe; well at least for now.'

It rankled Alfie to think Franny had spoken to Vaughn without mentioning it last night when they'd had a heart to heart, but he wasn't going to show it. 'She's good; well she will be. I've got a lot of making up to do with her, but she's going to be a credit.'

Vaughn raised his eyebrows. 'A credit? A credit to what?'

'The Jennings name.'

'Have you heard yourself, Alf? Your arrogance never ceases to amaze me.'

'Perhaps I'm not great with words, Vaughnie, but I've learned me lesson, I certainly don't mean it in any other way than pride. I'm proud of what Chloe did; proud and humbled by her. And there's no part of me which feels I was part of what she did or how brave she was. Calling her a credit was a crude and stupid way of saying that.'

There was another long pause and another shake of the head, but it was Vaughn this time who spoke. 'Fair enough Alf, but it's too little too late wouldn't you say?'

'Not if you don't want it to be.'

'What difference does it make to me? I'm looking at a lump, mate. Ten stretch, maybe fifteen.'

Alfie tried to give comforting words. 'It won't be that long, not now Casey's awake.'

Vaughn stared at Alfie incredulously. 'Oh well that's alright then, I'm only looking at an eight-year stretch; I'm laughing.'

'Sorry... I'm sorry. This ain't going how it should. It sounded a lot different in me head when I was thinking about it on the way here...

312

Look, I came here to say, I want to make it better. You, me. The whole thing. Tell me what I can do to help.'

'Alf, I dunno what to say, mate. Suddenly you get a streak of conscience and you want to put the world to rights. Do me a favour. Ain't nothing no one can do, I'm up in court for a bail application in a couple of days, and you know as well as I do I won't be getting it. What you going to do, magic me out of here? Just drop me out, Alf.'

'Look, I'm not stupid, I know how it all works and I also know too many things have happened between us to be bosom buddies again, but what else? There must be something else I can do. You want me to make a statement? No problem. You want me to sort out some money and keep things ticking over whilst you're inside; I can do that, but you gotta tell me. Tell me how I can make your life better, considering the circumstances.'

Vaughn studied Alfie. The geezer seemed so sincere, and if he'd been anyone else he would be taken in by it all. 'You've had a wasted journey. I'm glad the kid's okay, and I appreciate the fact Del and Frankie have put themselves out to make sure of it, but they can go back home now. I don't suppose they really wanted to come over here in the first place. So all's well that ends well.' Vaughn began to stand up.

'Stay!... Give us a minute.'

'What for, Alf? I ain't got nothing to say, and there's nothing you've got to say that I want to hear.'

Vaughn turned and nodded to the prison officer, letting him know he wanted to go back to his cell, listening to Alfie as he called out to him. 'I'll sort it, Vaughn. Whatever it takes, I'll sort it. I'll get you out of here.'

The visit to the prison to see Vaughn had depressed Alfie. He hadn't assumed anything, but he certainly hadn't thought he would be going away with nothing. Vaughn hadn't wanted to know, and although Alfie could see where Vaughn was coming from, he also thought he was cutting off the proverbial to spite his face.

It wasn't as if Vaughn didn't know the rules of engagement when it came to gangland London. Arguments happened. Threats were made; people got hurt and even killed. That was how it had always been and always would be, but Vaughn was acting like this was new to him and as a result he wouldn't allow himself to let go of their rivalry.

It wasn't as if Alfie was asking Vaughn to apologise, or even to make amends for *his* behaviour, *his* childish ways. No, he wasn't going to mention or insist on that – although perhaps by rights he should, there were a lot of things Vaughn Sadler had cause to be contrite about – but Alfie was going to be the bigger man; deciding he'd take full responsibility without pointing any fingers at anyone. And how was he being repaid? To have it all thrown back in his face. But unlike the Alfie Jennings of old, he wasn't going to go back on his word, he was going to sort it. And like he had told Vaughn, he'd get him out of Belmarsh somehow, and make everything like it had been.

'Alfie? What are you doing here?' Casey turned to look at Alfie as she opened her eyes. She'd been sleeping; partly because of the painkillers and partly because what else was there to do but sleep?

'I just wanted to see how you were getting on, girl. And besides, I owe you.'

'No you don't, Alf; I should be the one apologising to you... I made a real spectacle of myself didn't I?'

Alfie winked. 'We've all been a few lashes to the wind at one time or another.'

Casey smiled. 'You're being kind. And it's not just that is it? The whole thing with Vaughn, I'm responsible for it.'

Alfie took Casey's hand which surprised her, but she didn't pull it away. 'No darlin', you ain't. And who's being kind now? You know full well the ball started in my court. I made everyone think it was just Vaughn and his vendetta... I went to see him.'

Casey's eyes brightened at the thought of Vaughn. 'How is he? Lola told me he wasn't doing so good.'

'She's right, he ain't too clever and he wasn't thrilled to see me either. He's up in court in a couple of days for a bail app. Doubt he'll get it.' He shrugged. 'Anyway Cass, I'm not here to give you a sad song; just coming to try and sort out all me wrongs and tell you I'm going to get Vaughn out of there.'

Casey stared at Alfie. 'What?... How?'

'Course, that's the part I ain't figured out yet;

315

but I will. I ain't leaving it like this. I ain't leaving him to rot for some shit I did. I don't know quite what happened to me, maybe it's Chloe-Jane coming into me life, or you getting shot, or even something to do with Franny; fuck knows, but I've changed.' Alfie saw the way Casey was looking at him. He threw his hands up in the air. 'I don't blame you for looking at me like that, I know you've heard me say this bullshit before over the years but it's a strange thing... I can't look at meself in the mirror and know I've caused pain and ultimately been part of putting someone inside. Someone who shouldn't be there. Believe me, if I could go back to me old ways I would, there ain't nothing I'd like more than to bury me head in the sand and get on with me life. But somehow I woke up and got meself a conscience.'

'Alf, I don't want to put a dampener on it, but...'

'I know it sounds like I'm talking out of my arse but I'm going to figure it out. I guess that's why I came to see you. I want to know if you'll be up for it.'

Casey frowned. 'Up for what?'

'For helping.'

'Alf, you aren't making sense.'

Alfie threw a grape into his mouth from the fruit bowl sitting on the side. 'All I need to know is if you'll be on board with helping get Vaughn out.'

'You know I want that as much as you, and I'll do whatever I can but I can't imagine what use I'll be when it comes to breaking him out. I'm

316

not really sure if anything went wrong I could stand doing time. Vaughn's always told me how bad it is.'

Alfie gazed at Casey, open-mouthed, before bursting into loud and infectious laughter. It took a minute or so for him to be calm enough to talk.

'Oh I needed that, Cass! That did me the world of good. It's been a long time since I did a belly laugh. The idea of you doing a breakout... I don't know what movie you've been watching, but take my word for it, Casey, I'm certainly not suggesting anything remotely like that; though seeing you with a sawn-off shotgun in your hand and a balaclava on your face would be something I'd like to see. Maybe it'd be worth doing it just for that.'

Casey grinned, she could see what a ridiculous assumption it was. 'But if it's not that, what?'

Alfie sighed. 'Like I say, Cass, I ain't worked it out yet, but even if I have to take the blame myself, I want to make sure you're on board.'

Casey looked horrified. 'You can't do that, Alf!'

'Unless I can come up with something else, Cass, then taking the blame is the only way.'

58

'Oh look; here he is.' Lola spread her arms wide, greeting Alfie in a warm embrace. 'It's like the good old days. You're all here. All me boys, well apart from Vaughnie, that is. But it's good to see you all putting your differences aside.'

The raised eyebrows of the men said it all. And the frozen expression on Alfie's face as he entered Lola's lounge made Franny shuffle uncomfortably. It was only Lola herself who was blissfully ignorant of the tension in the room.

'Ain't you going to say hello, Alf?' Lola pushed Alfie forward, looking like a proud mum in the playground.

'Hello.' Alf put his head down, feeling stupid.

Lola roared with laughter. 'It's like you don't know one another. Come on boys, turn it in and give each other a proper welcome.'

Del snapped, then regretted it immediately when he saw the look of hurt on Lola's face.

'Drop me out, Lola... Look, I'm sorry, I'm just tired. A long journey and a bit of stress. Ignore me.'

'He didn't mean it, you know what a plank he can be sometimes.' Frankie nudged Del, attempting to make light of the situation.

Lola smiled, appreciating them trying. 'So who wants a cuppa?' As an afterthought, Lola said, 'It's good you've come. Chloe will be pleased.'

'Though I think we had a bit of a wasted journey if she's safe and well. Where is she, anyway?' Del spoke, not really very keen on seeing Chloe after his last run-in with her. But remembering what his daughter Star had said to him about coming over to help, he added, 'I'm pleased she's okay.'

Franny turned to Del. There was still a lot of unfinished business between the two of them; things left unsaid, after all, the last time any of them had seen each other had been in Alfie's club when Casey had been shot. It was, as she'd so often thought over the past few weeks, a mess.

She sighed, not wanting to concentrate on the things that had passed, but rather on the things that still needed sorting out.

'I think okay is too strong a word. She's coping, but the problem's moved on. It's certainly not a waste of a journey.'

Del looked embarrassed. 'I didn't mean it like that. I was only saying now the girl's been found perhaps there isn't the urgency like there was when Vaughn called... How is he by the way, Fran?'

'Not great, he's up in court in a day or so apparently. I don't think any of us are too happy at the moment how everything is going... And I didn't mean to sound like I was having a go at you, Del, for not wanting to be here. I understand all too well. Who wouldn't swap a bit of Marbella for Soho? How's Star?'

Del smiled at the thought of his daughter. 'She's good. It was her who made me see sense about coming across and helping. She put me to shame.'

Frankie joined in. 'And it was Gypsy who had me packing too. Behind every man, hey?'

Lola chuckled. 'Exactly darlin'. What would you lot do without us girls, hey?'

Del, remembering the conversation with Franny, picked it up again. 'What were you saying about moving on, babe?'

This time it was Alfie who shuffled, not appreciating Del calling Franny babe. He fought the urge to say anything, gritting his teeth as he listened.

'Jodie, Chloe's friend, she's in trouble. We need to go and get her out of there. What Chloe tells us, it's vital we do it as soon as possible. That Mr Lee...'

Before Franny had time to finish, Lola butted in. 'He's a sick bastard. The stuff she's told us would make you sick.'

'Keep your voice down, she might hear you,' Franny warned Lola, hating the idea of Chloe walking in and catching them talking about her.

'Don't worry love, she's fast asleep still. Poor kid must have been exhausted.'

Frankie Taylor spoke up. 'Listen, I ain't being funny but you're not seriously asking us to put our necks on the line for some girl we don't even know?'

Del nodded in agreement. 'He's right, Fran, I didn't sign up for that.'

'Jodie's a kid, guys. And like Chloe, she hasn't got anyone either. Or rather, she's only got us. Lola, why don't you go and wake Chloe so she can tell them herself?'

'You sure, love?'

'Yeah, maybe they need to hear it from her.'

As Lola walked out to wake Chloe, Franny continued to plead her case. 'You're seriously not trying to tell me we're going to turn our backs on her, are you?'

'I'm not trying to tell you anything, Fran. You can do what you like, obviously. But when it comes to me, I dunno...' Del trailed off.

'Guys, listen. I know you're not feeling too clever about me, and I understand that. In fact ... in fact...' Alfie paused, finding it more difficult than he'd thought to apologise to the two men.

As he looked at both Del and Frankie, he was sure he could see a glimmer of a smirk on each of their faces, and everything in his being told him to grab them by the scruff of their collar to show them who was boss.

Franny, seeing Alfie was struggling, encouraged him. 'Go on Alf, say it.'

'Yeah Alf, we're intrigued.' Frankie winked at him.

Alfie, having no other option but to continue, took a deep breath. 'I'm sorry. There I've said it... I was a wanker, and I was wrong.'

Del coughed. He stared at Alfie, sitting forward on the couch. 'I didn't hear that last part, mate, don't suppose you can say it again can you?'

Alfie swung round. 'You're enjoying this, ain't you?'

'No, just making sure I hear every word of this

apology. Never thought the day would come... Did you, Frank?'

Frank, not having quite the same beef Del had with Alfie, gave him a half smile. He knew only too well how easy it was for things to get out of hand. He only had to look at his own life and the mess he'd made of it at times to know just how Alf was feeling. He'd made the wrong decisions and paid a heavy price; a very heavy one. Although it wasn't a case of no harm having been done by Alfie's actions, Frank didn't have the desire of putting the boot in either.

'I ain't making any excuses for Alf, but I think we've all been in the same boat at one time or another. And I'm not saying it was right, but I am saying we live in a world where you've always got to be at the head of your game. We're forever ducking and diving and sometimes we can dive too far with it all. Get carried away. I know I have in the past, and I know you have, Del.'

Alfie winked at Frank, grateful for his support. Del, however, wasn't as understanding.

'There's one thing diving too far and there's another thing taking your friends to the bottom with you. Frank's business went up in smoke, Lola's got petrol-bombed, and look at Vaughn; look what happened to him, let alone Casey. Fuck me, that was just the start of it really, 'cos now your niece is caught up in it all. It was flat out of order, no matter what you say, Frank. The only reason I'm sitting here now being so frigging cordial is because if I don't, claret is going to get spilled.'

Alfie, having tried to keep his cool, exploded at

the underlying threat. He leapt at Del, who hadn't expected such a reaction and dropped the cup of tea he was holding.

Alfie, although injured, pinned Del to the back of the couch. His face was red. His eyes projecting with anger. He bellowed the words into the face of a taken-aback Del Williams. 'This ain't a game, mate. Don't try and wind me up, 'cos as much as I'm sorry, I'm still not having the piss ripped out of me. Tell me what it is you want me to do, 'cos I'm willing to do anything to make amends. If you want me to get down on me frigging knees and beg your forgiveness I will, 'cos all that matters is I get things back to how they were. But for fuck's sake, Del, let me–'

'She's gone!' Lola came running into the room, stopping Alfie in mid-flow.

Franny stared at her. 'Chloe?... But she can't have done. Did you check in the bathroom?'

'Ain't no mistaking it, darlin'. Look...' Lola shoved a quickly written note in Franny's hand.

Franny shook her head as she read out loud Chloe's words.

Franny, I know you'll be pissed off with me for going without telling you but I didn't want you to stop me. Please don't be angry with me. I understand it's a lot to ask of you all to help me and I understand I've caused a lot of trouble since I've arrived but I can't just sit around and do nothing. Jodie's my friend and I know she needs my help, so I'm going to find her, like she found me.

Ten minutes before Lola had discovered Chloe-

Jane had gone, Chloe had been standing by the door of the front room, listening to the conversation between everyone. She'd been glad Franny and Alfie were finally talking, because although both of them had told her she shouldn't feel responsible for their fallout, she did. Chloe felt responsible for a lot of things.

When she'd heard Franny tell the faces about Jodie, her heart had soared but as quickly as her hopes had been raised, they had been shattered when she'd heard what Del had said. And it was then she'd decided to scrawl Franny a quick note before she'd tiptoed out of the fiat, careful not to let anyone hear her and try to stop her. Because no one was going to do that. No one was going to stop Chloe finding her friend, Jodie.

Outside, Chloe hurried down the street, clutching Jodie's letter in her hand. There was no way she was going to be part of hurting anyone else, and once again it looked like there was no one willing to help her.

She pulled out her phone and dialled a number. It rang but eventually went to answering machine. She tried again. It rang first, then she heard the voice.

'Hello?'

'It's Chloe-Jane.'

'And what do I owe this call to, Chloe-Jane?'

Chloe-Jane swallowed, her whole body shaking. 'I was calling for Jodie, Mr Lee.'

'And why would you do that?'

'I ... I want to know she's alright–'

'Oh, she's fine.'

Chloe hesitated before speaking. 'Can I talk to her?'

'Not now.'

Chloe pushed on. 'When?'

'Well, that all depends. You and your uncle have caused a lot of problems, Chloe. And now you're not here, the only person who'll pay for it is Jodie.'

'She didn't know!... She didn't know it was me Uncle Alfie, I swear.'

'And you really expect me to believe that?'

'I'm telling you the truth.'

'And what if I do believe you, what then, Chloe?... What actual difference does it make, because it still leaves Jodie to take the blame. Unless... Do you want to see Jodie again?'

Chloe couldn't answer quickly enough. 'Yes ... yes.'

'Then you'll meet me by the bottom entrance of Highgate Cemetery, you do know where that is don't you?'

'Yes, but...'

'Either you want to meet or you don't want to, Chloe-Jane.'

Chloe spoke in a tiny voice. 'I can't.'

'Can't – or *won't*, Chloe-Jane, the two things are very different. So come on, what do you say? Which is it going to be?'

Chloe closed her eyes. She knew it was a trap but what was she supposed to do?

'I don't think I'll be able to do that, Mr Lee.'

'Then I don't think I'll be able to guarantee your friend's safety. It's absolutely your choice.'

Chloe began to walk down the street as she held the phone to her ear. She crossed the road, turning left near Charlotte Street. Once she'd got to the corner she spoke, quietly, resigned. 'Fine, I'll meet you. I'll be there in an hour.'

'Good choice, Chloe-Jane, but come alone. If I see you with anyone else or I think you've said anything to anyone, there'll be no more Jodie. You understand?'

'Yes.'

'Good. Then the cemetery it is. A perfect place, wouldn't you say?' Without waiting, Mr Lee clicked off the phone; he turned to Lin. 'She's coming.'

'You think she'll show?'

Mr Lee grinned. 'Oh yes, she'll show alright; she's stupid and sentimental enough to; they all are. Come on, I don't want to keep her waiting.' And with that, Mr Lee and Lin walked out of the room, leaving Jodie's body swinging gently from the rafter.

59

The two Range Rovers seemed to almost lift off the ground as they flew out of the underground car park, screeching into Berwick Street before heading north up Tottenham Court Road.

Fuck. Alfie rubbed his head in exasperation as he saw the late-afternoon traffic in front of him had blocked any quick access to Euston Road.

'What the fuck are we supposed to do now?' He glanced quickly at Franny as he headed the two-car convoy. He smashed his fist down on the horn, causing the other drivers to look around to see what the furore was.

Without warning, and at the last possible moment, Alfie swerved left into New Cavendish Street. The sharp turn threw Franny into the passenger seat door. Clinging onto the handle to stay upright, she shouted. 'Alf, slow down!'

Alfie rammed his foot on the accelerator. 'You want us to get there don't you?'

'Yes, but...'

Keeping his eyes on the road, Alfie reached out to touch Franny's leg. 'Trust me, Fran, I'll get us there in one piece. We'll find her.'

'Are they still behind us, Fran?'

Franny turned round, seeing Del's silver Range Rover looping in and out of the traffic.

'Just...'

In the car behind Alfie it was all Del Williams could do to keep up and to keep from crashing into any of the other cars. He cursed, annoyed with himself at his waning expertise. Once were the days when he'd been able to give any car a run for its money, outracing or outsmarting any driver, police or otherwise on the road. But now it seemed, and Del hated to admit it, age was catching up with them all.

Guessing Alfie was planning to head East for a bit before hanging a right further down, Del was shocked to see Alf choose Harley Street; a wide *one way* street coming the other way to them. The wrong way to them.

Realising there wasn't any other option but to cut through the street the wrong way, Del spoke to Lola who sat behind Frankie, wide eyed, clinging onto the white leather seat for dear life.

'Ready?'

She raised her eyebrows. 'No, but do what you have to do, darlin'. You won't hear any complaints from me.' And with that, Del Williams, like Alfie, pushed his foot down on the accelerator.

The two four by fours weaved in and out, avoiding the oncoming cars. Blaring horns and screeching tyres, raised fists and outraged faces sped past them, as all those present in the Range Rovers realised it was actually the perfect way to avoid the traffic jams heading out of town.

In no time at all the two cars were out on the Euston Road, racing down the clear bus lane towards Paddington where Alf, still closely followed by Del, slowed down, turning right and eventually parking round the corner from the place where he and Chloe had been held captive by Mr Lee. Only this time, he was going to be the one calling the shots. This time he had back-up.

In truth Alfie hadn't been keen for Franny to come along in case there was trouble, but in actuality he'd really had no choice. She'd reminded him how capable she was of looking after herself and others, bringing up the past and recalling the times she'd helped out in other, similar situations where lives had been on the line.

As for Lola, once she'd realised Franny was coming along, there'd been no stopping her. And now they were here, ready to confront whatever it was that would be waiting for them, Alfie found comfort in knowing he had people around him who cared.

All of them made their way on foot towards the building. Alfie kept a lookout; remaining vigilant and on high alert. Out of all of them, he was the only one who knew what Mr Lee looked like. He spoke to Franny, his eyes darting about all the time.

'When we get there, you and Lola keep walking; find a café or something and wait for me to call.'

Franny looked surprised. 'No, Alf, we do this together. All of us.'

As they continued to hurry along the street, Alfie knew it was pointless arguing with her. He could see the steely determination in her eyes and once Franny had made up her mind to do something, no one was going to change it.

Glancing at Lola, Alfie spoke authoritatively. 'I can't stop Franny, but there's no way I'm letting you come in, Lo. It's bound to be dangerous; I don't want you getting hurt.'

'You mean you don't want an old bird slowing you down.'

'You know that's not what I mean.'

'It's alright Alf, I ain't here to make things harder for you. All I want is to see Chloe back where she belongs. I'll stay around here and if I see anyone coming, I'll call.'

'And if you do see Chloe, I want you and her to get as far away from here as you can.'

Lola took a deep breath, looking around at the other four. She held onto Frankie's hand.

'Guys, be careful. I want you all coming back in one piece.'

Alfie quickly led the others round the back;

towards the basement entrance at the side of Mr Lee's building. He was angry. Real angry, and ready for payback. He owed Chloe big time, and not bringing her back safely wasn't an option. Failure wasn't an option.

'Coast clear?' Frankie called to Del who stood by the corner of the building. He quickly glanced around before nodding, whilst Alfie and Frankie began examining any possible entrances. The only way in was the tiny gap in the air vent which Chloe had showed Alfie and it was clear none of them could squeeze through it.

Moving to the far end of the wall and pressing his ear to the steel security door, Frankie waved to the others to be quiet as he listened, checking there wasn't anyone about.

'Seems okay. Come on.'

Stepping forward, Franny reached into the brown holdall she was carrying and pulled out a bright red set of eighteen-inch bolt croppers. She gave them to Alfie who, with surgical precision, nipped through the two security padlocks, before swapping the croppers to give Frankie a crowbar.

'You do the honours.'

Frankie took them, then deftly levered the heavy door frame away from the deadlocks and with one final controlled heave popped open the door. He looked around, signalling to Del to join them. 'After you, gentlemen.'

'Nice one,' Alfie whispered to Frankie as he stepped past him, entering into the basement first. Again he listened, and once he'd established the coast was clear he gestured to the others to follow him.

Alfie immediately recognised the passageway that he and Chloe had been down. He shivered as he saw the line of cell-like rooms again, not wanting to remember the fear he'd experienced whilst being held captive.

Del and Frankie held guns in their hands as they quickly checked every room, kicking open each of the doors – with each door opening to reveal nothing inside. With a flick of his head, Alfie directed the others towards the stairwell and gestured with his thumb to head up. He held Franny's arm, holding her back as she was about to pass.

'You okay, sweetheart? You can go back to the car if you want.'

Franny shook her head, appreciating his concern. 'I'm fine, but thank you.'

With their guns drawn, they crept up two flights of wooden stairs, avoiding the discarded needles and treading as quietly as possible. Leading the way, Alfie winced at every creak in the floorboards. He glanced back at the others; he could see them stepping round every noisy stair. They looked at him, alert and ready for action, and although he was definitely up for it, he sensed that the last few days or so had taken their toll as he heaved himself onwards. Alfie was determined but unclear exactly as to where he was leading them.

The plan was simple. Basic. Old school. Find Jodie and force her to leave before Chloe even got here – or if Chloe had come here already and been caught like before, they'd simply outgun any of Lee's men, then get the fuck out as quickly

331

as possible.

As Alfie continued to ascend the stairs, he realised how quiet the building was. Eerily quiet; he had an uneasy feeling they were walking straight into a trap. But there was no other choice but to try and find Jodie before Chloe did, or more importantly, find Chloe before Mr Lee.

From the fire door in the stairwell, Alf peered through the safety glass down the dimly lit second-floor corridor. No sign of anyone. Frankie pushed his head alongside to have a look.

'I don't like this, Alf; something doesn't feel right. The place is like a frigging ghost town.' Frankie cocked the trigger of his revolver. 'My suggestion is we take the place head on. Storm it, rather than play the mouse to their cats. There are four of us, so let's just kick open all these doors, get what we came for, then get the hell out of here. I ain't waiting to be ambushed by people who know the layout round here. What do you say?'

Alfie nodded. 'I say you're on, mate.'

And with that, they swiftly ran from down the corridors, bursting into every door, guns pointed and at the ready. All of them together, moving with one mind and one goal.

One by one they discovered the rooms had been stripped bare; no people, no furniture and no Chloe-Jane. Breathless, they gathered in the last room. Frankie closed the door as they all stared at one another.

Franny was distraught. 'The building's been abandoned. Everything's gone. She isn't here, is she Alf? What the hell are we going to do?'

'What about upstairs? We haven't tried there.'

Del seemed puzzled. 'There ain't an upstairs, Alf, we're on the top.'

'No, I counted five floors from outside. Five sets of windows and this is only the fourth. I saw a door at the end of the corridor I didn't try, and I'm guessing it leads to the top floor but by a different flight of stairs.'

Frankie looked at Alf. 'Then what are we waiting for?!'

With Alfie still leading the way, they ran through the door at the end of the fourth-floor corridor and up the stairs.

'Bingo.' Alfie gave a thumbs-up as he found himself on the top floor. The four of them hurtled along and like before, burst into rooms, only to find nothing.

Alfie glanced around at the others. Pride, shame and revenge ran through him. Pride for his friends, shame for himself, and revenge for Chloe. Mixed emotions raced through him as the pain from the exertion clutched hold of his body. But the adrenaline drove him on. *Revenge* drove him on.

Kicking open the next door, he heard a scream. It was Franny. Frantically swinging his gun round the room, a movement in the corner of his eye made Alfie pivot and instinctively fire three rounds.

Feeling the familiar numbness in his ears when he fired his gun, Alfie experienced ten seconds of deafness, not hearing the words of Del, as he burst into the room behind him.

'Alf get down! Get down! I got you covered.'

Del pointed his gun, assuming one of Mr Lee's men had targeted Alf, but only a splattered rat lay bleeding, shot into the floorboards by Alf.

Del breathed out, and shook his head. 'Fuck me, Alf. Wanna give me a heart attack? Carry on shooting up the rodents. Jesus...'

As Alfie's hearing slowly returned, both he and Del heard another scream. Alfie's blood ran cold.

'Franny!... Fran, where are you?' he shouted desperately, not caring who heard or who might shoot at him as he ran towards her cries.

Chasing down the corridor, with Del closely behind, as well as Frankie, who had also heard the screams and gunshots, Alfie was relieved to see Franny standing in the last room with the gun he'd given her in her hand.

'Fran, are you okay?... Fran?' From where he was standing in the corridor he could see she was pale and shaking. 'Fran, can you hear me? What's going on? It's me, babe.'

But Franny didn't say anything. She just stared ahead.

Alfie hurried into the room, with Del and Frankie directly behind him. A powerful smell hit them. Alf turned to follow Franny's gaze until his eyes rested on the swollen purple face staring back at them, a limp body hanging only inches from the floor. It was Jodie.

Alf shouted, 'Cut her down!... Cut her down! It's Jodie!' He ran forward, tugging at the belt, then stood on the chair to try to get her down. He called out to Del and Frankie.

'Help me guys, help me!' They ran forward, lifting her body weight up, allowing Alfie to undo the loop.

Jodie fell into Alfie's arms. 'Call the ambulance! Call the ambulance!'

Franny put her hand gently on Alfie's shoulder as he knelt on the floor by Jodie's body.

'She's gone, Alf... She's gone.'

Alfie buried his face into his hands. 'She was only a kid. She was only a kid.'

'I know sweetheart. I know... Look, you guys better go.'

Alfie looked up. He wiped the tears away. 'We can't leave her here. I can't leave her on her own.'

'I'll call the ambulance and wait for them,' Franny answered. 'It's better that way. Fewer questions. And I'll see you back at Lola's.'

Del put his hand on Alfie. 'Franny's right. She can say she was looking for her niece and came across this... Well, you know what I mean.'

Alfie got up, he touched Franny's face gently, then kissed her on her forehead before turning to the others. 'Okay. But Lee's going to pay for this. And I ain't going to rest till I put him in the ground.'

60

It was gone one in the morning. They were all crammed into Lola's tiny kitchen, all subdued by their grim discovery and all fearful but not speaking about their deep concern for Chloe-Jane. Lola's kettle clicked off.

'Tea, anyone?' No one answered. 'Alfie, come on love, have some tea.' Alfie shook his head.

'Fran, you'll have a cup won't you?' Franny didn't say anything, looking down to the tiled floor.

'Del, Frankie... Anybody. A cup of tea.'

With an empty mug in each hand Lola held open her arms, bursting into inconsolable tears. Her whole body shook. 'For the love of God, someone have a cup of tea... *Please*... Oh my God, the poor kid... Poor Chloe... Oh, Jesus, what we going to do?'

It was Franny who spoke first. 'On second thoughts, I'll have a cup of tea, and so will Alf, won't you, Alf?'

Alfie nodded. 'Let's all have a brew, Lola. That would be good.'

Del chipped in. 'Yeah, and perhaps even a biscuit or two, then we'll see if we can't get our heads together and come up with a plan.'

Lola smiled gratefully, happy she had something to do to try to avoid just thinking about Chloe.

Alfie watched Lola busying herself about. He had an overwhelming fear that finally his luck, or rather Chloe's luck, had run out. They had no idea where to even start to look for Chloe; the only real lead had been the building in Paddington and Jodie. Thinking about her made him pull his breath in. He didn't think he'd ever get rid of that image out of his mind. He'd seen a lot, but that... That kid hanging there was another thing completely. A tragic waste of life. And the saddest part? The saddest part was besides everyone congregated here in Lola's kitchen, none of whom really knew Jodie at all, no one would care that she was dead.

As Lola counted out the PG tips, Alfie thought of all the times he'd knocked back Chloe when all she wanted to do was belong. Even with his own daughter Emmie, he'd never stopped to listen. Of course her mother had driven him mad with her nagging but it wasn't Emmie's fault. All the designer gifts he'd bought her to smooth things over and to replace him being there a lot of the time, along with his behaviour, had hurt his daughter to the point where she didn't want anything to do with him.

Chloe had been a second chance to care for a Jennings kid. Someone who'd needed him, like he'd needed someone when he'd been growing up. But he hadn't cared for her properly. Not even a tiny bit. And even though he'd known about her childhood, Alfie's care of his own niece had been so inadequate she'd still needed to turn to the likes of Mr Lee for help.

The image of Jodie came into his mind again.

Again it made him shudder; a tight knot in his stomach. She'd risked her life to save him and Chloe and now she was gone; taking her own life had been better than living. He took a sip of his tea to stop him feeling more physically sick than he did already.

Half an hour later, they were all sitting in the front room, the fear and worry still palpable. Inwardly Del Williams felt uncharacteristically shaken at having seen that poor kid obviously so desperate she'd do that to herself. It made him think of all the times his missus Bunny had talked about her miserable childhood in care, the abuse and God knows what else. He wondered if she ever came close to ending it all herself. When he got back to Marbella, he was going to take her in his arms and not let her go.

Frankie also sat and thought about Jodie. His heart broke for the tragedy of it all. He knew only too well from his own difficult, neglected childhood how it was easy to find yourself lost and alone. He had been lucky, he'd got through it and he had a wonderful family of his own now, and the first thing he was going to do when he got back was tell them how much he loved them.

Alfie had been a prick who'd brought a lot onto himself. But not this; no one deserved this. And he would do everything he could to help him bring Chloe back. Frankie sighed. He wasn't used to feeling useless, powerless, but that's exactly what they were all feeling as they all drank their tea, each one of them silently wondering what

338

they were going to say, and what they could possibly do next.

Franny Doyle sat quietly by the window in Lola's lounge, holding Chloe's note in her hand, barely able to contemplate the guilt she now felt for pushing Chloe away. She'd taken Chloe in and given her hope and support, then, despite knowing how vulnerable she was, had taken her lifeline away for purely selfish reasons.

Alfie's phone started to ring, interrupting everyone's thoughts. He answered, urgently. 'Yes? Hello?' As the voice on the other end started to talk, Alfie kicked the table in front of him in frustration, and before the caller had even had time to finish his sentence, Alfie cut in, 'I ain't got time for this now, just put everything in the club and don't bother me with anything. I couldn't give a flying fuck where you put the frigging beer.' Clicking the phone off, he stuffed it back in his pocket.

Almost immediately, Alfie's phone rang again. Enraged, he snatched it off again, barking down the phone. 'Christ, al-fucking-mighty, I told you, just leave everything at the club.'

But then, Alfie froze. Instead of the heavy cockney accent of his driver, a much softer voice spoke calmly.

'Mr Jennings, I too have a club, an exclusive club that I think you might be interested in.'

Then the line went dead.

Franny who'd been watching Alfie, saw the mix of anger and confusion on his face as he looked down at the blank screen.

'Who was that, Alf?... Alf?'

339

Before Alf could reply, a text message pinged out from his phone.

V.I.P. – You are invited to enjoy a special event.

As Alfie opened the message in full, it triggered an internet link which opened directly into a video stream. What Alfie saw next made him visibly pale, and for a moment he wondered if he was going to throw up
'Alf, what's going on?'
Franny took the phone, turning it round so she could see it. They both stared in horrified disbelief at a scantily clad Chloe-Jane tethered to a chair with various torture tools hung neatly behind her; a rolling footnote passed across the screen.

R.I.P. Chloe-Jane, click here *to subscribe.*

When Alfie clicked on the link, he saw a counter ticking down. 0 days 18 hours and 10 minutes, 9, 8, 7, 6, seconds.
Dropping the phone onto the table as if it were suddenly burning into his hands, Alfie slumped into the chair next to Franny. 'Oh, fuck Fran. Fuck... I don't believe this.'
The others gathered round the table and everyone stared at the horrifying video. Del and Frankie caught each other's eye. Franny placed her hand on Alfie's arm partly to comfort him but more to steady herself as she felt her head start to spin.
Looking up from the phone, Lola spoke, 'What

the hell is this, Alf?'

Alfie buried his head in his hands. 'It's my worst nightmare.'

Lola's voice was shrill. 'You mean it's Chloe's worst nightmare. Look at her. Alfie, you've got to sort this. Don't matter what you do, whatever it is, you have to get her back, Alfie!'

They were interrupted by Alfie's phone ringing again, the number withheld.

Lola leaned forward. 'Answer it, quick Alfie!'

Snapping into movement Alfie picked up the phone. 'Yes?'

'Ah, Mr Jennings.'

'Lee, just tell me what you want. You can have it. You can have anything.'

There was a chuckle. 'I don't want anything. I have *everything* I want right here.'

'You're dead, Lee. Do you hear me ... dead.' Alfie gripped the phone, spitting his words.

The sarcasm dripped from Mr Lee. 'No, Mr Jennings, I'm clearly not. That's Jodie's department.'

'You fucking bastard.'

'That's as maybe, Mr Jennings, but like I told you, right at the beginning. You brought this on yourself. And besides, this is just a courtesy call. I can't help but notice that your introductory free subscription to my video service is about to expire. Just about eighteen hours left.'

Alfie was desperate. 'What do you want, Lee? This has gone too far, I want her back.'

'Mr Jennings, she's not yours to take back.'

'Just answer the question. What is it you want?'

'I don't want anything.'

'Stop playing games, Lee. How much? Name your price.'

'I don't think you're listening to me. I said I don't want anything.'

'You want me to beg? Is that it? I'll beg, I'll do whatever it takes.'

'No, Mr Jennings, I expect you to watch. Watch the clock and watch what happens. People pay a lot of money for this, and you're getting it free.'

'What the hell are you going to do?'

'I think the clue's in the title. R.I.P. Chloe-Jane. There's nothing left for you to do now, except sit back and enjoy the show.'

61

They all sat out in the car. All five of them, squeezed into Del's Range Rover.

'You sure this is going to work, Alf?'

Alfie stared at Frankie. 'No, but I ain't got any other ideas. But if I know this man, I know he'll do anything to get what he wants. Wouldn't you say, Lola?

Lola nodded, looking around at them all. 'He's right. From what I hear through the Soho grapevine the man would put his grandmother on the street if it meant he was going to get a catch.'

Del shrugged. 'It's not the way we usually do things. Feels ... I dunno, unclean somehow. Makes me feel dirty. But okay, I'm in.'

Franny agreed. 'We're all in.'

Alfie's eyes brimmed with tears. He was feeling overwhelmed with all the emotion. He choked on his words as he spoke. 'Thank you guys... Thank you. I know you're going on the line to do this.'

Del winked at Alf. 'Don't worry about it, mate... After all, we're family.'

Detective Spencer leaned back in his chair. He pushed his hands against his desk, forcing out a loud noisy fart, letting the cannelloni he'd had for lunch have a final word. A knock at the door came, before his sergeant popped his head round. 'Gov, there's someone here to see you.'

'I'm busy, so tell whoever it is they need an appointment.'

'Actually Gov, it's...'

Del Williams pushed into the room, followed by Frankie, Alfie, Franny and Lola. Del gave a hostile stare to the sergeant, before turning his attention to Spencer.

'We ain't got time for all this; we need your help.'

Detective Spencer stared at them incredulously. To see a handful of gangland faces standing in his office, *voluntarily*, was something he thought he'd never get to see.

'To what do I owe this ... this dubious honour? You lot shot any more of your girlfriends?'

Stepping forward Frankie Taylor grimaced, partly at Spencer's attitude but also at the rancid smell that hung in the messy office.

'We're trying to find a missing person and much

as it pains me to say it, we can't trace her without your help.'

Spencer roared with laughter, much to the annoyance of all assembled, but his laughter soon turned into a sneer. He banged on his desk. 'You lot have some front. You come here wanting my help, yet I recall only a small while ago, all of you had either conveniently gone AWOL or had a severe case of amnesia about events which happened right under your nose.'

Del spoke, hating every moment of talking to the Old Bill. 'Well we're here now, and strangest thing is, we seem to have got our memory back.'

Spencer leaned forward. He shook his head, not believing what he was hearing. 'Come again.'

'You heard Spencer, we've got our memory back. All of us. And we'll all give you a statement about what happened. About us being there ... when Casey was shot.'

Spencer nearly choked on his own saliva. He stared, pointing his finger one at a time at them. 'You ... you lot are going to give a statement?'

Franny sat down on the chair next to her. 'That's right. All of us, even Lola here. If... If you help us.'

'Always a catch with you lot.'

Lola joined in the conversation. 'Ain't no catch, darlin'. You want the statements, we want Chloe back, and because of that, you'll get what you want.'

Spencer chewed on his pen top, managing to bite his own tongue. Irritated, he spoke, directing his conversation to Alfie. 'I don't do missing per-

344

sons, not my department – unless they're dead, and I take it this...'

'Chloe.'

'Yes, this Chloe isn't. Problem you've got is I don't trust any of you. What's to say I help and you decide to back out of giving me the statement? I reckon I should get the sergeant here to deliver you back out onto the street where you belong, don't you?'

Frankie Taylor's face flushed as he went to lunge at the detective but before he could speak, Del Williams gently pulled his friend's arm down and spoke carefully.

'Look, you'll get your sworn statements about the Casey Edwards shooting. You can have it now.'

Spencer raised his eyebrows. 'Now?'

'Well, part of it. You see, the feeling's mutual. We don't trust you either. What's to stop you not helping us once we give you the statement?'

Spencer fell silent. He could tell they were desperate. There was no way the likes of Alfie Jennings, Del Williams, Frankie Taylor, Franny Doyle or that creature Lola Harding would ever step foot in a police station without being cuffed. He'd waited a long time to put Vaughn Sadler away; a very long time. The man had been the scourge of his career, having always escaped the heavy weight of justice by having a watertight alibi or a slick lawyer to hand. But now, now they were willing to grass on their own, all in the name of this person, Chloe.

He spoke to Franny. 'And if I agree to this?'

'We'll give you the statement you want. I've

345

spoken to Casey and she'll give you one too, and then you help us. Tell us what we need to know about where our girl is being held.'

'Being held! I thought you said they were missing.'

'Jesus, what's the difference?' Frankie snapped.

'There's a lot of difference, Mr Taylor. Kidnap isn't my department either.'

Lola blurted out. 'I don't care if your department is the shoe section in flipping Harvey Nicks, we need you to find her, and fast. Del, show him.'

Without saying anything, Del Williams opened his laptop and placed it on the desk. The screen burst into life and Spencer gazed mesmerised at the streaming of the girl tied up on the chair. He was transfixed by the grainy picture of Chloe staring back at them in a bleak concrete room, dressed only in flimsy underwear, occasionally tugging at her restraints, her eyes bulging in terror as she breathed hard around a tight gag.

And in that moment, Detective Spencer realised just how much they needed him. And just how far they'd go to save her; including grassing on Vaughn Sadler. He hid the smile, but finally, finally he'd got him. The sweetest thing was, Vaughn wouldn't be brought down by Spencer, oh no, he would be brought down by his so-called friends.

'Et tu, Brutus.'

Frankie snarled. 'You what?'

'It's Shak– You know something, Taylor; forget it. I was about to explain, but I doubt you'd understand.'

346

Frankie clenched his fists and it was only the image of Jodie and the thought that Chloe-Jane was still out there and her life hung in the balance that stopped him from smashing Spencer right in his face.

'Okay, gentlemen and *ladies.*' Spencer turned to look at Lola as he emphasised the last word. 'The sergeant here will take you into the interview room, and take your statements officially, so there can be no cock-ups and no getting out of it. Agreed?'

Alfie looked concerned. 'Agreed, but as you can see by the countdown, we ain't got much time.'

'The moment I've got the statement in my hand, I'll get onto internet vice and tracking.'

Forty minutes later, Detective Spencer held the signed statements of all of them in his hand. He read each one. Each one short and brief. Apart from their names, each one said the exact same thing as Alfie's did.

I, Alfie Jennings, admit that on the day of the 18th April this year, was present at the club, Whispers which is situated in Old Compton Street when Casey Edwards was shot.

This is a true and accurate statement.
Alfie Jennings.

Spencer looked up, placing the statements carefully on his desk as he stared at them all. He spoke to Del.

'Is that it?'

'That's all you'll need for now – or get. You've

got what you want, we're admitting we're there. There's no backing out now. You'll get the rest of the statement when you've done what we asked. Just in time for Vaughn's court appearance. You should be dancing on the ceiling, mate. You win.'

Detective Spencer didn't say anything but he certainly *felt* something. Del was right, he had won. At last, Vaughn Sadler was going to get his comeuppance.

62

'For fuck's sake how long is this going to take?' Alfie paced around the room. The time it was taking for them to trace the video link seemed to be dragging on, yet the time they had left was speeding by. And it was doing his head in.

'Calm down, Alf, they're doing their best. I know it's tough, but try to hold it together.'

Alfie whispered to Franny, not wanting anyone else in the room to hear what he was saying. 'No Fran, they're doing fuck all. I think they're taking the piss. How do we know that they're actually doing anything?'

'Come on, Alf, they aren't going to play games. Chloe is in trouble, they know that. They'd have to find her, even if we didn't come here. What we've done is shove her to the top of the queue, and Spencer is making sure she's top priority. That's good isn't it?'

'Yeah, if we had all the time in the world, but we ain't got time, babe; look at her.' Alfie gestured his head towards the large screen on the wall of the internet tracking crime office which monitored and streamed the live link of Chloe-Jane. But neither of them could bear to look up at it. Neither of them could bear to see Chloe's life being counted down in minutes and seconds.

Alf, looking like a broken man, turned to one of the police officers sitting at his desk. 'Do you have to keep that up-there all the time? That's my niece for Christ's sake, and I don't need a constant reminder of how long she's got left, as well as a constant reminder of how long you fucking lot are taking.'

Franny didn't say anything. She felt the same way as Alf did, but understood that the police officers probably needed to keep an eye on Chloe, just in case...

'Come away, Alf, leave them to it.'

Franny was grateful to see Del and Frankie arriving back from the coffee machine, and she noticed how neither of them looked towards the screen either. It was too raw. Too real.

Del enquired, 'Any news?'

Alfie shook his head, glaring hatred at the police officers who in his mind, were deliberately taking longer than they had to.

'Sweet FA, they just seem to be typing away, doing nothing much. It's doing my head in; Fran's the only thing keeping me from losing it completely.'

He leaned over the nearest police officer's

shoulder. 'Look mate, how much fucking longer is this going to take?'

Detective Spencer spoke from behind him. 'Mr Jennings, I advise you to just let these men do what they have to do; they'll work much quicker without, how shall I put it, without your *constant encouragement.*'

Alfie glared at the detective. He'd never liked coppers. Never. But this one; this Detective Spencer was an oily, smarmy bastard. Alfie hissed at Spencer, feeling the comforting hand of Franny on his back.

'Then I suggest that this lot hurry up or...'

Spencer interrupted, giving Alfie a smug smile. 'The deal's off? Oh no Jennings, our deal's certainly not off. There's no going back. You lot said that yourself.'

As much as Spencer pissed Alfie off, he was right about one thing. There was no going back; not now. Not now they were here forty-five minutes later, watching Chloe-Jane's life tick away.

'I think we've got something, Gov,' one of the officers shouted.

Detective Spencer, along with Del, Frankie and Alfie, ran across to where the police officer was sitting, whilst Lola clung onto Franny, scared to raise her hopes. Spencer spoke, authority in his voice. 'What have you got?'

'Sir, we've traced it to Limehouse in the Docklands.' The man paused, tapping a few more keys. 'I've got the address.'

Alf pushed past Fran, grabbing the officer's shoulder. 'You know where she is? You know where Chloe-Jane is?'

Spencer stepped in, pulling Alfie's hand off the officer. 'It seems so, Mr Jennings.'

Pulling his arm free from Spencer's grip, Alf snarled, 'So if you've found her, what the fuck are we waiting for?'

Spencer leaned in to Alfie. '*You're* not waiting for anything. This is police business now, and as you see, we're dealing with it.'

As Spencer spoke, Frankie watched some of the other officers picking up their phones, urgently requesting the search warrant as well as the armed response team. Others were quickly collecting various bits of technical kit, along with their protective jackets.

'Just tell me where in Limehouse she is! I want to go and get my niece. I ain't leaving it up to you lot.' Alfie squared up to Detective Spencer, who nonchalantly waved him away as he turned to follow the other officers out of the room. He stopped at the door to speak to Del before he left the room.

'You lot can't be involved in this; there are procedures to follow which don't involve you. Now I am warning you, stay out of this.'

Alfie and Del drove their respective Range Rovers hard as they followed in the wake of a convoy of police cars with lights and sirens blaring. Spencer may not have wanted them to have or given them the address but there was no way he was going to stop them tailing their obvious presence.

Alfie carved through the heavy traffic towards London's Docklands. His voice boomed out as he spoke to Franny. 'What the hell did he think we were going to do? Sit there like friggin' muppets whilst they messed it up?'

'The one good thing is there are a lot of them. Hopefully it'll make all the difference.'

Alfie gave a quick sideward glance to Fran. The speed they were going, he needed to keep his eyes firmly on the traffic.

'Me too, but I'm telling you, Fran, I ain't taking my eyes off them for a moment.'

Three minutes later, the police cars, along with the two Range Rovers, emerged from the Limehouse link tunnel. The sirens stopped, and the flashing lights ceased as they all sped with ease down the quieter industrial roads of the Isle of Dogs.

'We must be getting closer, Alf.'

Alfie didn't answer Franny, his stomach was in knots and his heart raced faster. He gripped the steering wheel hard, glancing at Del and Frankie in the rear view mirror, who both stared intensely ahead.

'You okay?' Franny looked at Alf, and this time he answered.

'I will be. When we've got her back.'

The convoy swept quietly into Hertsmere Road. Some of the police cars began to peel off into different side streets. The other cars, including the Range Rovers, surrounded an old warehouse; a stark and imposing structure, complete with original winches and pulleys. Franny felt a chill, knowing that Chloe-Jane was in there; tied up, scared and alone. But worse, much worse, was knowing Mr Lee wouldn't care about killing her in an attempt to escape the police raid. She began to question the wisdom of involving the police, but what choice had there been?

Alfie also looked on helplessly, watching the team of officers in riot gear smash open the wooden doors. He listened to them calling out, shouting orders to each other.

'Right, right, right. Head towards the back. Collins, Davies, Daniels, head to the east entrance.'

That was it. It was too much for them all to contemplate. To sit back and do nothing. It went against the grain of who they were. All of them had seen enough. Stood back for long enough. And there was no way they were doing it for a moment longer.

Alfie called out to the others. 'Ready?'

'You bet we are.'

All of them except for Lola ran forward, unable to stop themselves going in. They darted past a couple of uniform police officers and joined the police-coordinated ascent of the warehouse stairs.

Detective Spencer glanced over his shoulder, and stared back in disbelief to see Alfie, Del, Frankie and Franny creeping up the stairs with guns drawn in their hands.

'What the fuck are you doing? This isn't an episode of *Magnum P.I.* This isn't a game. Put them away... Now!'

Before any of them had the chance to speak, an urgent voice sounded out from further up the stairwell. 'Gov, I think you'd better come and see this.'

Something in the officer's tone didn't fill Alfie

with any confidence. He took a deep breath to steady himself, then pushing past a couple of armed police, he clambered up two more flights of stairs, desperate to see what was there. Who was there.

Arriving in the main upstairs area of the warehouse, Alfie's heart sank to the pit of his stomach as he saw what was in front of him. There was Chloe-Jane. Sitting on the chair. Hands tied. Gag in mouth... But he could only see her on another computer screen. A lone laptop computer sat on the floor, displaying the now-familiar image of Chloe tied to a chair with the counter still running down.

As the technical guys surrounded the laptop, opening their tool cases, a breathless and desperate Alf managed to gasp, 'What the fuck is this?... What the hell is going on? Where is she?'

For a minute no one answered, it was obvious to all of them apart from Alfie what had happened. It was Spencer who explained. 'It appears we've been deliberately led on a wild goose chase. Chloe-Jane was never here.'

Alfie sank to his knees and stared in horror at the vision of Chloe on the laptop.

'I don't understand... I...' Alfie said it as much to himself as to the police officer starting to work on the laptop.

The officer answered sympathetically. 'What they've done is, make a short film of her. What you see is the same two minutes rolling round and round with the timing counter embedded on top. It's not even a hi-tech job, anyone could do this.'

Coming up behind Alf, Franny sat down on the floor next to him. She didn't speak, nor did Alf as he reached to the side of him, taking her hand in his.

Del's voice came from the back of the room. He spoke to the officer. 'Please, just turn it off, turn that fucking film off.'

Detective Spencer nodded to the officer, who then clicked off the image of Chloe. The officer spoke to Spencer. 'Sir, the link was definitely from here. From this laptop. There's nothing else to go with this now.'

Spencer nodded to the armed team and support groups to stand down and move out.

'I think it's time we took this back to the station.'

Alfie jumped up. 'What do you mean, back to the station? Spencer, you promised you'd find her.'

'I promised to try, and I have. And of course the team will keep on looking, but if there's nothing else to go on, I can't just make her appear.'

One of the uniform constables approached Spencer, 'Sir, if this link is a dead end, what about the other link? The signup page. That might be a separate upload.'

The constable pointed to the signup page which had remained on the screen after the video of Chloe was shut down.

Spencer cut him off. 'I told you to ship out of here, and constable, do yourself a favour and leave the clever stuff to the tech officers, will you?'

'But sir, the tech guys have been tracing the link

to the main...'

Spencer cut him off again, angered at the constable's insolence. 'I'm not asking, I'm ordering you to keep out of this or I'll...'

It was Alfie who cut in this time. 'Let him speak, Spencer. For fuck's sake we need every lead we can get.' Turning to face the constable, Alfie nodded to him to carry on.

'Well, I'm just saying the tech guys have been tracing the main page, but it's clear that the signup page is a different upload. Maybe – and I know it's a long shot – but maybe it's worth putting a trace on the IP address of that as well.'

Everyone apart from the tech officers and the constable looked blank, not understanding the technology of it all. Spencer spoke to the officer who'd been working on the laptop.

'What do you think?'

'I think it's worth a try. It'll take a bit of time though.'

Alfie growled. 'How long? Don't you get it, mate, we ain't got long.'

Spencer turned to Alfie. 'Mr Jennings, we don't know if she's even alive.'

Alfie grabbed hold of Spencer shaking him hard, as Del, Frankie and Franny tried to pull him off. He yelled at Spencer, distraught. 'Don't you say it! Don't you dare write her off before we've even tried. Everyone, everyone, including me, has written Chloe-Jane off all her life and we ain't doing it now; not when she needs us the most. You hear me?... You hear me, Spencer?'

Spencer's face was red with rage, matching

Alfie's. 'Get him off me... Now! Before he gets himself arrested!'

Del managed to pull Alfie off, gripped him hard. 'Calm the fuck down, Alf. I get it, mate. I get it, but we ain't giving up on her. None of us are.' He pulled Alfie into a huge embrace, holding him tightly, not caring who saw his tears or Alfie's.

An hour and a half later, they were still in the warehouse. Franny and Del watched as the tech officers battled away with links and hyperlinks, IP addresses and hidden embedded codes.

'We've got it!' Everyone stared in amazement. There was still a glimmer of hope, and they were amazed and cautiously delighted all at the same time. The tech officer continued to speak.

'Astonishingly he was right, sir. The signup page was uploaded from a different address. The only problem is it's a Wi-Fi connection.'

Alfie wondered what the problem was. 'And?'

'Being an open, unlocked Wi-Fi connection means it's accessible to anyone within a twenty-five-metre radius of it. The registered person of it means nothing, because other people can use it.'

Spencer asked, 'But you know where the Wi-Fi connection is coming from?'

'Yes sir, we've got the name of the street, Royster Road, but like I say it's accessible to anyone within twenty-five metres of it.'

Another tech officer interjected. 'More like a fifty-metre radius.'

Alf got to his feet. 'So you're saying if we go to

the street where the Wi-Fi address is registered, within fifty metres or less of that we'll find Chloe.'

Spencer answered. 'If she's there, Mr Jennings. It could be another wild goose chase.'

Alfie snapped, 'I ain't talking to you, I was talking to this geezer.' He turned back to the tech officer. 'So is that right? Within fifty metres of the hub point, she'll be there?'

'Well, assuming she's there. Give or take a few metres or so, technically, yes!'

Alfie nodded to himself. He looked at the tech guy and then to the constable. 'I owe you, mate. Look me up in Whispers, I'll sort you out. Got some nice designer gear and bags you can have for your missus.'

The constable was about to thank Alfie, but the warning *'don't you dare look'* from Spencer shut him up.

'Let's go then.'

Spencer rolled his eyes. 'We can't get a warrant for that, and we can hardly kick down every door in a fifty-metre radius, can we?'

Alfie began to run out of the room. *'You* may not be able to, Spencer, but *we* certainly can.'

63

The noisy convoy of police cars had to drive hard, struggling to keep up with the two high-powered Range Rovers as Alfie and Del sped round the tiny streets of the Isle of Dogs, heading towards Royster Road. Tyres screeching and cars overtaking cars made it difficult at times to tell if the police were chasing Alfie and Del or they were chasing the police.

'We've lost them!' Franny turned round to see the three police cars being held up behind a large crane on the back of a lorry reversing awkwardly into the road. 'There aren't any other ways round, unless of course they head round by Canary Wharf, which will take them at least forty minutes because of the road works. I reckon we've got fifteen minutes' head start on them. They should be stuck there for a while. Do you think fifteen minutes is okay?'

'I think it'll have to be. Is Del still behind?'

'Yeah, he's still... Look, there's the road!' Franny shouted to Alfie as she saw Royster Road coming into view.

The sight of the road ahead had Alfie pushing the car to the max to get there.

'Shit...! Shit!... Hold on!' Alfie shouted out as he saw, too late to slow down, the no-entry bollards stopping him entering Royster Road. He pulled on the emergency handbrake, taking the car from four wheel drive to two, making the Range Rover turn into a spin to stop crashing into the bollards. Alfie's wheels screeched, sending up smoke and gravel.

The scream of Alfie's tyres was echoed by Del's, who also had to make the sharp handbrake turn to stop his car crashing into Alfie's Range Rover.

The men jumped out, discarding the cars in the middle of the road.

Frankie turned to Alfie. 'What's the plan?'

'Simple. We crash out every house in the street. It's less than fifty metres, so it should be relatively easy. Four houses on each side. So if we bang up every house, then we're bound to find her.'

Del looked and sounded worried. 'You sure, mate?'

'No, I ain't but that's all I've got. Spencer will be here biting on our bums soon, so we need to get a move on if we're going to do this.'

Franny agreed. 'I can't see any other way. The one thing we've got going for us is that on either side of the street there's either wasteland or the river, which means the fifty-metre range they talked about can only be within this street, because basically...' She stopped to look round the bleak environment of Royster Road then added, '...This is it.'

Frankie could see the logic in it, although when they'd first suggested it he'd thought it was the kind of plan Del's daughter, Star, would have come up with. 'It's not as crazy as I thought then. Eight houses altogether... Piece of piss.' He winked at Franny.

Franny looked at them all. 'So what are we waiting for, boys?'

Alfie, Del, Frankie, Lola and Franny ran into the street. Alfie knew the pressure was on and it was probably only a matter of minutes before Spencer and his band arrived. But they could do it if they were quick; real quick. Eight houses in total. Two each. As Frankie had said, a piece of piss. He called out to the others.

'I'll take this side with Del, and you, Franny, can you go with Frankie and take the other side. Lola, take your pick girl.'

They all nodded, making their way to various spots in the street of old, rundown detached houses.

Taking the nearest house first, Alfie ran down the path, adrenaline flowing, determined no one would stop him. He looked at the door, agitated, deciding whether to ring the bell first or kick the door down.

Choosing the former, Alf gave a quick buzz but before he'd even taken his finger away from the bell, he shook his head, talking to himself out loud. 'Fuck it!'

Turning to take a run-up he lifted his leg, kicking out at the door to let his full weight flow from the sole of his shoe to send him crashing through the front door. Running into the hall-way, with gun drawn, Alfie shouted out to the occupants, warning anybody present.

'Everybody down! Everybody down!' He ran into the front room, finding an old man asleep on his couch, oblivious to the disturbance. Disheartened but still pushing on, Alfie ran through each room, knowing in his heart – but needing to check anyway – this wasn't the house.

Rushing out into the street and down the next path, Alfie didn't bother ringing the door this time. With one violent kick he booted it hard enough to leave the front swinging awkwardly from its hinges.

Further down the street, Del raced to a house where an elderly couple stared from an upstairs window, clutching onto each other in terror at the scene unfolding. Del slipped his gun into his jacket pocket and quickly tried the door handle; having no wish to kick the door down or frighten them any more than they were already.

It opened and he ran in, but instead of calling out warning threats, he feigned cheeriness. Speaking to the couple who'd come to the top of the stairs.

Del waved up to them, eyes darting round at all times. 'Sorry sir, don't worry, just some urgent police business. We're checking all houses.' Not waiting for a reply, Del continued to race through the house, but like Alfie, he had a sinking feeling Chloe-Jane wouldn't be there.

On the opposite side, using a mixture of charm and the occasional wave of her gun, Franny was also checking houses. Quickly and as speedily as she could, aware there was no time to waste, aware like the others the likelihood of finding Chloe was getting slimmer by the moment.

Franny, opening the bathroom door in one

house, was greeted by the sight of an overweight man sitting in his bath with his dog, playing with an array of toy soldiers. They both stared open-mouthed at each other before Franny politely said, 'Sorry!' and quickly closed the door again.

She took the stairs two at a time, running out into the street. Right into Detective Spencer. He snarled at her.

'Give me a good reason why I shouldn't nick you.'

'Because you're as bent as we are and you're looking for our statements on what happened in the club.'

Spencer glared at her. 'This is a dead end. You know that don't you?'

Franny's voice was full of emotion. 'Then help us, Spencer. Get your men to bang on some doors. You don't need a warrant for that. There's only a couple of houses to go. Get them to do them.'

Franny looked over Spencer's shoulder to see what could only be described as chaos. There was a melee of half a dozen police officers trying to calm down irate and frightened residents standing in the middle of the road, where three flashing police cars were abandoned as carelessly as their Range Rovers.

She turned to her right, Del and Lola moving and making their way from house to house.

Spencer, not having answered Franny yet, leaned in, breathing coffee and cigarette fumes at her. 'Fine, but your statement better be good, Doyle. Real good.'

As Spencer hurried across to his men to order them to start banging on the last couple of doors, Franny waved across to the others to join her. She called out, not sure whether they'd hear over the noise. 'We have got to stop!... Spencer is getting his men to do the last couple of houses.'

Franny sighed and looked around her. She could see the police were becoming confused as to who they should arrest, as more and more local residents came out of their houses to find out what was happening. It was chaos. A mess. A dead end.

Frankie Taylor crossed over the road to join Franny.

'What's going on, darlin'?'

'Spencer's getting his men to do the last couple. We've got to stop or get ourselves arrested. But I think whatever way, it's a no go. Chloe-Jane isn't here.'

Lola hugged Franny. 'There must be something else. It can't stop here. Not now.' Her voice cracked with emotion. 'Frankie, tell me there's something else we can do.'

Frankie didn't say anything. He was over-whelmed with raw emotion just as much as Lola was.

Alfie, having separated from the others, ran back to find them standing by the wall, worry etched in all their expressions. It said all he needed to know. Without bothering to talk to them he turned away, a cold realisation coming to him that they might never find Chloe-Jane, and she might never be coming home at all.

He rushed to where Detective Spencer was standing with a couple of his men. Alfie yelled out, full of pain, 'You said fifty metres. A fucking fifty-metre radius you said. Well she ain't here.'

The tech officer looked pale; terrified. 'I didn't say she'd be here. I said *technically.*'

Alfie stood inches away from the man, towering above him. 'You were wrong though weren't you?'

The man stepped backwards. 'No, no. It should be about fifty metres, give or take. The fifty-metre radius of a domestic Wi-Fi goes along or up. It's not complicated.'

Alfie paused quizzically. 'What you talking about, up?'

The man swallowed hard. 'Well, a Wi-Fi range doesn't just run along, it runs up. For example, if you were on a hill out of the fifty-metre range, say one or even two hundred metres away, you'd still pick up a connection. I don't want to bore you with the technology of it all but it's the way the frequency travels.'

Lola, along with the others, had walked across to join Alfie. She looked bemused, not understanding in the slightest anything to do with computers. 'But there ain't no hills.'

The man looked at Lola. 'No, I know, but of course it's not just hills. It could be anything high up.'

Alf enquired, 'Like buildings?'

The man nodded. 'Exactly, like high buildings.'

'Like that one there.' Alfie pointed to a large

high-rise office at the other side of the waste-land.

Franny looked at Alfie. 'Are you thinking what I think you are?'

Alfie began to run to his car. 'Too damn right I am... Too damn right.'

64

'She's in there, I can feel it.' Lola looked at Alfie as they stood outside the disused office block. Her eyes appealed to him not to shatter her hopes, however unlikely it was.

Alfie shrugged. 'Maybe, but...'

Lola interrupted, not wanting to hear anything to dispel her longing for Chloe to be safe and well inside the offices. 'I can hope, can't I?'

'Yes, Lola. We can hope. We can all hope.'

She looked up at him. 'Be careful; all of you. I'm going to wait out here; me bones have seen younger days and I'm not sure if they'll manage another flight of stairs.'

Alfie held onto the door of the derelict office block, mustering up all the strength he could. He felt desperate, after so many dead ends, and he had to wonder if this one was just the same thing. Raising hope, only to have it cruelly snatched away. Time was almost up, and this was the end of the road. But for now, he had a job to do.

He clenched his fists and took a deep breath. 'Let's get in there and bring her back.'

Franny, Del and Frankie all followed into the main entrance area but Spencer and his core team of five stood back. Alfie turned to him. 'What the hell are you waiting for?'

'We can't go in without a warrant, Jennings, you know that of old.'

Alfie rushed towards him but slowed down when he felt Lola's hand on his arm. 'Take it easy, Alf.'

He nodded to her, but kept his eyes on Spencer. 'My niece is about to die and you lot are talking about fucking paperwork.' He paused, feeling a new level of rage swell inside him.

'As the Old Bill you may be able to live with yourself if you walk away, knowing there are rules and frigging regulations to abide by, but what about as a human being? What about as a man, hey Spencer? Can you honestly turn your back because of crosses and ticks? There might be a kid in there who needs our help. We... *You* might be the difference between her living or dying.'

'It won't stand up in court if there isn't a warrant. He'll walk.'

'I don't care about court, I care about Chloe, and mark my words Spencer, Lee ain't walking anywhere if I get my hands on him. You have a choice, help Chloe live, or help her die, which is it going to be?'

Spencer stared at Alfie, chewing on his lip as his men looked at him awaiting orders. 'Okay... Okay Jennings, but anything ... *anything* you do which crosses the line; I'm arresting you.'

Regaining an air of composure and authority, Spencer spoke to everyone assembled as he took a quick glance round. 'This place obviously has two main stairwells, one at each end of the building. We'll take the left side, and you lot take the other... And Jennings, I meant what I said about crossing the line.'

Alfie didn't say anything. He watched Spencer disappear out of sight, and then almost in one synchronised movement, Del, Frankie, Franny and Alfie drew their guns, finding themselves once more creeping silently up stairwells of a deserted, derelict building, with Frankie taking the lead and Alfie taking the rear.

The first and second floors had nothing but large office spaces, with little or no furniture, and occasionally the group got a glimpse of the police on the other side of the building. But that was it. No Mr Lee, no Chloe-Jane.

Dust and dirt, and large open office spaces, boarded-up windows, graffiti and human waste. And with each step, each stair they took as they headed for the top floor, they sensed it was finally over. Reaching the top, the group hurried into the office space, and a moment later Spencer and his men came from the other side.

Spencer looked at Frankie. 'Nothing. There's nothing here.'

'Nothing this side either.' Both groups looked at each other, not wanting to say the inevitable words. Del was the first to speak.

'What now?'

Frankie answered him flatly. 'I think we both

know what. I'm sorry Alf.' He turned round to look at Alfie.

'Where's Alf?'

Del and Franny along with Frankie ran to the top of the stairs. They called out. 'Alf!... Alf!'

Frankie stared at Franny. 'When was the last time you saw him?'

'I dunno. He was at the back. Maybe the first floor...'

'Shit, come on!'

Two floors down, Alfie, overwhelmed by the frustration of finding nothing, had doubled back on himself for a quick look in the empty office space, letting the others head on up.

He hurried through the rows of empty desks. A wave of nausea hit him again, cold sweat prickling onto his forehead. Alfie leaned on a tall display screen for support, breathing deeply to stop the sickness taking hold. He closed his eyes, desperate for it to pass.

After a couple of minutes, he began to feel better. Opening his eyes, he frowned, peered forward. Christ, how could they have missed it? Behind the five-foot screen, he could see a door. A door they hadn't seen or checked behind. Alfie turned, about to run to get the others but too much time had been wasted already.

Reaching for the door, Alfie swung it open. It led into another stairwell, only this time the stairs were walled on either side, twisting only up or down.

He paused, listening for any sound. Nothing. Only the sound of his own breathing. Heading upwards, Alfie gripped onto his gun. The stairs twisted around so much he couldn't see round the corner. Slowly... Slowly...

Fuck!... Jesus!... Oh Christ! His foot stood on a nail, puncturing through his shoe. Then as the sharp pain ripped through his body he heard it. He heard the banging. He froze. Was he hearing things?

Alfie continued up the stairs, watching his step much more carefully. He stopped suddenly. There it was again. It was coming from the left side of him. He touched the wall, tapping it at first before banging it. It was hollow. Then came another bang, but not his. A bang from within the cavity of the wall.

Alfie's heart began to race. He called out, not caring who heard.

'Chloe! Chloe-Jane!' His voice echoed all around him. Then the noise again.

He ran, feeling the wall, trying to figure out what was behind it.

'Chloe!'

Each time Alfie called her name he was sure, so sure the bang answered back. It had to be her. It couldn't be just his blind hope. And then it came to him. Suddenly he realised what was on the other side of the wall and why it sounded so hollow. It was a lift shaft. And if there was a lift shaft, there had to be a lift.

Scrabbling up the stairs, Alfie tripped and stumbled, wanting to go faster than his body could take him. He felt the sweat dripping down his back, but he didn't care; he pushed on. His. breathing rasped as the tightness clasped his chest. Dizziness and waves of sickness flowed over him as he refused to stop and rest, even though his body was crying out for it. Nearly there... Nearly there.

Alfie could see the top of the stairs, twisting round to a landing beyond. Once at the landing, he sped round the corner. And he could see it. The old silver rusting doors of the lift. Rushing over, Alfie quickly examined it Even though it was old, the lift was still sealed tight shut.

He jammed his fingers in the centre of the doors, trying to prise them open, desperate to pull them apart. He gritted his teeth, grunting through pain, sweating through the effort of it all, and digging deep inside himself for strength.

Pull... Pull... He had to pull harder. His arms shook, trembling with the exertion as he tried to crank the doors apart. It was no good. Alfie let go, falling forward and resting his head against the two metal lift doors.

Fuck. Fuck. Fuck. He kicked out at the doors, echoing the sound down the lift shaft. Then he heard it again. The banging. The banging back.

Alfie charged down the stairs, but he missed his footing and tumbled forward. He tried to grab onto something to break his fall, but there was nothing there. He cried out as the steel stairs slammed into his back and smashed his head.

The stairs rolled and spun him around before he eventually slowed down almost to a stop. Alfie lay head first on the stairs. He groaned at the thumping pain, hesitant to move in case he'd broken anything. He looked up and what he saw had him scrabbling up to his feet.

The sign said, *Danger Keep Out – Service Users Only* – but to Alfie, it was a way into the lift shaft.

He opened the door, and immediately stepped back. On the other side was a sheer drop. He didn't know how far down it went, but Alfie did know if he did fall, there was no way he was surviving it.

Switching on his phone light, he leaned forward, surveying the lift shaft. On his near side, an access ladder ran up the length of the shaft wall. And below him, Alfie could see the top of the lift.

'Chloe!... Chloe! Bang if you can hear me.'

Multiple bangs, loud and insistent, came from the lift. Chloe-Jane was in there. But more than that, she was alive.

Alfie fought back the overwhelming sense of emotion. He needed to shut down. Focus. Be the hard bastard he knew he could be. Because it was only then he'd have a chance of getting Chloe-Jane out.

The wall ladder looked precarious; brown with rust, and no wider than a foot. Alfie wasn't certain it could take his weight. But there was only one way to find out. Reaching round to the side, Alfie took a sharp intake of breath before stretching one foot and one hand onto the ladder. It seemed strong enough, but he was also aware a good part of his weight still rested on the stairwell.

Alfie pulled his whole weight on the ladder, bringing his body round. The size of the ladder seemed inadequate and he once more had to battle to push away the sense of vulnerability he felt.

'Chloe... Baby... I'm coming. Hold on, sweetheart.' To the sound of the banged reply, Alfie carefully lowered himself down the ladder. One foot after the other. One hand after another. All the time calling out to Chloe. All the time ignoring his own fears.

'Chloe, just a couple more minutes. Then it's over. You hear me, Chloe? It's over.'

The top of the lift came into sight and Alfie cautiously placed one foot on the top of it. The lift seemed to scream out, as the rusting cable wires creaked and groaned, loud and jarring. He pulled his foot away, back on the ladder. Shit.

'Chloe!... Don't worry about the noise, it's only the lift. All lifts do that, babe.'

Alfie wanted to believe his own lie but he knew by the sound of the cables they were weakened and damaged.

Still holding onto the ladder with one hand, he reached down to the lift hatch which sat to the near side of him. He tried to push it across, but he couldn't get enough strength behind it because of the angle he was at.

Slowly he placed one hand on the top of the lift. It groaned, swaying about on the cables. From there Alfie put one knee down, then the next and finally let go of the ladder, putting his full weight on the roof of the lift.

The lift buckled and instinctively Alfie wanted to grab back hold of the ladder but instead he stayed motionless, almost daring not to breathe. 'Chloe, I'm on top of the lift now. I want you to stay real still, baby, whilst I push this hatch back. You might hear the lift making a really loud noise but don't panic. Okay? Don't panic.'

Now in the perfect position, Alfie pushed the hatch. It was old and had clearly been unused for a while and as a consequence it seemed to be jammed. He pushed again. It wouldn't budge. Wiping away the sweat from his forehead, Alfie gave everything he had and was rewarded by a tiny movement from the steel access point, making the lift begin to move.

The hatch ground on its metal runners but eventually it pulled back enough for Alfie to see Chloe.

Through his tears and smiles, Alfie fell over his words. Feeling delight of a kind he'd never experienced in his life before, and for just for a moment it didn't matter where they were. He had found her.

'Chloe... I... Chloe... I... Oh Jesus, Chloe, you don't know... Oh shit, it's good to see you, babe.'

Although Chloe's hands were tied behind her back and a tight gag jammed cruelly in her mouth, Alfie knew she was smiling. Her eyes twinkled with joy, deep pools of love and warmth.

The first thing he had to do was get her hands untied, helpless as she was. Ignoring another loud groan of the lift, Alfie expertly lowered himself in. The moment his feet touched the ground, he grabbed hold of Chloe; hard, tight and loving.

He pulled her gag off, holding her face in his hands.

'Uncle Alfie... You came... You came for me.'

He could hardly speak for his tears. 'Like you came for me. Jesus, Chloe, I thought I wouldn't find you.'

Chloe-Jane smiled. 'I knew you would, Uncle Alfie. I just knew it.'

Alfie bent down to untie her hands. 'Okay, it's a bit of a climb but I'll have you home in no time. I'll climb back up, and then I'll pull you up. You ready, babe?'

Chloe nodded enthusiastically. 'You bet I am.'

Alfie turned to jump back up on the roof of the lift, but before he did he turned back to Chloe-Jane. 'I don't know what I'd have done if I hadn't found you. I ain't ever going to let you go again.'

Alfie jumped up, catching the edge of the roof. The lift was high but narrow enough for him to splay his legs and use his feet to edge back up to the top, ably assisted by Chloe-Jane giving him a push from underneath.

The effort of getting back out of the lift made it sway back and forth, banging against the sides, frightening Chloe.

'Uncle Alfie...'

'It's okay sweetheart. Remember what I–'

A bright light shone from above Alfie. He looked up, dazzled by it, realising the lift doors at the top had been opened. A voice called down.

'Mr Jennings, one thing I admire about you is, you're persistent.'

'Lee, you bastard!'

'Indeed... However now you've found Chloe-

Jane. I hope it was worth it.'

The first bullet from Mr Lee ricocheted round the lift shaft. Sparks of light blasted into the air. Alfie dived down, thudding down hard on top of the lift roof. The lift screeched, banging into the sides, creaking loudly as Chloe-Jane began to scream.

'It's going to fall!... Uncle Alfie!'

Alfie, still lying on his stomach, called out to Chloe. 'It's fine...' The next bullet whisked past Alfie's head, penetrating the metal of the lift.

'Chloe! Get down... Huddle in the corner, Chloe!'

Pulling his gun out of his pocket, Alfie fired upwards, not able to see where he was shooting. The sound of more bullets was heard within the lift shaft but Alfie didn't know if they were ricochets and echoes or Mr Lee firing multiple bullets.

He tried to stand up and hold onto the cable which held the lift, but it caused it to clatter too far to the side, smashing into the steel wall. Alfie crouched down with the sparks still flying around him.

Trying to picture where the lift doors were at the top of the shaft, Alfie aimed. There was silence for a moment... And then... And then... Oh my God. He looked up. The noise was deafening as the roar of grinding and whirring began above him. The hum of the cables broken, whistling, unlooping from their tethers as they picked up speed came towards him. And then Alfie felt the vibration, the groaning, the shaking as the lift began to give way.

He yelled out, hanging onto the edge of the hatch whilst his cries were drowned out by the clatter of steel thudding and pounding against the wall as the lift hurtled down, careering towards the ground, plunging down as sparks whisked out from the sides, sending out a glow as metal scraped against metal at high speed.

Then it was over. Obscure silence... Darkness ... stillness... And then, a voice.

'Chloe-Jane?'

'Uncle Alfie.'

'Are you okay?'

'Yes. Are you?'

'Yes.'

Alfie slowly felt for his phone, switching on the light. He moved slightly to the side, and to his horror and Chloe's screams the lift juddered down another foot into the darkness of the lift shaft.

'Chloe, stay still baby.' Alfie wriggled over, slowly stretching his arm downwards towards his niece. 'Chloe, slowly move towards my hand.'

The movement from Chloe trying to move across from her spot in the lift made it plunge down another two feet as the cable at the top threatened to give way. Alfie shouted out.

'Stay where you are! Don't move!... Chloe, don't move... Chloe, listen to me. I'm going to...'

Chloe interrupted. 'You can't leave me! Uncle Alfie, you can't!'

Alfie closed his eyes for a moment, wanting to take her in his arms. 'I ain't leaving you... Remember what I said, girl. I ain't leaving you again. But I am going to go and get help. Franny, Del, Lola and Frankie are here. They're all here, sweetheart. They've all come to help you, but I need to go and tell them where we are. So I need you to be brave. Which ain't no trouble for a Jennings girl, hey!'

'Okay... Okay.'

'That's my girl. But Chloe, don't move babe. Just don't move.'

Alfie gave one last look to Chloe as he carefully backed up towards the ladder. He reached behind him, pulling his full body slowly off the lift roof.

He called once more. 'I'll be back, Chloe, I promise you and then there's no getting rid of me, darlin'.'

Alfie began to climb up the ladder faster than he'd climbed down it. Once more it felt like he was against the clock. Before he reached the service access door, the climb took Alfie past a large air conditioning tunnel. He was about to ignore and climb on but it struck him if Mr Lee was still about, the obvious place he'd be waiting would be at the service door.

At least going through the tunnel he'd avoid being seen, and from his days long ago as a burglar he knew that any air vent tunnel in old buildings not only led to the outside of the building but also had regular maintenance points accessible through unlocked grilles.

The tunnel was large enough for Alfie to shuffle comfortably through on all fours. He passed two grilles but they were jammed shut; at the third grille he stopped, making sure there was no one about. Satisfied it was safe to continue, Alfie pulled on the grille, surprised at how easily it opened.

He paused again, double checking that the sound of the grille being moved hadn't attracted attention, then slowly he lowered himself down into the dimly lit room. It felt like the middle of the night, but a large clock on the wall told him it was still only five o'clock.

In front of him was a door which led to the outside fire exit and, wanting to waste no time, Alfie ran over to it, preparing to smash the glass. But once close up, he could see it was already ajar.

Outside on the fire escape, Alfie immediately got his bearings. He was at the side of the building, near to where he'd parked his car. Which meant the entrance and more importantly, help, was round the corner.

Running down the stairs and into the car park, Alfie began to head towards the front of the building to raise the alarm. As he raced on, a sound of an engine, loud and clear, came from behind him. He turned, expecting to see a familiar face or one of Spencer's men – but sitting at the wheel of the car was Mr Lee.

A smiling Mr Lee revved the engine hard of the stationary car as Alfie locked eyes with him. The car began to crawl forward, then a second later it sped towards Alfie at high speed. Alfie drew his gun and pulled the trigger. It clicked, but nothing else happened. He clicked again, desperately over and over again, realising he was out of bullets.

Closing his eyes, Alfie threw his whole body to the side, diving to the ground and covering his head as he waited for the impact of the car; but as he did so, he heard the sound of two shots and then an explosion.

He looked up in time to see Mr Lee's car bursting into a ball of flames before it plunged into the canal.

Alfie watched, mesmerised, not by the torrent of smoke, not by the car sinking into the murky waters but by Franny Doyle as she walked towards him, smoking gun in hand. She smiled.

'Fran... I, Jesus, you saved my life.'

Franny looked at him and smirked playfully. 'It was nothing; I only shot out the tyres; thought it was best that way. I don't want Spencer pulling me up for murder. Anyway, I owed you one.' She winked knowingly at Alfie, then her face fell. 'Alfie, I'm sorry, we haven't found Chloe.'

Alfie, helped up by Franny, began to run to the front entrance. 'Well, I have.'

Without question Franny ran behind him. They raced across the car park to be greeted by Spencer and the others.

Frankie nodded towards the flames. 'What the hell?'

'It's a long story, I'll tell you later but for the time being it's going to go like this. I've found Chloe.'

The cry of relief was sounded out by everyone, including Spencer.

'But we need to move fast. She's in the lift, and

it's about to give way. It dropped down...'

Del spoke up. 'Jesus, that must have been the noise we heard. One fucking almighty bang. We thought there'd been a bomb. Jesus...' Before Del had finished his sentence another car sped past them, skidding round, sending billows of dust and grit in the air.

Spencer looked startled. 'What the...'

Alfie, getting a glimpse of the driver, gave Spencer the answer he was after. 'It's Lin. That's Lin. He's Lee second-in-command, but we can sort him out later – we need to go to Chloe, now! Lola, you call the ambulance and fire brigade and whoever else you think can help. Come on guys, this way!'

They all followed Alfie as he rushed through the building and back up the service stairs, taking them as many as he could at a time. He shouted loudly.

'Chloe, Chloe-Jane, we're coming babe!'

At the top landing, by the open lift doors, Frankie caught up with Alfie. 'Where is she?'

'Down there, in the lift somewhere between halfway and the bottom.' He flashed his mobile phone torch on, trying to light up the lift shaft to show Frankie, picking out the service ladder as it ran down into the distance.

Del arrived, and a wave of vertigo hit him at the sight of the sheer drop. 'Oh, shit.' He stared at the ancient-looking winch mechanism and the badly frayed steel cable which quivered under the strain of holding the lift car which swayed precariously, metres below them.

'Chloe!... Chloe! We're going to get you out of there. You hear me? But remember babe... Don't move.'

Frankie turned to Alfie, lowering his voice, not wanting to have what he said echo down to Chloe. 'How the hell are we going to do that? Look at it, it's going to give any minute.'

They all looked at the cables which continued to creak and move, tiny millimetre by tiny millimetre. Del spoke anxiously. 'When those cables get to the end, the whole thing is going to fall.'

'Uncle Alfie!'

'Yes baby, I'm here. We're all here.'

Del fought back the emotions. 'Hello, Chloe.'

Frankie had to bite on his lip. 'Hello, Chloe.'

Franny paused, too overwhelmed for a moment. 'Hello, Chloe.'

And then another voice came from behind them. 'Hello darlin'.' It was Lola, red-faced and panting hard. She looked at them all shrugging. 'I may be old and me bones might be giving up, but Chloe needs me, and I ain't letting a flight of stairs get in me way.'

Pulling Del and Frankie in close, Alf whispered, 'How the fuck are we going to do this? Del's right, that wire will snap any time; we ain't got time to wait for engineers or nothing.'

Frankie agreed. 'You're right, the only thing for it is we go in and get her ourselves.'

'It's no good, you can't touch the lift; it'll give straight away. I tried to pull her up but the whole thing fell a couple of feet when she moved towards me.'

'Then she doesn't move towards us. *We* move towards her.'

Alfie frowned. 'What do you mean, Frank?'

'Remember the game we played as kids; monkey chain? When you hold onto each other's arm, then swing off a high wall?'

Del shook his head giving Frankie a crooked smile. 'I think you're on your own there, mate. Ain't no one doing anything like that, apart from you.'

'Anyway, that's how we're going to get Chloe out.'

Alfie looked incredulous. 'By a monkey chain? Turn it in Frank, we ain't kids, we're frigging grown adults, with grown-up weight.'

Frankie began to get annoyed. 'Look, the weight is relative. Adult with adult. We go down the ladder, and instead of making Chloe move towards us or put any kind of weight on the lift we do a monkey chain.'

Alfie snapped. 'Do you have to keep calling it that?'

'Well if you have any better ideas or any better names come to think of it, let me know.'

Alfie took a deep breath. 'I'm sorry, Frank.' He paused to think. It was crazy. Fuck knows it was. But what else did they have to work with? And it could work in theory, whether in practice, he didn't know, but the opening of the lift roof was directly next to the ladder, so by rights as long as they could get deep enough into the lift, there was a chance of grabbing hold of Chloe. 'Okay... Let's do it.'

Without another word, Alfie stepped out

through the service door placing his expensive leather soles on the first rung, ready for the descent down.

Franny gripped hold of his arm. 'Alf, I know you want to help Chloe but I'm the lightest, it's better if I go down first, isn't it? Del tell him.'

'She's right, Alf. It should go, Franny, me, Frankie, then you. It's pointless asking you to stay up here with Lola, I know that, but you've been proper battered about, mate, and you're not in the best shape because of it. We don't want to take any chances. This is about Chloe.'

To the surprise of the others, Alfie didn't argue. He smiled at them all, simply saying, 'Thank you.'

Franny, not having ever been fond of heights, made her way down.

Del called down, 'Fran are you okay?'

'Oh, never better!'

They climbed down in silence. As the lift came into sight, Alfie from his position on the service ladder, called out.

'Chloe... Chloe, we're nearly there. You're nearly home, babe but I need you to listen to me really carefully. Del is going to lower Franny through the hatch and when I say ready, you grab her hand. But not before. Understand me babe. Not before. You got that?'

Chloe's voice sounded tiny. 'Yes ... yes, okay.'

Alfie continued. 'But here's the thing, I don't want you to panic but when you reach for Franny's hand, the lift might give way... But no matter what baby, no matter what happens you hold on. You got that?'

'Yeah.'

'Good ... good.' Alfie spoke to the others. 'Okay, guys, let's do it.'

Frankie grabbed hold of Del. 'I got you mate. Ain't no way you're getting out of this grip; champion monkey chainer I was.'

Del nodded gratefully then placed a steel-like grip round Franny's wrist. He stared at her, before letting her lean down towards the lift. 'I won't let you go, no matter what happens, I'm holding on.'

Franny didn't say anything, she only smiled weakly then leaned back, feeling the jerk from Del's grip as he leaned down from Frankie's who held onto the ladder with formidable strength.

Franny hovered over the lift hatch, carefully making sure she didn't hit any part of it. She called up to Del. 'I need to be let down a bit.'

Alfie called out to Chloe. 'Chloe, can you see Franny? But I still don't want you to move.'

'I can see her.'

'Okay Chloe, how far away are you from her? Do you think you would be able to reach her hand?'

Chloe edged forward to try to reach for Franny, and the moment she did the lift dropped down a foot, crashing into the wall to now swing at an angle.

'Chloe! Don't move! I said, don't move!'

Everyone heard her terror through her tears. 'I'm sorry... I'm sorry.'

Alfie called back down. 'Ain't no need to be sorry, not you, Chloe. Not you.'

Del spoke quickly, feeling the pull from Franny

on his arm. 'Alf, you better make this quick, mate.'

'Okay, can you lower Franny any more?'

'Only by about a few inches.'

'Then do that.' Alfie watched as Del leaned even further back, letting Franny drop down. Once she had gone as far as she could go, he called to Chloe.

'Okay Chloe, listen to me. I'm going to count down to one. Slowly, and I need you to be ready to grab hold of Franny's hand. Just grab it. Grab it hard. You got that?'

'Okay.'

'Baby, the lift will move but don't panic because Franny will have you. Just hold on, and she'll hold onto you. Got it?'

'Yeah... Yeah, I got it.'

Alfie paused, beginning the countdown. 'You ready Chloe, I'm going to start to count down now. Five... Four... Three... Two ... One... Jump Chloe! Jump Chloe, hold on baby.'

The whole of the human monkey chain jerked downwards, as Chloe's weight added to the group. She screamed but her screams were drowned out as immediately beneath her, the lift fell away in deafening roars as the frayed wire burst apart, crashing the lift to the ground, sending up a billow of smoke.

'Franny... Franny, I can't hold on!' Chloe looked up, wide-eyed in terror as she held onto Franny's arm with both hands as the rest of her body dangled, suspended in mid-air. 'I'm losing my grip... I'm losing my grip... Help me!'

'I got you, Chloe! I got you. But don't wriggle.

Try to keep still.'

'Uncle Alfie, help me. I can't hold on!'

Franny shouted to Chloe again. 'Chloe, please stop! Please stop!'

Chloe's movements acted like a domino effect to the chain link. From the top of the group, Frankie felt himself losing his grip on the ladder, and moved slightly, causing Del to instinctively hold on tighter to Frankie, but his actions made Franny try to reposition her hand but with the pull of the weight of Chloe, she felt herself slipping. She cried out.

'Del! I'm slipping!'

Del tried to pull her back up but he couldn't lift the weight of two people. He yelled up to Alfie.

'Alf, we need help! Fucking hell, we need help!'

Alfie cried out to Del. 'Don't you let them go! Don't you fucking let them go!' He could see the strain on Del and Frankie as they battled to find whatever strength they had left. He called out again, but this time to Chloe and Franny.

'You two... You two hold on. You hear me? You hold on 'cos I ain't losing you. I ain't living my life without you.'

Alfie reached down, holding the ladder, trying to reach far enough to help Frankie. He stretched. Then some more, feeling the burn on his hand from the rusty steel. Just a little further. Just a little further. There. He grabbed hold of Frankie, helping him to lift his own arm which lifted Del higher up towards them and in turn, Franny.

'Franny... Franny, can you reach your foot onto

the ladder? Chloe, hold on baby. Hold on.'

In the darkness Franny stretched out her leg to the side. She couldn't speak, she needed all her strength to hold onto Chloe. She could feel the sweat dripping down her, she could feel the tear and burn of her muscles as they struggled to cope.

Her foot hit the side and then the rung of the ladder which held her steady and spurred her on, helping her to find her voice.

'Chloe, I've got you sweetheart, stretch out your leg to the side; stretch it out.'

'I can't ... I can't.'

'Sweetheart, *you* can do anything. Go on... I'm here.'

In that moment through her terror, Chloe-Jane finally found a reason to live. For the people who cared, for the life she would live but for the first time ever she wanted to live for herself.

Closing her eyes, Chloe-Jane stretched over towards the side. Feeling her foot on the rung of the ladder she pulled herself in to safety.

At the top of the ladder, they were greeted by Lola and Spencer, along with the emergency services. Seeing Chloe, Lola grabbed hold of her, pulling her in and holding her tightly. She gestured for the others to join her; Del, Frankie, Franny and of course, Alfie.

Chloe-Jane looked at them all, her face enchanted by them. 'You came for me. All of you.'

They all looked at one another; bashful, humbled, thankful. Frankie shrugged, winking at Chloe. 'Well what else would you expect from us, darlin', because after all, we're family.'

65

Resting on the only bit of hospital table that wasn't covered with grapes and magazines, Casey Edwards carefully signed her name. Looking up, she held out the paper.

'There you go, detective, will that do you? The statement as promised.'

Detective Spencer having driven from UCH hospital straight to Snaresbrook Crown Court, walked in through the main entrance. He was spotted by the CPS barrister who hailed him from the first-floor balcony.

The barrister coasted down the sweeping marble stairs to greet Spencer, who held out a brown envelope.

'Are these the statements?'

Detective Spencer nodded.

'All of them?'

He nodded again. 'Oh yes, every last one of them. Taylor's, Harding's, Williams', Edwards' and of course, Jennings'.'

'Good, then all of it's in order. You read them?'

'Oh, I've read them.'

The court bailiff edged through a wooden door at the front of court fourteen and took his place by the court secretary. Reading from a card he loudly announced, 'Case 3465, Crown versus

Sadler, Judge Driver presiding, all rise.'

As the judge made his way slowly to his seat, Vaughn Sadler sat impassively as he watched his defence and prosecution lawyer.

It wasn't as if he hadn't been in this position before; he had, but there was something which made even the hardest of men feel vulnerable as they sat in the dock, evidence piled against them, looking at a stretch inside.

The judge nodded to the defence counsel to start to make their bail application.

'Your honour...'

The prosecuting counsel interrupted. 'Excuse me, your honour, but due to new evidence we need to approach the bench.'

Vaughn Sadler sat straight up in the dock He looked over to his defence barrister in alarm, who looked none the wiser himself. Vaughn watched as both barristers spoke in hushed tones to the judge.

Eventually, the judge waved the counsel back to their seats before beginning to address the court.

'Mr Sadler, can you stand up.'

Vaughn stood slowly, taking a deep breath, staring directly at the judge.

'Mr Sadler...'

'I plead...'

'Mr Sadler...'

'I plead...'

The judge brought down his hammer, raising his voice angrily. 'Mr Sadler, in the light of new evidence which the prosecution has brought this morning for my attention I find there is no case to answer. Therefore you are free to leave the court.'

'But, I don't...'

'Mr Sadler...'

'But your honour, I...'

'Mr Sadler, unless you'd like to be held in contempt of court, I suggest you leave now.'

Vaughn looked at his barrister, puzzled, then he heard the sound of a clap, then another clap, which turned into thunderous applause. He looked up to the gallery to see them all there. All clapping, all with smiles on their faces. Del, Frankie, Franny, Lola, Chloe-Jane and of course, Alfie.

Vaughn sat listening to Lola tell the story; partly in shock and partly not quite believing he wasn't actually going to spend the next ten years inside.

'So you see Vaughnie, Spencer was desperate to put you away, and Alfie here had the bright idea to use it to our advantage when Chloe went missing. We agreed to give him a statement but first up, only a part one saying we were all there. He was well chuffed about that, 'cos it placed us right there at the shooting. What he didn't expect was the second part of the statement to point the finger at Lin.'

Vaughn frowned. 'Lin?'

'You know, that geezer who worked for that Lee fella. Do you remember he turned up at the club? Well, Alfie here had CCTV of him entering the club, so it was easy for us all to say he was the one who shot Casey. Bleedin' genius.'

'But didn't Spencer think it was suss you didn't tell him that before?'

'Oh yes, he thought it was suss and he knew it

was bullshit, but we all said the exact same thing. We told him we hadn't said it before 'cos of fear and threats from Lin and Lee. Turns out they'd been after Lin for a while but couldn't get anything on him. The finishing touch was when Chloe went to find Alfie in that building in Paddington, she went with Franny's gun but during everything it was left behind there. Lin apparently had it in his possession, proper stitched himself up and he never even knew it. Apparently he squealed on the rest of the gang so he wouldn't get extradited back to Hong Kong, so the whole lot of them have been bang to rights and all due to that gun of yours.'

Vaughn nodded. 'Because that was the gun I shot Casey with.'

'Exactly. It all falls nicely into everything that has been going on in Soho. But Spencer of course was bleedin' fuming not to be able to bring you down. Can't tell you, like Puff the Magic Dragon with smoke coming out of his nose and ears, he was. I tell you Vaughnie, you should have seen it.' Lola paused adding, 'And Cass was in on it too.'

'Casey?'

'Oh yes, she's waiting at the hospital for you.'

EPILOGUE

They were all there. All of them. The faces of London coming together and putting their differences aside. Del Williams and Frankie Taylor, Alfie and Franny, Lola and Chloe-Jane all sitting sharing stories, memories, and friendships as they sat in Lola's café.

The door opened and Vaughn walked in, much to the exclamation of Lola.

'What the bleedin' hell?'

'One moose head, as promised.'

The sound of laughter echoed round the room. 'Vaughnie, you're the best.'

Alfie shouted across to Del. 'Did I tell you, me and Franny and Chloe are off on holiday, thought we'd look you up in Marbella, you can show us how the better half lives.'

'Well you are welcome, mate, I know Bunny will be pleased to see you.' Then Del turned to talk to Vaughn. 'What about you, what are your plans?'

Vaughn shrugged, feeling slightly melancholy. It felt like an end of an era. Soho had been his life, but now it was time to move on to something new. 'Now Casey is okay to come out of the hospital, we're going to take some time out, probably to the States. Always fancied my chances out there.'

Alfie grinned. 'I have always thought of you as

393

a cowboy.'

Vaughn smiled. He was going to let bygones be bygones. 'And what about you, Alf? What are you going to do when you come back from holiday?'

'Oh, I'm thinking of opening a casino.'

The place fell silent then Alfie grinned a huge smile. 'I was joking. Guys, I was *joking*.'

A flannel from Frankie landed in Alfie's face. 'That is not funny, that ain't funny mate. Franny, I don't know how you put up with him.'

Franny grinned. 'I ask myself that every day.'

Vaughn shouted to Frankie, 'And you, what are your plans?'

'Going back to Gypsy so she can chew me ear off some more. But listen up, I know things won't ever be the same, but none of us are losing touch. You hear me?'

Lola joined in. 'That's right, none of us are. Family stick together.'

Alfie raised his tea cup. 'A toast. To family.'

'To family!'

Chloe looked on and smiled. She was finally a part of something. An odd, strange, unique family. But a family nevertheless. A family that loved, argued, then loved some more. A family who'd always be there. She raised her cup but her toast was to someone else. To her friend who'd be dearly missed. 'To Jodie!'

'To Jodie!'

Lola waved her cup in the air again. 'I got another toast. Ladies and gentlemen, please, I would like you to meet my new manageress. Chloe-Jo.'

Everyone threw their arms in the air. A united cry of voices shouted at Lola. 'It's Jane!'

'Where?'

The publishers hope that this book has given you enjoyable reading. Large Print Books are especially designed to be as easy to see and hold as possible. If you wish a complete list of our books please ask at your local library or write directly to:

Magna Large Print Books
Magna House, Long Preston,
Skipton, North Yorkshire.
BD23 4ND

This Large Print Book for the partially sighted, who cannot read normal print, is published under the auspices of

THE ULVERSCROFT FOUNDATION

THE ULVERSCROFT FOUNDATION

... we hope that you have enjoyed this Large Print Book. Please think for a moment about those people who have worse eyesight problems than you ... and are unable to even read or enjoy Large Print, without great difficulty.

You can help them by sending a donation, large or small to:

**The Ulverscroft Foundation,
1, The Green, Bradgate Road,
Anstey, Leicestershire, LE7 7FU,
England.**
or request a copy of our brochure for more details.

The Foundation will use all your help to assist those people who are handicapped by various sight problems and need special attention.

Thank you very much for your help.